Shot Through the Heart

Matt Cain was born in Bury and brought up in Bolton. He spent ten years making arts and entertainment programmes for ITV before stepping in front of the camera in 2010 to become Channel 4 News' first Culture Editor. Now a full-time writer, *Shot Through the Heart* is his first novel. He lives in London.

You can follow Matt Cain on Twitter @MattCainWriter

MATT CAIN

Shot Through the Heart

PAN BOOKS

First published 2014 by Pan Books,
an imprint of Pan Macmillan, a division of Macmillan Publishers Limited
Pan Macmillan, 20 New Wharf Road, London N1 9RR
Basingstoke and Oxford
Associated companies throughout the world
www.panmacmillan.com

ISBN 978-1-4472-3829-4

1 3 5 7 9 8 6 4 2

A CIP catalogue record for this book is available from the British Library.

Typeset by Ellipsis Digital Limited, Glasgow
Printed and bound by CPI Group (UK) Ltd, Croydon, CR0 4YY

For my Nana Irene Clough,

who was brave enough to follow her heart.

1

'Well it sure is good to meet you, Miss Sinclair.'

'You too, Dan.'

'You know, I can't believe I'm actually on a date with the First Lady of Love.'

Mia tried not to wince – that nickname was starting to become a curse.

'Don't be silly,' she said, flashing him what she hoped was her best movie star smile. 'And please, call me Mia.'

Oh I hope tonight goes well, she thought. *I'm not sure I can cope with another disappointment . . .*

Mia's date was taking place in Sky High, an exclusive lounge club perched above the outdoor pool of the Mirage Hotel with some of the best views of Los Angeles. Sitting opposite her was Dan Morrison, a solidly handsome thirtysomething dressed in an understated navy suit. Dan was sipping a glass of Merlot while Mia was working her way through a rather bitter pomegranate juice.

'So I hear you're new to LA,' she purred. 'Why did you decide to move here?'

'Oh things in Seattle were getting way too stressful,' Dan explained. 'I was a doctor in an Emergency Room but wanted a more relaxed lifestyle. Now I've re-trained as a carpenter I'm much happier.'

'A carpenter?' Mia breezed. 'Oh how creative and . . . manly.'

Did I actually just say that? she thought. *That was way too corny!*

Dan fiddled with his tie and looked down bashfully.

Mia had been fixed up with Dan by her trainer Cole, a black guy with pecs so big you could shelter from the rain under them. Not that it ever rained in Los Angeles. In fact, in the eight years that Mia had lived here she could count on one hand the number of days when there hadn't been a bright blue sky over the city. Which was one of the things that she loved so much about the place, having grown up in Cleveland, Ohio – a dreary city where the sky always seemed to be grey. She'd dreamt for years of escaping to LA and when she eventually arrived here, it had turned out to be everything she'd wanted it to be. Since then, she'd worked hard to create what she sometimes thought of as a fairytale life for herself; she had a great career, wonderful friends and a fabulous home high in the Hollywood Hills. In fact, the only thing that she didn't have right now was a man to share it all with. And according to Cole, Dan could be just the man to fix that.

'I guess I just love making things,' he explained rather earnestly. 'And I know it might sound dorky but I love the feel of wood. I just think it's a beautiful material.'

'Wow,' breathed Mia. She couldn't think of anything else to say. 'Wow.' She stared wistfully at the indentation at the bottom of his neck.

According to Cole, Dan Morrison was kind, dependable

and very much one of the good guys. In fact, Cole always called him Nice Man Dan and from what Mia had seen so far, he wasn't wrong.

Being fixed up with potential boyfriends could be difficult for Mia because invariably she knew very little about them and they knew so much about her. This unsettling one-way intimacy gave her date a massively unfair advantage. For a start, if he liked going to the movies, chances were he'd already seen her naked in one of her many love scenes. And if he read the papers or had access to the internet, it was more than likely that he knew some very private things about her already – the kind of things that were quite revealing and which you wouldn't normally give away on a first date. Details about her unhappy childhood in Cleveland for example, her youthful dreams of becoming a film star, and her mother's death just as her movie career was taking off. A quick Google search would also reveal the media's nickname for her – the First Lady of Love, a title she'd earned after appearing in a string of hit chick flicks. Dan was obviously well researched on this front and she hoped he wouldn't mention it again. The irony was that Mia wasn't sure she'd ever been in love – despite countless attempts, many of them soul-destroying. In fact, she was starting to wonder if she even believed in love anymore – and to worry that she was becoming cynical and jaded. But that was the kind of thing she kept private. There was no way Dan could have learned *that* from the internet.

'So tell me about your relationship history,' she asked. 'How come a great guy like you's still single?'

'Oh well, I recently broke up with someone so am only just back on the market, I guess.' Dan explained that his last girlfriend, Angelique, was a nurse in a plastic surgeon's who'd left him for one of her clients, a famous porn actor who'd gone to the clinic for a penis enlargement. 'What a douche-bag,' he moaned. 'I could never cheat on a woman – I've too much respect for them. In fact, I don't think I've ever been unfaithful in all my life.'

Hmm, that's another tick, thought Mia. *He's doing pretty well here.*

Whenever Mia went on a first date there was a checklist she always worked through, imagining cheesy sound effects from a TV quiz show when contestants got the answers right or wrong. Is he punctual? Bleep bleep – correct answer. Does he have his own career? Bleep bleep – full marks. Has he ever cheated on a girlfriend? Bleep bleep – three out of three.

It wasn't that Mia was being cold or ruthless in her search for a man, just that she was trying to look after herself. She'd seen her mother lose her security, dignity and, for a long time, her happiness after her father had walked out on the family when Mia was still very young. Her mom had had to take on extra shifts at the hospital where she slaved away as a nurse and worked herself into the ground over the next ten years, just to survive and bring up her daughter. Ever since then she'd warned Mia not to make the same mistake with men as she had. 'Don't fall for a bad boy,' she'd lectured, time and time again. 'Find yourself a nice, dependable good guy – someone who isn't trouble.' Over the years, Mia had vowed never to fall into the same trap as her mom. There was too much at stake; she'd seen first hand how much could be lost through falling in love with the wrong kind of guy.

'You know,' Dan went on, 'maybe I'm not the most exciting

of guys but I never thought Angelique would cheat on me like that. Maybe that's my problem though – maybe I'm just too nice.'

Bleep bleep! For Mia, a man could never be too nice. She didn't understand why so many women fell for bad boys, those sexy scoundrels who had trouble written all over them. She was different. She wanted her very own good guy – and perhaps she'd just found him.

*

'So Leo, let me get this straight. Are you saying you're breaking up with me?'

Across town, Leo Henderson was in Dirty Dick's, an English-themed pub popular with LA's expat crowd, just metres away from the seafront in Venice Beach. Dirty Dick's was one of his favourite drinking haunts as it was really close to his house, served more than twenty different real ales, and had the atmosphere of a British pub, which reminded him of home. And with its candlelit recesses at the back, it was a surprisingly good setting for a quiet, intimate date. In fact, Leo had used it for that very purpose on several occasions. Tonight though he was here with a completely different purpose. Tonight, he was here to have a difficult conversation with his girlfriend Eden. And by the end of the conversation, she'd hopefully be his *ex*-girlfriend.

'Yeah, I'm sorry Eden but I've thought about this a lot and things just aren't working for me at the moment.'

'But I don't understand,' she said. 'Is it something I've done?'

The problem was that it *was* something she'd done. But he

didn't want to upset her by saying that. He paused for a moment to choose his words carefully.

'No, no, it's nothing you've done. I just think our lives are moving in different directions, that's all.'

Is that a cliché? he wondered. He hoped not but he was really struggling to get through this. And anyway, it was true.

When he'd first met Eden six months ago her name had been Barbara and she'd been a Pilates instructor teaching stay-at-home mums and former film stars in a local old folks' home. He couldn't deny that he'd been attracted to her stunning good looks and incredible body but more importantly for Leo, she'd been a Buddhist with a bit of a hippie outlook on life. As a paparazzo, he had more than enough madness in his professional life and liked nothing more than a laid-back, calm personal life. Eden had seemed like the perfect fit.

But ever since she'd signed a deal to appear on a daytime TV show as a fitness expert, things had changed. It was as if her first taste of fame had somehow corrupted her. She'd adopted her stage name, given up Buddhism almost overnight and started talking endlessly about her 'profile' with a manic glint in her eye. When she released her first Pilates DVD she treated herself to a boob job and went out for a 'relaunch', which basically consisted of going to a film premiere in a low-cut top, perspex hooker heels and a mini skirt that looked like a pelmet. When she saw the photos in the press she became almost crazed in her desire for more. She kept pestering Leo to snap her coming out of restaurants with a few semi-famous friends – and he started to wonder if that was the only reason she was going out with him in the first place. As she got more and more angry with him for refusing, it began to dawn on him that the two of them couldn't last much longer.

'I'm so sorry, Eden.' He gave her a smile that he hoped wasn't too sympathetic or patronizing.

'Well all I can say is, you sure know how to pick your moments. You do realize I'm on *The Wendy Williams Show* tomorrow?'

He took a swig of his beer. 'Well I guess that's kind of it to be honest, Eden. Boob jobs and TV shows – it's not really what I signed up for.'

She suddenly perked up, as if hit by a good idea. 'Actually, I could always tell Wendy about being dumped – open my heart on air and turn on the tears. She loves a good sob story.'

Leo was beginning to struggle not to sound impatient. 'Eden, will you just listen to me for a minute? It's this obsession with chasing fame that's my whole problem.'

'Well maybe it wouldn't *be* such a problem if you'd actually bother to pap me now and again.'

'But we've already been through all that – you know I don't like to mix work with pleasure. It's way too complicated.'

'It's not complicated at all, Leo. In fact, it's quite simple. My career's moving to another level and you just don't want to deal with it.'

'But Eden, it's not that I don't want to deal with it. It's that I don't want to give up my job – not when I love it so much. And I just don't see how a pap can possibly date a target.'

How many times have we had this conversation? The fact that they were having it yet again only strengthened his resolve that he was doing the right thing.

And it wasn't as if he had many rules in life. In fact, he only had one, and that was never to let his relationships get mixed up with his work. A paparazzo dating someone famous could never work. For a start, both sides wouldn't know when they were being used. And the way Leo saw it, whatever trust there was between them could only ever break down.

'Oh, Leo,' Eden pouted, 'but we've always been so good together . . .'

She swivelled on her seat and crossed her legs – legs that had always driven Leo wild. As he looked at them stretching out beside him he was reminded of just how gorgeous she was and couldn't help thinking back to the great sex they'd had. Eden was right: they *were* good together. So was he really doing the right thing by ending it?

She leaned forward and began nibbling on her finger flirtatiously. 'Oh it just seems such a shame to throw it all away. I mean, we both know there's a real chemistry between us. And chemistry like that doesn't come around every day . . .'

Leo was starting to feel a bit hot and undid another button on his shirt. He had to admit, most men would kill to have a girlfriend as good-looking as Eden. As he breathed down his neck to cool himself down he thought about how tough it would be never to sleep with her again. *Oh maybe just one last time*, he thought. *That couldn't hurt, could it?*

Just then he sensed a buzzing sound from his jeans pocket and realized he'd received a text message on his phone. 'Look, I'm sorry Eden but I really need to get this.'

As he keyed in his security code he felt relieved to have been rescued from a moment of weakness. The last thing he needed right now was to end up back in bed with her – it would only make things even more difficult. Eden must have realized that her last-ditch attempt to save the relationship had failed as she gave a loud huff and swung her legs back under the table.

On the screen of his phone Leo read a text from his photographic agency, Shooting Stars. 'Mia Sinclair on date in Sky High – arrived 9 p.m.'

Straight away he wanted to take the job as pictures of the First Lady of Love with a new man always sold for good money. But he couldn't leave Eden before they'd properly talked things through. He wondered how much longer it would take.

Because this assignation with Mia Sinclair was his kind of date. Totally uncomplicated – and purely professional.

*

As Nice Man Dan told her about his charity work helping to build a village in a remote part of Africa, Mia Sinclair leant back on the heavily cushioned sofa and relaxed into a date that she was enjoying more and more. She often chose Sky High as the venue for first dates as she loved its tasteful gold and green furniture and the pulsing Brazilian music they played. Most of all though, she loved the fact that the bar was private and heavily guarded from the paparazzi.

Because Mia hated the paparazzi. Without doubt they were her biggest enemy. Ever since she'd had her first hit movie and suddenly become public property, they'd ruined every attempt she'd made at starting a new relationship. In the last month alone there'd been three casualties of their unrelenting pursuit of pictures. First there was Seth, a shy but sexy writer who spent all his time indoors hunched over a computer and consequently looked a bit like a mole. But he was sweet and sensitive and Mia liked him a lot. After their first date she'd kissed him goodbye in front of the restaurant and the two of them had been almost blinded by the camera flashes as the paps had pounced, each of them desperate for an exclusive. As someone terrified of any attention at all, Seth had completely freaked out and ended it with her later that night.

It was all very upsetting but she'd picked herself up again and soon felt strong enough to start dating a guy called Hart, a real head-turner of a model who she knew would be used to having his photo taken. He did indeed seem to love being in the spotlight. But when she'd found out that he'd tipped off the paps about their third date so that he could be photographed basking in *her* spotlight, she'd forced herself to dump him without a second thought. The truth was, though, that she'd been devastated and had gone on to spend the entire weekend stuffing herself on takeaway pizza as she YouTubed over and over again his two-minute guest appearance on *America's Next Top Model*.

And finally there was Buck, a tough-talking baseball player with a soft centre who'd said he wanted to take things slowly after recently coming out of a painful break-up. Just when she'd started to think she might be falling for him, photos of them stepping out together had been splashed across trashy tabloids and gossip websites, one of which quoted a so-called friend to come up with the headline 'Marriage within a month for the First Lady of Love' – not the easiest read for someone wary of getting serious. Unsurprisingly, Buck had ditched her like a shot. Again, she'd been devastated but this time she'd had to deal with the public humiliation as well.

She sighed slowly like a deflating tyre. The way Mia saw things, the paparazzi really did have a lot to answer for.

'You know I've seen all your movies,' Dan said, interrupting her thoughts. 'You're very talented. And if you don't mind me saying so, from what I've seen on screen you sure do seem like a lovely lady.'

Now it was Mia's turn to be bashful. 'Oh that's very kind of you,' she said. 'But I have to let you know that in real life I'm nothing like the characters I've played.'

Mia felt that she had to make this point on first dates as she was starting to worry that men were confusing her with the kind of needy, clingy characters she played on screen. Not that there was anything wrong with that kind of person but she'd played so many of them that she sometimes thought men would assume she was a total desperado and run a mile.

Her first hit had been a movie called *Harassment*, in which she played a naïve young secretary whose boss suggests they fake a case of sexual harassment, sue their employer and split the proceeds. Only their plan falls apart when they fall in love, the harassment suit collapses and they're left with nothing but each other – although by this stage they're so in love that they realize that's all they need to be happy. Then there was *Lapping it Up*, in which she played a lapdancer with a heart of gold who gives up her dream of becoming a prima ballerina to elope with a customer who tells her he's a billionaire businessman but is actually a gangster on the run from both the police and the Mob. Obviously, he's heart-breakingly handsome, so she forgives his deception and falls for him anyway, joining him as he flees across the border to a new life in South America. And her last big hit was *The Princess and the Pauper*, in which she played a plucky British royal who renounces her title and claim to the throne to marry a dashing American divorcee who whisks her away from the glamour of her family's palace to live happily ever after on a pig farm in rural Tennessee.

Mia sipped her drink and thought back over her film roles. They might be weak and needy but none of them seemed to have any problem finding somebody to love them. Why was it so difficult for her? Sure, she had more to contend with – a public persona as the First Lady of Love and a squadron of hairy, sweaty paps trailing her everywhere. But however much she reminded herself of this it didn't stop her from feeling increasingly lonely, an emotion she'd never had to portray on screen. What she wanted now more than anything else was to be on a solid team of two, to know that she always had someone on her side, whatever happened. And she really hoped Dan would be that guy.

'So how about you?' he said. 'How come you're still single?'

Mia breathed in confidently. This is what she was good at – this was where the acting came in.

'Oh, you know, I'm so busy with my career at the moment that I just don't get the time to sit around pining for a man. Although, then again, if one should happen to come along . . .' She allowed herself to trail off with a giggle.

Was that all right? she wondered. *I hope I'm not coming across as too cold.*

Dan asked about her next film and Mia explained that she was about to finish making a movie with Billy Spencer, who everyone was calling the hottest actor in town. It was a period piece called *War of Words* and she was hoping it would be a big departure for her. True to form, she played a romantic novelist volunteering as a nurse on the frontline in the Second World War who has an explosive and passionate affair with a radical war poet. But the difference this time was that there was no happy ending and her soldier lover dies on the battlefield, leaving her character desolate and heartbroken. Mia had never starred in a weepie before so there was a whole different emotional journey for her to get her teeth into. And because the film didn't have a formulaic happy ending, it was being taken much more seriously – it wasn't even finished yet and there was already talk of film festivals and awards.

'I just heard we have to do a few reshoots for the ending,' Mia explained. 'But we're all excited about it – and I'm hoping it means I get to play more serious roles from now on.'

'Well I think we should drink to that.' Dan held out his glass and she brought hers to meet it with a cheery chink.

'To new beginnings!' Mia smiled.

'New beginnings!'

They sipped their drinks and held each other's gaze.

All I need now, Mia thought, *is someone to walk me down the red carpet.*

*

'Well I don't need you,' Eden spat. 'My DVD was the fourth biggest seller in Walmart last week!'

Leo sat there and took the flak. As he was breaking up with her he thought it was only right to let her express her anger – even if it was all directed at him.

'Exactly,' he offered, 'I'm sure you'll find someone much better than me. Someone who's famous too and then you can go out and be photographed together.'

'You know, when I think of all the men I turned down because I was dating you,' she ranted. 'You do realize I was hit on by Hart Blakemore last week? I mean, he's only the most famous male model in the world! His last girlfriend was *Mia Sinclair*!'

At the mention of Mia's name, Leo wondered how her date was going in the Mirage. He really hoped he could make it across town in time to catch her exit.

'You know, I always knew you'd be trouble,' Eden rattled on. 'My girlfriends warned me you were a bad boy. And man were they right.'

Leo wondered what time it was and if he could have a quick look at his watch without her noticing.

'And don't think I don't realize that all your bullshit about hating fame is just a cover. I can see right through you, Leo. You just don't want to admit that you're a dog – a dirty dog who can't commit.'

Leo was happy to sit there and take it like a man but this kind of comment really hurt him. He tried not to show it.

'You'll probably have another girlfriend by next week – if you haven't got one already!'

He stared at his beer and tried not to let her get to him. It was proving difficult.

Leo was aware that lately he'd built up a reputation as something of a bad boy, purely because he'd had so many girl-friends. His friend Ronnie joked about him being irresistible, having to fend off female admirers wherever he went. He had no idea why they all seemed to fall for him. Was it the British accent? Was it the motorbike? Was it that wonky grin they all seemed to talk about?

Whatever it was, the problem was that he had a knack of attracting girls who wanted to be famous – and who wanted his help to get there. Before he knew it he'd racked up a string of failed relationships, Eden being just the latest example. But the truth was, he'd only ever wanted one special girl – just one who *didn't* want to be famous.

Leo's phone vibrated again and he apologized and fished it out of his pocket.

'The problem with you paps,' Eden snarled, 'is you've got no feelings. You're just a bunch of cold-hearted sleazeballs!'

He tried to block her out and read the message. Apparently Mia Sinclair had just asked for her check and looked to be winding up her date. He really needed to get going soon or he wouldn't make it to the Mirage in time. If Eden didn't hate him enough already, she was going to hate him a whole lot more when he walked out on her, leaving her with a wad of cash to pay the bill.

'Well screw you, ass-wipe. *Screw you!*'

He took a deep breath and prepared to tell her that he was leaving. Across town he had an urgent assignation with Mia Sinclair, the First Lady of Love.

*

A nicotine-blonde waitress with a face like a King Charles spaniel brought over the check and plonked it down on the table between Mia and Dan. 'Have a great night!'

They finished the last of their drinks and Mia felt a glow of satisfaction that the evening had gone so well. Dan really did seem to be everything she was looking for in a man. But she couldn't allow herself to feel totally satisfied yet – it remained to be seen how he'd cope with the paparazzi, who were no doubt waiting outside the hotel that very moment. She gulped at the idea of subjecting him to the final – and without doubt the biggest and most difficult – test of the evening.

*

Leo was on his bike zipping down the Santa Monica Freeway, winding his way in and out of the traffic to get to the Mirage as fast as he could.

He was trying to relieve his guilt about dumping Eden by telling himself that there was no way things could have ever worked out between them. And she was wrong about him having no feelings; the problem was that he couldn't photograph anyone he did have feelings for. In fact, when he went to work it was almost like he had to switch *off* his feelings and adopt a different persona. And if he stopped being able to do this, he wouldn't be able to carry on doing the job he loved.

When he eventually made it to the hotel and parked up outside, he spotted a cluster of faces he recognized; the pack of paps in LA might have been big but most of them knew each other well from working the circuit. At the back of the pack Leo spied a bald head and a pair of little sticky-out ears and recognized his best mate Ronnie. He worked his way over to talk to him.

'Evening, partner.'

'Hey buddy, how'd it go with Eden?'

'Oh you know – it went. But at least it's out of the way now.'

'That's the spirit. And you still made it here in time to collect your pay check.'

'Looks like it. She's not come out yet then?'

'Not yet. But she's due any second – one of the valet boys has just gone to get her car.'

Leo followed Ronnie's eyes to the small group of people standing by the main entrance – two sniffy-looking doormen who were clearly gay but trying to butch it up, a pair of rich kids kissing like it was a whole new experience, and a fat man smoking a cigarette with the concentration of an addict about to catch a transatlantic flight. Mia Sinclair was nowhere to be seen. *Phew! Looks like I made it in plenty of time.*

Leo was just about to turn away when he spotted the faces of the doormen light up. And he knew just what that meant; they'd caught sight of Mia Sinclair.

When she emerged, it was hard not to stop and stare at her. She had baby blonde hair, a fresh complexion and piercing blue eyes. Tonight she looked incredible in a figure-hugging pastel blue dress with matching high-heeled sandals and a striking diamond necklace. And in case there was any doubt that the show was about to begin, she was glowing with an almost visible aura which Leo had come to recognize as good old-fashioned star quality.

Her date must have gone well as she was smiling brightly on the arm of a rather handsome man who was focused on her so intently that he almost tripped down the first step. Whoever he was, his presence next to Mia meant the paps had their story.

'Ker-ching!' beamed Ronnie.

In a matter of seconds, Leo and the rest of the pack jumped into Mia's path and snapped away, all the time shouting her name so she'd look into their lenses. As the couple pressed forward and fought their way down the steps, using their hands to shield them from the brightness of the exploding flashbulbs, Leo darted around them to get the best shot, sometimes holding up his camera as high as he could and angling it downwards without looking through the viewfinder – a trick known to paps as the 'Hail Mary'.

To the casual observer, this sudden eruption of noise, movement and relentlessly blinding flashes must have looked frightening and almost violently intense. The balding fat man dropped his cigarette and watched from the entrance open-mouthed. But for Leo – and Mia too – this was simply the reality of everyday life.

'Mia!'

'Over here, Mia!'

'To me, Mia!'

'No, to me, Mia!'

'Who's the dude, Mia?'

'Who's your new man, Mia?'

'Oh come *on*, Mia!'

Within seconds, Mia and her date had reached the bottom of the steps and slid into their waiting car. Leo spotted the man take the driving seat and thrust a bunch of notes into the hand of the valet. For a few seconds he sat there frozen, clutching the wheel with a horrified expression on his face. Then he hit the accelerator and the pack of paps scrambled out of the way and rushed to their cars and bikes. Whoever this guy was, if they got a shot of him kissing Mia goodnight, or better still going into her place, then it really would be payday.

*

'Phew!' gasped Dan. 'That was intense.' He whistled and shook his head.

'Welcome to my world,' chirped Mia, desperate to defuse the tension. 'Don't worry, you kind of get used to it after a while.'

Dan raised his eyebrows and punched the steering wheel. He didn't look like he wanted to get used to it.

Oh no! she thought. *Here we go again . . .*

Mia gazed out of the window and saw the bright lights of Sunset Boulevard whizzing by. Film posters glared down at her from all angles, often so big that they covered the sides of entire buildings. Right ahead was one for the DVD release of her last film *The Princess and the Pauper*. It featured a huge image of her wearing a tiara and gazing into the eyes of her leading man with a regal yet familiarly love-struck expression. Under the picture was the tag line 'Can love truly conquer all?' Right now she sure hoped it could.

They turned off Sunset and onto Laurel Canyon Boulevard.

'Wait a second,' said Dan, looking in the mirror, 'are they following us?'

She twisted her neck and saw four or five paps on motorbikes hot on their tail. 'I'm afraid so,' she soothed, patting his knee. 'Don't worry – it's perfectly normal.'

'Normal? This is what you call *normal*?'

Mia shrugged and sank back into her seat. She didn't like to tell him that as well as the motorbikes, they were also being followed by the cars behind and in front of them as well as four or five others she recognized trailing further back. In her head she heard a loud nee-noo sound effect from the TV quiz show she'd been imagining earlier. If coping with the paps was Dan's final test of the evening, it looked like he was about to fail miserably.

One of the motorbike riders inched alongside their car and edged just in front of them to get a clear view. Mia spotted a sticker of the British flag attached to the back of the bike. The pap held out his camera and turned it round at them, flashing away on the off-chance he'd get a decent shot.

Dan held out his hand as if to bat him away. 'Jeez, this is insane!'

'I'm sorry, Dan. It isn't always like this, I promise. They just haven't seen you with me before so they're chasing a story.'

'But I don't do drama, Mia. I'm just a regular guy.'

'Yeah, well there are ways to deal with it, you know. I have a car with blacked-out windows, which I drive if I don't want the paps to see anything. And there's always security . . .'

'Security? Blacked-out windows? I make furniture for a living, Mia. This really isn't my thing.'

Uh-oh. It sounded like Dan would definitely be joining Seth, Hart and Buck on the casualty list. Mia bit her lip to stop a tremble becoming anything else. For just a moment this evening she'd dared to imagine a future for her and Dan. She'd dared to imagine that she might finally have found love. With Nice Man Dan, who unfortunately wasn't quite nice enough to put up with the reality of dating Mia Sinclair.

*

Leo and the other paps raced down Mulholland Drive, heading off Mia's car to arrive at her place before she did. They'd worked this route several times before so knew exactly where they were going. After a few minutes they turned off Mulholland and down a much quieter side street, stopping when they recognized the entrance to Mia's house.

One after the other they parked their cars, threw down their bikes and quickly assumed their positions, cameras at the ready to start snapping away. At times like this, paps like Leo not only had to put to one side all emotion and sensitivity; they had to stop viewing the stars they were following as human beings and see them simply as targets. He knew that to many people this might seem cruel but if he was going to be any good at his job there was only one thing he could focus on – and that was the picture. And right now Leo was wondering what would happen with tonight's big picture.

He was surprised when the car eventually appeared but pulled up outside the property and didn't go through the gates. He assumed that the date hadn't gone well after all and the man wasn't being invited to spend the night. *Never mind*, he thought. *If we're lucky we might still get a kiss.*

*

'Well thanks for a lovely evening. Are you sure you don't want to come in for a nightcap?'

'Gee, I'd love to Mia but I've got an early start tomorrow.' For a fraction of a second his eyes flickered towards the paps snapping their conversation through the windscreen.

'Oh, OK,' she swallowed. 'I understand.'

Mia was crestfallen but didn't want to show it. She could

feel her chin start to wobble but did her best to smile through it. By now she was *really* glad she was an actress.

She wanted to kiss Dan goodbye but knew that the paps would go crazy if she did and she'd be answering marriage rumours for the next few weeks. Before she had time to think about it, Dan moved in to kiss her and she puckered up, ready to meet his lips. He went for her cheek but the flashbulbs exploded anyway. *Oh great*, thought Mia. *Tomorrow it'll be all over the papers: 'The First Lady of Love – dumped again!'*

'Well, goodnight then, Dan.'

'Yeah. See you around, I guess.'

But as he said it, she knew he didn't mean it.

She clutched the door handle and, before pulling it, stopped for a moment to compose herself. *Whatever you do, don't let the paps see you're upset.*

She took a deep breath and opened the door.

*

As Mia stepped out of the car, Leo was at the front of the pack, snapping relentlessly as she walked over to the security gates and began tapping in her code. The look on her face was steely and no-nonsense; she was obviously determined to give nothing away.

Leo stood watching as the gates to the house slowly opened and Mia disappeared behind them. The rest of the paps looked at each other and shrugged. The show was over.

But not for Leo.

Like most stars, Mia lived in a heavily gated property surrounded by bushes and trees and Leo knew from previous experience where to find a good peephole. As the other paps began looking back over their pictures, Leo slipped away and started scaling a huge tree with his bare hands, his camera dangling from around his neck. He straddled a thick branch with his legs and inched along until he came to a spot where, if he held his camera at the end of his outstretched arm, he could just about shoot through the leaves.

Leo would do almost anything to nail an exclusive shot. And right now he might just nail a dynamite one of the First Lady of Love at the end of another disappointing date.

*

As Mia walked up her driveway she could hear the pack of paps on the other side of the gates, chatting amongst themselves as they compared the shots they'd taken.

'Mmm, not bad.'

'That's a good one!'

'That's freakin' awesome!'

She stopped for a moment and sighed. The night had ended in disaster and she just wanted to go inside and forget about it. *Those damn paps! Why do they always have to ruin everything?*

Following her every move from several feet above, Leo was just about to start snapping when Mia sloped off and disappeared into her front porch. *Oh no! Why can't she stand still and look towards the camera?*

Sheltered from his lens under the roof of her porch, Mia's whole face began to tremble. She remembered her strict rule of not letting down her guard until she was safely behind the walls of her home. She took out her keys and prepared to enter her sanctuary.

Leo frowned and switched off his camera.

*

Mia opened her door and entered the empty house, slamming the door shut and slumping back against it. *Thank God*, she thought. *Safe at last.*

She loved her home but at times like this it felt like a prison, barricaded away from the rest of the world. And she found it exhausting to have to live her life as if she were permanently under siege.

She tried to snap out of it by reminding herself of how lucky she was. It wasn't so long ago that she'd been stuck with her mom in a tiny apartment in Cleveland struggling to make ends meet and dreaming about one day leading the privileged life of a movie star. But it was no use; however strong those memories were, they couldn't stop her from feeling overcome by a devastating feeling of loneliness.

And yeah, she didn't want to turn into one of those needy, desperate characters she played on screen. But as she stood staring into her empty house, all she could think was that there was a big, gaping emptiness in her life too. And however brave a front she put on for the world, she knew that only love could fill it. The problem was, she was beginning to lose hope that she'd ever find it.

She sank to the floor and buried her head in her hands. Within seconds she could feel the tears trickling down her face.

Outside she could just about make out the sound of the last pap's motorbike as it revved its engine and sped away into the night.

2

The following morning Leo woke up feeling terrible about his split from Eden. It wasn't that he regretted it or was worried that he'd made a mistake but that didn't stop him from feeling sad that someone he'd once been so fond of would no longer be part of his life. He couldn't help remembering that she hadn't always been a monster; and that at one point he'd even thought he might fall in love with her.

He'd decided to take a day off work and was trying to take his mind off things by strolling along Ocean Front Walk, the famous pedestrian promenade that was at the heart of Venice Beach. On his left was the beach itself, bordered by palm trees and tourists lounging on benches licking ice creams. Between them were dotted every variety of tarot readers, buskers, caricaturists, human statues and street masseurs. On the other side of the walkway were blocks of brightly coloured buildings facing the sea, many of them with elaborate murals painted along their fronts. Spilling out of the buildings were cafés with outdoor seating, noisy tattoo parlours and shops selling souvenirs, sun hats, knock-off sunglasses and all manner of ethnic and tie-dyed tat.

Padding along just ahead of Leo was his pet dog Watford,

an affectionate, permanently dribbling British bulldog named after his owner's hometown. Watford not only reminded Leo of home but also of how far he'd come from the drab reality of life in the English suburbs. It all seemed a million miles away from Venice Beach.

Watford pulled him forwards past the famous Muscle Beach outdoor gym towards a group of shirtless acrobats performing energetic routines for amazed tourists. A little further on was a fully costumed and made-up clown twisting balloons into animal shapes for groups of delighted children. And sauntering up and down the walkway was a man dressed as Spiderman, who didn't seem to be performing to anyone at all but was just soaking up the atmosphere.

Once again Leo's thoughts drifted to Eden. Although she lived in the Los Feliz neighbourhood just north of downtown LA, she'd always loved it here in Venice. Leo wondered how she was feeling this morning. At one point he'd thought about watching her appearance on *The Wendy Williams Show*. But then he'd thought it would be better to clear his head and decided to come out for a walk instead.

Whizzing past Leo one after the other were cyclists, runners, skateboarders and rollerbladers, as well as shell-suited seniors on their way to tai chi club on the beach. As he pressed on he passed through wave after wave of different music – from the bongo- and banjo-playing buskers to the summery pop shimmering out of sleek new sound systems in the shops and cafés. The only constant sound was that of hundreds of pairs of flip-flops slapping their way up and down the busy street.

When Leo had first come to LA five years ago he'd lived

in a neighbourhood called Silver Lake but had decided to settle here in Venice Beach once he'd made enough money to buy his first place. Sure, it was out of town but with his motorbike he could get anywhere quickly. And with its grungy, alternative vibe, Venice was easily the most British-feeling part of LA, often prompting Leo to wonder if that was why he'd settled here. There were times when it reminded him of Camden Town in London but with a pronounced Californian twist and, of course, never-ending sunshine.

On Leo's left he passed an acne-encrusted teenager with a snake draped around his neck. He remembered that Eden had had her photo taken with the snake the first weekend she'd stayed with him in Venice. Again he felt a surge of sadness and realized that he was missing her. Or more accurately, that he was missing the girl he'd hoped she'd be.

Coming up on the right Leo spotted one of his favourite Venice characters – a stoned tramp zonked out and slumped over a begging sign he'd made saying 'Need for Weed'. Leo couldn't help chuckling to himself – weed was clearly the *last* thing this guy needed. Leo loved the fact that Venice was full of characters like this, rather than Hollywood's interchangeable personality-free models of physical perfection. Characters like this were what gave Venice its colour and unique feel. Another of his favourites was coming up now – a heavily tattooed bull dyke who worked in the newsagents and always saved him a copy of his favourite British newspapers. 'Hey, Leo,' she boomed. 'How's my favourite Limey?'

Next appeared the tarot reader from Texas, who'd dyed his hair so badly that it looked like a cheap wig. 'Hey, dude, how's it hangin'?'

And then he saw the contortionist with ears the size of rhubarb leaves, who always wore a leopard-print thong and shuffled up and down the seafront in unimaginable positions. 'Whassup Leo? Where's Eden?'

Leo sighed, wondering why everyone was so fixated on him and Eden being together. *I tried my best!* he wanted to shout. *It wasn't my fault she turned into a monster!*

Watford let out a loud fart and Leo quickly scanned round to check that no one had heard. This was a long-standing habit of Watford's and whenever Eden had stayed over at Leo's apartment, he'd had to follow the dog around lighting matches to neutralize the various bad smells he left around the place.

Now that it was just the two of them he wouldn't have to bother.

*

'*Señora*, Meester Bob ees here!'

Mia's Mexican housekeeper Ramona was shouting up the stairs.

'I'm coming!' she yelled back at her. 'Just a second!'

She threw on a thick white dressing gown and skipped downstairs with a new bounce. That morning she'd woken up to memories of last night's disastrous date hitting her with a dull thud. But now that Bob had arrived, things were hopefully about to perk up.

Bob was Mia's Thai masseur, who she'd been using regularly for three years. She always thought it funny that he had such an English name as he'd managed to live in LA for more than a decade without learning a single word of the language. But he was perpetually polite and never seemed to stop smiling so over time Mia had grown comfortable with his long silences, particularly as everyone said he was the best masseur in the business. Her assistant Hector liaised with him to book her appointments and she had no idea how they communicated – she'd given up trying long ago. Ramona, however, hadn't. As Mia reached the kitchen she saw that the two of them were engaged in their usual giggly round of flirtation – despite the fact that neither of them spoke a word of the other's language.

'*¡Ay Bob, que chulo estás hoy!*'

'*Phom yaak cha non kab khun.*'

'*Quiero que me chingues lo más pronto posible.*'

They stopped as they spotted her, Ramona touching her neck and colouring with embarrassment.

'Will you two knock it off?' Mia joked fondly. 'Come on, Bob, we're ready for you upstairs.'

In their usual silence she led him out of the enormous, gleaming kitchen and into what she called her den. This was the entertainment room she'd fitted out for fun nights in with her girlfriends. It boasted a movie-sized TV screen, a fully stocked bar, a karaoke machine with its own stage, and a revolving dance floor complete with top-of-the-range lighting rig and a huge rotating glitter ball in the centre. There was even a pole for dancing around, which Mia had learned how to use when preparing for her role in the film *Lapping it Up*. An enormous framed poster for the film was hanging on one of the walls, together with other movie posters and framed magazine covers, all featuring Mia modelling various different fashions.

Next she led Bob through to her lounge, which was much warmer and cosier. Here, Mia had gone for a very simple look, with white walls, sofas and countless cushions, and a huge chandelier in the centre of the ceiling. On the glass coffee table there was an oversized vase of gigantic white calla lilies, and dotted around the room were pictures of Mia with her mother, girlfriends and a smattering of famous co-stars. Asleep on the sofas were her pet Russian Blue cats, who she'd bought as kittens when her first film had hit number one at the Box Office. At the time she'd been overwhelmed that her Hollywood fairytale was coming true so had named them Bogie and Bacall after one of Hollywood's golden couples. One of the cats yawned as Mia and Bob passed through.

Mia swept him through her marble-floored hall, awash with sunshine streaming through its stunning domed skylight, up the grand staircase with its elaborate wrought-iron banisters, and past the entrance to the home's master bedroom. As the door was only slightly ajar, all Bob could see was a glimpse of pastel pink. Mia hadn't been able to resist decorating it in her favourite colour.

Next door was a guest bedroom, which Mia had converted into a walk-in wardrobe, with endless racks of clothes arranged by colour, and entrances to two other closets – one for shoes and one for accessories. As she walked past she told herself that she may still be looking for love but at least in the meantime she had every girl's dream wardrobe. And she'd never stop appreciating it.

Just before their destination was Mia's favourite room of all – her very own hair and beauty salon, complete with huge cylindrical hairdryers and light-studded mirrors. She didn't think she'd ever get used to this, and every time she saw it she felt like the luckiest girl in the world. *What man could compare to this?* She let out a dreamy sigh but couldn't stop her voice from cracking.

Finally she led Bob through to her treatment room, which was Moroccan themed and decorated in various shades of dusky green, lit by genuine North African lanterns and scented by numerous Diptyque candles in her favourite jasmine. Sitting on a sofa waiting for them was Mia's best friend Serena. Bob gave her a little bow and began quietly unpacking his bags.

Serena was Mia's agent but they'd moved on from the usual actor–agent relationship years ago; Serena was more like a big sister to Mia now, always on hand to give her personal as well as professional advice. It was a role in which she excelled, being a few years older than Mia and having accrued a solid store of wisdom since she'd arrived in LA from her hometown of Harlem at the age of eighteen. Serena had been toughened up by an early career working as a model – not easy for a black woman in a largely white industry. Now she wasn't afraid to speak her mind, even if it was sometimes difficult to take.

As Mia removed her robe and lay down on her front for her massage, Serena sat back and sipped a green tea. 'Hey, sister,' she said, 'have you looked online this morning?'

'Oh no, I couldn't face it.'

'Well, when you do, take a look at Perez Hilton. He has a pap shot of you and some boring-looking dude on your way home from a date. Says he's a carpenter or something?'

'Yeah that'll be Dan – Nice Man Dan. Although he didn't turn out to be quite so nice once the paps showed up.'

'You don't say.'

'Oh, you know, it was the usual story: a quick car chase home and then he was falling over himself to dump me.'

'Man, that is such a pain in the ass. Well, at least the bloggers got their story straight for once.'

'Oh yeah, great, thanks Serena – everyone'll be having a good old laugh at me this morning then.'

'Don't say that Mia. Being unlucky in love hasn't done you any harm in the past – your fans go crazy for heartache, you know that. It only makes them love you more.'

'Yeah but you're not the one who has to read those headlines about yourself. "Mia Sinclair may be the First Lady of Love but in real life she can't get a man." Have you any idea how that feels, Serena?'

'I know, baby. But you're going to have to be brave because it'll be all over the papers later.'

'Yeah well, I was really upset last night but I'm over it now. I mean, it's not as if it comes as a surprise anymore when the paps screw everything up. I just don't know what to do about it, that's the problem.'

In the corner, Bob was busy preparing his various potions and warming up his hands.

'Mia, I've told you before – I don't mind helping you out with decoy cars and stuff like that. We've fooled their ass before so I'm sure we can do it again.'

'Yeah but we couldn't do that forever – sooner or later any man who dates me would have to face the paps. And if he's going to dump me I'd rather it happened straight off than months into a relationship.'

'Well there is that, I guess. At least the paps are your built-in bullshit detector.'

'Hmpf, well they've sure been working overtime lately.'

The two of them laughed and Bob moved over to begin

working on Mia. Within minutes she could feel herself starting to relax.

Very soon she'd have forgotten all about Nice Man Dan.

*

In his home nestled away in a secluded corner of the Hollywood Hills, Billy Spencer was lying in a bed so big that his interior designer had joked it could sleep a family of four. Of course, he was aware that some people might find a bed so big sickeningly extravagant but it was also damn comfortable. And not only had Billy worked hard for everything he'd achieved in life but he'd also made major sacrifices along the way – which in his book meant that he was entitled to enjoy the perks of being a movie star.

Right now he was supposed to be reading a pile of scripts his agent had sent over but he just couldn't concentrate. Instead, he'd settled into a daze, looking out through the bedroom's glass walls at the view of the city, opening and closing his remote-controlled floor-to-ceiling shutters so that the famous Hollywood sign appeared and then disappeared as if it were winking at him. *Man, it's good to be me.*

That morning Billy could justify lounging around in bed as he'd been up late attending a fundraiser thrown by the trophy wife of a studio boss in aid of some obscure charity she ran in order to boost her social life. The dinner had gone on for hours and he'd been sitting in between a pair of crushing bores with terrible halitosis but at the party afterwards he'd been bombarded by admirers telling him how wonderful he was, how much they enjoyed his work and how much they loved him. He'd only had to make the occasional banal observation and everyone had thrown their heads back and given off gales of uncontrollable laughter. Even though he'd originally intended to dip in and out of the event and do only what was expected of him, he'd ended up staying for hours, lapping up the adulation.

Ooh, he remembered, *I might have a little look online to see how the photos turned out.*

He reached down for his laptop at the side of the bed, fired it up and entered the name of the official photographers who'd been hired to cover the event. Straight away he was hit by several images of himself; his chestnut hair, square jaw and muscular frame complemented by a fitted Dior suit and slim tie, staring into the cameras, flashing the trademark smile he'd perfected through years of studying photos like these. There he was, smiling with his hands in his pockets, leaning slightly forwards – a pose he always knew delivered great results. And there he was again standing to one side fiddling with his cuff, as if casually distracted – another tried-and-tested favourite. In shot after shot his smile looked exactly the same but that didn't bother him. As long as he looked good, that's what was important.

And these were the kind of photos Billy loved, ones which he knew were coming and which he could prepare for. They were so much more flattering than the photos the paparazzi took when they caught him off guard. He hated those – they always managed to capture him at his worst, with his nostrils flared like a carthorse or his mouth straining at a funny angle, as if he were curling out a huge dump. Of course he knew that was the point but all the same, it didn't make him feel particularly good about himself.

And people always assumed that because he was one of the most famous men in the world, Billy didn't need any help feeling good about himself. But nothing could be further from the truth. In fact, the only reason he'd become famous in the first place was because he desperately wanted people to like him – then perhaps he could like himself that little bit more.

He clicked off the site and was automatically redirected to Google's homepage. Staring out at him was the empty white box into which he'd entered his name so many times. And right now it was very tempting . . .

B-I-L-L-Y

He began typing his name.

I really should get up and start reading those scripts.

S-P-E-N-C-E-R

His finger hovered over the Enter key.

Oh come on, just one little Google search first . . .

He hit the Enter key and in an instant the page flashed up the top ten search results. He scanned down and quickly took in a couple of news stories about last night's fundraiser, a lengthy blog speculating about his love life, a preview of his next film *War of Words*, and an article reporting that last month he was the fifth most Googled celebrity in the world. Now even allowing for his own considerable activity Googling himself, that must mean a lot of people were interested in him. And a lot of people liked him. And that felt good – it felt really good.

Forgetting that he'd rationed himself to just one little search, he was soon logging onto fan sites and forums such as *ilovebillyspencer.com* and *billylicious.org*. He already knew the most popular ones off by heart and had even set up fake accounts and usernames so he could join in the discussion.

Oh he knew that most people would think what he was doing was vain and egotistical but the truth was that he found reading what other people thought about him relaxing. Some stars might have a massage or a facial but he liked to read nice things about himself. Where was the harm in that?

'I love you Billy Spencer!' read one posting. 'I wanna have your baby!'

'Billy Spencer is so hot,' read another, 'I'd eat his shit with a rusty spoon.'

As he clicked through page after page, Billy couldn't help smiling brighter and brighter each time. Sure, some of the fans sounded a little unhinged but what was important was that they loved him, they really loved him. And it made him feel so *right*.

Of course he didn't need a therapist to tell him that the only reason he was so desperate for validation was because he'd been so cruelly rejected by his own parents, the very people who were supposed to love him the most – and unconditionally.

You're disgusting, Billy.

You're no son of ours!

No amount of adoring comments on fan sites could ever take away the pain insults like these had caused, a pain that felt just as strong all these years later.

Get out of our sight, Billy.

We never want to see you again!

He tried to block out the hurt by looking at a photo of a fan who'd tattooed his name around her belly button. But it was no use; he needed something much more powerful. And he knew just where to find it.

The problem with fan sites was that they didn't give you a particularly balanced view of how you were perceived in the world. For that Billy knew he had to search for his name on more democratic social media sites like twitter. Here, people famously spoke their minds – and didn't hold back if they were feeling vicious or angry. For this reason Billy could only look on twitter when he was having a good day. But if he did and he happened to find positive comments then it meant so much more to him than anything written on a fan site – and for a moment he could almost forget the pain of parental rejection.

He reassured himself that today *was* a good day and began typing the web address into his tool bar. He entered the details of his false account and username, and as soon as he hit the Search key, hundreds of responses appeared.

'Man, Billy Spencer is so freakin hot! No one can be that perfect. He's got to have a tiny dick! ;-)'

He chuckled. It was a backhanded compliment, but still a compliment.

'Just watching Billy Spencer in *Foreign Affair*. What a kick-ass performance. And a major hottie too!'

Again he smiled brightly.

But then one tweet caught his eye which caused his smile to droop. It had been posted by *alphamale007*.

'Billy Spencer is such a loser. He's cheesy as hell and can't act for shit. Man, he's a total DICK!'

Straight away he could feel anxiety sweep through his body. How could somebody think that about him?

He stared at the tweet till the letters spun out of focus. And as they did his self-doubt started to rise.

Did *alphamale007* have a point? Was he a lousy actor? Maybe he *was* a dick after all. If someone thought that enough to say it on twitter then maybe others were thinking the same thing. And how many people had read the comment already? He looked on the user's profile and saw that he had 197 followers. Nearly 200 people who'd probably read the tweet and laughed at it – laughed at *him*!

Billy's day had been ruined. He felt crushed and rotten to the core.

Maybe Mom and Dad were right about me after all . . .

He sat up in bed and snapped his laptop shut, trying to block out an overpowering feeling of self-loathing. But it was no use – the words he'd just read kept spinning round and round in his head.

At times like this he knew there was only one thing he could do to make himself feel better. He needed to go out into the world and prove to himself that he *was* still loved.

Those scripts would have to wait until tomorrow.

*

Leo strode forward and gulped in a huge breath of sea air. He'd walked north of Venice Beach and was just coming into the centre of Santa Monica. The more he ploughed on, the more he felt that he was shedding his sadness about breaking up with Eden. Rather than getting increasingly tired, with each step he felt more energized and positive about life. Unfortunately, at the same time, Watford's energy was gradually waning and his pace slowing. Leo was now leading him and had to give his leash a little tug to move him forward.

'Come on boy! Off we go!'

Santa Monica was much less rough around the edges than Venice and more representative of what people in the rest of the world imagined LA to be like. The lifeguards wore the red uniforms made famous in *Baywatch* and sat scanning the waterfront from the porches of painted wooden huts scattered the entire length of the gorgeous sandy beach. Between them were groups of stunning sunbathers and unfeasibly ripped surfers standing in the ocean waiting to catch the waves. The occasional dolphin bobbed in and out of the sunlight-dappled water, and stretching out to the horizon was the old wooden pier, home to the Pacific Park fairground and its famous Ferris wheel. Leo took it all in as he and Watford walked on. It really was a beautiful sight.

Leo realized at that moment just how much he loved LA. It was the eternal optimism of the place that he'd first fallen in love with, the sense of everything being possible. No one had wanted to pigeonhole him or hold him back here. And he'd discovered that the cliché about LA was true; no one was interested in where he came from, just in where he was going. It had been a relief to shake off the pessimism and cynicism of the old world and come to a new world where you could practically smell the self-belief in the air. La La Land. City of Angels. Leo's adopted home.

It wasn't as if he could pretend he'd had a difficult childhood or a traumatic past to escape from. He'd been brought up in a perfectly comfortable family home; his dad was a policeman and his mum a primary school teacher and he had three older sisters who'd doted on him throughout his youth. It was just that he'd grown up, moved on and discovered there was more to life than the deadening mediocrity of the English suburbs. He'd started to notice how seldom his parents ever expressed happiness – or any vital emotions for that matter. He used to look at them and worry that if he stayed in Watford he'd end up just like them, plodding through the motions of life without really experiencing everything it had to offer, without really *living*.

And then he'd come on his first trip to LA and it had all changed. He could still remember gliding down Rodeo Drive in a convertible Audi, the sun dodging in and out of the palm trees. He hadn't been able to stop himself shouting out at the top of his voice, overwhelmed by a new feeling he soon recognized as happiness. He made up his mind there and then that he was never going back to Watford.

When he looked back at his past now, Leo was so thankful that he'd fallen into this life – he'd never really had any kind of master plan and had only tried his hand as a paparazzo when a photographer he'd met at a party had seen how nifty he was on his bike and suggested that he use it to earn himself a living. He'd worked the circuit in London for a few years before coming to LA on holiday with an old schoolfriend who had wealthy relatives living in Beverly Hills. And then happiness had entered his life and he'd never looked back.

Beep beep!

It was a text alert from his photographic agency Shooting Stars. Apparently Billy Spencer had just been spotted arriving at the Beverly Center. Leo had no idea what he was doing in a shopping mall surrounded by members of the public but he told himself that it didn't matter; today was his day off, his healing day. And anyway, Ronnie would be sure to cover the job – that is if he made it in time. Right now none of that was

Leo's concern and he decided to put work right out of his mind.

Watford had started to wilt in the sunshine, panting louder and louder and dragging his hind legs along the pathway, a mournful expression on his face. It was about time Leo turned back and took him home; he might even have to carry him some of the way.

Before he left, he stopped to take one last look at the view of Santa Monica stretching out before him. *What a wonderful day and what a wonderful city*, he thought.

Sure, he hadn't had much luck in finding someone special to share his life with. But now that he'd had a chance to think everything over, he knew that he had nothing to feel sad about. Nothing at all.

*

Mia slumped onto the sofa and settled into a post-massage mellow. In fact, she felt so mellow that she was even happy to initiate the kind of conversation about her love life that she usually found difficult.

'Serena?'

'Mmm-hmm?'

'Do you think I'll ever find the right guy?'

Serena was still in a decidedly *pre*-massage mood. 'Sure I do,' she said. 'And when you do he won't give a rat's ass about fame – or the paps!'

She lay down on the table, ready for Bob to start work.

'But you know what I think,' she went on, 'it's not going to happen until you take a serious look at your approach to dating.'

'Uh-oh,' Mia joked, 'here we go again.'

Bob leaned forward and began kneading Serena's flesh.

'Well, it's true,' she said, letting out a little groan of pleasure. 'It's way off the mark. You're too freakin' businesslike about it and totally inflexible in what you're looking for. You need to quit searching for a boyfriend as if you're casting a leading man in one of your movies.'

'OK, OK. Well what do you suggest then?'

'Haven't we been through all this? I've been telling you for years that you need to get yourself a man who's in the industry.'

'But I tried that with Hart and look how that finished up.'

'Yeah but that doesn't mean that every guy in the industry's going to be an asshole. You know, at least they get the pressure you're under and understand how it works with the paps. How about dating an actor?'

'No way. Actors are all trouble – you know that. I mean, come on, Serena. The only one I actually like is Billy and he's gay!'

Serena put her finger to her lips and nodded towards Bob. 'Sssh!'

'Oh it's OK,' Mia breezed. 'Bob doesn't understand a word of English.'

Serena raised her eyes as if to say, *Even so*. Bob carried on kneading her flesh without the slightest reaction; he clearly wasn't following their conversation and they didn't have to worry.

'Well, I still think you're making things way too hard for yourself,' Serena went on, her speech slowing as she became gradually more relaxed. 'Look at me and Mitchell – he wasn't my type at all. I'd spent my entire life dating ball players and jocks – I never thought I'd end up with a dorky accountant for Christ's sake. But it's only when I looked outside my usual casting that I found the right guy. We've been together eight years now and I couldn't imagine life without him.'

'So what are you trying to say here exactly? That I should date an accountant?'

'No! You *know* what I think – that you're managing and controlling things too much. If you start off with a precise checklist then you're leaving no room for magic. And you can't control these things, Mia. If you want my advice, you need to loosen up a little and go with the flow.'

'But is it really so bad to be a little cautious? All I'm trying to do is stop myself from being hurt. I'm frightened, Serena. I know it sounds stupid but I'm really frightened.'

There was a pause and they both listened to Bob working his fingers along Serena's shoulders.

'Look, sister,' she began gently, 'I just think you're being a little too guarded. You need to give up some of that precious control. And those barriers need to come down – big time.'

'But I've already had my heart broken once, Serena. And there's no way I'm going there again.'

'Wait a second. I know you've just had a run of bad luck, but I didn't realize one of them had broken your heart.'

'Oh I'm not talking about any of those dumb guys! I'm talking about my dad, Serena. My dad broke my heart – he really did. And I've never been able to forget it.'

'Hmpf. Well unless you do, you'd better get used to being on your own a whole lot longer. Sometimes you have to take risks to win big in this life. And at the moment, sister, you ain't even playing the game.'

Mia gave out a loud huff and decided she was through with this conversation. If it went on any longer, pretty soon she was going to need another massage.

*

Boy, it sure was great to be Billy Spencer.

That was the thought going round Billy's mind as he strode through the Beverly Center. On either side of him people stopped in their tracks, some of them staring in amazement, others gasping out loud. He'd only parked his car five minutes ago and already he'd been asked to pose for several photos and sign a handful of autographs. As he watched people's faces light up at the sight of him, that morning's nasty tweeter seemed less and less important.

Who cares what he thinks anyway? Billy thought as he glided on. *Everyone else loves me!*

'Welcome to Bloomingdales, Mr Spencer!'

At the entrance to the department store he was greeted by an efficient-looking sales assistant whose eyes sparkled as she shook his hand. Word had obviously reached the store that a famous actor was in the mall and they'd only needed a few minutes' notice to roll out their special VIP welcome. This kind of attention was one of the perks of being a star – and Billy revelled in it.

'Hello ma'am,' he grinned. 'Good to meet you.'

'Good to meet you too. My name's Latona. Is there anything I can help you with today?'

He quickly invented some cock-and-bull story about

needing to buy a present at the last minute for his cleaner's birthday. Of course it was totally implausible; everyone knew a star as big as Billy could have whatever he wanted sent over to his home in an instant and didn't need to go out shopping himself. But that wasn't the point. He'd learnt from previous experience that nobody ever doubted his story – they were all way too pleased to see him for that.

Unfortunately he'd also learned from experience that he didn't have much time to enjoy himself before the paps arrived and spoiled the fun. Once they appeared the public tended to lose their cool and there was a real chance chaos would break out. His security team had warned him on numerous occasions that dropping into busy shopping malls like this represented a major risk to his safety. But he reckoned he'd have fifteen minutes or so before he'd be in any real danger.

'I was thinking of maybe buying her a nice perfume,' he lied, treating Latona to his full-wattage red-carpet smile.

Although she was clearly used to dealing with celebrities, he could see her composure waver. 'Of course, Mr Spencer,' she croaked. 'Follow me.'

The perfume counter was less than fifty yards away but Billy was stopped en route by a string of fans asking for his picture. His presence in the store was like an electric charge sparking off excitement all around him.

'I love you, Billy!' drooled a middle-aged woman in chunky jewellery and free-flowing crafty clothes.

'I love you too!' oozed a generic blonde, the joins of her cheap hair extensions clearly visible.

'You're even better looking in real life!' gushed a skanky redhead with a lipsticked cold sore.

'Thank you, ladies,' Billy smiled, feigning embarrassment. 'You're too kind, really.'

When he eventually made it to the perfume counter he found a trio of sales assistants slouching around twiddling their hair. Once they spotted him they immediately straightened up, lurching forwards with a collective squeal.

'Good morning, ladies,' he breezed, playing up his Southern accent, 'and how are y'all today?'

They broke out in nervous giggles and one of them dropped a bottle of Jean-Paul Gaultier onto the tiled floor. This was even better than Billy had imagined.

As the assistants busied themselves clearing up the mess, Latona stepped in and began spraying various scents onto cards.

'This is the latest Stella McCartney,' she explained, as businesslike as she could manage.

'That's real nice,' Billy quipped, paying no attention whatsoever. He was distracted by a goosebumped girl with train-track braces hovering shyly and clutching a camera phone.

'Well hi, sugar,' Billy cooed. 'Would you like a photo?'

'Y-y-y-y-yes please,' she managed, her parents ushering her forward.

'Well come on over here,' he coaxed. 'There ain't nothing to be afraid of.'

As she stepped forward he put his arm around her stiff shoulders and her parents snapped away with their phones.

Take that, alphamale007!

The family thanked him and then huddled together to look at the photos. As he heard them whooping with glee he couldn't help thinking about his own parents and his heart contracted with sadness.

The truth was that his own family had never been as close as the one he was looking at now. His parents were fanatically religious, making no secret of the fact that they cared about God more than their only son. When he'd told them he was gay at the age of eighteen, they'd bundled him off to a Christian rehab clinic in Arizona where they'd tried to cure him of what they called his 'evil urges' through a long course of fasting, aversion therapy and hours and hours of prayer. For weeks he'd had no contact with the outside world and was repeatedly told he was possessed by the demon of perversion, which a group of the course 'mentors' tried to drag out of him in a series of torturous exorcisms. He only got out of the clinic by summoning up all his powers as an actor to convince them that not only was he now straight but he was also the most committed Christian ever to walk the earth. He shuddered at the memory; it had been a brutalizing, traumatic experience and he really didn't want to re-live it now.

'And how about this one?' asked Latona. 'It's by Hermès and is very popular at the moment.'

Billy leaned forward and pretended to sniff it.

'Mmm that's the one! I'll take your biggest bottle please.'

Latona nodded and began unrolling the gift wrap. As Billy took out his card he casually glanced at the crowd of customers gathering around to stare at him.

'Excuse me,' came a voice, 'but may we have a photo?'

A pair of shy young men approached, one of them covered in freckles, the other wearing Harry Potter glasses. They were holding hands and clearly a couple.

'Well of course you can, boys,' Billy beamed, used to the attention of his gay fans. Even though he wasn't remotely camp, he deepened his voice a little just to be on the safe side. 'It would be my pleasure.'

The one with the freckles slipped in next to him. 'He takes such *terrible* photos,' he told Billy, loud enough for his boyfriend to hear. 'Try not to cut my head off this time!' he called out teasingly.

The boyfriend shot him a look of mock offence but genuine affection.

Billy was touched by how much they clearly loved each other but felt a flicker of sadness when it reminded him of what was missing in his own life.

'You know, we've only been in LA for a week,' said the one with the freckles, 'and already we've met our favourite movie star!'

As Billy smiled for the camera, he cast his mind back to his own first week in the city. Shortly after his experience in Arizona, he'd told his parents that he'd fallen in love with a former lesbian he'd met in gay rehab and wanted to go and say goodbye to her before she left her home in LA to do some work on a Christian mission in Africa. Once he'd arrived in the city he wrote his parents a letter explaining that there was no lesbian, he was definitely gay and, what's more, he was never coming home.

He'd then dipped his toe into the gay area of West Hollywood, still only tentatively as he was just growing comfortable with his sexuality after so many years of being told it was sinful. But for the first time in his life he'd felt free, exploring gay bars, shops, clubs and gyms and even going on a few dates with prospective boyfriends. It had all been intoxicating and he'd been blown away by the discovery that his sexuality was something to be celebrated rather than a source of shame. But unfortunately, this happy time had lasted only a few months. To his utter shock, everything had changed once he'd pursued his dream of becoming an actor.

Billy had been lucky enough to land himself a top agent relatively quickly and before he knew it he was being offered small parts on television. But when he'd told his agent that he was gay, the agent had freaked and Billy had felt like he was coming out to his parents all over again. Men he'd dated had had to be paid off and he was forced back into the closet after only a few months of freedom. He soon came to realize that his sexuality was even more of a problem in LA than it had been at home in Mississippi.

'My turn!' cheeped the young man in the Harry Potter glasses as he thrust the phone into his boyfriend's hand. 'You know we're such big fans of yours Billy, we've seen all your movies! We saw *Stroke of Midnight* on our first date!'

'Well I'm glad it worked out so well for you,' Billy replied, smiling for the camera but starting to feel a little uneasy.

Can they tell that I'm gay too? he wondered.

He imagined what they'd say if he just came out with it. Of course, there was no way that he would; he'd learned long ago to keep his sexuality strictly under wraps. And the more successful he became, the more important it was not to let the secret out. Over the last few years, as his profile had grown bigger than he'd ever imagined, his sexuality had begun to feel like a permanent burden weighing heavily on his shoulders – the only cloud ruining an otherwise bright blue sky. Only a few people in the industry knew that he was gay, including his agent and publicist and a handful of close friends such as Mia Sinclair. Which meant that he had to live life permanently on the defensive, worrying about ever letting slip the slightest clue.

He looked at his watch and realized that he had to make a move soon before the paparazzi arrived. Billy couldn't help feeling on edge around them, worried that they could see through his façade – or that they'd pounce and out him as gay if they spotted the slightest chink in his armour.

'Well, nice meeting you, boys,' he said to the young couple, anxious to wind up the encounter, 'and I hope you go on enjoying the movies!'

He gave them each a hug and a manly pat on the back. The boys backed away slowly, eager to prolong the experience as much as they could.

As he paid for the perfume, Billy spotted a couple of paps pretending to browse in the lingerie section as they shot him across the crowded store. There was one he vaguely recognized with a bald head and little sticky-out ears. Just being in their presence made him bristle with anxiety and he could feel an air of aggression beginning to spread its way around the store. He reached onto his head and pulled down his face-swallowing sunglasses. *I really need to get out of here.*

He thanked Latona for all her help. 'It's been a real pleasure to meet you, ma'am.'

'You too, Mr Spencer. Come back soon!'

As he turned to leave he wondered how long it would take to get to his car. Now that the paps had arrived the fun was most definitely over.

'Excuse me, Mr Spencer!'

He stopped and turned back. 'Yeah?'

Latona was holding out his bag of perfume. 'Aren't you forgetting something?'

'Oh yeah, erm, sorry.'

He took it off her and dashed out. 'Thanks!' he called out behind him.

Out of the corner of his eye he could see the paps shooting away.

*

Once Bob had worked his magic on Mia and Serena, they said their goodbyes and moved downstairs to have lunch in the garden.

Mia's garden was set out like a Spanish hacienda with a tiled patio, bougainvillea trailing along the walls and Mediterranean palms providing the odd spot of shade. Its immaculate green lawns stretched out onto an expansive view of the city while a full-sized infinity pool added an undeniable wow factor. When Mia had first seen it, when she'd stopped shooting back-to-back movies for long enough to buy her own place, her jaw had practically cracked the patio tiles.

Now Mia and Serena were sitting at a long dining table under an awning at the back of the house, with Bogie and Bacall lounging at their feet. Ramona was busy in the outdoor kitchen grilling fish and steaming vegetables for lunch.

Today was the first day of Mia's crash diet to get back in shape for a new sequence they were shooting for her upcoming film *War of Words*. Principal photography had taken place months earlier, before which Mia had put herself through hell to diet and exercise her way down to a size zero – a strict stipulation of her contract. Now that they were about to start shooting again, she'd have to match her previous weight exactly. Which meant working out with her trainer every day and eating nothing but grilled fish and vegetables for the next two weeks. She knew from previous experience that this was going to be tough.

Mia wished that she could be one of those girls who ate what they wanted, did no exercise and still managed to be stick thin. But biology was working against her; her mother and grandmother had been naturally hefty and her only aunt back in Cleveland had always been a big girl too. There was no doubt about it, Mia had to work hard at her figure. And today the hard work was about to start all over again.

'So what did the producers say?' she asked Serena, munching on a stick of celery. 'What exactly am I doing in these new scenes?'

'OK, here's the deal. They've test screened the picture and audiences loved it. They *loved* it, Mia – the studio said they've not had a movie get such high scores in more than ten years.'

'Brilliant! So what's the problem?'

She paused and took a breath. 'They loved the picture but *hated* the ending.'

'Oh no. But what about my big crying scene, all that grief on the battlefield?'

'I'm not going to bullshit you, Mia – they want to cut it.'

'You've got to be kidding! But isn't the whole point of the movie that it's a weepie?'

Serena raised her eyebrows.

'Oh no. Don't tell me I have to reshoot a happy ending? Jeez, not again.'

'Not exactly. What they want to do is work out the tension that builds up during the love story. Remember how Billy's character is always dismissive of the books your character writes?'

'Yeah, there's that big scene where he says there's no place for romance on the battlefield.'

'OK. Well what they want to do is end with you discovering that he's been shot and killed but *then* you find a romantic poem he secretly wrote for you before he died. Do you see? So it's still a sad ending but—'

'But love wins through. Love conquers all, yet again. Great. Now they'll never quit calling me the First Lady of Love.'

'Well you've got to admit, it *is* kind of clever. And if it's giving audiences what they want . . .'

'Oh don't get me wrong, Serena, I like it – it's a brilliant ending. I just thought that for once I'd get to do something different.'

'Oh come on, Mia, this *is* different. Your character just gets to feel loved at the end, that's all.'

Mia reached down for Bogie and settled him on her lap.

'Hmm, maybe that's why I find it so hard to take. It kind of rubs salt into the wound, I guess.'

'Now you do realize that you're only saying that because you're feeling sorry for yourself . . .'

'Yeah, yeah, I know.'

Mia gazed out at the garden, stroking the cat.

'Well at least I'll get to hang out with Billy again . . .'

Serena gave a wry smile. 'And you know they're already promising a big Oscar campaign . . .'

Ramona broke in, plonking what looked like a thoroughly lacklustre lunch on the table. '*¡Buen provecho, chicas!*'

'*Gracias*,' chirped Serena.

Mia ignored the food and carried on stroking Bogie.

'OK,' she said. 'You win – I'll do it.'

'That's my girl!'

She looked at the food and rolled her eyes. She was dreading surviving on nothing but this for two whole weeks. 'All I have to do now is get down to a size zero. *All over again.*'

'Well look on the bright side – it'll take your mind off trying to find a man.'

'Hmpf! I'll be way too hungry to get a man.'

'Yeah, well be careful, sister. Hunger can make a girl do funny things . . .'

3

'Man, this job sucks!'

Leo and Ronnie were crouching in an overfull skip at the side of La Cienega Boulevard, somewhere between West Hollywood and Beverly Hills. The sun was beating down, the skip stank of rotting fish and there was some kind of metal skewer poking into Leo's back.

'Definitely not one for the top ten,' huffed Leo. 'What's she *doing* in there?'

The two of them were doorstepping Mia Sinclair after receiving a tip-off that she was working out with her trainer in celebrity gym The Ab Lab. What they were really hoping for was a shot of her coming out of the gym looking sweaty and bedraggled but they knew that they wouldn't nail this if Mia had even the slightest inkling they were outside. Which is why they found themselves hiding in an overflowing skip stinking of rotting fish with no protection from the blazing sun.

'Man, it's so freakin' hot in here,' whistled Ronnie, 'I'm sweating like a virgin on a date with a porn star.'

'Yeah well, Mia's been in there all morning – she can't be much longer now.'

'Dude, I sure hope not – I'm starting to get real grouchy.' He reached for his cigarettes and lit his fifth smoke of the day. 'Which smart-ass came up with this idea anyway?'

'OK, OK, guilty as charged. Maybe I do get a bit carried away sometimes. But you know what I'm like about nailing the best shots.'

'What, like the time you had us disguised as Mexican mariachi to pap Gwyneth Paltrow and Chris Martin on their honeymoon?'

'Yeah and if you remember, if your comedy moustache hadn't fallen off we might have got away with it!'

'Or the time we blacked up as refugees in Darfur to snap Angelina Jolie handing out food?'

'Yeah and we would have pulled that off too if you didn't have a tattoo that said "I love Rosie" on your arm!'

With a cheeky grin, Ronnie held up his hand as if he weren't listening. 'You know, it's about time you faced it, bud. The thrill of the chase really swings your balls. You're a junkie, Leo – a serious adrenaline junkie.'

Before Leo had time to come back at him, the two of them heard text alerts coming from their mobile phones. It was their agency Shooting Stars tipping them off that Destiny Diament, a washed-up reality TV star with a serious prescription drug habit, would be having open-air sex on a quiet beach in Malibu with her new boyfriend Hank Haslam, an ageing bodybuilder turned actor who hadn't had a hit movie in years and had recently earned the nickname Hank Has-been. Apparently Destiny was about to launch a discount underwear range and was pulling out all the stops to ensure she got maximum pub- licity. Any snappers taking on the job were promised they wouldn't be disappointed. Destiny and Hank might not be big stars but for a pap this was an easy assignment. As the whole thing was set up, the job would be over and done with in half an hour.

'What do you reckon, buddy?' asked Ronnie, stubbing out his cigarette. 'Malibu Beach sure has to beat this stinking dumpster.'

'OK, I'll toss you for it.'

'Well I'm heads. And I'm going to whip your ass!'

Leo smiled and took out a quarter. He flicked it, caught it on his palm and then slowly revealed the head of George Washington.

'Ker-ching!' beamed Ronnie. 'Looks like I'm off to Malibu Beach.'

'Go on, mate, you enjoy it.'

'Well you've got to admit, it sure makes a change. It's usually you who has all the luck.'

'Yeah but aren't you forgetting it's me who just split up with his girlfriend?'

'Well in that case you could do with some quality healing time on your own.'

'What? In a skip?'

'In America we call them dumpsters, Limey. And you'd better start healing 'cause I'm out of here.'

As Ronnie leapt out of their hiding place Leo wriggled around, stretching out to fill the extra space.

'Go get 'em, partner!' he shouted after him.

As he settled into his new position he realized that the skewer was no longer poking into his back but he was now sitting on what felt like some kind of hat stand. He really hoped Mia wouldn't be much longer.

*

Inside The Ab Lab, Mia was hanging from a steel cube attached to the ceiling balancing a hula-hoop on the end of her big toe.

'Are we done yet?' she croaked.

'Not yet – another thirty seconds!'

Cole was an exceptional trainer but sometimes Mia wondered why she put herself through this. So far today she'd done half an hour of Pilates on his new reformer machine, half an hour of skipping, hopping and jumping on a treadmill, and was now suspended in his own patented cube holding excruciating yoga positions for what seemed like an eternity. She was exhausted. And she *hated* exercise.

'Are you sure your watch isn't broken?' she gasped. 'I don't think I can do this much longer.'

Cole smirked and shook his head. 'Five-four-three-two-one. And relax, girlfriend!'

He stepped forward to help her down and she practically crumpled into his arms. The sheer size of Cole never ceased to amaze Mia; his chest was more than the width of a double wardrobe and she was sure his neck was thicker than her waist. But there was nothing remotely threatening about him – far from it. He insisted on working out to dance remixes of Madonna or Britney, minced around the studio in spangly silver hot pants, and had such a squeaky voice that he sounded like somebody was permanently standing on his foot.

'Now then, girlfriend, time for some *serious* fun!' he trilled.

She tried not to groan as he attached weights to her wrists

and ankles until she was shackled like a convict. She then had to haul herself up into the cube, balance her core along a cushioned platform and hold out her limbs in a star shape for a whole ninety seconds. Even as she assumed the position she was in such pain that she knew her face must look like a chewed-up blood orange.

'Atta girl. Now off we go!'

Mia often worked out with Cole at home or in her garden but today he'd dragged her to the gym where he kept a fully equipped studio and could vary her routine. Unfortunately, every time Mia walked into the studio her heart sank – it looked like some kind of serial killer's lair lifted straight out of a horror film. There were bands, cubes and straps hanging from the ceiling and Cole liked to keep the room heated to a sizzling 40°C. As usual, the sweltering atmosphere was making Mia sweat buckets and giving her shockingly bad hair frizz. To make things worse, the rest of the gym was packed at the moment; she really hoped that nobody could see into the studio. Next door was the hardcore free weights studio where it was currently Power Hour, during which heavy metal was played at teeth-loosening volume and the serious weightlifters could work out with their shirts off. Mia could hear their grunts and growls through the wall. She desperately hoped that none of them peeked in and recognized her.

'And relax, girlfriend!'

'Oh thank God.' She struggled down and he helped her to her feet. 'I'm not sure I can do much more of this, Cole.'

'We're nearly done, I promise. And I've saved the best till last.'

He nodded over to Mia's least favourite piece of equipment

– a studded trapeze covered in leather hand-grips with chains hanging off it from every angle. Apparently Cole had appropriated the contraption from the set of the last Bourne film, on which he'd worked as cast trainer and in which the trapeze had served as a prop in a toe-curling torture scene. Mia knew just why.

'Oh no, do I really have to?' she moaned.

'Quit bitching, girlfriend! And let's kick some ass!'

She took a deep breath and heaved herself up.

*

Ronnie had been right – this job really did suck.

Leo had now been waiting on his own for an hour and there was still no sign of Mia. On the floor of the skip he shuffled around his bottom, desperately trying to dig himself into a more comfortable position. The stench of decaying fish was getting worse as the day grew hotter. This was fast turning into one of the worst door-steppings ever.

Whenever he and Ronnie were on a stake-out, they liked to while away the waiting time compiling an ongoing list of their top ten favourite jobs ever. Without doubt, job number one was the time they'd been sent to St Tropez to chase David and Victoria Beckham around on the ultimate boys' toy – a top-of-the-range private yacht which they'd taken turns in steering and onto which they'd proudly attached British and American flags. That was closely followed by the time they'd managed to infiltrate a party for a James Bond film by hiding inside a huge statue of a golden gun; they'd quickly taken the snaps they needed through the gun's open barrel and then spent the rest of the evening being served vodka martinis by a seriously hot waitress dressed as Pussy Galore. And definitely making the top ten was the time they'd trailed Colin Farrell and his gaggle of playmates around Miami on a major bender, until halfway through the night (when they'd already shot five different sets of blinding pictures), they'd started downing shots themselves – only to wake up eight hours later in Sleeping Beauty's castle in Disney World, with no idea how they'd got there.

But despite all this, Leo wasn't in the paparazzi game for the glamour. What he loved about the business was the heart-thumping moment when he nailed a pic he knew would be a huge seller and make the front pages around the world. And if nailing that shot involved a high-speed car chase (or a 'follow' as it was known in the business), then his adrenaline levels hit the roof. Pursuing a car on his bike reminded Leo of the computer games he used to play as a boy in Watford. Except now it was all happening for real and the buzz was incredible. Ronnie was right – Leo was a serious adrenaline junkie.

He sometimes looked at the lengths he'd go to in search of a fix and, in moments of conscience, the way it led him to treat people, and wonder if his addiction was a problem – and one that needed treating like any other. But now wasn't one of those times. And as usual he'd managed to switch off his feelings to concentrate on the job in hand – and securing his next fix.

But Mia had been in the gym for such a long time that Leo was starting to worry that she might be doing her hair and make-up after her workout. At times like this he always remembered a photographer he knew in his early days on the job telling him that a good pap pic was one that showed someone looking amazing or amazingly bad. Mia Sinclair always looked amazing so if Leo wanted to earn some decent money, he needed to melt her looking amazingly bad. But the longer she took to emerge from The Ab Lab, the less likely it looked that he'd be hitting today's jackpot. Which meant going without his much-needed fix of adrenaline.

He really hoped Mia turned up and got his heart thumping soon.

*

Mia put down the hair-drier and felt a twinge in her arm muscles. She was aching all over but now that she'd finished her workout felt pleased with herself for seeing it through. She might hate exercise but no one could fault her for hard work and dedication.

She turned on the hair straighteners to warm them up. She'd decided to dress down in a pink tracksuit and trainers but even so, was determined to look her best. Soon she'd be ready for the rest of the day – and not just ready but camera-ready.

One of Mia's worst fears was being caught out by the paps on an off-day and ending up in the pages of one of those tacky magazines that revelled in showing celebs looking rough. Unfortunately, to avoid this she had to spend at least an hour on her hair and make-up every day before she dared even to step outside. Sometimes all the preening exhausted her and made her feel like a slave to the fame game. There were times when she was desperate for a day off and her only option was to stay in the house all day. But there was no question that the effort was worth it. So far she'd never been papped looking a mess and she'd no intention of starting now.

Across the changing room a woman with a weirdly long face which looked like it had been trapped between the doors of an elevator was parading around with no clothes on. Mia tried not to stare and applied a dollop of her favourite anti-frizz pro-gloss serum to her hair. It was time for her to start on her make-up.

As a child in Cleveland, Mia remembered watching a famous movie star being interviewed about her glamorous life on a TV chat show. For some reason the woman had insisted on banging on about how *un*glamorous her life was, how working in films was really hard work and how stars like her were just normal people really. Mia had felt utterly let down. *I don't really want to hear this*, she remembered thinking. *I want fantasy – I want magic!* She'd vowed there and then that if she ever became a successful actress, she wouldn't shatter the public's illusions but would keep the flames of glamour burning at all times – whatever the cost.

The woman with the long face was now sitting on a bench behind Mia, crouching over and plucking a grey hair out of her slug-shaped pubic strip. Mia tried not to gasp and reached for her mascara.

Her stomach rumbled and she hoped nobody could hear it. It was nearly lunchtime and she was ravenous – the only thing that had passed her lips all day was one lousy glass of palm syrup with lemon and hot water. Waiting for her at home would be her usual meal of tasteless fish and bland vegetables. *What I'd give right now for a cheeseburger and fries*, she thought. *And to not have to bother applying full make-up just for the journey home.*

The things she put herself through. She let out a long sigh and twisted open her lipstick.

*

Leo rummaged in his pocket to find his phone. He was going to text Shooting Stars to find out if Mia had somehow left the gym already through a back door or some kind of decoy system. He couldn't bear the stench of fish one moment longer and was ready to resign himself to missing out on the action for the day.

But just then the doors to The Ab Lab swung open and Leo spotted her. In an instant his sparkle returned and he looked through his viewfinder for a closer examination. He zoomed in, only to find that she was fully coiffed and made-up. His sparkle faded. *Gutted*, he thought. *What a waste of a morning.*

Leo observed her looking around surreptitiously to see if there were any paps watching her. She wouldn't be able to spot him as he was more than a hundred yards away with a lens so long it could pull focus on someone if they were on the moon. He knocked off a few shots anyway, even though he knew that none of them would sell, let alone make him any decent money.

As Mia turned the corner and disappeared into the car park, Leo leapt from the skip and jogged around it to find his bike, which was parked out of view behind. He reached for his helmet and put it on, ready to follow her at a safe distance. The chances were that she'd be heading straight home. But he'd already missed the Malibu Beach job so was free for the rest of the afternoon. He might as well follow her. Just in case.

*

Mia shut the door of her car and checked her face in the mirror. She looked immaculate but wished she hadn't bothered making the effort now. There wasn't a single pap anywhere to be seen so she might as well have saved herself the trouble. *Never mind*, she thought. *Better to be safe than sorry.*

Her stomach gave another rumble and she suddenly felt overwhelmed with hunger. She'd have to get home soon before she started to feel faint. She put the keys in the ignition and hit the accelerator.

Mia was just four days into her new diet and already finding it really tough. The problem was that she had a naturally big appetite. When she'd first arrived in LA she'd lived with a dumpy costume designer called Shanice who had a seriously sweet tooth and had just broken up with her childhood sweetheart back in Michigan. After every meal Shanice would sit on the sofa pigging out on chocolate and cakes and Mia had found it really hard to resist joining in. Soon she was ten pounds heavier than she'd been in Cleveland, which was already hovering high above the ideal weight for a movie star. Shortly after that she'd been to her first ever audition and a movie producer had told her that she had no future in Hollywood unless she did something about her 'fat ass'. She still had painful memories of the stinging humiliation all these years later.

She put her foot down and cruised up La Cienega, coming to a stop at the junction with Sunset. She remembered that soon she'd be passing a drive-thru fast-food joint called Gobble and Go and was hit by a sudden craving for junk food. She turned on the radio to try and distract her. *You'll be home soon*, she told herself. *Hold on a little longer and the craving will pass*. The last thing she wanted was to return to her days of overeating, which she'd had to work hard to beat in her first few years in LA.

Shortly after that early audition, Mia had moved out of the apartment she shared with Shanice and rented her own place. But her big appetite moved with her and every time she had a knock-back or received some kind of rejection in her career, she'd feel an urgent, uncontrollable need to trough as much unhealthy food as possible. In order to resist temptation she'd often have to throw any chocolate she had at home into the trash can and pour washing-up liquid over it so she couldn't scoop it out later and eat it. Even then she'd occasionally been known to salvage what she could and rinse it under the tap before shovelling it into her mouth in a crazed frenzy. It was almost like an addiction and she could still remember how her heart would thump in her chest mid-binge, her head buzzing with a sweet rush of adrenaline.

She glided down Sunset and spotted a block of outdoor cafés she'd eaten in several times over the last few years. She knew that none of them served what she was craving right now – a great big juicy burger with fries on the side. Her heart started pounding just at the thought of it and she felt dizzy and weak with longing. She told herself to snap out of it. She wasn't even driving the car with blacked-out windows so there was no way she could risk pulling into a place like Gobble and Go. And anyway, it had been years since she'd eaten junk food and she had no intention of giving in to temptation now.

The problem was that everyone who was anyone in LA was so healthy. Since starring in her first movie, Mia had been forced to crack down on her binge-eating by keeping nothing sweet or fattening in the house. That, unfortunately, was the only way that she could be sure of removing every trace of temptation from her life, as she obviously couldn't risk being papped driving to the shops for sweets or junk food. Or could she . . . ? Just that morning she'd gone to all that effort with her hair and make-up and there hadn't been any paps around anyway. If she sneaked into Gobble and Go now no one need ever find out. Her heart began pumping even faster and she felt close to hyperventilating.

Nothing tastes as good as being thin feels, she told herself sternly. *And you need to look amazing for filming in ten days' time.*

One day off won't do you any harm, said another voice inside her head. *Nobody will notice through your nurse's uniform anyway.*

She spotted the sign for Gobble and Go and inside her something clicked. From now on she knew there was no turning back.

She switched off the radio, put on her wrap-around sun-glasses and checked in her mirror. She definitely wasn't being followed.

As if powered by an alien force, she found herself turning into the entrance to the drive-thru restaurant. Her stomach gave a little flip as she drove under a welcome sign and fol-lowed the lane around. She was so high she could barely think straight, let alone speak. She was sure she could actually feel her heart thudding at the back of her throat.

She took a deep breath and drove up to the serving hatch.

Slouching behind the window was a surly black girl with large lips that didn't quite fit together and a name badge saying 'Tiara'. Mia was worried that she might be able to hear her heart beating it was so loud.

Thankfully the assistant didn't even look at her but spoke her lines like some kind of automaton. 'Welcome to Gobble and Go. What can I do for you today?'

'Oh hello.' Mia tried imitating Billy's Deep South accent just in case Tiara recognized her voice. 'I'll have a triple-decker cheeseburger with extra cheese please and three large portions of fries. With ketchup *and* mayo. Oh and some chicken dippers on the side.'

Tiara didn't bat an eyelid. 'Any drink?'

'Just a water please.' *No point wasting calories on a boring drink.*

'Anything else?'

Oh what the hell! I might as well go the whole hog . . . 'Erm, yeah, an apple pie please. Just to round it off nicely, you know. Actually, make that two – one's never quite enough.'

Tiara turned to look at her. 'You sure is hungry, ma'am.'

'Oh it's not all for me,' Mia spluttered, her accent straying into Texan. 'I'm meeting a friend for lunch.'

Tiara looked at her flash, clearly expensive car and raised an eyebrow. Mia didn't know why she was so suspicious – stars like Britney Spears and Kirstie Alley came to places like this all the time.

'That'll be forty dollars and fifty cents,' Tiara yawned.

'Oh right, yeah, just a minute.' She began fumbling in her purse but in the shade of the serving hatch couldn't see anything behind her dark glasses. Reluctantly she took them off. As she clutched manically at dollar bills she gradually became conscious of a pair of eyes watching her. *Oh no*, she thought. *Here we go. . .*

'Wait a second,' Tiara said, her voice suddenly perking up, 'aren't you—?'

'No! You must be mistaken!'

Tiara took a good look at her, blinking. 'But aren't you—?'

'Honestly, I don't know what you're talking about.' By now she'd completely abandoned her Deep South accent and her voice had drifted into the higher pitches of the borderline psychotic. 'Now let me find . . .'

'But you look just like . . .'

Mia thrust out a handful of notes, which she hoped would be enough. 'There you go.'

'Mia Sinclair! *That's* who you are! Mia Sinclair!'

Mia pulled a face and raised her arms in surrender – there was no point pretending any longer. 'OK, the game's up. You're right, it's me.'

'But what are *you* doing in a rat-hole like this?'

'Well you know, when a girl needs a burger she *really* needs a burger.' She looked plaintively at Tiara, who smiled back brightly. Mia suddenly noticed that she was actually quite pretty.

'Listen,' Mia went on, 'you won't snitch on me, will you? I just desperately need a burger right now. Do you know what I'm saying? Girl to girl? Please could you keep it a secret?'

'Hell, yeah! You enjoy it, girlfriend. Go knock yourself out!'

'Thanks, Tiara, thanks. I really appreciate it.'

Mia gave her a huge smile and hit the gas.

'Pick up your food at the next window!'

*

As Mia's car slid forwards, Leo watched with his mouth open from behind the building next door. He couldn't believe what he was witnessing. Not only was Mia Sinclair letting down her guard like never before, she was getting seriously sloppy and hadn't even noticed that she was being followed by a predatory pap.

He whipped out his camera just as an assistant handed Mia bags and bags of food to take away. He quickly began snapping but Mia had her back to him and he couldn't get a clear shot that would identify her. The action was over in seconds and he knew instinctively that he'd missed his chance. *Not to worry*, he thought, *the big money's on nailing Mia actually eating the food. And I haven't missed out on that yet.*

Mia put the food on the passenger seat next to her and drove off and out of the restaurant.

Leo wasn't letting that shot get away now. It was time to play his favourite game – a game at which he really was one of the best in the business, if not *the* best. He revved up his bike and roared off after her.

Finally his adrenaline was pumping. What had started out as a boring day was now turning into a bonanza.

*

Inside her car, Mia felt like she was going insane with hunger. She was overpowered by the smell of the hot food and absolutely desperate to shovel it into her mouth as soon as was humanly possible. She couldn't help swerving the car all over the road and was even starting to hallucinate. When she looked in her mirror she realized with horror that there was actually a trail of dribble down her chin.

It was no use – there was no way she was going to make it home before eating the food. Besides, it would be stone cold by the time she got up into the hills. And she may not have eaten junk food for years but she could still remember that a cold burger was gross. She spotted a dirt track at the side of the road and indicated that she was about to turn into it.

This time she forgot to check in her mirror to see if she was being followed.

*

Leo stopped his bike a few yards behind Mia's car and practically threw it to the ground. Between him and the shot he so desperately wanted was a strip of wasteland overgrown with thick foliage. Blinded by a seriously hardcore head rush, he plunged into it without thinking and began wading through to assume his position on the frontline. By now he had tunnel vision and nothing was going to stop him nailing his shot.

Whipped, grazed and stung by a mini jungle of wild plants, after a few minutes he spotted his prey. Raised in front of her was the biggest burger he'd ever seen. And she was about to cram it into her mouth.

This was truly amazing – for the first time ever, right there waiting for him, was a shot of the real Mia Sinclair as she'd never been seen before.

All he could think of was what Ronnie would say if he were here: 'Ker-ching!"

*

As she felt the hot sticky meat wrapped in delicious melting cheese dance around her tongue, Mia almost felt like she was close to orgasm. The physical impact of the taste was incredible and it somehow managed to send waves of a sensation she could only think was sheer joy racing around her body. Gradually all the pressures of her life simply fell away and she regressed to a state of natural, primal bliss. Sitting there eating her burger just felt so *right* – it was a beautiful, beautiful feeling and one she couldn't believe she'd deprived herself of for so long.

Before she'd finished swallowing, her mouth was already open for the next bite. She couldn't stop herself from groaning aloud with pleasure; it was as if her entire body had been sedated by a heavy dose of pure, raw ecstasy. And she hadn't even started on the fries yet. She took a fistful, smothered them in mayo and rammed them into her mouth.

Just as she prepared to go for the swallow she heard a familiar snapping sound coming from the bushes. She froze in terror. It couldn't be, surely . . .

She wound down the window and poked her head outside. The sound was there again.

Snap, snap.

Oh shit!

Shit, shit, shit!

Throwing her food onto the passenger seat, she swallowed

what was in her mouth, leapt out of the car and raced over to the tangle of foliage.

She followed the sound and used her arm to clear the branches. As she drew back the leaves she saw that her worst fear was actually coming true. Standing in front of her was a pap, camera in hand.

She was still on a high from her food binge but a surge of anger added itself to the mix and she couldn't splutter out her words fast enough. 'Excuse me but what the hell do you think you're doing?'

The pap smiled. 'Erm, hi Mia. I think you've got some mayo on your chin.'

'What? Oh right.' She wiped it away on her sleeve; it was a bit late to worry about her dignity now. Determined not to let him get the better of her, she folded her arms and gave him a sneer.

As she looked at him she saw every pap who'd ever screwed her over and caused her heartache. And she wasn't going to let any pap defeat her this time.

*

'Look, I don't know who you are but I need you to give me that camera,' Mia Sinclair growled at him.

As she looked him in the eye, Leo could feel his tough front start to crumble. Sure, he'd been shouted at by celebrities before but as soon as they engaged with him he found it difficult to pretend they weren't real people. And there was another thing disconcerting him right now; he'd never been shouted at by a celebrity as beautiful as Mia Sinclair. In fact, he wasn't sure he'd ever *met* anyone as beautiful as Mia Sinclair.

Just then he felt a twinge right in the middle of his heart. He told himself that it must be where he'd been poked and prodded in that skip. He began to rub it and tried to pull himself together. *You're a paparazzo, remember? Now try to focus on the job!*

'No way am I handing this over,' he said. 'This camera's my livelihood.'

'Well OK, just give me the pictures. You can keep your lousy camera.'

'Well that's very nice of you but those pictures are worth a lot of money.'

'Money you wouldn't have earned if it weren't for me – which means if you were any kind of gentleman you'd hand them over.'

Was he imagining this or was the energy between them tipping over into something else?

'Nah, you see it doesn't work like that,' he couldn't help teasing. 'Some of us paparazzi actually have a strong sense of moral duty.'

'Oh yeah, to do what?'

'To show the public what stars like you really get up to when you're not on show.'

He flashed her a cocky grin but the joke had obviously missed the mark; Mia returned it with a scowl.

'Look, I'm starting to get major pissed now. Just give me the pictures, asshole.'

'The name's Leo actually. And it's very nice to meet you, Mia.'

He held out his hand for her to shake. She turned up her nose and kept her arms firmly folded.

'OK, how much do you want for them?'

He shook his head mischievously. 'They're not for sale, sorry.'

'Hmpf! You expect me to believe that? You guys are only in this game to screw as much money as you can out of people like me.'

'Look, I told you, Mia – I do this job to provide a public service.'

'Public service my ass!'

Leo had never seen someone usually as composed and together as Mia get so angry and he was surprised to find it actually quite sexy. He reminded himself that he'd only just broken up with Eden and wasn't ready to start flirting with other girls. And that flirting with one of the biggest stars on the planet had to represent the greatest possible collision of business and pleasure. *What on earth am I doing?*

But for some reason, he just couldn't help himself.

He was suddenly hit by a crazy – but possibly brilliant – idea.

'OK,' he grinned. 'I'll do you a deal.'

*

'Go on,' she snorted, 'I'm listening.'

'You come out for dinner with me and I'll hand over the pictures at the end of the night.'

Mia burst out laughing. 'You've got to be joking. *Me?* Go out for dinner with *you*?'

'Yeah. You might even enjoy it.'

'Oh I'm sure that plenty of others have,' she mocked, 'but

maybe I'm not like the kind of girl you usually date. I know all about your sort. And I stay well away.'

'So I see. Which is why I'm intrigued.'

Mia raised her eyebrows in disbelief. She had to hand it to him – this guy really did have some front. She pursed her lips as she reminded herself of all the trouble the paparazzi had caused her.

'Listen, Liam, there's no way—'

'Erm, it's Leo actually.'

'*Whatever.* Liam/Leo, there's no way I'm going out on a date with some ass-wipe paparazzo.'

'Well in that case, there's no way I'm handing over the pictures.'

Mia stood still for a moment and looked him over.

He held her gaze and for a split second she couldn't help feeling just a frisson of attraction. If he weren't a paparazzo, she'd happily admit this guy was a major hottie. He was tall, well-built, with sun-kissed fair hair, sparkling eyes and dimples so deep you could swim in them. And she could just imagine the effect that wonky grin had on most girls. *But I'm not most girls*, she reminded herself. *And I don't go anywhere near this kind of guy.* Paparazzo or not, Leo had trouble written all over him. He was obviously just the kind of bad boy she tried her best to avoid. But what choice did she have if she wanted the pictures back?

'OK,' she sighed, as if defeated. 'I'll go for dinner with you.'

'Hurray!'

'But only to get the pictures back.'

'Yeah? Well it sounds like you've got yourself a deal.'

'Fine. Oh and there's one condition.'

'Mm-hmm? What's that?'

'*You* take care of the paparazzi. This is one date that I *really* don't want splashed all over the papers.'

'Done!'

Their eyes lingered on each other for a little too long. Mia tried her best to stop it but she could feel a smile begin to spread its way across her face. Just then she felt her heart flutter. She told herself that it must be a touch of heartburn from stuffing that burger down so quickly. Or was it? *Uh-oh*, she thought. *What am I getting myself into?*

'Oh and by the way,' she snapped, keen to show that she wasn't warming to him.

'Yeah?'

'You might want to take a shower before we go out.'

Leo looked at her, confused. 'Oh yeah, why?'

'Because I don't know if you realize, but you totally stink of fish.'

4

It was the first day of reshoots on the set of *War of Words* and Billy Spencer was sitting in the make-up chair being prepared for his big death scene. He was having war wounds applied by a make-up artist called Dominique, who'd recently come to work in the US from Paris and was proving to be unusually chatty.

'So how does it feel to be back on set?' she asked in a thick French accent.

'Good,' he replied. 'Real good. I can't wait to see Mia later.'

'Oh, are you two . . . dating?'

'No, no. I mean, *no*. We're just good friends.'

'Aha.' Dominique looked reassured.

If Billy wasn't mistaken, she wasn't just chatting but flirting with him, too. And most men would probably welcome her advances; she was a stunning brunette with full, pouty lips and sky-high cheekbones. He couldn't help noticing that she wasn't wearing a bra and her ample, natural breasts were jangling around as she worked, directly in his eye line. But Billy wasn't most men and she just wasn't his type. *Don't waste your time on me, sugar*, he wanted to say. Instead, he took a sip of his chai latte and kept quiet.

'So, have you always lived in LA?' she cooed.

'No, I only pitched up here seven years ago. I was born and raised in Mississippi in the South. Do you know it?'

'Of course! Tom Sawyer and Huckleberry Finn?'

'That's the one.'

'Oh Billy, how *adorable*!'

Although he usually lapped up admiration, this was starting to get embarrassing. Billy hoped no one else in the trailer could hear their conversation. She moved in even closer to continue painting a trickle of blood onto his face, just below a wound on his cheekbone where his character had supposedly been grazed by a bullet. Her close proximity meant that she could easily look him in the eye and, judging by the flirtatious fluttering of her eyelashes, there was no question now that she was hitting on him – big time. He took another sip of his hot drink and hoped this wouldn't take long.

'So what was it like growing up in Mississippi?' she purred.

'Oh you know, the typical American thing. Lots of apple pie and Little League.'

'Oh Billy, that's so cute!' She jumped around on the spot, her breasts bouncing up and down in front of him.

He tried not to squirm. 'Yeah, it was kind of cool, I guess.'

He didn't like to tell Dominique the truth about his unhappy childhood – or how hard it had been growing up knowing that he was different to other boys and that, once they found out, his parents were only going to hate him for it. And man, had they hated him.

He shuddered as he thought back to the aversion therapy they'd forced him to endure at the clinic in Arizona. Over and over again he'd been made to look at pictures of handsome men in swimwear while Church leaders had called out insults and spat in his face.

You dirty fag!

You disgusting queer!

The idea was that he'd associate gay desire with negative emotions and his sexuality would be 'reprogrammed'. He'd even had to wear a tight rubber band around his wrist and snap it hard whenever he'd had sexual thoughts about a man – sometimes until his skin bled. Dominique reminded him of a photo of a big-busted brunette in a bikini which the Church leaders had repeatedly thrust in front of him as they tried to 'pray out the gay'. It had made him feel sick with shame and self-loathing but however hard he tried, he just couldn't find women attractive. And despite all the treatment, he still felt the same now.

'So,' breathed Dominique, oblivious to his discomfort, 'do you have a girlfriend back in Mississippi or are you dating anyone here?'

He couldn't help feeling a little sorry for her. If she were parading her charms in front of any other leading man in LA, she'd probably have received an invitation to dinner by now. And who could blame her for coming to LA and wanting to date a film star? Wasn't that everyone's romantic dream? It wasn't her fault that she'd chosen a dud target this time. He decided he'd do his best to let her down gently.

'Erm, no,' he muttered, 'I don't really have time for dating right now.' It was the official line he trotted out whenever he was asked in public about his love life.

'But you should always make time for love!' gushed Dominique, clearly undeterred. 'Being in love is the most beautiful thing in the world!'

Billy smiled at her awkwardly. She was leaning in so close that he could taste her cloying perfume at the back of his throat. He didn't want to be impolite but this was starting to become difficult. *If only she'd get the message!*

He suddenly felt a shiver of suspicion and wondered if he'd misjudged the situation. He was used to girls getting gooey around him but there was something aggressive about Dominique that was starting to ring warning bells. *Is she only flirting with me because she's digging for dirt? Is she looking for a story to sell to the press? Or am I just being paranoid?* Whatever was going on, he was getting nervous and wished it would all stop.

'Come on, you can tell me . . .' she cooed conspiratorially. 'You must have some little secrets hidden away somewhere?'

In an instant he was back in gay rehab, being probed by a team of so-called therapists trying to work out why he'd developed what they termed 'perverted' sexual urges. Had he been abused as a child? Had his father neglected him, forcing him to empathize with women? Just who was to blame for his sick diversion from God's 'natural design'?

All Billy knew was that to him, being attracted to men seemed like the most natural thing in the world. But no matter how much he tried to hold onto that, the sustained attack of anti-gay therapy had ended up contaminating his self-respect and eating away at his soul. Even now, all these years later, he couldn't imagine ever being able to enter into any kind of healthy, loving relationship. His heart felt shot through.

'Honestly, Dominique,' he said emphatically, 'I don't have

any secrets. There really is no one special in my life right now – and that's just how I like it.'

'*Quel dommage*!' she sighed, sticking out her bottom lip in an exaggerated sulk.

Billy felt bad about upsetting her but knew that he had to see this through. There was just no way he could risk revealing his sexuality to someone he'd just met like the bra-less Dominique. For all he knew, she could be a journalist recording the entire conversation on a secret camera. Worse things had been known to happen in Hollywood. And yeah, over the last few years a handful of emerging indie actors had come out of the closet and Jodie Foster had made her famous 'coming out' speech when she won the Lifetime Achievement Award at the Golden Globes. But none of it made any difference to the attitudes of studio bosses, who still refused to believe that mainstream audiences would accept a young, openly gay actor playing a straight romantic lead. As his agent insisted on telling him at every opportunity, if the press or paps ever found out Billy was gay, his career would be over. Which was why he was becoming increasingly paranoid, even when talking to make-up girls.

'To tell you the truth,' he said, just to cover himself in case she *was* digging for a story, 'there hasn't been anyone special in my life since I came to LA. And I'm pretty sure it's going to stay that way.'

Dominique nodded as if she'd finally got the message. She fell silent and topped up her brush with fake blood.

Before he had time to fight it, the sight of the blood transported Billy back to the most distressing episodes in his anti-gay therapy. On three or four occasions he'd been taken to a church hall where several pastors had surrounded him, thrown him onto the floor and then beaten him as they tried to exorcize the homosexual 'demon' which they were convinced was inside him. Each exorcism could last for hours and by the time it had finished Billy would be lying on the floor exhausted, often in horrendous pain and usually covered in vomit and blood. As he looked at the fake blood now he could still hear the pastors chanting in his ears.

Come out in the name of Jesus!

Foul queer be not here!

He started to feel sick and could feel a sense of panic taking hold of him. He needed to get out of the trailer quickly and breathe some air. But he didn't want to arouse Dominique's suspicions – or let her see that anything was wrong.

'So how am I looking?' he struggled. 'Beat up and bruised?'

'*Oui oui*,' she stated matter-of-factly, as if to blot out her earlier flirtation. 'You're quite the injured soldier. Just a few more minutes and you'll be ready for battle.'

He breathed a sigh of relief and couldn't help smiling to himself.

If only she knew.

*

Leo and Ronnie were in the offices of their agency Shooting Stars on the top floor of a skyscraper in downtown LA. Having caught up on paperwork and serviced their camera gear, they'd spent an hour flicking through celebrity magazines researching new targets and keeping abreast of who was dating who. Now they were sipping Starbucks cappuccinos and being briefed on possible jobs for the day.

Over the last few years, paparazzi around the world had come under increasing pressure to come up with dynamite pictures. The rise in popularity of camera phones meant that anyone could now take a photo of a star, particularly in a city like LA. It was up to the professionals to deliver something extra special – and Leo and Ronnie were all too aware of this.

Shooting Stars was run by Chip and Biff Mahoney, a pair of wise-cracking wide boys from Chicago who, although they were brothers, managed to look nothing like each other. Chip was skinny with spiky hair and a pock-marked face that made him look a bit like a pineapple. He constantly chewed gum, was always fidgeting or pacing the room and had a permanent build-up of white foam in the corners of his mouth. His younger brother Biff on the other hand was bald, immensely overweight and a dead ringer for Jabba the Hutt. As usual he was leaning back in his reinforced swivel chair wearing a Chicago Cubs baseball cap, stinking of last night's weed and scratching the hairy muffin top that hung out over the stretched-to-breaking-point waistband of his already baggy jeans.

'OK,' began Chip, chewing furiously. 'First up we have Cooper Kelly laid up in the Sickbay to the Stars.' He explained that ageing movie legend Cooper was in LA's famous Cedars-Sinai Medical Center recovering from an operation for the rather unglamorous condition of gout. Despite the actor's strenuous efforts for his condition to go unreported, a hospital porter working for Shooting Stars had confirmed that the patient was due for an X-ray at precisely ten twenty that morning and would be transferred from one building to another just beforehand, conveniently passing a spot from where paps could take a clear shot. 'What do you reckon, guys?' chirped Chip. 'Are you in or out?'

'Nah,' frowned Leo. 'Hospital jobs are boring. We need something to put fire in our bellies.'

Chip rolled his eyes fondly. 'I thought you'd say that.'

Leo couldn't help looking at the white foam in the corners of his mouth. *What is that stuff?* He tried not to stare but it was putting him off his frothy cappuccino.

'All right,' drawled Biff. 'Next up is Layla Lloyd, due in to LAX from London at eleven ten a.m.' Ronnie raised an eyebrow with interest. Layla Lloyd was a British topless model who flew into LA every few months for a regular round of false nails, hair extensions and Botox. She wasn't a big star in the US but pictures of her sold for staggering sums when syndicated all over Europe. And the market was particularly hot for her right now as there were rumours she was pregnant by her new boyfriend – a world-champion heavyweight boxer with a penchant for cross-dressing. 'If we're lucky she might be wearing something nice and tight,' drooled Biff, 'and give us friendly paps the first ever shot of that bun in the oven.'

'Not these paps,' said Ronnie, shaking his head. 'Layla's hated us ever since we busted her cheating on her last husband. There's nowhere to hide in the airport and once she spots us she won't give us shit.'

Chip stood up and began to pace the room. 'OK, well there is another job that's just come in. There's a new movie called *War of Words* shooting at a secret location out of town.'

'But I thought the studios were cracking down on pap shots?' said Leo. 'Last time we covered a film shoot we got chased all over the desert by security.'

'Yeah and if you remember,' grunted Ronnie, 'you got away while I got my ass kicked. As usual.'

'Well it's not my fault if you can't keep up,' teased Leo. 'Maybe it's time you laid off the fags.'

'We call them smokes in this country, Limey. And a word like fag isn't very nice.'

'Oh cut it out, ladies,' piped Chip. 'And trust us – you won't have any problems on this set.'

Biff leaned back in his chair with a loud creak. 'One of the make-up girls is working for us – a smoking-hot French chick new to LA and keen to earn some extra dough. Word is she's hawking gossip and pictures all around town. She reckons she can smuggle two paps onto the set as extras so it'll have to be a hidden-camera job.'

Leo and Ronnie looked at each other, thinking it over.

'What do you say, guys?' asked Biff. 'You interested?'

'What kind of scene are they shooting?' pressed Leo.

'Some big battle scene. So you'd get to dress up as soldiers and play around with guns . . .'

'Cool!' crooned Ronnie. 'Count us in!'

Chip nodded. 'Awesome. There's a great buzz about the movie – they reckon it's going to be a big hit. It stars Billy Spencer and Mia Sinclair.'

Leo almost choked on his cappuccino. This was the last thing he expected. He couldn't go on a film set with Mia now that he'd met her – she'd instantly spot him and he'd be kicked out straight away. And besides, they were going on a date in a few days and he knew that it was daft but he kind of liked her.

'Obviously we want a shot of the two stars together,' Chip

rattled on. 'There's big money on any picture that proves Billy's banging Mia for real.'

Leo squirmed. He might have only met Mia once but now that he'd spoken to her he couldn't do his usual trick of switching off his emotions and seeing her as prey rather than a person. 'Is that true?' he stammered. '*Is* Billy sleeping with her in real life?'

'Fact is we don't know,' said Biff. 'The French broad was digging this morning and said she had ways of getting info out of any dude. I can only imagine what they are . . .' He trailed off and gazed out of the window wistfully. He checked himself and cleared his throat. 'For some reason this time she drew a blank. Which means it's now your job to find out.'

'OK, we're definitely in,' confirmed Ronnie. 'What's the address?'

'Coming right up.'

Chip and Biff began tapping into their computers to access the co-ordinates of the shoot. Leo leaned into Ronnie so no one would hear him whispering.

'Listen, partner, don't you think we should talk about this?'

'Talk about what? You love this kind of shit. Soldiers, battlefields, dodging security . . . What's the problem, bud?'

'Erm, no, erm, there is no problem.'

'Good,' said Ronnie. 'It'll be a blast. Maybe even one for the top ten.'

Leo drained the last of his cappuccino. This was going to be tough.

'Here you go,' interrupted Chip, handing them a computer printout. 'When you get there call Dominique on this number.'

Biff whistled and shook his head. 'Man, that chick is seri-ously hot.'

'Yeah,' agreed Chip, 'but the dumb broad obviously hasn't learned that if word gets around she's a snitch the studios will fire her ass.'

'So you two try and keep your heads down,' Biff warned. 'She could be real useful to us in future.'

'OK, boss,' said Ronnie. 'We'll do our best.'

Leo nodded weakly. He had other more important things on his mind. He was far more worried about being spotted by Mia Sinclair. And messing up his chance on their big date.

*

'Excuse me? You're doing *what*?'

'I'm going on a date with a paparazzo.'

'Sugar, have you gone out of your mind?'

Billy and Mia were lounging on the sofas in his trailer. He was fully dressed in his soldier's uniform while she was wearing her nurse's costume complete with headdress. They'd just run through their lines and were now catching up on each other's news since they'd last spoken. And there was one piece of news that hadn't gone down well with Billy.

'Oh don't get mad with me, Billy, I'm only doing it to get the pictures back.'

'Well in that case, why are you smiling when you talk about it?'

'I'm not smiling!' She turned to look at herself in the mirror and her face froze. 'Was I really smiling?'

'You so were! Don't tell me you're falling for a paparazzo,

Mia! I mean, I've heard about sleeping with the enemy but this is something else.'

'I haven't slept with him, Billy. I've no intention of sleeping with him. And I promise you that there's even less chance of me falling in love with him.'

'Well your mouth might be saying that but that's not what your eyes are saying. If you need the pictures back then why don't you get Violet to sue him? Isn't that what publicists are for?'

'Oh I don't know, I just thought it'd be easier for me to sort it out on my own. And anyway, I've agreed to it now so I can't back out.'

He looked at her disapprovingly. 'You do realize if you go on this date you won't be able to relax the entire time. You'll be worried sick that whatever you say will wind up in *The Enquirer*.'

Mia pulled a face. Maybe he had a point.

'This asshole will probably sit down to dinner with a hidden camera poking at you.'

Another good point.

'And as soon as the date's over his buddies will pop up all wanting their piece of the action.'

'All right, all right! Oh maybe I am being stupid. I don't know what it is, though, but part of me *wants* to go on the date. It's only a little part, I promise. But is that really terrible of me?'

Billy leaned back and stretched his arms behind his head. 'Well what do you know? The First Lady of Love is about to take a tumble for some low-down, dirty paparazzo.' He poked her in the ribs with a taunting grin.

'Oh shut up, Billy,' she giggled, picking up a cushion and hitting him over the head.

He mimed outrage. 'Hey, sugar, watch my make-up!'

'Oooh, "Watch my make-up!"' she teased. 'Listen to the big tough soldier!'

He snatched the cushion off her and threw it in her face. 'Hey, that's no way to speak to your leading man! You just remember who's got top billing on this picture!'

The two of them launched into a play-fight, rolling around on the sofa before collapsing in giggles in each other's arms.

*

Leo and Ronnie had been met by Dominique at the entrance to the set and she was now rushing them through costume and make-up. She was hard-faced and businesslike, nothing like the flirtatious tease they'd imagined from what Biff had said. Although, as Ronnie kept pointing out, Biff had been right about one thing – she *was* smoking hot.

'Now don't forget,' Dominique warned sternly, 'if anyone catches you taking pictures, you keep quiet about me. Just make up some story about sneaking in through a gap in the fence or something. *D'accord*?'

Leo and Ronnie looked at each other, clueless. '*D'accord*,' they echoed.

'Hey buddy,' whispered Ronnie once they were at a safe distance, 'am I imagining things or is that chick wearing no bra?'

The two of them chuckled like naughty schoolboys. It was the first time Leo had been able to relax since joining the set. The rest of the time he'd been too busy looking around for

Mia and being nervous in case she spotted him. It wasn't like him to be on edge and he really wasn't enjoying it.

Once they were fully dressed and made up, Dominique left them in the holding area for supporting artists. '*Bon courage!*' she nodded briskly.

'Yeah, erm, thanks,' said Ronnie, sneaking one last look at her breasts.

As soon as they could, the two of them slipped away into the toilets to remove the little cameras they'd stashed down their underpants. They each attached one of the tiny devices to their collar, which was operated by a cable release in their pocket. Within minutes they were ready for battle.

They returned to the holding area and found a pair of seats under the shade of a cluster of trees. Experience on film sets had taught them that they could be in for a long wait. Leo glanced around to check there was no sign of Mia and Ronnie lit a cigarette.

'So come on then, bud, are you going to tell me what's making you so jumpy?'

'What do you mean? I'm not jumpy.'

'Bull*shit*. I've never seen you like this. What's going on?'

For a split second Leo considered lying but knew that there was no way he could pull it off. At least not with Ronnie – he knew him too well. 'OK partner,' he shrugged. 'I suppose I'd better come clean.'

'Hmm, this sounds serious.' Ronnie took a thoughtful drag on his cigarette. 'Go ahead, shoot.'

'Well this might seem a bit mad to you . . .'

'Yeah?'

'But the reason I'm a bit nervous is . . .'

'Go on.'

'. . . is-because-I'm-basically-going-on-a-date-with-Mia-Sinclair.' He blurted it out in one breath before he had time to change his mind.

Ronnie looked at him in disbelief. 'What? You've got to be shitting me.'

'No, mate. I'm afraid not.'

As Ronnie shook his head repeatedly, Leo explained at length how he'd met Mia the previous week and had come to ask her on a date. Ronnie was so intrigued that he forgot to smoke his cigarette and by the time Leo reached the end of the story, he was holding a long length of ash in his hand.

'But surely you're not taking this date seriously?' he grunted, flicking the ash onto the floor and taking one last drag. 'Whatever happened to never mixing business with pleasure?'

'Erm, yeah, well maybe it would be different with Mia Sinclair. I mean, she doesn't need me – she's a huge star already.'

'No but she needs you not to release those pictures. What's the difference?'

'Oh I know it sounds completely bonkers, Ronnie. But I just want to go on one date and see what happens.'

'But can't you see that she's only stringing you along because she wants to get her hands on your shots? Girls like Mia Sinclair don't date dudes like us, Leo. We're the paparazzi. We're the *enemy*.'

'Really? Are you sure it's that simple anymore? Because the whole thing's made me think. You know as well as I do that celebs tip us off about pictures all the time – it's much more of a two-way relationship these days.'

'Yeah, but they don't *respect* us, buddy. They still look down on us like pieces of shit they stood in on the sidewalk. When was the last time you heard of a pap dating a target?'

'Erm, didn't Britney do it once?'

'Exactly – and look how that ended up.'

Leo nodded thoughtfully.

'You've broken up with enough girlfriends over it,' Ronnie went on, 'and you've got to be crazy to consider giving it a shot now. You should have sold the photos to Mia's publicist or cut yourself a nice deal for non-publication. It's not as if it hasn't been done before. I mean, what were you *thinking*, Leo?'

Leo shrugged and said nothing. Maybe Ronnie was right. Maybe he was being stupid. Maybe he was breaking his golden rule and letting his feelings get in the way.

'LA's a battlefield,' Ronnie went on. 'The stars are on one side and we're on the other—'

'OK guys, listen up!' They were interrupted by the sound of the Third Assistant Director, who'd come to round them up for the big scene. He was wearing thick-framed plastic glasses and had long yellow hair, which gave him an unfortunate look of Donatella Versace. He was speaking into a megaphone so that everyone could hear. 'Now I want the good guys on my left,' he boomed, 'and the bad guys on my right.'

Ronnie looked puzzled and began searching his uniform for clues. 'Hey Leo, which one are we?'

'You just said it, didn't you? We're the bad guys, Ronnie.'

'Oh yeah, course we are.'

Leo stood up and felt his collar to check that his camera was still in place. 'Now come on, partner – it's time for battle.'

*

As two long lines of German and American soldiers filed onto set they were observed by Mia and Billy, sitting in their personalized canvas chairs just a few metres away. Several of the extras smiled or waved in their direction as they passed.

'What do you reckon, sugar?' Billy joked. 'You see any hotties out there?'

'Mm-hmm,' she mused, 'there are some *major* hotties. And I've got to admit, there's something about a soldier's uniform . . .'

They lapsed into a loaded silence as they gazed at the soldiers longingly, both lost in a delirium of desire.

'Check out this one coming up now,' gushed Billy. 'The Latin-looking one with the big machine gun. Now he's really got it going on.'

'Yeah, he's cute.'

'Cute? He's gorgeous, Mia!'

The Latino soldier looked over in their direction and caught Billy staring. Their eyes lingered on each other a little too long and Mia sensed a mutual murmur of excitement. She remembered experiencing a similar sensation just a few days earlier when she'd met Leo. She tried not to think about it now.

'I think he likes you . . .' she sing-songed. 'It looks like he's checking you out.'

'Do you really think so?'

'Oh come on, Billy, his tongue's practically hanging out.'

'Yeah, well it's no use – it'll have to stay hanging.'

Mia looked at him sympathetically. 'You know, you could always go and chat to him,' she offered. 'See if he's a nice guy.'

'Nah, it's way too risky. This place could be crawling with paps. It's just not worth it, sugar.'

He picked up his script and began reading his lines.

Mia carried on gazing at the soldiers as they filed past. Before long her mind drifted to Leo. She wondered what he was doing right now, who he was shooting and whether he'd thought about her since they'd met. She told herself not to be stupid. *He probably sees me as a pay check rather than a person*, she thought. *Right now he'll be shooting some other star, trying to screw as much money out of her as he can.*

Whatever he was up to, Mia had to accept that Billy was right; there was no way she could ever trust Leo. There was one fact that was never going to change: the paparazzi were the enemy.

*

As he shuffled forwards at the end of a long line of German soldiers, Leo could make out Mia sitting next to Billy Spencer in a shaded area near the monitors. While Billy was reading what looked like a script, Mia was looking straight at them. He could feel his mouth go dry.

He wanted to make it past her as quickly as possible but the soldiers in front of him were dragging their feet along slowly. There was no backing out now; he pulled his helmet as far down as he could and inched forwards.

He knew that if he were spotted he'd be in serious trouble and could even be prosecuted for trespassing. The funny thing was that this sense of danger on a job usually gave him a real thrill. Today it was making him feel nauseous.

'Well, what do you know?' Ronnie mocked. 'Leo Henderson has got the fear.'

'Shh!' Leo hissed, keeping his head down. 'Shut it, Ronnie!'

'Oh come on, buddy, what happened to wanting some fire in your belly? Or are you too scared of upsetting your new girlfriend?'

Leo ignored Ronnie and pretended to have an itch on the side of his face. After scratching his cheek for what felt like ten minutes, he moved his hand away and realized that he'd made it past Mia undetected. He was in the clear.

Phew!

Ronnie looked at him and shook his head with a wry grin.

The two of them were led onto set by the yellow-haired Third. He explained that today's scene was being shot in a huge field which had been made to look like a bombed-out village somewhere in 1940s Europe, with the remains of several buildings scattered around and a church standing more or less intact in the centre. Everywhere Leo looked there were cameras, tracks, dollies and cranes, and hundreds of soldiers were being put into position in every corner of the fake battlefield. Ronnie looked mesmerized.

The Third eventually led them to a crashed, partly wrecked German tank, marooned in front of what must have been a rather twee café before it had been blasted to smithereens. He explained that they were supposed to be playing a two-man tank team who'd been forced to fight for their lives when the back of their vehicle had been blown away by the Americans. Ronnie was to peep out of the cockpit and operate the tank's machine gun while Leo's character had jumped out of the vehicle and was to crouch by the side of it firing his gun.

'Way to go!' yelped Ronnie, jumping straight into position. 'This rocks!'

He grabbed hold of the fixed machine gun and began swivelling it around, making his own shooting sounds as he fired at imaginary enemies. '*Achtung!*' he shouted. '*Achtung! Achtung!*'

'Do you actually know what that means?' Leo joked.

'No but it's the only German I know. And what do you care anyway? You keep an eye on your girlfriend over there – it looks to me like she's getting pretty close to Billy.'

Leo looked over and saw that Mia was sitting in the same position but now chatting to Billy next to her. She'd taken hold of his hand and was stroking it as she talked to him. Leo wondered if they were actually a couple after all. He had to stop himself feeling a snag of jealousy. *Don't be daft*, he thought, *she's not interested in you. You're a paparazzo, remember? Just concentrate on taking your pictures.*

He took his first shots of the day by pressing the cable release wired into his pocket. He was thankful of the tank to hide behind and ducked down whenever Mia glanced in his direction. He soon started to relax – there was no chance he'd get caught as the tank provided more than enough cover. And best of all, he was near enough to the star couple to get his shots but far enough away not to be spotted.

Mia and Billy burst into a fit of giggles and Leo snapped away. He had to admit, they did look like they were pretty close. He tried not to think about it but to revert to seeing them as simple targets for his shots.

'Ra-ra-ra-ra-ra-ra-ra-ra-raaaaar!'

Ronnie was spellbound by his new toy. In fact, he was so carried away that he'd forgotten why they were on set in the first place and, as usual, was missing out on the important shots. It didn't matter – Leo always shared his pictures with him anyway.

'Ra-ra-ra-raaar!'

Mia threw her arms around Billy and Leo pressed again on the device in his pocket. He couldn't help replaying in his mind his meeting with Mia – he'd been sure that right at the end of their conversation there'd been a frisson of attraction. He told himself not to even think about it. And anyway, like Ronnie said, she probably hadn't given *him* a second thought. Even if she had, she wouldn't be thinking of him as a person but only as a paparazzo.

He watched as Mia leaned over to Billy and kissed him on the cheek.

With a lump in his throat Leo continued shooting.

*

'OK kids,' barked the director. 'Let's get this show on the road.'

War of Words was being directed by Tyler Bracket, a fifty-something redhead who somehow managed to combine a professional flair for visuals with a shockingly bad sense of personal style. Today she was wearing some kind of traditional ethnic costume, including a long lace skirt, a colourful shawl and a turban-style headscarf, all of which she'd accessorized with Ugg boots and Ray-Ban shades.

Tyler sat down with Mia and Billy to talk them through the scene. She explained that they were about to shoot the moment when Billy's character, seriously wounded and nursed by Mia in the middle of a violent and chaotic battle, dies tragically in her arms. This wasn't any different to what they'd shot last time around, except that this time, when Mia ripped open Billy's shirt to treat his injuries (handily exposing his impressively muscular chest in the process), she'd find a romantic poem he'd written for her taped to his heart. This would then prompt a whole new sequence to end the film, one that would hopefully go down much better with cinemagoers around the world.

'Come on kids,' rasped Tyler with a flounce of her shawl, 'it's show time!'

They began rehearsing and, as usual, Mia drew on her own experiences to turn on the tears at just the required moment. It wasn't difficult. All she had to do was think of how it had felt to come home at the age of nine to find that the charismatic, sparky father she'd worshipped and adored had suddenly walked out on his family without even saying goodbye, leaving them with an avalanche of his gambling debts and the humiliation of being told in a brief note that he'd dumped them in favour of a trashy blonde who lived in a trailer park and worked in the local gas station. As well as dealing with her own pain, Mia had been forced to witness her mother's sparkle instantly fade and then continue to gradually ebb away over the next decade, until she eventually died a few years ago after a long and devastating battle with breast cancer. Mia only had to picture her mother lying in her hospital bed the last time she'd seen her for the tears to start welling up in her eyes.

By the time she received her cue to find the poem strapped

to Billy's chest, she was in full flow. As she held up the crumpled paper to read it, angled towards a camera ready to zoom in on her shattered expression, she was surprised to find her mind drifting once again to Leo and to what Billy had said about their date. Maybe she was making a big mistake going out with him after all. Maybe he *would* film the whole thing on a hidden camera and then sell his story.

However the date turned out, something inside her told her that she simply had to go through with it. *Just for curiosity*, she reassured herself, *not for any other reason*.

*

'Final checks!' came a booming voice over a loudspeaker.

Leo stopped snapping as Mia and Billy were separated by an army of hair and make-up girls and disappeared under a buzz of activity. In the midst of the mêlée he spotted Dominique reappear to touch up Billy's wounds.

'You know, I've been thinking about this date,' said Ronnie, finally stepping back from his machine gun. 'How are you going to make sure you're not followed? I mean, have you actually thought this through? What happens when the rest of the paps see you out on a date with one of the biggest stars in town?'

'Standby!' shouted the same voice over the loudspeaker.

'Aha,' said Leo, stepping into position, 'I was hoping *you'd* help me out with that one. What with you being my trusted partner and everything.'

'Me?'

'Yeah. You see I've come up with this genius plan. And with you on side I know it can't go wrong . . .'

'Uh-oh. Now you're starting to sound like a major suck-up. What *exactly* have you got in mind, Leo?'

Before he had time to elaborate, he was interrupted by another blast of the loudspeaker.

'ACTION!'

They picked up their guns, aimed at the enemy and began shooting.

5

Ronnie was standing in his living room wearing a long blonde wig, pale pink lipstick and mascara that was getting in his eyes and making him twitch. He'd already had to shave off all his stubble, endure his entire body being waxed of its considerable covering of dark hair, and then struggle through the agony of having his eyebrows plucked to near-obliteration. If this was what being a woman was like, then he sure was glad to be a guy.

'Man, the things I do for Leo.'

His wife Rosie was putting the finishing touches to her creation. A Boston-born beautician, Rosie had met Ronnie when he'd papped Destiny Diament having her nails done through the windows of her salon and she'd stormed outside to defend her client armed with a hose normally used for washing hair. Within seconds Ronnie was drenched and his brand-new camera ruined. It had been a fittingly tempestuous start to a relationship that ever since had lurched from one fight to another. But their bust-ups were always followed by passionate make-ups and after being together for three years both of them knew they'd struggle to live without each other.

'You look real beautiful, honey,' cooed Rosie. 'Quite the leading lady.'

'Man, I need a smoke.'

'I've told you, Ronnie, not in the house.'

'Huh! You think I'm going out like this?'

Ronnie lit a cigarette and Rosie gave a loud huff.

'OK, I'll let it go – just this once. But I'll kick you back into touch once you've got through tonight.'

Ronnie smiled weakly and took a deep drag on his cigarette.

Laid out on the sofa were three dresses for him to try on. Only five feet tall and of a petite frame herself, Rosie had had to borrow some larger dresses from a big-boned hulk of a girl called Patty who worked as a rather hopeless junior stylist at the salon. Ronnie always joked about her looking like a man in drag so had suggested that her wardrobe might be a good fit. Of course Rosie hadn't told Patty the real reason she needed the dresses, inventing some fiction about a cousin visiting from Boston and her luggage going missing on the plane. The whole thing was being done in top secret, which was why they couldn't risk hiring a female decoy. And Rosie was off the hook as her mixed-race skin meant there was no way she could pass for baby-blonde Mia. Which was where Ronnie came in.

'I'll try that one,' he said, pointing to a rather Eighties-looking, sequinned dress with shoulder pads.

'Ooh, you like that one, do you?' Rosie teased.

'Give me a break, babe. I just picked the black one because Mia's assistant told me she'd be wearing black.'

'OK, OK! Don't be so touchy.'

Ronnie slipped on the dress over his underwear, managing

to knock his wig skew-whiff in the process. Rosie fixed the damage then stood back to take in the finished look. Thankfully the dress was a perfect fit.

'Hmm, not bad,' she nodded. 'Not bad at all.'

Ronnie suspected that he looked grotesque but she didn't have the heart to tell him. He looked in the mirror and couldn't help thinking that he looked like some kind of cross-dressing psycho from a dark, intense crime thriller.

'Let's see you walk up and down,' Rosie chirped. 'You know, get into character a little.'

'Hi Rosie, I'm Mia Sinclair,' he grunted, plodding across the room. As if to make up for the fact that he was dressed as a woman, he deepened his voice, was walking bow-legged like John Wayne, and smoked with his cigarette pinched between his thumb and finger, like some kind of hoodie from the Bronx. It was quite a combination.

'Great,' managed Rosie feebly. 'You look real great.'

'Yeah,' he sighed. 'I sure hope Mia's car has blacked-out windows.'

*

Leo stood waiting in the underground car park of the offices of Mia's agent in Beverly Hills. This had been designated as the rendezvous point by her assistant Hector, who she'd appointed as co-ordinator of tonight's activities. Leo had only spoken to Hector on the phone a few times but he sounded nice enough. He always seemed to have lush Latino power ballads playing in the background and made no secret of the fact that he thought the whole escapade was thrillingly romantic. As Leo stood on his own in a drab concrete car park, he'd have struggled to imagine a less promising start to a romantic evening. Was he being completely insane? He was starting to wonder . . .

He heard a car coming through the security gates above and hoped it wasn't Mia. As usual, Ronnie was late and Leo was starting to worry that she'd arrive before him and end up in a bad mood before their date had even begun. He breathed a sigh of relief as he recognized Ronnie's car.

Ronnie parked alongside Leo and stomped out of his car in a sulk.

'Don't you dare say anything, Leo.'

'But mate, you look amazing.'

'Yeah, right. Sure I do.'

'No, honestly, I could almost fancy you – you actually look quite fit.'

'The word's "hot", Limey. And quit hitting on me – I'm way out of your league.'

Before Leo could carry on the banter they heard another car approaching from upstairs. Leo gulped. He hadn't realized just how nervous he was until now. *What is it with this woman? How does she do this to me?*

Mia slid her car into the space next to Ronnie's and Leo was relieved to see that it had tinted windows; without them there'd be no way the paps would mistake Ronnie for Mia. Sure, he was the right colouring but he was too stocky and his little ears stuck out way too much to ever pass for a female film star.

The butterflies in his stomach began fluttering up his throat as he watched Mia park up and swiftly step out. She closed the door and strode towards them without so much as a smile.

Leo saw that, like Ronnie, she was wearing black but unlike him she looked stunning. He felt like he'd been punched in the stomach and struggled to catch his breath.

'Come on then,' she said, without saying hello to either of them, 'let's get on with it.'

'Erm, hi Mia,' he mumbled, 'this is my partner, Ronnie.'

Mia looked Ronnie up and down with a straight face, as if his get-up were totally normal. 'Nice to meet you,' she quipped matter-of-factly. 'Now what's the plan?'

Leo explained that Ronnie would drive out of the building in Mia's car to fool the paps on her trail. He'd take them on a wild goose chase around town for an hour or so until the coast was definitely clear, at which stage he'd drive the car up to Mia's house, where Hector would be waiting for him.

'OK and how do we get to the restaurant?'

Leo gestured to his motorbike.

'Huh!' Mia snorted and turned up her nose. 'There's no way I'm getting on that thing!'

'Why not? It's perfectly safe. I've brought you a spare helmet.'

'Yeah and I can imagine how many girls have worn that.'

Leo looked down bashfully. Ronnie shot him a look that clearly meant *I told you so*.

'Look, I'm sorry,' Mia said, 'but I just can't do it. I mean, how would I hold on?'

'You'd put your arms round me.' He held out his hands and gave her a smile.

'Yeah, nice try punk but it's not going to happen.' She turned to Ronnie. 'Listen, if you're driving off in my car, can't we take yours?'

'And how would I get home?'

'On the bike?' offered Leo.

'Great,' he sighed, throwing his arms up in the air. 'I'll ride across LA dressed like some ugly chick.' He gestured to what he was wearing. 'No problem at all.'

Leo looked at him beseechingly. 'Please, partner.'

'Oh give me a break, bud. Why does this shit always happen to me?'

He stood with his hands on his hips, as if thinking it over. After a few seconds he reluctantly held out his palms and Leo and Mia handed him their keys. He let out a loud groan and dragged himself over to Mia's car, exaggerating the effort, as if his entire body were a dead weight. 'Dude,' he shouted back to Leo, 'you're going to owe me for this – big time.'

'Mate, I really appreciate it.'

'Just as long as you do!'

Ronnie got into Mia's car and drove off, screeching the tyres along the tarmac as he disappeared up the ramp. Outside, Leo and Mia could hear the pack of paps zoom after him into the night. The noise echoed around them in the empty space. They were all alone.

There was an awkward silence and Leo told himself he had to snap out of his nerves and take control of the evening. He'd never been nervous on a date before and girls had always seemed to like him. Obviously, Mia was a huge star but surely she couldn't be that different from the other girls he'd dated. All he had to do was be himself and everything would run smoothly, just as it always did.

He gave Mia a wide grin. 'Well it's nice to see you,' he offered, 'and you look really lovely.'

'Oh cut the crap, Leo. And don't look at me like that.'

'Like what?'

'Like that! That little wonky grin-smile thing you do. It might win over the other girls but it won't work on me. Honestly.'

Despite her protests, Leo noticed that she was having to purse her lips together tightly to stop herself from smiling. He took this as a good sign but still found it hard to relax. He hoped she couldn't tell how nervous he was – or that his confident swagger was just a front he put up to hide it. He tried his best not to smile.

'Come on then – this way.'

He held out his hand and showed her the way to the car.

*

Stepping out of the car around the back of the restaurant, Mia chatted away on her mobile phone. She'd made the conversation last the entire journey, forcing Leo to listen to her talking to Serena about a single pair of shoes she wanted for a whole twenty minutes. Of course she wanted to make it clear that she was only here because she had no choice. But the truth was that the phone call was also a good way of covering up her nerves.

Still chatting on her phone, she watched as Leo stopped at the back door to the restaurant and raised his hands in supplication. She grudgingly said goodbye to Serena.

'Oh come on, Mia,' he begged, 'can't you at least *try* to enjoy yourself?'

She tutted as if the suggestion were ludicrous. 'I was under the impression I had to have dinner with you, Leo. Nobody mentioned speaking to you in the car.'

'All right, all right, point taken. But we're here now so do me a favour and put the phone away.'

With an exaggerated sigh she switched off her phone and dropped it into her handbag. 'Listen,' she piped, 'while we're out here we might as well lay down some ground rules.'

'OK. Go on.'

'Firstly, I don't want to have to watch what I say all night so if I let anything slip about any famous friends of mine, you have to promise me you won't act on it.'

'Fair enough. I give you my word.'

'Hmpf! The word of a paparazzo – that sure counts for a lot.'

'Well, you know,' he smirked. 'Honour amongst thieves.'

She found it hard to keep up the tough front when he smiled at her like that. And she had to admit, he was even more handsome than she remembered. She looked down to avoid catching his gaze.

'Wait a second,' she said, spotting something suspicious, 'what's that bulge?'

'What bulge?'

'The one in your trousers.'

He chuckled naughtily. 'Woah! Slow down a bit, Mia. Shouldn't we save that for later?'

Now she was really struggling not to smile and had to make a big effort to sound firm. 'Don't get fresh with me, Leo. Come on, hand over the camera. I know you've got one in there.'

'There is no camera, Mia. I don't know what you're taking about.'

'Then what's that . . . that . . . *thing* in your pocket?'

Leo reached into the pocket of his jeans and drew out a

small box with a memory card inside it. 'All I've got here are the pictures you want. Happy now?'

'Oh right. Erm, good. Yeah, thanks.'

'Honestly, you can frisk me if you don't believe me.'

'No, no, that won't be necessary. Just as long as you know that's the only reason I'm here – to get the pictures.'

'Of course.'

'And while we're on the subject, how long till I can have them? I mean, how long does this whole date thing have to last?'

'Calm down, you'll get your photos. I'll hand them over just as soon as we've eaten.'

'Good. Just as long as you do.'

He reached forward and pulled the door handle, holding it open so she could walk inside.

*

As Mia walked inside the restaurant, Leo reflected that he'd never been on a date with someone so feisty. Usually by this stage girls were fawning all over him. But it didn't matter – he'd just have to up his game to win her round. He only hoped he didn't overdo it and put her off by being too cocky. Because there was something about her toughness that he was starting to find seriously attractive.

Mia looked around the restaurant and couldn't help raising a smile at the cheery atmosphere. Leo had brought her to a tiny Mexican place called El Burrito Alegre, which was on a hidden little back street in a quiet corner of East LA. He explained that he was friends with the owners, a middle-aged couple called Luis and Luisa with elderly parents and a gaggle of teenage children, all of whom helped out in the restaurant when it was busy. He'd already spoken to them about tonight and wasn't remotely worried that they'd tip off the press. And they'd saved him a private room at the back of the restaurant so that Mia wouldn't be spotted by any of the other customers.

'*Encantada*,' Mia beamed as she was introduced to the entire family. Leo noticed how easily she dropped her hard front. *So I was right*, he thought, *she's only putting it on for my benefit*. He wondered at which stage of the evening the two of them would feel relaxed enough to actually be themselves.

Whether it was a front or not, as soon as they were left alone in their room, Mia's tone changed back to snappy. 'Right then, let's get on with it. The sooner we get our food, the sooner this'll be over.'

Unruffled, Leo cast his eye over the menu. 'I guess you'll be wanting a big fat burger,' he teased. 'I'm afraid they don't do them here.'

She just about managed to keep a straight face. 'Ha, ha, very funny. I'll have you know that when you papped me the other day that was the first burger I'd tasted in years.'

'Yeah, yeah – I've heard that line before.'

Before she had time to reply, Luis came in to take their drinks order. Leo asked for a Corona while Mia ordered a still water. As soon as he'd gone, Luisa appeared, asking what they'd like to eat. Leo ordered chicken quesadillas followed by the house speciality, seafood fajitas.

'Erm, could you just do me some grilled fish with vegetables, please?' asked Mia. 'I'm really sorry to be awkward, it's just that I'm on a special diet right now.'

'*Sin problema, señorita*,' smiled Luisa.

'*Gracias.*'

'So what's this diet?' Leo asked when she'd gone.

'Oh you know, just my usual shooting diet. No dairy, no alcohol, no sugar, no bread, no wheat, no fat, no carbs.'

'That sounds pretty hardcore. Aren't you permanently starving?'

Mia sensed that their conversation was drifting dangerously close to pleasant and realized she'd have to act quickly to avoid blowing her front. 'Yeah but what can I do with you guys following me around all day, all of you desperate to get a shot of me looking like crap? Don't you realize how much pressure that puts me under?'

Again, Leo was unruffled. 'Well don't worry about it so much – fans love pictures that show stars are only human. You know, shots of you guys putting the rubbish out, pushing a trolley around the supermarket, eating a greasy burger . . .'

'Yeah well that's easy for you to say. It's not you they're seeing looking gross.'

'I'm serious, Mia. Pictures that make ordinary people think stars are just like them always sell really well. They work for you guys too because they help the public identify with you more. And they work for the public because they make them feel better about the boring reality of their everyday lives.'

Mia was just about to say that maybe he had a point when she reminded herself that the paparazzi were her enemy – her arch enemy. And she wasn't going to let this one win her round that easily.

'Oh spare me the public service broadcast,' she piped. 'Do you actually expect me to buy that? That you only snap us off duty to make the public feel better about themselves?'

'Well that's not the only reason I do my job but it is a big part of it. If you want to, see it as supplying a demand in the entertainment industry. And when you look at it like that, it's not so different to what you do, is it?'

Mia wasn't sure how to reply. She didn't want to let him win the argument but she was finding the effort of being an ice queen totally exhausting. *How much longer do I have to keep this up?* she wondered.

Leo's phone beeped and he lifted it out of his pocket to read a text from Ronnie. Their plan had worked and he'd successfully shaken off the paps.

'Well you can relax for tonight at least,' he told Mia. 'From now on you won't be bothered by any paps.'

'Apart from the one sitting opposite,' she sniffed.

She was starting to hate being so cold. Would it matter if she stopped snapping at him and relaxed just a little?

Luisa appeared with their drinks and Leo's starter and he tucked right in. Mia was ravenous and the food looked and smelled really good. She took a sip of her water and tried not to stare. What she'd give for a mouthful of chicken with melted cheese. She hoped that Leo couldn't spot the desperate, almost crazed look in her eyes – it really wasn't attractive. She quickly reminded herself that it didn't matter whether or not Leo found her attractive. It wasn't as if she was taking the date seriously.

'So while I'm eating,' Leo managed, 'how about you do the talking? Tell me about yourself, Mia.'

'That's like the worst interview question ever,' she mocked. '"Tell me about yourself." Totally annoying. Most interviewers have done their homework before they meet me.'

'Well I'm sorry but I haven't. I mean, I know what the

magazines and papers say about you but I want to hear about the real you. Who are you when no one's watching, Mia?'

'Oh right.' For a second she was stumped. This was the kind of thing she'd always wanted a man to say to her on a date.

'I mean, obviously I know where you live,' he broke in, 'what car you drive and what you do for a living. Oh, and that you like burgers.'

'Yeah yeah, I wish you'd drop that one.'

'But that's about it.'

'All right, fine. That's not a problem. But surely you can do better than "Tell me about yourself"?'

'OK, well how about this – what's going on with you and Billy Spencer? Are you two seeing each other?' The question came out before he had time to think about it. He hoped it didn't make him sound jealous.

'Well that's none of your business but no, we're not actually. We're just very good friends.'

'You looked more than just good friends the other day.' Now he was sounding completely jealous – he decided to quit before she rumbled him. 'Mmm, this food is really good. Want to try some?'

'No thanks. And what do you mean "the other day"?'

Leo realized what he'd said and knew he'd have to backtrack. 'Erm, in the erm, in the pictures of you two on set. I saw them on Perez Hilton today.'

'Oh right, yeah. My publicist was thrilled – she reckons it'll be great press for the movie.'

'Oh really? So the paps aren't always the bad guys then?'

'Erm, I didn't say that exactly.'

'No but you did say the pictures would help plug your film.' He popped a fork full of food into his mouth, pleased with the way he'd regained the advantage.

'Erm, yeah, erm, I suppose so. But that's not the point.'

She realized that she'd walked into a trap and screwed up her face in mock anger. In a way it was almost a relief to know that he'd got one over on her. At least now she had an excuse to be a little nicer to him and stop pretending to be such a bitch.

'Don't worry,' Leo smiled, sensing that she was warming to him, 'I'm glad you liked the pictures. I was pretty chuffed with them myself.'

'Hang on a second – *you* took those photos?'

'I might have done.'

'But I didn't spot you. Were you on set?'

'Yep – got it in one. Dressed as a German tank commander.'

She slammed her glass onto the table. 'But Leo, that's outrageous! You must have told all kinds of lies to get past security.'

'Oh come on,' he shrugged. 'It wasn't that big a deal. I was just doing a bit of acting, that's all – just like you.'

She gripped her glass with both hands and glared at him. 'But how can you say that, Leo? What you were doing was completely different – and you know it. And anyway, what if I hadn't wanted to be photographed that day?'

'But Mia, you were there on set to be shot by the film cameras, fully styled and made-up. And, if you don't mind me saying, you were looking particularly beautiful too.'

She did her best not to smile; it was difficult to stay angry with him when he insisted on being so charming. And hadn't she just decided to be less of an ice maiden anyway? She pursed her lips as she thought things over. She wasn't sure she really wanted to be outraged. 'Well I've got to hand it to you,' she managed, 'what you did was very impressive.'

'Thanks.'

'They were nice pictures too. For what it's worth, you're obviously good at your job.' Mia checked herself – she might have got out of being a bitch but now she was overdoing the niceness.

'Cheers,' said Leo. 'So are you. I saw the scene you filmed with Billy – it was actually really moving.'

Mia caught herself blushing. 'Yeah, well we're all hoping this movie will be a big step forward for me. You know, I'm starting to get real sick of making the same old chick flicks.'

Leo put down his knife and fork. 'I'm sorry, Mia, but I guess this is when I have to make a really bad confession.'

'What? What is it?'

'Oh it's just that I haven't seen any of your films.'

'What? You haven't seen *any* of them?'

He frowned in apology. 'Sorry. But to be honest, chick flicks aren't really my bag.'

Well this makes a change, thought Mia. Men had usually seen every film she'd made and fell over themselves to tell her how much they'd enjoyed them, even if she could tell they were lying through their teeth. If she was working through her usual checklist for first dates, she wasn't sure whether that answer deserved a tick or a cross. She decided to look on the bright side: if he hadn't seen any of her films then at least he hadn't seen her naked.

'I suppose it's because I grew up with three older sisters,' he explained. 'They spent the whole time watching chick flicks so I kind of got sick of them.'

'Three sisters? Hmm, I bet they spoiled you.'

'Yeah, why do you say that?'

'Oh just a hunch.'

He took his last mouthful of food and pushed his plate away. 'Anyway, I think growing up in a female environment taught me to understand women better.'

Mia stifled a laugh. She'd never heard anyone so cocky. That wasn't a tick on her checklist but a very heavy cross. And if she could have underlined it she would – *and* put a ring around it.

'It's true,' he went on, as if reading her thoughts. 'I mean, I've got you completely weighed up for a start.'

'Oh yeah. And what am I thinking now then?'

He looked her in the eye, but this time struck a serious expression. 'That you're actually attracted to me. But you're fighting it because you don't want to be.'

There was a tense silence; his forwardness had caught Mia off guard. She hoped that he'd stop there.

'That you're frightened to death of losing control of your emotions,' he went on, holding her gaze. 'And you see me as a serious danger.'

This was starting to get really unnerving – she felt like she'd just had her cover blown and was left sitting there completely disarmed. She really wished he'd stop. But part of her wanted to hear more.

'And I think you spend your whole time putting up this front to the world but the truth is that it's starting to wear you down. And if I'm not mistaken, you're getting ready to drop your guard. Really soon.'

What is it with this guy? How's he able to read me so well?

'Oh that's bullshit and you know it,' she managed to trill, as if undaunted.

There was another tense silence and Leo took a swig of his beer. His look told her that he didn't believe her.

Luisa entered to clear Leo's plate and Mia was glad of the brief respite. While Leo complimented Luisa on the food, she gave herself a little pep talk. She told herself that it didn't matter what he thought about her. *It's not as if I'm seeing him again so who cares what he thinks?* The realization was quite liberating and she could feel herself starting to relax.

'I told you,' he went on as Luisa left, 'I was brought up watching romantic films. I can read you like an open book.'

'Well for your information, the key to understanding women isn't watching romantic movies. And just because I act in romantic movies doesn't mean my life's like one.'

'OK so what *is* your life like?' He adopted the voice of a cheesy TV interviewer. 'Mia Sinclair, *tell me about yourself.*'

So she did.

*

By the time their main course had been cleared away, Mia had told Leo things she hadn't spoken about on dates ever before. She'd told him about how she sometimes felt no different from the frightened, lonely eighteen-year-old who'd arrived in LA desperate to make her dream come true. She'd told him she'd completely lost touch with her father and was sometimes tormented by the thought that he might have died and she wouldn't even know about it. And she told him about her fear that, after working so hard to make her dream come true, her career could end tomorrow, leaving her with nothing but a loveless, empty shell of a life. She surprised herself by how frank she was being but on some level she understood that if she didn't tell the truth he'd see right through her anyway.

As Mia talked and talked, Leo relaxed into the situation and didn't feel such a need to cover up his nerves. The more she revealed about her true self, the more he started to like her. And he gradually came to realize that he'd been completely wrong about one thing; Mia was nothing like the other girls he'd dated. None of the other girls had made him feel like this. Ever.

He felt suddenly unnerved by his feelings and decided to crack a joke. 'Don't worry,' he teased, 'if your career hits the skids, I can think of a great silver lining.'

'Oh yeah and what's that?'

'You could give up your ridiculous diet. And eat as many burgers as you wanted.'

She'd say one thing for Leo; he treated her differently to all the other men she'd dated. Sure, he was cocky and forthright but maybe that wasn't such a bad thing after all. As the night went on she started to see that deep down he was sensitive and caring. And she surprised herself by how much she was enjoying his company.

She stirred her peppermint tea while he sipped his espresso.

If she focused back in on her usual checklist then she had to admit that Leo was scoring a lot of ticks. He was punctual, he had his own career, and he had a big edge over everyone else she'd dated as he was utterly unfazed by the paparazzi. He even knew how to lose them for the evening. The one stumbling block was that he was obviously some kind of ladies' man. In the course of their conversation he'd already mentioned four or five ex-girlfriends. But maybe she could change that. Maybe he'd be different with the right girl. She wondered if her mom had thought the same thing when she'd fallen in love with her dad.

The thought of her mom made Mia wonder if she was letting her down. She realized that she'd got so carried away talking about herself that she'd forgotten to ask Leo some crucial questions. Going back to her trusty checklist, there was one area she hadn't even touched on yet; she had to find out about his past relationships and in particular whether he was reliable and, most importantly of all, faithful.

'So tell me about you, Leo,' she said, blowing on her hot tea. 'What's your relationship history?'

'Wow, that's a heavy question. Talk about in at the deep end.'

'Well I just told you my story. Now it's your turn to tell me yours.'

He looked into his espresso as if for reassurance. 'Erm, I just split up with someone so I'm recently single.'

'OK and why did you two break up? Did you cheat on her?'

'What is this? Some kind of grilling?'

She put on the face of an arch interrogator and adopted the accent of a Russian Bond villain. 'Shut up und answer zee question, *asshole*!'

A smile flickered over his face like sunlight over shadow. Whatever she'd said to him in the parking lot about not liking his smile, she could admit to herself now that it was actually very charming, especially when it wavered with the tiniest hint of vulnerability. She wondered if behind his confident front he'd actually been nervous about taking her out to dinner. If he had, then that only made her warm to him even more. She felt something flutter inside her and took a sip of her tea.

'No, I wasn't unfaithful, no,' he said. 'I never have been, to be honest. At least not since I grew up, if you know what I mean.'

Hmm, she mused, *maybe he isn't such a bad boy after all. Could that even count as a tick?*

'I can't see the point in infidelity,' he went on. 'If I'm not into someone I have to come out and say it. I'm all about honesty, Mia. Guess I always have been.'

'Don't tell me,' she smirked. 'I suppose that's why you became a paparazzo?'

'Yeah, maybe it is.'

'Well,' she joked, 'that and wanting to pick on innocent, defenceless actresses while they secretly eat burgers.'

'OK, I'm sorry about that.'

'That's OK. Apology accepted.'

'But the way it works is, when you're on the job you have to forget about your conscience. You train yourself to take pictures first and ask questions later. Because you don't want to miss out on a picture and sometimes if you blink it's gone. So you take it anyway and you can always decide not to sell it later. For the record, I've done that myself – several times.'

Mia nodded, taking it all in. She hadn't realized the paparazzi had a code of ethics but now that he'd explained himself, it did kind of make sense.

'And while we're on the subject,' he smiled. 'Dinner's over so it's time I gave you your pictures.'

He reached into his pocket and handed her the package.

'Thanks. Thanks very much.' For some reason she felt a bit sad to have the pictures back. She slipped them into her bag and snapped it shut. 'It's very gallant of you to help me out like that. I really appreciate it.'

Hang on a minute, did I really just say that?

'Oh and just for the record,' she added swiftly, 'I wasn't defenceless. I could easily have set my publicist on you. And you wouldn't want to mess with her.'

'Yeah but you didn't,' he grinned. 'You set yourself on me. And I'm glad you did.'

He sure was forward. But damn it was sexy.

At a nod from Leo, Luis appeared with the check and Leo insisted on paying it.

'Erm, just so you know,' she ventured, 'I much prefer to pay my half of the check – if you don't mind.'

'Well I'm sorry but you're not paying anything tonight. This is my treat.'

For some reason, letting him pay felt like a big mistake – it was almost like admitting he'd won, that he'd broken through her defences. It was about time she pulled herself together.

'Erm, actually,' she struggled, 'that's very kind of you but would you mind if I paid my share?'

He looked at her with a twinkle in his eye. 'OK, well how about I do you another deal? Seeing as tonight's arrangement worked out so well . . . ?'

'OK. Go ahead.'

'If you don't want me to pay then there's only one thing for it.'

'Oh yeah, what's that?'

'You pay next time.'

She finally let a huge smile sweep over her face.

'Looks like you got yourself another deal.'

6

It was nearly midday and Hector Molino had only just dragged himself out of bed. After downing two coffees and then brushing his teeth with whitening toothpaste so strong it burnt his gums, he'd jumped into the shower, where he was now standing under the powerful jets of hot water, singing along at the top of his lungs to his favourite power ballad by Ricky Martin.

'*Vuelve, que sin tí la vida se me va.*'

Hector lived right in the centre of West Hollywood, where he'd recently bought his own little apartment above a Chinese takeaway called Phat Phuck. His boss Mia Sinclair paid him well so over the last couple of years he'd saved enough money for a deposit and had then signed the deeds to his very first home. It might not be a patch on Mia's place and towards the end of the day it did tend to stink of Peking duck but despite all this, Hector was proud of being a homeowner at the age of twenty-four. It really wasn't a bad turn-out for the son of Cuban immigrants who'd started with nothing.

'*Vuelve, que me falta el aire si tú no estás.*'

Listening to Ricky Martin reminded Hector of being a young boy in Miami and watching his mother and father dancing and smooching in the garden of the family home. The two of them had been childhood sweethearts in their native Cuba but his mother's family had suddenly emigrated to the US in great secrecy when she was just sixteen. Realizing that he couldn't live without her, Hector's father had sent love letters via other Cubans fleeing the regime, telling his sweetheart to wait for him as he'd follow her as soon as he could. A few years later he kept his promise and risked his life to cross the Caribbean on a makeshift raft, joining his patient beloved in Miami, where they eventually married and lived happily ever after. Hector had always adored hearing the story of how his parents got together and thought it was all so deeply romantic. One day he hoped to experience a love story of his very own.

Because Hector Molino was in love with love. Songs about love, films about love, books about love, plays about love – whatever the medium, he couldn't get enough of it. So it was kind of fitting that he now worked for the First Lady of Love, particularly as he was such a big fan of her films. His favourite movie of all time was *Harassment*, which he'd originally watched on a date with his first ever boyfriend, shortly before losing his virginity round the back of the cinema. Of course he'd never told Mia that he was a big fan as he worried this would be considered unprofessional, which couldn't be further from the truth. Hector took great pride in his role as Mia's personal assistant, always working to the very best of his abilities and loving every aspect of the job. The only slight disappointment he'd experienced had been the discovery that the life of the First Lady of Love was singularly lacking in the very thing that had made her famous. But maybe all that was about to change. Hector had been working for Mia for two years now and he'd never seen her with such a spring in her step. The romantic in him was convinced that it was all down to Leo.

'*Oh vuelve, nadie ocupará tu lugar.*'

Planning the couple's big date over the last week had been a joy for Hector from start to finish. Mia's agent Serena had been so worried about her friend's safety that she'd insisted Hector speak to Leo about every last detail of the date and, best of all, that he personally waited in the house last night until Mia arrived safely home. Which meant that Hector had been thrilled to become the first person in Mia's circle to find out how the date had gone. And if he wasn't mistaken, it had gone very well indeed.

He switched off the shower and reached over to find a towel. As he patted himself dry he began replaying the events of last night in his mind. After all the comings and goings with Ronnie, who'd dropped off Mia's car at the house but then had to be driven back to the underground parking lot so that he could pick up Leo's motorbike, Hector had sat with the cats for what felt like hours watching the CCTV cameras for the first signs of Mia arriving home. When a car eventually pulled up at the entrance and swung into the driveway, he'd had to stop himself from squealing out loud; if Mia was inviting her date onto the other side of the gates then things had obviously gone well.

What Hector had been most looking forward to was finally finding out what Leo looked like. He obviously knew what he sounded like from their numerous phone conversations and there was something about his deep, manly voice and British accent that he found seriously hot. Hector only hoped that he lived up to it in the flesh. As the car crunched to a halt in front of the porch, Hector dropped Bogie and Bacall and dashed to the hall window to peek through the curtains and take a look.

To his immense relief, he wasn't disappointed. He saw that Leo had a cutely crooked grin, deep dimples and a real twinkle in his eye. And to top it all, the short-sleeved fitted shirt he was wearing hinted at a killer body underneath. There was no doubt about it; Leo was easily the hottest man Mia had dated since Hector had been working for her, including that gorgeous model Hart, who'd unfortunately only lasted a few weeks. Hopefully Leo would last a whole lot longer.

Hector carried on spying as Leo leaned forward to plant a kiss on Mia's lips. It was only a little kiss and it only lasted a few seconds but it was quite definitely a kiss. And it was all so romantic!

As Mia opened the door of the car Hector rushed back to the kitchen, where he grabbed both cats and a magazine to flick through. The last thing he wanted was for his boss to think he was some kind of nosy gossip. A few seconds later he looked up, pretending to be surprised as Mia appeared in the doorway.

'Oh hi, Mia, I didn't hear you get home.'

She leaned against the doorframe and gazed into the air with a dreamy, distant look. For Hector, there was no mistaking the look of love.

'So how did it go?' he asked. 'Did you like him?'

'What? Oh, sorry yeah. Erm, it was OK. Yeah.'

'Only OK?'

'Yeah, erm, OK.'

There was a pause while Hector waited for more. As Mia plunged back into her dewy-eyed dreaming he realized he wasn't going to get it.

She let out a long sigh. 'Listen, Hector, I hope you don't mind but I'm kind of beat. I'm going to head up straight away.'

'Oh OK, that's fine. You don't want a drink or anything before you go up? Something to help you wind down?'

'Sorry, what?'

There was no point; she was already halfway out the door.

'Oh nothing,' he mumbled half to himself, 'just sleep well.'

'Yeah, you too, Hector.' She turned again to face him. 'And thanks so much for everything. You've been brilliant, you know. Totally brilliant.'

'No problem, Mia.' He forced a smile but couldn't help feeling disappointed. He was dying to know more but it looked like he'd have to wait.

As he towelled himself dry the following morning, he realized that he *couldn't* wait. Today was a Sunday so he wasn't due in to work for another twenty-four hours. And twenty-four hours was such a long time – he simply wouldn't get through it. He'd just have to invent an excuse and pop round to the house this afternoon. He began devising possible stories as he moved over to the mirror to apply a long series of premium skincare products lined up neatly on the shelf.

He began massaging the first cream into his skin and thought back to last night and how carried away he'd been by the romance of it all. In fact, he'd been so excited about his boss falling in love that he knew he wouldn't be able to sleep so once Mia had gone to bed, he'd dashed across town to meet some friends at a gay bar called The Man Hole. He was thrilled that Mia was so clearly in love but the look on her face had reminded him of how much he wanted to fall in love himself.

Looking around the bar for his very own romantic hero, he'd been sorely disappointed. The only people who'd chatted him up all night were an almost identical-looking couple with stubble and skinheads, who introduced themselves as Sexy Rob and Sexy Tom and bluntly announced that they were looking for a threesome. When he politely refused they gave him their phone number just in case he changed his mind. When he looked closer he saw that they'd written it on the back of a leaflet for a sexual health clinic. He spotted the leaflet now, lying in the trash can next to the sink.

He slipped into his bedroom and pulled on his Sunday clothes; sweat pants, a T-shirt and a matching baseball cap. He wondered what Mia was doing right now and if she was thinking about Leo. He always felt pleased when somebody else fell in love as it made him think there was hope for him yet. And if it was happening to Mia after years of disappointment, then maybe it would happen to him too. More than anything in the world he wanted to meet the right person and fall in love. And falling in love had always come easily to him. It was finding the right person that was the difficult part.

Already this year Hector had fallen in love three times. First there was a giant of a stuntman known as Deep Pan Dan because of his massive appetite. Hector had fallen for him almost instantly, only to be dumped a few weeks later once Dan had found out the only thing he could cook was a bowl of cereal. Next there'd been an Argentinian who claimed to be from the same village as Eva Perón and taught Hector how to tango. But he'd flown back to Buenos Aires after just a few months, ending it with Hector by email as soon as he arrived, quoting lyrics from *Evita* as he did so. And finally, just a few weeks ago there'd been a statuesque dancer known throughout West Hollywood as Black Beauty. Hector had assumed he'd earned the nickname because of his stunning appearance but later found out that it was because he'd given a ride to almost every man in town – including several while he was supposed to be dating Hector.

With each break-up Hector had been utterly heartbroken. And the injustice of it all only rubbed salt into the wound. All he wanted was someone to love. He wasn't even that bothered about being loved in return. Sometimes he felt he had so much love to give that he might even explode. And with every day that passed he became more and more desperate to share it with someone.

For now he supposed he'd have to settle for loving vicariously through Mia. He slipped on his trainers and began looking for his car keys. All he had to do was invent some excuse to get him back to the house.

That's it, he thought, *I'll pretend I've left my cell phone charger in the office*. He had genuinely left his phone charger, but Mia didn't need to know that he kept a second one at home. It was the perfect excuse; he could say he needed to make some important personal calls but his battery was almost flat so he'd had to stop by the house to pick it up.

He spotted his car keys on a table by the door and scooped them up. As he began trotting downstairs to the street he felt giddy with excitement. He was so happy that Mia was in love – and very soon he'd be hearing all about it.

*

I'm not in love, thought Leo, *I can't possibly be.*

Watford let out a long fart.

The two of them were lounging around Leo's home, which stood right next to the water in a quiet spot on the Venice Canals. It was a house he'd designed himself and very much his kingdom. It was split into three levels and filled throughout with bright light streaming through several large windows and glass doors. The floors were all made out of hard wood, which was complemented by exposed steel trimmings and granite surfaces, yet the place still managed to exude warmth and character. On the walls were a mixture of stylish abstract paintings and a selection of some of Leo's own more artistic photos, blown up and framed. At the top of the house there was a roof garden with bamboo borders, cushion-filled hammocks and stunning views of the canal. On the ground floor, there was a large waterfront patio where Leo often held barbecues for his friends or raucous drinks parties for his expat mates when there was a big football match going on back in Britain. But without doubt Leo's favourite part of the house was the huge open lounge, where he was sitting now with Watford. It was dominated by a long leather sofa, which snaked its way around the walls and had been kitted out with a giant plasma TV, full entertainment centre and every games console on the market, one of which he was playing while a yawning Watford stretched out across his feet.

He was trying to stop himself thinking about last night's date, which was what he'd been doing all morning. He really liked Mia and couldn't remember ever being as keen on anyone he'd dated after just one night. Part of him was excited about the way he felt but another part of him was scared and a bit confused too.

Does she really like me or was I just imagining it?

Am I only interested in her because she's much harder to get than anyone else I've dated?

And could a relationship ever really work between a pap and a target?

All he wanted to do was see Mia again, or just speak to her on the phone. But as her assistant had taken care of the arrangements for their date he didn't even have her number. Already this morning he'd used his professional contacts to send her a little surprise by special delivery but now that it had been dispatched there was nothing he could do but sit and wait for her reaction. Which was why he'd decided to distract himself by playing *Speed Demon 2* on his Xbox.

Just as he was about to steer his futuristic sports car off the roof of a huge skyscraper and onto the wing of a passing aeroplane, the phone rang. He hit Pause and picked it up. It was Ronnie.

'How was the date, bud?' he asked gruffly.

'Oh, you know,' Leo breezed, 'it was all right.'

'Only "all right"? Don't tell me you didn't get laid?'

'No, I didn't get laid. And for your information, last night wasn't about getting laid in the first place.'

'What was it about then?'

'Well, it was, you know . . . It was about me and Mia getting to know each other. And I'm pleased to say that she's a really great girl.'

Ronnie grunted. 'So are you going to see each other again? Or has she lost interest now she's got the pictures?'

'No, I think we will see each other again. Hopefully . . . Yeah . . . But anyway, how about you, partner? Did you get home OK?'

'Well if by getting home you mean riding across town on a motorbike dressed like some whacked-out trannie, then yeah, I guess it was OK.'

'Look, I'm really sorry about that, Ronnie. But it honestly wasn't part of the plan, I promise.'

'Yeah and neither was getting pulled over by the LAPD.'

'Seriously? You got stopped by the cops?'

'Yeah, for some reason they thought I was acting suspiciously. Can't think why. I tried telling them I was going to a costume party but they looked at me like I was a total weirdo.'

Leo tried not to laugh. 'Well in that case I suppose I owe you an even bigger favour than I thought.'

'You sure do, bud.'

'So it's just as well I've got us a pair of tickets to see the Dodgers game later.'

'You've got to be kidding me! Are you for real?'

'Too right I am.'

'That's awesome, man. But how did you swing it?'

'Oh you know what it's like in our business – we've got accomplices dotted all around town. I just work them more than you, I suppose. So do you fancy joining me or what?

'Big time. The only problem is Rosie. I already promised I'd go with her to visit some chick she works with who's just had twins. She's in a bitch of a mood and I can't bail out on her now, she'd totally whip my ass.'

'Well give it half an hour and then ask her. By that time a huge bunch of flowers should have arrived with her name on it.'

'Man, are you serious?'

'Yep, it's all sorted.'

'Dude, you're so good at that kind of thing. If only I could be more like you – my life would sure be a lot more peaceful.'

'Well, I've sent them from you so all you need to do is make out the whole thing was your idea. And then I'll see you at the game in a few hours.'

'Man, you think of everything.'

'Mate, that's nothing. Wait till you hear what I've sent Mia.'

*

Mia had to admit, Leo was good. He was really good. Laid out on the office table in front of her was the exact pair of shoes she'd talked to Serena about wanting in the car on the way to their date. She'd assumed Leo had zoned out and hadn't listened to a word she'd said, but not only had he managed to have them sent over from Prada first thing this morning but they'd come in her exact size too. She had no idea how he'd done it but she was really impressed. And kind of touched that he'd taken the trouble to do something so thoughtful to make her happy. The only thing was, she'd been trying not to think about him all day. How was she going to avoid it now?

Hector wasn't helping in the slightest. '*Dios mío!*' he

squeaked when she showed him the shoes. 'It's like something out of *Cinderella*!'

'Do you really think so?' she asked, trying to sound as cool as she could. 'You don't think it's a little hokey?'

'Not at all! It's so *romantic*!'

Mia's instincts agreed with Hector but something inside her was making her hold back. 'But what if he's only done it because he wants to get laid?'

'Excuse me but didn't you notice how hot he is? A guy like that could easily get laid without going to the trouble of buying shoes.'

'But what if he just wants to sleep with a movie star? You know, to brag about it to all his friends? Isn't that what men do?'

'*Some* men. But did he strike you as that kind of guy?'

'Not really but . . .'

'But nothing. Quit freaking out and enjoy this, Mia. It's like something out of one of your movies!'

'I know. But maybe that's what I'm afraid of.'

She knew that he meant well but the last thing Mia needed when she was trying to rein in her feelings about Leo was Hector doing his best to whip her up into a love-struck frenzy. He'd turned up a few minutes ago muttering something about leaving his phone charger in the office, but she could tell he was lying. It was blatantly obvious that he was only there because he wanted to find out more about last night's date. Right now he was making a big show of scouring the room for his charger while he bombarded her with questions about Leo.

'So is he a good kisser?'

'What does he smell like?'

'Do you feel tingly when you look him in the eye?'

Mia was doing everything she could to avoid Hector's questions and play down how much she'd enjoyed last night. She was immensely fond of Hector but at times he came across like an over-enthusiastic puppy.

'You know, it's just like my mom and dad,' he gushed. 'Did I ever tell you that Dad had to sail across the ocean on a raft so they could be together?'

'Yes Hector, you did tell me – several times.'

'Well, every day she came to the sea front to look out for him. And when he finally arrived he whisked her into his arms and they danced along the sand, blissfully happy and totally in love.'

'Don't tell me, to the sound of Ricky Martin?'

He frowned. 'No, that came later. And anyway, quit being so cynical. You need to open yourself up to love, Mia. You and Leo could be like a modern day Romeo and Juliet – sworn enemies who, against all the odds, find true love in each other's arms.' Once again he squeaked with excitement.

'Erm, correct me if I'm wrong but don't Romeo and Juliet die?'

'Well, erm, yeah . . . But that doesn't mean that you and Leo wouldn't have your happy ending.'

Mia rolled her eyes and smiled. 'Hector Molino, you are something else.'

'And Mia Sinclair, you're just frightened because you know I'm talking sense.'

Just then she spotted his phone charger peeping out of the desk drawer. 'Yeah well, I might quite like Leo but not enough to die for him.' She yanked out the charger and handed it to him. 'Is this what you're looking for?'

'Oh yeah, erm, thanks.'

'Now that's all you're getting for now. Run along and find your own Romeo. Because the sooner you do, the better for all of us!'

*

The roar of the crowd was almost deafening. The batter had just hit a blooper and scored a triple. Unfortunately the Dodgers were pitching.

'Man,' groaned Ronnie, 'we totally suck today.'

Leo and Ronnie were in Dodger Stadium watching their team take on the New York Yankees. When Leo had first arrived in LA he hadn't really enjoyed baseball; it used to remind him of playing rounders at school but with much more complicated rules. But Ronnie had always been a big fan so over the years Leo had grown to love it. And from the very start he'd loved coming to Dodger Stadium. There was something about the Chávez Ravine location with its amazing mountain views, the live organ music inside the stadium and the constant call of the peanut vendors working their way through the stands that created an incredible atmosphere. It was just a shame today's game was going so badly. It was the sixth innings by now and obvious the Dodgers were getting thrashed.

Ronnie was just about to roar his disapproval at an outfielder who missed a catch when he was hit on the head by a stray beach ball. Impromptu volleyball games often broke out in the stands during Dodger games and the fans loved them. Leo took hold of the ball and punched it far away behind them.

As he refocused on the game he spotted a not very pregnant-looking but heavily Botoxed Layla Lloyd and her boxer boyfriend sitting in prime courtside seats. Part of him wished he'd brought his camera. He didn't normally leave the house without at least a little pocket-sized camera, just in case he came across something worth snapping. Thinking about Mia all morning had obviously made him sloppy. He decided to concentrate on the game.

The batter whacked the ball high into air and began belting his way around the field. The Yankees fans' cheers grew steadily until their man scored a home run, by which time it felt like the stadium would erupt. Ronnie looked gutted.

'Man, this is just my luck,' he moaned. 'Every time I watch a game the Dodgers get their ass kicked.'

'I'm sorry, mate, I wish I could have fixed it for you.'

'Don't worry, bud. I reckon you've fixed enough for today already.'

Leo suddenly remembered to text his contact in the Prada shop to say thanks for sorting out the shoes. Kiana Kamaka was a rather severe-looking lesbian from Hawaii who over-used the words 'eclectic' and 'iconic' and spent the whole time either fanning herself or loudly clicking her fan open and shut. She regularly tipped off the paps when any stars came into the store so Leo had got to know her well over the years. He took out his phone and texted a quick thank-you.

Once again, Leo found himself wondering what Mia thought of the shoes. They must have arrived hours ago by now and he still hadn't heard anything from her. He was starting to worry that he'd missed the mark somehow and managed to cause offence.

During the seventh inning stretch, when he and Ronnie were happily chomping away on Dodger dogs with all the trimmings, he decided to ask his friend's opinion. 'Mate, do you think the whole shoe thing was a good idea?'

'Sure it was, dude. Chicks go crazy for shoes. You'll totally get laid now.'

'But I keep telling you, I don't want to get laid.'

'Sure you don't, buddy.'

'I don't! Well OK, I don't *just* want to get laid.'

'That's more like it.' He smiled and took a huge bite of his hotdog.

'I don't know,' Leo went on, 'for some reason with Mia things feel different. It's like I just want to make her happy, if that makes sense. I'd have loved to have seen her face this morning when she opened the package.'

Ronnie pretend to be choking on his food. 'Dude, did you hear what you just said? You need to take a step back and listen to yourself. She's a target, remember?'

Leo thought back to his strict policy of never mixing business with pleasure – a policy that had led to him ending countless relationships. But now here he was, wanting to break all the rules after just one date. *My God, what's happening to me?* he thought. *Maybe I am falling in love after all.*

'All I can say,' piped Ronnie, 'is I just hope Mia feels as strongly as you do.'

'Yeah,' gulped Leo, 'so do I.'

*

'Now before you ask, I'm not falling in love with anybody.' Mia was standing in the doorway with her arms folded. 'Can I just make that perfectly clear?'

'Loud and clear, sister,' boomed Serena, standing to attention and giving her a little salute. *Hmm*, she thought, *somebody's got it bad*.

That morning Serena had received a text from Mia telling her that the date had gone well. She'd been desperate to speak to her ever since but had already arranged to have lunch with Mitchell's parents that day and couldn't get out of it. She'd sat in her in-laws' dining room for what felt like forever, not enjoying a minute of it and wishing it would end soon. Mitchell's parents were academics in the department of molecular biology at UCLA and fiercely intellectual. And although Serena was confident that she could more than hold her own when it came to worldly wisdom and knowledge about the entertainment industry, she felt completely out of her depth whenever she spent time with Mitchell's family and often couldn't follow their conversation, let alone join in. As usual, she ended up feeling like, however much she progressed in life, however much she matured and grew as a person, deep down she was still the same foul-mouthed, tough little girl from a single-parent family in Harlem, and one who wasn't even as tough as people thought. After nearly three hours of torture, she'd finally managed to extricate herself and had plonked Mitchell in front of their house and then rushed straight round to Mia's.

Serena had a hunch that last night's date was potentially the most important one her friend had been on for years, if not ever. And now that she was here she could tell that she'd been right – however much Mia protested.

'So do I get to hear about this man you're *not* in love with?' she teased.

'Of course you do.' Mia grinned, kissing her on both cheeks. 'Come on in.'

They'd arranged to have an early evening swim so made their way through the house to the pool in the garden. It was Mia's day off hardcore exercise but she'd promised Cole she'd do at least fifty lengths and somehow Serena had landed herself the job of making sure it happened – even though she hated swimming as she had to stick her neck out of the water like a turtle to avoid wetting her straightened hair. The truth was, she actually quite liked her naturally kinky hair but she'd discovered from experience that other people saw a black woman with an Afro as some kind of angry, political activist. It was a conclusion that Serena had learned many Hollywood execs were only too quick to jump to – and one that she had to spend a lot of time avoiding if she wanted to continue being successful in the movie business.

Mia led her over to the small summerhouse at the edge of the pool and slipped off her bathrobe to reveal her bikini underneath. She'd obviously been sticking to her extreme diet and exercise plan as her figure was looking better than Serena had ever seen it. And even though they were best friends and she knew all about Mia's struggles with binge-eating, Serena always felt conscious about her own figure when stripping off in front of her. Since her days as a model, when she'd had to starve herself and used to suffer fainting fits and stomach cramps on a daily basis, she'd decided to go much easier on herself and eat what she wanted. She never went crazy but now that she was approaching thirty-five her natural body shape was catching up with her and however much Mitchell loved her ever-expanding booty (or her 'ghetto blaster' as he called it), there were days when she felt like a water buffalo and wished it weren't so damned big – or at least that her boobs would grow and balance it out a bit. She reassured herself that she only felt like this because she'd spent so much time around skinny white models at the height of the craze for heroin chic. And she hoped that being unhappy with her body shape didn't mean that she was any less proud of her identity as a woman of colour.

As Mia crouched into a sitting position at the edge of the pool, Serena shyly slipped into her swimming costume and went over to perch next to her. From where she was sitting she could see out over the entire city and hear the sound of the water softly cascading down the hillside. Swimming would have to wait.

'So come on then,' she started, 'I promise not to mention the L-word if you promise to tell me *all* about him.'

Mia laughed. 'Oh, Serena, he's great. Really, really great. He's funny, intelligent, sexy, charming, thoughtful, gentlemanly, sexy—'

'Yeah, I think you mentioned that one already.'

'Oh did I?'

'Yeah but I get the picture.' They looked at each other and giggled. 'So if he's really that great, then what's the problem?'

'The problem is that he's a paparazzo.'

'Oh yeah, I'd forgotten about that.'

'I mean, however great he is, can I ever really trust him?'

Serena dipped her feet into the water and began gently paddling. 'You know, I think you're right to hold back a little but you need to cut this dude some slack.'

'Do you really think so?'

'Totally. At least give him a chance to prove himself, to prove that you can trust him.'

'OK, well what do you suggest?'

'Well it's pretty early days to be talking about long-term compatibility but I think in your case you need to find out if you would ever feel comfortable integrating him into your life.'

'And how would I do that?'

'By introducing him to your world, I guess. Giving him a little try-out.'

'OK, and how do I do that?'

She began kicking her legs faster. 'Well how about taking him to Cooper Kelly's birthday party this week?'

'Are you serious?'

'Deadly serious. Think about it, sister – it's perfect. Cooper's turning eighty and wants to show the world that he's still in the game, especially since everyone knows he was in hospital last week. The word is the party's going to be freakin' awesome.'

'But the whole of Hollywood's going to be there. Billy's been excited about it for weeks.'

'Exactly. So if Leo wants to do the dirty on you by secretly taking shots of people or just doing some sneaky research then he'll have ample opportunity.'

'Hmmm, I see what you mean. But if he is going to stitch me up then won't everyone get real pissed at me for bringing him along?'

'Well that's a risk you'll have to take. I suppose the question is, how strongly do you feel about this guy? I mean, is he worth taking the risk?'

Just then Mia blushed. She turned away, almost hiding her face. At that moment Serena knew she'd got her answer.

She touched Mia on the arm to get her attention. 'Do it, sister. If you feel like that then you've got to do it. Take your man behind enemy lines and see what happens. See if he sinks – or swims.'

And with that she slid into the water and swam off.

7

The driver opened the door of the limousine and in stepped Billy.

'Hey, sugar,' he beamed at Mia. 'How's my favourite girl?'

'All the better for seeing my favourite boy.'

They leaned forward and kissed each other.

'Well you look real beautiful – just like a princess.'

'Oh thanks, Billy. And you look very dashing, my handsome prince.'

Billy did look even more dashing than usual; he was dressed for the party in a tuxedo, which really set off his square jaw and sparkling eyes. It confirmed Mia's assessment of him as attractive in a safe, non-threatening way – sweet rather than sexy. *At least to me he is anyway*, she thought. *But then again, he is my gay best friend.*

The two of them were on their way to Cooper Kelly's eightieth birthday party and had been told that there'd be a red carpet for photographers and TV crews at the entrance; Cooper obviously wanted the whole world to know about his relaunch. Mia and Billy shared the same publicist and she'd suggested that they arrive together to help plug *War of Words*, which now that they'd finished the reshoots would be released in less than two months' time. Leo had accepted Mia's invitation but arranged to wait at the far end of the red carpet; he'd only join her once they were out of sight of the photographers. She hoped that Billy wouldn't feel pushed out but when they'd run through the plan on the phone he'd seemed perfectly happy.

As soon as Billy had fastened his seatbelt Mia nodded to the driver and the limo glided forwards. They were driving way out of town to Santa Barbara, where Cooper had lived for decades now. A true Hollywood legend, he'd been playing lead roles since the 1950s, when it was rumoured he'd seduced Jayne Mansfield, Lana Turner *and* Marilyn Monroe. Now entering his ninth decade, he'd only just given up playing romantic leads and had recently married his fifth wife, a Venezuelan beauty queen forty years his junior and the daughter of a former president deposed in a coup. Over the years, Cooper had himself sired a huge family whose amorous antics often made the newspaper headlines. He'd also amassed enough money to design and build a house so grand it was rumoured to have been the model for the Carrington mansion in *Dynasty*. The last time Mia had been there she'd been knocked out by the extensive landscaped gardens bordering the ocean and the huge ballroom, which she guessed would serve as the main hub of tonight's party. And the theme for the party was simple – Gold. She really hoped Leo wouldn't find it overwhelming.

'That dress rocks,' piped Billy. 'Is it Gucci?'

'Oscar de la Renta. Isn't it a dream?' In keeping with the party's theme, she was wearing a shimmering gold open-backed halter-neck gown with extensive embroidery. 'They sent it over with a whole bunch of stuff weeks ago,' she added excitedly. 'Honestly, I didn't step out of the closet for hours!'

What she didn't tell him was that before she'd left home that night she'd spent hours in the closet trying on different outfits, all the time working herself up into a panic about the party. She'd been less nervous for her last premiere and this year's Oscars, when she'd had an army of stylists fussing around her and speculating on what people would think of her dress. She was under no illusion as to the reason behind tonight's nerves; her frantic state was clearly all down to Leo. And her mind had been racing all day imagining the worst.

What if we run out of things to talk about?

What if the spark just isn't there anymore?

What if I've put him off by revealing too much?

It had taken a great effort of willpower and concentration to stay calm and now that she was on her way to the party she tried her best not to let the worries build up again.

'And what do you think of the shoes?' she asked Billy, kicking her feet playfully so that he could take in her sleek shoes with their accents of metallic gold leather and mirrored heels shiny enough for her to check her lipstick in.

'Man, they're the bomb.'

'Aren't they just? Leo bought them for me.'

'Oh, so he's buying you shoes now, is he? Things must be getting serious.'

'Well I wouldn't say that exactly. But I definitely want to get to know him more.'

'And you're not worried that all the time you're getting to know him he's planning how he's going to screw your ass? You know, conmen can be very charming, Mia.'

'Billy, he isn't a conman.'

'No but he's a paparazzo. Is there a difference?'

There was an awkward silence while Mia fiddled with the buckle on her clutch bag.

'Well, you know, I guess that's what I need to find out,' she breathed, brushing down her dress with her hands. 'Which is why he's coming along tonight.'

Billy pulled a face. 'You know, I've been thinking about that. Couldn't you have chosen a less intense way of figuring him out?'

'But don't you see? That's why it's so perfect.' She found herself repeating Serena's lines. 'If he behaves himself tonight then I'll be able to trust him anywhere. That's the whole point.'

Billy looked out of the window and shook his head. 'I sure hope you're right, sugar. I sure hope you're right.'

Another awkward silence fell between them and Mia too turned to look out of the window. They'd already passed through Thousand Oaks and were cruising down the Ventura Freeway with the ocean on their left.

After a few minutes, Billy turned to look at her with a grave expression. 'Mia, you do feel safe with this guy, don't you? I mean, I know I'm being hard on him but it's only because I'd hate for anything bad to happen to you.'

She smiled and squeezed his hand. 'That's very sweet of you, Billy. But yeah, I do feel safe with him. That's the weird thing. I know that on paper I shouldn't but for some reason in real life I kind of do.'

He gave a resigned shrug. 'Well I'm no expert on these things but that must count for something.'

'I hope so. And I know you think I'm going crazy but sometimes I think I've been way too sane for years now. Do you know what I mean? I'm starting to think that maybe it's time I let myself go a little crazy.'

He seemed lost in his thoughts and didn't reply.

'And if Leo *is* a conman,' she went on, 'maybe it's best that I find out for myself. Otherwise I'm going to spend the rest of my life wondering what might have been.'

Again there was a thoughtful silence. The low hum of the limo's engine filled the space between them.

When they passed the Four Seasons on the left and the entrance to the Montecito Country Club on the right, both of them knew that they were approaching their destination. Soon the car turned off the road and onto Cooper's driveway, where it joined a queue of purring limos.

'Now this is your last chance, Mia,' said Billy. 'Are you sure you know what you're doing?'

'Yep. One hundred per cent sure. Well . . . maybe ninety per cent.'

'OK then let's do it. If anything goes wrong I'll be right behind you.'

As the car inched forward, Mia realized that just because she was sure she was doing the right thing, that didn't mean she wasn't nervous.

She took a deep breath and swallowed.

*

At the top of the red carpet Leo stepped aside to let through Tyler Bracket, dressed in an outfit that made her look like Big Bird from *Sesame Street*. A few paces behind strode an actor Leo recognized as Morrison De Vere, a former wild child who'd recently announced that he'd conquered his long-standing addiction to casual sex and hookers by settling down with his new wife, an Eastern European skiing champion who always reminded Leo of a transsexual he used to see hanging around the bus station in Watford on his way home from school.

He looked down at a carpet that was so red it was almost psychedelic. Leo knew from experience that even though it looked garish in real life it would be the perfect shade of red for the cameras. At the opposite end of the carpet he spotted a cluster of event photographers, who the public often confused with the paparazzi although in reality they were an entirely different breed who'd opted to spend their careers shouting out stars' names from behind crash barriers at the entrance to parties and premieres. Standing just ahead of them was the usual line-up of TV crews dressed in black, a mass of middle-aged, jaded cameramen accompanied by anxious-looking young reporters clutching stick mics, knowing they'd get only two minutes with each interviewee in which to nail a dynamite sound bite. Amongst their ranks he spotted the familiar on-screen faces of *E.T.*, *Access Hollywood*, *Extra*, *E News Daily* and *Jillian and Dorothy*. Leo felt a sudden surge of conviction that he'd chosen the right job in life; he knew that being part of the world on view before him would bore him to tears.

But his commitment to his job was about to be put to the test as he stepped behind enemy lines. He had no doubt that he'd be able to resist using any gossip he heard for his own professional gain. But he did have one big worry: after he'd mixed with stars and chatted to them about their lives, how was he supposed to switch off his feelings and think of them only as targets? He remembered that this was one of the reasons he never mixed business and pleasure. He quickly dismissed the thought – he was in way too deep to worry about that now.

He adjusted the collar of his shirt and breathed up onto his forehead to cool down. It was a hot night and he hated being buttoned up at the best of times. He felt much more at ease in casual clothes and the rigid formality of wearing black tie was doing nothing to calm his nerves. He began looking forward to his first drink and then remembered that at this kind of party it was highly unlikely they'd serve his favourite beer. *Oh well*, he thought, *I'll just have to drink champagne*.

But if he was honest with himself, Leo wasn't nervous about what he was wearing or what he'd be drinking. He wasn't even that nervous about how tonight would affect his work as a paparazzo. No, there was one thing that was making him much more nervous. And that was seeing Mia.

What if I don't fit into her world?

What if next to all these film stars she thinks I'm boring and dull?

What if we find out we have nothing in common after all?

In his hand he was holding the invitation to tonight's event, which in his nervous state he realized he was grasping a little too tightly. Mia's wide-eyed assistant Hector had been round to his house earlier that week to drop it off. Delivering it in person had seemed above and beyond the call of duty and Leo had wondered whether Hector was also checking out his place – either to satisfy his own curiosity or Mia's. Needless to say, he hadn't spoken to Mia since their last date and still didn't have her number. And the shoes hadn't been mentioned at all, which made him think that she obviously hadn't liked them. He supposed that she was sent free clothes all the time so was probably blasé about that kind of thing and wouldn't even have noticed the sentiment behind the gift. That'd teach him to be cheesy in future.

Just then he spotted Mia stepping out of a stretch limo in the distance. His stomach did a little somersault and he held onto the railings to steady himself. *Phew!* he thought. *She's properly fit.* Or 'hot' as Ronnie always corrected him. Actually, he was going to make a point of using neither word tonight. It was much more polite to say 'beautiful' or 'pretty' when in the company of a woman he wanted to impress. And thankfully, Mia was both – and a whole lot more besides.

Stepping out of the limo behind her, Leo spied Billy Spencer. His stomach sank. He watched as Billy took his place next to Mia and the two of them posed together for photos.

'Mia!'

'Billy!'

'Are you two an item?'

The photographers yelled at their subjects, their flashbulbs exploding in a riot of light.

All Leo could see was Billy's hand on Mia's naked back. Everything else disappeared into the flickering brightness. And all he could feel was jealousy rising up within him. *What is it about these two?* he thought. *Why do I get so angry when I see them together?*

He told himself to calm down; he had no hold over Mia and she was free to do whatever she liked. And besides, she'd told him that she and Billy were just good friends and he had no option but to believe her – even if he was staring at evidence to the contrary.

He looked on as the two of them turned to face a new batch of photographers. Peeping out from under Mia's dress he spotted a pair of shoes he recognized.

He breathed a sigh of relief and felt a flutter of excitement. Suddenly he wasn't nervous anymore and he could almost sense his jealousy ebbing away. He felt a smile spread its way across his face.

It looked like he was in for a good night.

*

'Hi Mia,' Leo grinned. 'Nice shoes.'

'Thanks,' she beamed. 'A sweet English guy I know sent them to me.'

They looked each other in the eye and felt that by now familiar crackle of attraction almost buzz between them. *Forget 'sweet'*, she thought. *Make that 'sexy'*.

'That dress is a knock-out too,' Leo went on. 'You look beautiful – really beautiful.'

Well done, mate, he thought. *You didn't say 'fit'. Or even 'hot'*.

There was an awkward moment when Mia suddenly remembered that Billy was standing next to her. 'Oh, sorry. Leo, this is Billy. Billy, this is Leo.'

Billy stepped forward and shook Leo's hand but he didn't smile and there was something formal and noticeably cold about his greeting.

'Good to meet you,' he almost growled.

'Yeah, you too,' snarled Leo.

Mia picked up on a quite different energy buzzing in the

air now – the unmistakable crackle of aggression. *Uh-oh*. If tonight was her chance to see if Leo could fit into her world then his trial run had just hit a serious hitch.

Thankfully, Billy soon made an excuse about spotting someone he knew. 'Would you excuse me?' he smiled thinly. 'There's someone I've got to speak to.'

Leo nodded gravely as he turned to leave. *Hmm*, he thought. *If I'm not mistaken, that's the retreat of a guilty man.* His short introduction to Billy had only confirmed his worst fears: there was obviously something going on between him and Mia.

'See you soon, Billy,' Mia trilled somewhat desperately.

'Yeah, see you later,' Leo called after him, trying not to sound too taunting. Whatever was going on between Mia and Billy, it explained why she'd been holding back and playing hard to get with him. 'Just good friends' was nowhere near the whole story. No, he obviously had competition. And that was some serious competition – if you believed what you read in the magazines, Billy Spencer was only the most eligible bachelor on the planet. Any woman would give her right arm to be his girlfriend. And why should Mia be any different?

As soon as Billy was safely out of earshot, Leo couldn't resist making a comment. 'He seemed in a hurry to get away,' he ventured. 'What's all that about?'

'Oh mind your own business,' Mia snapped, frustration getting the better of her. Straight away she regretted it but she'd so wanted tonight to go smoothly and already it was looking like she'd made a major mistake. 'Sorry, Leo, I mean, I don't know.'

'OK. Well, erm . . . Shall we go inside?'

'Yeah but, you know, let's just go through those ground rules again first.'

'OK.' He felt like a naughty schoolboy being told off by the teacher. Maybe he'd been wrong to ever imagine they could make something work between them. 'Go ahead – I'm all ears.'

'Just, you know, if you see or hear anything tonight, you can't use it for professional gain – that's all. In fact, it's probably a good idea if you keep quiet about your real job. Tell people you're a photographer, sure, but then try and change the subject.'

'And if anyone asks, what should I say I photograph?'

'Erm, I don't know. Shoes?'

'*Shoes?*'

'Yeah, well somebody has to photograph them . . .'

'OK, right. In that case, for tonight and tonight only I'm a shoe photographer.'

There was a pause as they stood looking at each other stiffly. The earlier buzz of attraction had given way to a chronically nervous tension. Leo didn't care what alcohol they were serving anymore – he badly needed a drink.

He tried to lighten the mood and held out his arm for her to link. 'Come on then, princess. Shall we go in?'

She stopped him in his tracks. 'Oh and one other thing.'

'Yeah?'

'Please don't call me princess. I feel like I'm back on the set of my last picture.'

Leo nodded grimly. Things really hadn't got off to a good start.

*

It was nearly nine o'clock and Serena had been at the party for just over an hour. She was standing at the far end of the ballroom on a little balcony overlooking the action. The enormous ornate dance hall had been decked out entirely in gold for tonight's party and a small stage had been constructed in the middle in the shape of the number eighty. There were gold helium-filled balloons everywhere, waiters and waitresses dressed as characters from the Golden Age of Hollywood, and a 1930s jazz band wearing gold bow ties and little gold hats.

Not for the first time that evening, Serena felt a flicker of anxiety, worried that any minute someone would come over and denounce her as a fraud. She was perfectly fine when she was talking to people; she switched on her confidence and easily fooled everybody into thinking she'd never experienced a moment of self-doubt in her life. It was in quiet moments like this that she struggled. *What am I doing here?* she thought, *I don't belong here at all.* She took a deep breath and tried to pull herself together. She had just as much right to be here as anyone else. She took a sip of champagne and forced herself to smile.

Standing next to her and feeling even more awkward than Serena was her husband Mitchell. All night she'd made a big effort to look after him and make sure that he didn't feel too out of his depth. Mitchell was an accountant for a major multinational corporation in downtown LA and had nothing to do with the movie business. In fact, he was one of the few people in the city who wasn't even interested in film. Serena had a hard time persuading him to watch her clients' movies and once he'd even fallen asleep at a premiere. In a funny way that was one of the reasons she loved him so much. The fact that he was so different to everyone else she knew only made him more attractive. But it did mean that he struggled at parties like this, which was why she always made a special effort to put him at ease.

'You OK, Mitch?'

'Yeah, I'm doing fine. Isn't that Brad Pitt over there?'

She followed his gaze. 'No darlin', that's Matt Damon.'

'Huh? Who's Matt Damon?'

She smiled at him fondly.

Casting her gaze further around the room, Serena spotted Buck Andrews, a baseball player who'd once dated Mia and had recently been cast as an action hero in his first film. He was talking to the film's director, Randy Foster, a man with such a catastrophic alcohol problem that Serena always said he couldn't direct a wank and who, at the end of a particularly heavy night on the drink, would work his way around the room telling everyone he loved them. From the look of him now, Serena estimated that the guests in this particular room had only half an hour to wait before they were treated to that pleasure.

To Randy's left was Shereen Spicer, a bleached-blonde pop-star-turned-occasional-lousy-actress, who was showing off her collection of trampy tattoos to a crowd of dumb-looking teenagers famous for playing vampires in a popular but second-rate TV show. Even from a distance of twenty paces, Serena could hear her bursting into frequent fits of annoyingly flirtatious laughter; she guessed that at some point someone who wanted to get her into bed had told her that her laugh was cute and she'd been working it ever since. If she were one of

Serena's clients, she wouldn't waste any time in putting her straight.

Just then Serena realized that she was just as good as any of the people at the party. In fact, she was better than a lot of them. And she'd probably come a lot further in life to get here too. She treated herself to another sip of her champagne and took a moment to ponder on her humble start.

Much of her childhood in Harlem had been spent watching her mother being beaten up by her drunken, abusive father. By the time she was ten Serena had started to stand up to him but it had only made things worse and he'd turned on her too. A few years and countless beatings later, her dad had landed a lengthy prison sentence when his temper got the better of him in a bar brawl and he ended up killing the local coke dealer. Although at first Serena had been hugely relieved to be rid of him, she soon discovered that he'd left them saddled with massive debts. Utterly desperate, she was forced to take her brothers out shoplifting for food, and on one particular occasion, begging for money on the subway. The shame and humiliation had marked her for life but she'd survived – and gone on to earn enough money as a model then an agent not only to get out of Harlem but to get her mother and brothers out too. And now here she was at the eightieth birthday party of a man she used to watch as a little girl in classic movies on TV.

Hmm, she thought, *not bad for a girl from the projects.*

'Man, check that out,' gasped Mitchell. He pointed over to Cooper's wife Margarita, dancing to the jazz music in a huge puffball gown, matching Cinderella slippers and a sparkling gold crown. 'Does she look amazing or terrible?' he asked. 'I can't quite work it out.'

'Neither can I, darlin',' Serena smirked. 'But if anyone asks, she looks freakin' incredible.'

They looked at each other and chuckled.

As she continued scanning the room, Serena couldn't help noticing that, as usual, she and Mitchell were the only black faces there – apart from some of the security guards and glass collectors, obviously. Although this was now a familiar situation for her to find herself in, it didn't stop her feeling uncomfortable. And although she was fiercely proud to be African American, she sometimes felt under pressure to be some kind of figurehead for diversity in Hollywood. *Wait a second*, she thought. *There's Lucy Cantrell*. Lucy Cantrell was a former TV star who'd won the Oscar for Best Actress a few years ago after appearing in a period film as a gutsy slave girl repeatedly raped by her ruthless white master on a sugar plantation. Serena always felt better when Lucy was around, although she wasn't actually black but mixed race. *Hmm, just black enough*, she thought, trying not to be cynical.

'Hey, there's Mia,' said Mitchell, pointing to the other side of the room.

'And that must be Leo,' purred Serena, spotting a handsome man standing next to her. 'Looks like it's time to really get this party started.'

They walked downstairs and began inching their way over to the other side of the room. Serena was obviously excited about meeting Leo but checked herself with a reminder not to give him too much of a grilling.

And there was one thing she couldn't work out. Should

she or should she not mention the fact that he was a paparazzo?

*

Mia watched as Leo effortlessly charmed his way around the party. He might have got off to a shaky start but less than forty-five minutes into the evening, he'd already managed to turn the tanker around. She could only come to one conclusion: if this was a test then he was passing it with flying colours.

Leo's fight-back had begun when he'd met the often cantankerous Tyler Bracket and utterly entranced her with his cover story about photographing footwear. Mia had never heard a straight man talk about shoes in such detail or with such passion. Maybe it was chasing famous actresses around all day that made him so comfortable with his feminine side. Or maybe he was right and those three sisters had made their mark on him after all. Whatever was going on, the women at the party loved him and standing there with him on her arm made Mia feel somehow stronger and more self-assured than she would have done if she'd turned up on her own. As someone who'd been single for as long as she could remember, it was a feeling she wasn't that familiar with but one she knew she'd like to get used to.

And it wasn't just the women who loved Leo. The men couldn't get enough of him either; he'd even managed to impress Cooper. It turned out that Leo was a huge fan of their host's films and wasn't afraid to tell him so. Hearing that he was Leo's all-time hero seemed to be just what Cooper needed after the recent operation to cure his rather unheroic condition of gout. 'Wherever you found this guy,' the movie legend whispered to Mia, 'I think you should hold onto him.'

She felt another buzz of delight but then wondered whether Cooper would have said the same thing if he'd known Leo was a paparazzo. She realized she'd just hit on a fundamental flaw in her plan. Leo might be winning everyone over but he was only doing so by pretending to be someone else. *Mind you*, she thought, *isn't that what I've spent my whole career doing?*

She decided that now wasn't the time to get philosophical and took a swig of her champagne, her first alcoholic drink since she'd finished filming. Tonight was about finding out if Leo could be trusted in her world, not if the people in her world would accept him. That was something she'd have to tackle at a later date – if he really did pass tonight's test.

*

By the time they were joined by Serena and Mitchell, Mia had relaxed into the evening and was starting to really enjoy herself. Now it was Leo's turn to feel tense. Charming major movie stars didn't worry him at all but Mia had talked a lot about Serena and she was one person he knew he really needed to impress. The pressure was on.

Serena burst in with her opening line. 'So who've you papped lately, Leo?'

Leo almost choked on his drink.

'Man, what's the problem?' she went on, looking at the three incredulous faces staring at her. 'We all *know* you're a pap. Lighten up, you guys. I want to hear all about it.'

Everyone breathed a sigh of relief.

Leo suddenly realized that his job as a paparazzo had been

the elephant in the room until then. But with Serena confronting it head-on, it didn't seem like such a big deal after all. And once he started riffing, amusing everyone with funny stories about some of his more colourful jobs alongside his hapless sidekick Ronnie, it turned out to be a real ice-breaker.

As she listened to him holding court, it dawned on Mia that she was witnessing Leo at his best. Being a paparazzo was part of him and a part of him that she couldn't change and shouldn't even want to. It struck her that, while he might have charmed Tyler and Cooper by pretending to be someone else, he was even better at being himself – he was even better when he was being honest. She wondered if there was a lesson in there for her.

'So have you been to this kind of party before?' Mitchell asked Leo.

'Well, I've crashed a few if that's what you mean. Paps like me don't normally make the guest list for this kind of thing.'

'Oh I wouldn't worry about it,' joked Mitchell, 'neither do accountants. Unless they're married to hotshot agents that is.'

Serena smiled and turned to Leo. 'So what do you make of it anyway? Are you having fun?'

'Yeah. I mean, you know, it's great but the truth is it's not really my scene. Don't get me wrong, I can do this kind of thing and enjoy it too. But that doesn't stop me feeling like I don't quite fit in.'

'In what way?'

'Well, I'm British, I'm not in the film business, I've no idea who most of these industry people are. . . and that's *without* everyone knowing I'm a paparazzo.'

Mia laughed. 'If I were you I wouldn't get too hung up

about it. I mean, most people here act like they love me but it's all so superficial. Most of them don't really know me – not the real me anyway. And OK, I may officially be an insider now but I still feel like an outsider. I still feel like a fat girl from Cleveland who's in awe of everyone here and this whole world. I sometimes wonder if I'll ever lose that.'

Leo took hold of her hand and gave it a squeeze.

Serena couldn't believe Mia was being so open with him; she'd never heard her speak that freely with a man before. Maybe meeting him mid-food binge had actually been a good thing: her guard had been way down from the beginning, whether she liked it or not.

'Would you listen to you two?' Serena piped up with a wry grin. 'Outsiders? You want to try being black. *Then* you'd know how it feels to be an outsider.'

'Try being black and an accountant,' said Mitchell. 'I reckon I trump the whole lot of you!'

They all laughed freely.

Mia took a look around the party and wondered whether everyone there felt the same way as they did. Were they all turning it on to impress people, putting on their public faces to fool people into believing that they fitted in and that this was where they belonged?

'You know what,' said Leo, 'if this party were in London *everyone* would be feeling self-conscious and unsure of themselves – and they'd all get totally shit-faced to get over it.'

'Well who says that's not going to happen here?' Serena smirked mischievously.

Leo beckoned over a waitress dressed as Marlene Dietrich and everyone held out their glasses for a top-up.

'Cheers!'

'Cheers!'

As Leo cracked another joke, Serena realized just how much she liked him. OK, he was great to look at but she knew there was so much other stuff that was more important to get right – and as far as she could tell, he had all that other stuff going on too. She watched as he put a protective arm around Mia. And she couldn't help smiling as she caught Mia snuggling into his grip.

The touch of Leo's hand on the small of her naked back felt almost indecently erotic to Mia. There was no question that the spark between them had been reignited and was crackling away nicely. She felt light-headed and wondered if it was more than just the champagne. *Being with Leo just feels so right*, she thought, *even if he is a paparazzo*.

Leo felt a tingle of excitement running from Mia's back and up through his arm. He wanted to pick her up and snog the face off her. But he remembered that he was at a party and clearly still on some kind of trial. *So far so good*, he thought, trying to focus on the task in hand. *It looks like Serena and Mitchell like me. All I have to do now is face Billy . . .*

*

Billy felt like he'd conquered the world.

He'd expected the party to be good but this was surpassing even his wildest expectations. Absolutely everyone who was anyone in Hollywood was there, all of them glowing with an almost visible brilliance. And, best of all, everyone wanted a piece of him.

'Hey Billy, when are we going to make a film together?' fawned Lucy Cantrell.

'Why don't you drop by sometime and we can hang out?' crooned Buck Andrews.

'Honest to God, I really, *really* love you,' slurred a very drunk Randy Foster.

Each wave of admiration boosted Billy's sense of his own brilliance – and made him feel like the most special man in the world. This was better than any drug.

'Morrison, congratulations!' he beamed.

'Tyler, you're a genius!'

'Hey Cooper, *great* party!'

It was perfectly easy; all he had to do was open his mouth, smile and say nice things. It wasn't even as if he had to mean them.

'Margarita, you look *incredible*!'

Obviously he was aware that, even though everyone was supposedly off duty, the reality was that they were all working much harder than on any film set, checking each other out and trying to impress or strike up friendships with those who could somehow advance their career or social status. But that didn't alter the fact that they all wanted to make friends with *him*. And how could that fail to make him feel good about himself?

'Hi Billy,' came a girlie voice from behind him, 'would you like to see my tattoos?'

Of course the down side of being so loved was that he was sometimes targeted by female stars who spotted a rare single man in Hollywood – and the chance of boosting their profile by creating a new power couple.

'I'd sure love to show them to you,' cooed Shereen Spicer, dropping her bra strap to reveal a tattooed tit before Billy had time to argue.

After miming appropriate expressions of appreciation he was subjected to nearly half an hour of incessant flirting peppered with bursts of the most annoying laugh he'd ever heard. *Somebody really needs to tell her about that*, he thought. He also noticed that she had some food from one of the canapés stuck between her teeth. It looked like a red pepper and he couldn't stop staring at it. He decided to keep quiet and say nothing – this probably wasn't the place for honesty.

'Erm, would you excuse me?' he said, draining his glass so he could feasibly disappear for a refill. 'I'll catch you later, yeah?'

As he weaved his way through the guests he realized how much he missed Mia. The last time they'd been here, when Cooper and Margarita had renewed their wedding vows last year, they'd spent most of the evening together, working the party as a team of two. But right now he couldn't find her anywhere. And besides, she was bound to be with that sneaky pap who frightened the life out of him. *Oh what is she doing with him?* he wondered. The whole thing just felt so wrong. Obviously he was worried about Mia getting hurt and, selfishly, he had to admit he was also worried that Leo would somehow expose or 'out' him if he ever found out about his sexuality. But also, part of him wondered whether he was a bit jealous too. He and Mia had both been single for so long, and there was no denying that he found it reassuring to have her in the same position as him. Was part of him frightened of losing her? He shook it off; jealousy was such an unattractive emotion. It certainly didn't fit with the Billy Spencer that everyone here thought they knew and loved.

'Hi Billy!'

'Hey Billy!"

'Over here, Billy!'

He bounced through the room, emanating his usual upbeat disposition – a disposition he knew could make anyone smile. But as he reached the bar he was confronted head-on with a scene that made him stop dead.

Working as a bartender and dressed as Errol Flynn was Drew Boston, an aspiring actor Billy had dated during his few months of freedom when he'd first arrived in LA. For a couple of weeks they'd had fun together, training at the gym and helping each other prepare for auditions. They'd even flown to Las Vegas for a mad weekend gambling in the casinos. Billy had actually quite liked Drew at the time and he found that when he was with him he liked himself much more too. But when Drew had started calling him his 'boyfriend' and invited him for dinner at his sister's house, he'd panicked that things were getting too serious and ended up breaking it off. However much he wanted a relationship, he just hadn't felt ready to follow it through emotionally. And now, years later, he was in even less of a position to follow it through – for a whole different set of reasons.

He watched Drew pouring out the champagne and wanted to go over and say hi. Maybe it would be good to reconnect with a fellow actor forced to stay in the closet. Having said that, it didn't look like acting was working out too well for Drew so maybe he wouldn't appreciate the reappearance of a now hugely successful figure from his past. Billy hovered for a while as he tried to work out the best thing to do. He hoped Drew wasn't feeling too down about his career and wanted to check that he was OK. But he told himself it was far too risky to reintroduce himself to an ex-boyfriend at a party full of industry people. He turned around and walked away.

At that moment, striding directly towards him, he caught sight of Scott Lamont, a flamboyant gay comedian whose set consisted almost entirely of jokes about anal sex. He sometimes played outrageous supporting roles in romantic comedies and Billy seemed to remember that he'd been in a film with Cooper once. Billy knew that Scott was one person who could see right through his act and there'd always been bad energy between them. He really couldn't cope with bumping into him now. He pretended he hadn't seen him and ducked behind a giant statue of an Oscar. Suddenly this party was turning out to be far less fun than he'd expected.

Hiding behind the Oscar and having a quiet moment to himself, it slowly dawned on Billy just how lonely he was. Sure, he could put on his usual cheery front for everyone but right now that would only make him feel worse. The truth was that he didn't really fit in here and he was only trying to kid himself if he thought he did. He realized that he wasn't actually enjoying himself at all and he just wanted to go home.

He crept out from behind the Oscar and decided to find Mia – even if she was with Leo. After a few minutes scouring the room he finally spotted the two of them standing next to the entrance. He decided to go over and face them – he couldn't avoid them all night. As he got closer he saw that they were with Serena and Mitchell and the four of them were laughing and joking about something. He sensed that they'd bonded without him and didn't want to crash their group or spoil things for them. He wished he could join in with whatever they were joking about but he knew that he wouldn't be able to relax around Leo; he just couldn't trust him. And the fact that everyone else seemed to like him only made him feel guilty, on top of all his other emotions. He felt like the bad fairy at the ball in *Sleeping Beauty* and it was a truly rotten sensation.

Thankfully he was a good actor and knew just how to hide his emotions. After all, he told himself, this was his job: acting. And playing himself was arguably his greatest achievement. Good old Billy, happy-go-lucky and always fun to have around; he played the role so well that everyone loved him. But as he stood gazing out at the party now, he couldn't help wondering if the people here would love him quite as much if he came out of the closet and his career took a nosedive. Oh it was all such superficial bullshit.

He wouldn't let anyone else know how he was feeling and told himself that he'd be perfectly polite and civil to Leo. He took a deep breath and psyched himself up as if he was preparing for a scene.

As he walked towards them he heard a voice in his head saying just one word: 'Action!'

*

Mia couldn't believe how well things had turned out. It really had been the most perfect night. Until half an hour ago the only thing she'd been worried about had been Billy but he'd just had a drink with the group, entertaining them all with stories of his hopeless attempts to learn how to sword fight

169

for his first ever film, a remake of some old swashbuckler for which he'd actually had to wear a codpiece. As usual, he had everyone in hysterical laughter. Sure, he hadn't particularly hit it off with Leo and she'd sensed more than a prickle of hostility emanating towards Billy from Leo's direction but it was a big improvement on their introduction earlier that evening. They'd obviously both decided to call some kind of truce and Mia, for one, was massively relieved.

As Cooper took to the stage to begin the speeches, Leo suggested the two of them sneak off to be on their own. She agreed and they made their excuses to Serena and Mitchell, quietly slipping away before anyone noticed.

'Follow me,' whispered Mia, 'I know just where to go.'

She led him through the house, out of the back doors and down some stone steps into the garden. Coming up towards them in the opposite direction, Leo spotted Dominique, the make-up artist from *War of Words*. She was hanging off the arm of Cooper's youngest son Hunter, an infamous waster who'd had a promising start as an actor in a string of grossout comedies before messing it all up with a serious drug addiction and a stretch in jail for driving under the influence. His behaviour had been so erratic that no studio in town would touch him, however famous his dad was. But the rumour was that he'd finally got his act together and was about to make a big comeback. Leo thought it was a real shame that somewhere along the way he'd evidently fallen under the spell of the double-crossing Dominique. As they passed each other on the stone steps, Leo ducked his head slightly so she wouldn't recognize him.

For the first time in his life, he felt slightly ashamed of his career. How could he be proud of himself for colluding with the likes of Dominique to make a living by tricking people and exploiting them for his own personal gain? He told himself that now wasn't the time to think about this, although he knew that if things worked out with Mia, he'd have to revisit the thought soon enough.

Mia led him over to a bench at the edge of the garden, overlooking the moonlit ocean. It was a beautiful spot and impossible not to get carried away by the romantic setting. The only sounds were the low hum of laughter, the chinking of glasses coming from the distant ballroom and the lapping of the waves beneath them.

'So,' Leo smiled cheekily, 'did I pass the test or what?'

Mia did her best to look confused. 'What test?'

'Oh come on, Mia, you're not telling me I wasn't being put through some kind of test tonight?'

'Well . . . I suppose . . . Well yeah, maybe . . . I just wanted to see whether you could fit into my world, that's all.'

'And what do you think? Did I pass or fail?'

'You passed. With distinction.'

'Good to hear it. So what's my prize?'

She made a big show of thinking it over. 'Erm, how about my phone number? Will that do?'

'OK, I'll settle for that. But you're not having mine yet.'

'Excuse me?'

'Well, that wouldn't be fair, would it? I mean, I might have passed your test but I haven't worked out whether you can fit into *my* world yet. I might just have to set you a test of my own.'

'But I've already been out with you!'

'Yeah but you haven't met any of my friends. And I've just had yours giving me the once-over all night.'

Mia looked out at the ocean and pretended to sulk. 'Well you don't scare me, Leo Henderson. You come up with a test and just watch me pass it.'

'OK then, I will. But in the meantime, there's just one problem.'

'Oh yeah, and what's that?'

'Well you might be giving me your phone number, but surely I've earned a kiss too?'

Mia turned back to face him and couldn't resist smiling.

He gently touched her chin and leaned in towards her.

Under the shimmering light of the moon they melted into the kind of movie star kiss Mia was used to faking in her films.

Only this time she really meant it.

8

Rosie took one look at Ronnie and rolled her eyes. 'Honey, do you seriously want to go out dressed like that?'

'Sure I do, babe. What's the problem?'

She looked him up and down disapprovingly. He was wearing what he'd been wearing all day – chinos, a polo shirt and loafers without socks, the unofficial uniform of the LA paparazzi.

'Aren't you at least going to change your shirt?'

'But we're only going to the Ranch House. I go in my work clothes all the time.'

'Yeah but you don't usually go with a movie star. And I'm not saying we should dress up smart or anything but can't you make just a little effort?'

He huffed and puffed then began riffling through the wardrobe for a clean shirt.

With Ronnie taken care of, Rosie got back to concentrating on what she was going to wear. She was seriously nervous about meeting Mia and desperate to talk through her outfit with her girlfriends but she'd been strictly banned from discussing the event with anyone, even her sister. Worse than that, she couldn't even have a drink to loosen up; she and

Ronnie were trying for a baby and, after six months of nothing happening, she'd decided to stay off the booze to see if it made a difference. She'd offered to drive tonight so that she wouldn't be tempted and Ronnie had taken her up on the offer like a shot. Part of her wished she hadn't opened her big mouth.

She slipped into her new dress, a casual number she'd bought that afternoon which she hoped would show off her curves without making her look fat. She'd tried it on in the shop and had been so pleased with the result that she'd left thinking it would completely change her life. For some reason, now that she was wearing it at home she felt decidedly underwhelmed.

'Honey,' she simpered, 'does this dress make my ass look big?'

'Rosie, why do you always ask me that? That dress is exactly the same as every other one you wear – it makes your ass look just as big as it really is.'

She slammed the wardrobe door shut. 'And what exactly did I do to deserve a smart-ass sonofabitch like you for a husband?'

'Oh give me a break, Rosie. You asked me a straight question so I gave you a straight answer.'

'And didn't it occur to you that I might not have wanted a straight answer? Hmpf! I should have known better than to ask an asshole like you in the first place.'

'Oh cut it out, babe. You look just fine, I always tell you that.'

'Fine? *Fine?* Is that the best you can do?'

'OK then, you look real nice. How's that?'

'Nice. *Nice!*' She let out a deep sigh. 'Do you think Mia Sinclair ever settles for "nice"?'

'Man, I give up.' He finished buttoning up his shirt and stomped out of the room.

Staring at Rosie from the bedside table was a glossy magazine with a picture of Mia on the front. 'The 50 Most Beautiful Women in Hollywood' ran the headline. Mia Sinclair was number one.

Rosie took another look at herself in the mirror and her heart sank.

*

Rosie? Is that her name? Or is it Rosa? Or even Rose?

Mia was in such a flap that she couldn't even think straight. Whatever Ronnie's wife was called, Mia knew that she'd have to tread carefully if the two of them were going to get on. The last thing she wanted was for her to think that she was some stuck-up movie star with a superiority complex. And there was no getting away from the fact that when she'd met Ronnie the other week, Mia hadn't been particularly friendly. He'd probably told his wife all about it and she was expecting to meet a total bitch. How on earth was Mia going to convince her otherwise?

She'd decided that the best course of action would be to dress down. First of all she tried on plain jeans with a strappy top but looked in the mirror and worried that it showed too much flesh. Ronnie's wife would have no idea of the effort it took her to keep trim and she didn't want to come across as one of those smug, skinny women who were always showing

175

off their effortlessly toned arms. She slipped on a shirt and left it open.

The only problem now was that she still had to do her hair and make-up in case she got papped. Leo had promised her that he'd taken care of that but she knew from previous experience that she couldn't take any chances. There were so many things to think about: looking good for Leo, not looking too good for Ronnie's wife, and looking just good enough in case the paps caught her. She gazed at herself in the mirror and had no idea whether she'd got it just right or horribly wrong. *Oh well, it'll have to do.*

It had been a long time since Mia had stepped out of the world of the celebrity and back into the world of the civilian. Although it had been her own world for more than two decades, a lot had changed since then. And one thing celebrities always said when they were together was that once you were famous there was no going back. She wasn't sure whether or not that was true but Mia felt uneasy about the prospect of being recognized or hassled tonight. She decided to put on a baseball cap just in case. It wasn't her usual style but she told herself that she could never be too careful.

Now if only she could remember Ronnie's wife's name.

*

Leo rang the buzzer outside Mia's front gates.

'Leo!' screeched a slightly crazed voice through the intercom. 'What's Ronnie's wife called?'

'Erm, Rosie – her name's Rosie. And hello to you too, Mia.'

'Yeah, hi, sorry. Erm, wait right there – I'll be down in a minute.'

Hmm, he thought, *she sounds a little tense.*

He scanned to his left and right and was relieved to see that there were no paps around. Of course he knew all their hiding places so it didn't take him long to quickly check them all. It looked like his plan had worked. A few hours ago he'd called every picture agency in town and given them an anonymous tip-off that Shereen Spicer and Buck Andrews were having a top-secret affair and meeting in Venice Beach that very evening to have matching tattoos of each other's names. Part of him felt guilty for being disloyal to his work colleagues but the truth was that only one of them was a real friend, and that was Ronnie. All the other paps in town were fiercely competitive and although they often chatted to each other on jobs, they'd been known to pull far worse tricks than this simply to put their rivals off the trail of a good picture.

And more than anything else, he didn't want the paps to get in the way of whatever was developing between him and Mia. He'd called her on the phone a few times since the party and they'd had some really nice chats; he could tell she was a lot more relaxed with him now. Of course, just to wind her up he always kept his own phone number hidden and joked that she hadn't earned the right to be given it yet. Until she passed tonight's test, that was.

Just then the gates swung open and out stepped Mia. He leaned over to open the door.

'Hey Leo,' she smiled, a look of abject terror on her face. She sat in the seat next to him and they gave each other a quick kiss.

'So,' he grinned. 'Are you ready to step onto my side of the velvet rope?'

'Sure I am,' she almost shrieked. 'You're forgetting that it was my side too until not so long ago.'

He couldn't help chuckling to himself. 'Hmm, so you're not too nervous then?'

'Honestly, Leo, it'll be a piece of cake. Me, you, Ronnie and Rosa – just four regular guys on a regular night out.'

'Erm, actually Mia, her name's not Rosa, it's Rosie.'

She threw her hands up in the air.

A piece of cake? She might be kidding herself but she didn't fool Leo.

*

Ronnie was sitting with Rosie at the bar of the Beaver Creek Ranch House. The venue was dotted with hay bales and cow hides, had wood-panelled walls decorated with 'Wanted' posters, lassos and horse shoes, and was run by a team of staff who were dressed as cowboys and cowgirls. As it was just around the corner from the Shooting Stars offices, Ronnie often came here with Leo to unwind with a beer at the end of a long day. It was quite definitely a male domain and he wasn't sure what Mia would make of it. She'd seemed a bit stuck-up the last time he'd met her.

He and Rosie were sitting in silence and she was still clearly in a sulk with him, tutting, sighing loudly and banging down her glass every time she took a drink. He'd obviously put his foot in it earlier and knew that he'd be getting it in the neck for the rest of the evening. He was only thankful that she wasn't drinking because then she'd give him even more of a hard time. Oh if only he could be more like Leo; *he* never seemed to have this kind of problem with women.

Sitting next to them at the bar was a plain-looking girl wearing a T-shirt saying, 'How many frogs do I have to kiss till I find my prince?' Ronnie felt a pang of empathy towards her; before meeting Rosie, he'd had to get used to being the less good-looking friend always in Leo's shadow, perennially single while Leo seemed to be constantly fending off potential girlfriends. As he thought back to his years as a bachelor, Ronnie felt sorry for the girl and wanted to tell her that wherever her prince was waiting, it wasn't in here. But he knew that if he tried to be sensitive it would all come out wrong and he'd only end up offending her. So he took a sip of his beer and kept quiet.

Just then Leo and Mia walked in and Ronnie and Rosie stood up to greet them. First of all, Ronnie said hello to Mia and she leaned forward to kiss him on the cheek.

'Nice to see you again,' she said. 'And I'm sorry I had such bad attitude the last time we met – I was totally out of line.'

'Oh don't worry about it,' he mouthed, instantly entranced. *This broad's a class act*, he thought.

Next, Ronnie shook Leo's hand as Mia and Rosie came face to face. 'You look amazing!' they both screeched at once. There was an embarrassed silence before the two of them burst out laughing.

'I'm sorry,' managed Mia, 'I've just been really nervous about meeting you.'

'*You?* Nervous about meeting *me*?'

'Yeah. Is that such a surprise? And you do look amazing by the way – I wasn't just saying that.'

'Gee, thanks Mia. According to Ronnie this dress makes my ass look big.'

'Rosie, I did not say that!'

'You did too!'

He took a step back before things blew up into a full-blown argument. That wouldn't be good right at the start of the evening. He caught a glimpse of the single girl sitting at the bar and suddenly realized how lucky he was to have Rosie – even if she did give him a hard time.

'Rosie, I'm sorry about what I said earlier,' he said, 'and I honestly think you look really beautiful.'

In an instant she softened, her face visibly draining of hostility. She smiled sweetly at him and held out her hand.

'Come on, honey,' she cooed, 'let's all go and sit down.'

*

By the time they were sitting at the table, Mia's nerves had deserted her and she'd almost forgotten that she was a star. No one had batted an eyelid at her presence or even looked in her direction. She didn't know whether to be overjoyed or a little disappointed.

Now that she was getting to know them, she genuinely liked Ronnie and Rosie. They'd kicked off the conversation by having a laugh about Ronnie's attempt at drag a few weeks ago and the efforts Rosie had gone to in order to make him look anything like a woman. Then she and Rosie had branched off to compare stories about a Hungarian beautician nick-named Dora the Decimator, who was notorious throughout LA as the best but most brutal waxer in town. When their conversation drifted onto beauty treatments in general it was blatantly obvious that the boys had zoned out.

'Right,' said Ronnie, slapping his palms on the table, 'what are we going to eat?'

As Leo perused the menu, Mia couldn't resist peeping down the top of his open-necked shirt and gazing longingly at the subtle ridge between his chest muscles. It was sexy as hell but cuddly and snuggly too. She told herself not to stare.

After taking Leo to Cooper's party last week she now felt completely relaxed in his presence, especially as nothing he'd heard at the party had wound up in the tabloids since. She'd obviously been right in deciding that she could trust him and was actually starting to feel bad for having doubted him in the first place.

Ronnie beckoned over a waitress dressed as a cowgirl, who stood at the end of the table smiling down at them for their order. Mia had been worrying all day about what kind of food they'd serve in a venue called the Beaver Creek Ranch House. What if all they had to choose from was fatty junk and she ended up having a full-on binge? What if everyone else stuffed their faces and she couldn't resist the temptation? By the time she opened the menu she was in a blind panic and really starting to burn up.

As she tried to concentrate on the meal options staring back at her, Mia could feel the anxiety sweeping over her and hoped that she wasn't flushing bright red. She began to feel overwhelmed by a temptation to order a blow-out meal but the sensation was overshadowed by a terror that everyone else at the table was watching her to see what she'd order. Pictures of greasy burgers dripping with cheese exploded in her face like camera flashes and she began struggling to stop herself from hyperventilating.

'Is it me or is it hot in here?' she managed, her voice cracking.

'Yeah, it is kinda warm,' offered Rosie, 'maybe you should take off your baseball cap?'

She pulled a face. 'I know but I'm trying to avoid attention,' she explained, beginning to fan herself with the menu.

Rosie nodded with a smile of understanding.

While Ronnie ordered the Slurp and Burp special, Mia fanned herself more and more energetically. As far as she could tell his meal choice consisted of every cut of meat imaginable and a huge portion of fries; from the picture it looked like it could feed a family of four for an entire week. Her heart was pounding in her chest and she could feel a disorientating sound like white noise filling her ears.

Leo followed but thankfully only asked for a plain turkey steak with coleslaw and a baked potato. *Hmm*, she thought, *maybe this isn't going to be such a nightmare after all.*

And then good old Rosie made a joke about the men being greedy as usual and ordered a grilled chicken salad without any dressing. Mia relaxed as she felt her anxiety start to wane.

The waitress finally turned to her and there was a moment's silence as everyone listened to hear her order.

'Erm, I'll have a lean steak please,' she stammered. 'Just with a salad – no fries.'

To Mia's immense relief, nobody even commented on her order, apart from the waitress who asked how she'd like her meat cooked. She breathed out and felt her heart rate begin to slow down.

As the waitress took their drinks order, Mia told herself that her food choice for tonight probably represented the best dietary approach for her to follow in general – a happy middle ground between her usual twin extremes of rabid asceticism and rampant indulgence. It was quite obvious really. So why did she find it so hard to get it right?

'Man, I'm *starving*!' drooled Ronnie.

'Me too,' chirped Mia. 'I'm really looking forward to my steak.'

The Western-themed food prompted Leo and Ronnie to tell the girls about the time they'd hidden out on a cattle ranch in Texas for a whole week to try and nail the first shot of the almost decrepit Western actor Bolt Stephens and his teenage fiancée, an oil company heiress who'd appeared in a sex video and become an internet sensation, during their brief and now almost forgotten fling. Ronnie joked about how he'd been left without a single picture after they'd been caught up in a stampede of cattle, he'd dropped his camera onto the ground and it had been trampled to pieces. The next day Bolt and his fiancée had posed in the grounds of their ranch for an 'at home' special in a glossy magazine, ensuring that even if Leo and Ronnie had managed to get any pictures, they'd have been worthless anyway.

By the time Mia was on her third beer she couldn't think of a time when she'd laughed as much and had almost forgotten that she was a star. She realized how stupid she'd been to feel miffed that nobody had recognized her earlier, however momentary the feeling. It was nothing short of incredible to experience a night off being famous. And she knew one thing for sure – she was going to make the most of it.

*

Leo was thrilled the evening was going so well. He'd never seen Mia as relaxed as this and her laughter was so beautiful that it reminded him of sunshine. His only worry was that the venue was starting to fill up quickly. A crowd of rowdy jocks had just come in and were knocking back shots and playing a raucous game of pool. And a gaggle of out-of-town old boilers on a third-time-lucky hen night were cackling loudly as they eyed up the bucking bronco. He hoped that nobody recognized Mia or gave her any hassle.

When they'd finished the meal and their plates had been cleared away, Leo listened as Rosie steered the conversation onto a topic she'd clearly wanted to bring up all evening. 'So Mia,' she began with a twinkle in her eye, 'Ronnie tells me you're making a movie with Billy Spencer . . .'

Leo felt his heart sink.

'Yeah, it's all done now,' breezed Mia. 'In fact, it's opening quite soon.'

Rosie's whole face lit up with glee. 'Man, I know this is really uncool and everything but I'm such a big fan – I've seen all his movies.'

'Well I hope you like this one – he's very good in it.'

'So what's he like? In real life I mean.'

'Oh he's adorable, a total sweetheart.'

'Seriously?'

'Yeah, I've known him for years – we're really close.'

Good old Billy, thought Leo. *Who everyone seems to love – except me*.

'Man, that's so cool!' Rosie gushed on. 'You know, I saw him on *Oprah* once and I thought he looked like a nice guy.

I said to you, didn't I, Ronnie, "That Billy Spencer looks like a real nice guy"?'

'You did, babe, you did,' croaked Ronnie. 'Listen, no offence or anything but do we have to talk about Billy Spencer?'

Hear bloody hear, thought Leo.

'Oh shut up, Ronnie,' smirked Rosie. 'You're just jealous, that's all. And with good reason. I bet Billy Spencer knows how to treat a woman. I bet Billy Spencer wouldn't tell a woman her ass looked big.'

Ronnie rolled his eyes and took a swig of his beer. Leo knew just how he felt.

'So does he actually have a girlfriend?' Rosie went on, by now blatantly trying to goad Ronnie.

There was a knowing look from Mia. *There it is again*, thought Leo. *What's all that about?*

'No, no,' she smiled. 'I guess you could say Billy's happy being single. He does get a lot of attention from girls though.'

'You don't say. Man, what I'd give for a night with Billy Spencer. I bet he's dynamite in the sack . . .'

'Enough already,' moaned Ronnie, the tips of his sticky-out ears starting to burn bright red. Leo couldn't have agreed more. 'Can we change the subject please?'

Unfortunately Rosie paid him no attention. 'So do you have a love scene with him?' she pressed Mia. 'In the new movie I mean.'

'Yeah, we do actually. It's kind of raunchy for a period film.'

'Man, that's so cool! He has such a hot body – I bet he works out all the time.'

'Well he has to really,' smiled Mia. 'It's kind of his job.'

'Yeah but even so – that six pack is something else. You

know, the last time my Ronnie went to a gym was the week
before our wedding. He says he used to have a six pack but
I don't know what's happened to it now – it's all gone into
one barrel.'

'OK, I'm done with this conversation,' said a rather belea-
guered Ronnie. 'Who fancies a game of pool?'

'Me!' shouted Leo, practically jumping out of his seat.

Mia and Rosie looked unsure.

'Oh come on,' pleaded Leo. 'It'll be a laugh.'

'How about boys versus girls?' suggested Ronnie. He knew
just how to entice Rosie.

'Hmm,' she mused, an eyebrow raised. 'Sounds like a challenge.'

'Well I'm in if you are,' said Mia.

Rosie stood up and clapped her hands. 'Let's do it. And
we're going to whip your ass.'

*

Rosie took aim at the white, bounced it off the side of the
table and onto the blue striped ball, which dropped straight
into the pocket in front of her.

'Nice shot,' chirped Mia.

'Thanks babe.' She raised her hand in the air and they did
a high five.

The girls were beating the boys hands-down and loving
every minute of it. Rosie took another shot, positioning the
pink striped ball directly in front of a pocket for Mia's next
turn.

As Leo took to the table and she watched him take aim,
Rosie realized she was actually still hungry. She'd known when

she'd placed her order that a measly chicken salad wouldn't fill her up but she'd heard the story of how Leo had met Mia and hadn't wanted to do anything to make her feel uncomfortable. Rosie's work colleague Patty had a serious binge-eating problem and she'd often find her standing in a pile of crumbs, troughing her way through huge bags of Cheetos in the privacy of the staff room, only to burst into tears when she was discovered. It sounded like Mia suffered from something similar and Rosie hadn't wanted to do anything to upset her on their first night out. Unfortunately it was Rosie who was suffering for it now.

Thankfully, once they'd finished eating Mia seemed perfectly relaxed – and she'd surprised them all by being a really mean pool player. She'd explained that her dad used to take her to the local pool club when she was little and that was where she'd learned to play, although she'd protested about being rusty and not having played for years. It didn't seem to affect her performance though and Rosie watched as she potted the ball she'd lined up for her and then another for good measure.

Rosie couldn't help noticing that Mia didn't seem remotely bothered now about being recognized, even though the bar was by now completely packed. One of the jocks at the pool table next to them kept looking over as if she'd caught his eye but he couldn't work out how he knew her. Once the game was over, Rosie was going to suggest moving across the bar to the bucking bronco to get out of his way.

Unfortunately she wouldn't be able to have a go herself – not only were she and Ronnie trying for a baby but there was a small chance she might even be pregnant. Her period was due tomorrow so she couldn't do a test yet but she did feel different this time. Her boobs had gone harder and this morning she was convinced she'd felt the first stirrings of morning sickness. And after six months of trying to get pregnant she wasn't going to risk anything by jumping onto the back of a bucking bronco.

Ronnie would have a go though – and probably fall off after just a few minutes, as usual. Then Leo would get up and be brilliant as ever. It was a shame she couldn't jump on herself but she and Mia could stand at the side and cheer on their men. She might have shown that she was good at pool but Mia obviously wasn't the bucking bronco type. So Rosie would be ladylike for once, just like Mia.

*

'Yee-haa!' Mia was straddling the bucking bronco and gripping it as tightly as she could between her thighs. It was much harder than it looked but she was actually doing well and getting into quite a rhythm.

'Giddy up, cowgirl!' shouted an over-excited Rosie.

She spotted a group of drunken middle-aged women on some sort of bachelorette party, hollering and cheering in encouragement. 'Whooo!'

For a few seconds the bronco slowed slightly and Mia felt confident enough to lift one arm in the air and wave it above her head. This was really good fun and she'd surprised herself by how much she was enjoying it. Being off-duty and off-camera was liberating. This must be what life was like for regular girls all over America.

'Yee-haa!' she howled again.

Just when she thought it was getting easy, the bronco gave a tight jerk to the right and she had to tense all the muscles in her legs to hold on. Finally Cole's workouts were coming in useful.

The bronco then swerved to the left and she dangled off for a few seconds, her head almost touching the floor before she managed to pull herself back just in time. Unfortunately she'd lost her baseball cap in the process. But she didn't worry about it – right now she was totally focused on hanging onto the bronco. And loving every minute of it.

Out of the corner of her eye she spotted a group of drunken jocks gathering around and jeering from the sidelines. Before she had a chance to react, the bronco jerked upwards and she gripped the rope as tightly as she could to cling on.

'Keep going Mia!" shouted Ronnie. 'You're doing awesome!'

As the bronco tipped forwards a camera started flashing in her face and she couldn't see properly. She shielded her eyes with her hand just as the bronco gave a double jolt to the right. With only one hand holding the rope she didn't stand a chance and came tumbling to the floor, her hair everywhere and her face flushed. There was a huge round of applause from the bachelorette party but the camera carried on flashing and seemed to be getting closer.

'Give me that camera!' she heard Leo shout.

'Fuck you, asshole!'

She struggled to her feet and brushed her hair out of her eyes. She could see Leo standing in front of one of the jocks and holding out his hand for what she now realized was a camera phone. The rest of the bar had come to watch what all the fuss was about and were standing around staring.

'Leo, just leave it,' she begged, dusting herself down.

'Don't worry, Mia. All I want is those photos back.'

'And you ain't getting them,' taunted the jock. His friends gathered round him to back him up.

'Look,' Leo said, calmly but with authority, 'I'll give you one more chance. You give me that phone or—'

'Or what?' mocked the jock. 'What are you going to do about it?'

'You'll see.'

'Oooh, I'll see, will I? Well—'

Before he could finish his sentence, Leo punched him square in the face. The jock slumped to the floor, dropping his phone, which Leo deftly moved forward to catch. As the jock's friends fussed around him, Leo quickly went into the phone's menu and deleted all the photos.

'OK,' yelled a loud voice pushing its way through the crowd. As its owner emerged from the ranks of the bachelorette party, Mia saw that he was wearing a sheriff's outfit; he must have been the venue manager. 'Come on, I want you guys outside now!'

'What, us?' bleated Ronnie.

'No – them.' He pointed at the group of jocks. 'You guys are always causing trouble. I've told you before – any more and you're barred.'

The jocks helped up their friend and Leo handed him back his phone.

'Come on,' snapped the manager. 'Outside now.'

'This place is a total rat-hole anyway,' shouted a particularly ugly one as they slouched their way to the door.

'Yeah,' shouted another, 'and don't be surprised if we sue your ass!'

'Hmpf!' snorted the manager. 'Sue? After all the months of shit you've given me?'

'Just you try suing,' chipped in the leader of the bachelorette party from behind her veil. 'We witnessed everything tonight, didn't we, girls?'

'Yeah!' they chorused drunkenly.

'Look, just get out!' barked the manager, moving over to open the door for them. 'And don't ever come here again!'

As she heard the door slam behind them, Mia felt a strong hand touch her arm.

'You OK, princess?' asked Leo softly.

'Yeah, I'm fine,' she gulped. She looked into his eyes and was lost for words. He'd been absolutely brilliant and she didn't know how to thank him. Nobody had ever done anything like that for her before – nobody. And it was all so romantic; it even reminded her of a fight scene she'd filmed for her movie *The Princess and the Pauper*. She could feel herself welling up with emotion and her chin started to quiver. She looked him in the eye and knew that from now on there could never be any question, Leo was the man for her and she couldn't just trust him; she could trust him with her life.

Just then the emotion became too much for her and she started to cry.

'Come on, princess,' he soothed, stroking her chin. 'Let's get you home.'

*

Leo pulled up outside Mia's front door and brought the car to a standstill. It had been a long night.

Once the dust had settled after the fight, Mia had chatted with the bachelorette party and signed autographs for them and then they'd spoken to the manager and thanked him profusely for sticking up for them. Before jumping in the car home they'd said their goodbyes to Ronnie and Rosie on something of an emotional high and promised they'd all go out together again soon.

The drive to Mia's house had taken them half an hour and now that they were there Leo was starting to feel totally shattered. His hand ached too although he didn't like to say so as he didn't want Mia to feel bad. It had all been worth it anyway. And although it had been an eventful night there was one thing that stood out for Leo above all others; after looking for someone to love for so long, he now knew he'd finally found her. Even if she wasn't remotely the kind of girl he'd imagined himself falling for.

'So,' he smiled, switching off the engine. 'Is this when I give you my phone number?'

'Oh yeah,' she grinned. 'I'd forgotten about that.'

There was a nervous tension in the air as they looked at each other. More than anything else, Leo wanted to lean forward and kiss her.

'But did I pass your test tonight?' she butted in, before he had the chance. 'Or did I blow it when I accidentally caused a fight?'

'Not at all,' frowned Leo. 'You were amazing all night.'

There was another pause and the space between them almost buzzed with an energy so powerful it took Leo aback.

He might have spent his entire career chasing excitement but this was like nothing he'd ever experienced.

'Well in that case,' Mia went on, 'let's not end the night just yet.'

'OK,' he nodded. 'What are you suggesting?'

She gave him a penetrating gaze. Without saying anything she slipped out of the car and reached into her bag for her keys.

He watched as she stepped into the porch, under the roof that had sheltered her from his camera lens. As she opened the front door and turned to face him, he knew that he'd changed so much recently he almost didn't recognize the Leo who'd straddled the branch of a tree to try and pap her just a few weeks ago.

And something told him he'd never be the same again.

9

'Let's see sassy.'

'And sultry.'

'And smouldering.'

'That's *sensational*.'

Billy and Mia were being photographed for the cover of a prestigious monthly magazine to promote the release of *War of Words*. The photographer was Astrid Jensen, a Danish rock chick with Tina Turner hair and terribly obvious capped teeth. But she had a fantastic reputation and Billy had wanted to work with her for a while now. So far he hadn't been disappointed.

'If you just move to your left, Billy, and turn around slightly so that you're facing Mia.'

Billy happily followed her instructions.

'That's it. Sensational.'

The shoot was taking place in a huge house in the Doheny Hills that belonged to a bestselling writer of bonkbusting novels, all of which claimed to thrillingly reveal the real truth about life in LA. The photographs were being taken in an enormous library at the back of the house, which was crammed from floor to ceiling with thousands and thousands of books.

Billy and Mia were reclining on an old desk in front of a particularly stuffed row of bookcases, bursting with hardbacks, paperbacks and thick manuals that looked like dictionaries and encyclopedias. Initially Billy had thought the concept for the shoot a bit too obvious for a movie about the love affair between a poet and a novelist. But he'd checked a few of Astrid's shots on her laptop and he had to admit, they really did look sensational.

As he listened to her directions and struck poses on demand, he continued questioning Mia about her latest date. Leo was coming to visit the shoot in the next hour and before he arrived Billy wanted to hear all the news. 'So what happened after he slugged the jock?' he asked.

'Oh it was so romantic, Billy. He came over to see if I was OK and all he did was touch me but I've honestly never experienced anything like it. And that's when it happened – *I just knew.*'

'Well I've got to say, it does sound like a fairytale – your fans would knock themselves out if they knew.'

'And Mia, if you could just turn now to look at the camera,' piped Astrid. 'You too, Billy.'

'Oh I know it sounds corny,' Mia went on.

'Did I say that?' mouthed Billy.

'No but I bet you're thinking it. But, you know, in a weird way now that it's happening to me it doesn't seem corny at all.'

'Well I think it's brilliant, sugar. I really do.' Billy hoped that she didn't notice he was gritting his teeth.

'Can I have a more relaxed smile please, Billy?' drawled Astrid. 'A little more natural this time. That's it!'

Billy did his best to look more at ease and breezed on. 'So I'm assuming you spent the rest of the evening making out . . .'

Mia fluttered her eyelids coyly. 'I guess you could say that.'

'And by "making out" do I understand that Leo stayed the night?'

'He might have done . . .'

'Mia Sinclair, you low-down dirty ho!'

Billy began tickling her in a spot that he knew always made her laugh and she squealed out loud.

'Ooh, hold that pose!' blurted Astrid. 'That's *sensational*!'

Mia struggled to catch her breath through her giggles. 'Oh I know we've only been on a few dates,' she managed, 'but it just felt right. You know, after everything that happened with the fight and all. I mean, I can hardly go on worrying about trusting him now.'

Billy nodded his head. He knew that since Leo had proved he was trustworthy, if he continued to advise Mia to dump him, it would only sound like he was jealous. And he *was* jealous, however much he hated himself for it. He reminded himself that Mia had been unlucky in love for so long and more than anyone he knew she deserved to be happy. He should stop thinking about himself and concentrate on what was best for her. But why was it so difficult?

'Well in that case I'm sure you did the right thing spending the night with him,' he chirped. 'And I can honestly say I'm really happy for you.'

Mia saw right through him in an instant. 'Oh Billy, I know you don't really mean that.'

196

He opened his mouth to feign protest but knew there was no point.

'But if you're worried about where all this leaves me and you,' she went on, 'then I promise that whatever I feel for Leo, it doesn't mean I love you any less.'

Billy felt himself blushing.

'Can we turn up the air conditioning?' shouted Astrid to no one in particular. 'It looks like it's getting hot in here.'

Everyone turned to look at Billy and he could feel himself blushing even more.

'Oh I'm sorry, Billy,' whispered Mia. 'I didn't mean to embarrass you.'

'It's OK,' he stammered, wiping his brow. 'And thanks, sugar.'

'Thanks for what?'

'Oh just for understanding me, that's all. And for loving me all the same.'

'To hell with the air conditioning,' interrupted a voice from the back of the room. 'I've got a better idea.' Stepping forward from the crowd of stylists, designers, electricians, magazine journalists and assistants was the unmistakable figure of Violet Vaughn. One of the most powerful women in Hollywood, Violet not only looked after Billy and Mia's personal publicity but she'd also been hired to manage press for the film. A complete ball-breaker, Violet always reminded Billy of Cruella de Vil and she even had the same hairstyle as his childhood bogey woman – jet-black with a streak of bright white at the front. Violet had been a major player in Hollywood for as many years as anyone could remember and from the look of her cold, expressionless face, she'd had almost as many facelifts.

Whenever she looked at Billy, he had to make a real effort not to tremble.

'OK,' he mumbled. 'What's your idea?'

'Well why don't you take your shirt off?'

There was silence while everyone stared at Billy, waiting for him to respond. For years, Billy had been known for taking his clothes off at every available opportunity, in practically every photo shoot and film that he did. At first he'd enjoyed it, telling himself he had to spend so long working out in the gym that he might as well show off the results. But recently he'd realized his looks were getting in the way of being taken seriously as an actor and with this new movie he was really hoping things would finally change. He'd already had to get his body out when shooting the movie but now that filming was over he didn't really want to draw any more attention to it.

'What's the problem?' Violet brayed, picking up on his hesitation. 'It'd be great for the Box Office.'

'But I . . . I . . .'

'But nothing,' she bellowed, approaching her clients so that nobody else could hear. 'Fuck that, Billy. Remember the reaction to those pap shots of you and Mia on set, looking like you were about to make out? And how about the pictures of you two arriving at Cooper Kelly's party, smiling at the cameras like the happy couple? Don't forget that those photos ended up in every magazine in the world. Which proves that there are millions of people out there who want you two to get it on. All I'm saying is, let's tease them a little – have a little fun.'

Billy gulped. 'OK,' he mouthed. 'I understand.'

'So what do you say?' she asked, stepping back so that everyone could hear her. 'Shall we have some fun or what?'

He began to unbutton his shirt. 'I'll do it, yeah. But only if it's cool with Mia.'

*

Mia could feel Violet's eyes boring into her. She felt like a chicken being eyed up by a crocodile.

She was terrified of Violet. So terrified, in fact, that she'd never had the guts to stand up to her. And that wasn't about to change now.

'So?' Violet thundered. 'What do you say, Mia?'

The last thing Mia wanted was to end up in the middle of a raunchy photo shoot with Billy when Leo was due to arrive within the hour. But Violet could be very persuasive and there was no sense in arguing with her – she was in league with most of the major producers in Hollywood and had bigger balls than all of them put together. Everyone in town listened to her opinion. Violet Vaughn could make or break a career with just one phone call and stories abounded of how she'd done just that on many occasions.

'Erm, OK, yeah, great,' Mia stumbled. 'I'm cool with that.'

Billy finished unbuttoning his shirt and took it off to reveal an almost unfeasibly toned body. Mia knew how he felt about showing it off these days and shot him a sympathetic look. She wondered which of them felt more awkward.

'Come on,' she hissed under her breath. 'Let's get this over with.'

They moved from one pose to another with one common theme running through them – sex. The looks they were directed to give each other left little to the imagination and Mia was instructed to wrap herself around Billy's chest in more ways than she'd ever thought possible. She began to wonder what the point was of being in a library at all.

'Sensational!' cried Astrid, clearly much happier than she and Billy were.

'Hmmm,' nodded Violet. 'Looks like I was right again.'

As they ran out of poses to strike on the desk, Mia and Billy retired to their shared dressing room to choose new outfits while the crew changed the rig for the next set-up.

'What's going on, Billy?' Mia sighed as soon as she was through the door. 'How did we get ourselves into this position?'

'We didn't get ourselves into it, Mia – Violet did. Look, if you're really unhappy I can just tell her we're not doing any more sexy stuff.'

'Are you serious? And risk pissing her off? No way, Billy. We've worked too hard for our careers – both of us. And what if she's speaking for the producers?'

Billy bit his lip. 'OK, well we'll just have to ride it out then.'

Mia shrugged her shoulders. She might be able to justify what was going on to herself but she had no idea what she'd say to Leo when he arrived. It was one thing acting out a love scene when she was in character and following a script but this was completely different. Or was it?

She told herself that there was nothing she could do about it now and turned to the rack of clothes to decide what to wear. She looked through and saw that some of the outfits were very revealing, as if the shoot had always been intended to be raunchy. She couldn't help wondering if this had been Violet's plan all along.

As she perused rack after rack of skimpy underwear and little bra tops, she suddenly remembered that she hadn't been to the gym in days and had given up on her strict diet once filming had finished. *Oh it doesn't matter*, she reassured herself. *It's only a stills shoot so they can fix anything with the airbrush*. Unfortunately the airbrush wouldn't fix things with Leo.

She was just about to call for a stylist when there was a knock at the door.

'Coo-ee,' trilled Violet as she stepped inside the dressing room. 'It's only me.'

'Hi Violet,' the two of them said, standing to attention. They were half-naked but it didn't seem to matter.

'Listen, you guys,' she began. 'I've just this minute had another idea. And trust me, it's a damned good one.'

'OK,' said Billy, clearly apprehensive. 'Shoot.'

'I don't know how you'll feel about this but . . .'

'Go on, Violet.'

'Well, I was just chatting to the editor of the magazine and she was saying how the whole world's talking about whether or not you two are a couple.'

'And?'

'Well it suddenly hit me . . .'

'What did?'

'Why don't we pretend that you are?'

There was a long silence.

'Erm, what do you mean exactly?'

Violet's coyness gave way to a new energy. 'Well, why don't

we set up a good old-fashioned Hollywood show-mance? All you have to do is go on a few dates and I tip off the paps so that everyone gets to find out about it.'

'But isn't that, like, lying?' frowned Mia.

'Oh don't worry about that,' she breezed. 'Scams like this are as old as Hollywood. This town was built on fairytales like these!'

'But that doesn't make it right,' ventured Billy. 'And I'd feel really uncomfortable lying.'

Violet tightened her mouth into a curt smile. 'You do surprise me, Billy. I thought you were perfectly happy lying about your personal life.'

'That's not fair!' burst out Mia.

'"Fair"? Who ever said anything about "fair"? There's nothing fair about this business, Mia – surely you know that by now. And anyway, everyone in Hollywood lies about who they really are. Don't tell me there's nothing you haven't covered up from the public before.'

'Well . . .'

'Exactly. Fantasy is the name of the game. Sure, you act on camera, but you act off camera too. The public practically expects it of you.'

'Hmm,' said Billy, 'I'm not so sure.'

'Well I am. Sure as hell. And just think,' she went on with a twinkle in her eye, 'you'd be giving the public what they want . . .'

'Really?'

'Hell yeah. Everyone loves a good romance – especially *your* fans, Mia. Think of the Box Office.'

Mia and Billy looked at each other nervously. Mia couldn't

stop her eyes focusing in on Violet's thin lips painted a deep, blood red. She thought about Leo and something told her that she was being drawn into something that would end up being a big mistake.

'Actually, Violet,' she said, 'I'm not really cool with this. I'm sorry but I don't want to do it – it just doesn't feel right.'

Violet mimed brushing away her objections with her hand. 'Look, what's the fucking problem? It's not as if either of you has a boyfriend.'

'Well, erm, yeah,' muttered Mia, 'but what happens if, you know, we do meet someone?'

'Jesus, will you stop freakin' out about this? You're building it up into something much bigger than it is. You only have to play along with it till the film opens. And then maybe a month later, just to make it seem real. Oh, actually, make that two or three and then we can hit the DVD release.'

There was a long pause and Mia began chewing her lip. 'Oh I don't know . . .'

Billy stared at the floor blankly.

'Hmpf!' huffed Violet. 'I just don't understand what you guys are worried about. Billy, a good show-mance will be good for you. People buy the whole single-man-concentrating-on-his-career thing at the moment but pretty soon they're going to start asking questions. And Mia, it's about time you had a romance to flaunt to the press, otherwise people are going to start thinking you have serious issues and can't hold down a man.'

Mia felt like she'd been slapped across the face. This was exactly the kind of thing she'd started to worry people might think about her – before she'd met Leo. She could feel a heavy lump in her throat. The last thing she wanted to do now was cause problems with him.

'"I want to be on a team of two," that's what you told me,' Violet carried on. 'Well that's exactly what I'm proposing. In fact, it's practically your ideal relationship – just without the sex. So what do you say?'

Billy shuffled on the spot and was clearly trying to stop his whole body from squirming. He looked at Mia and scrunched up his face.

Mia wasn't sure what to say. She desperately wanted to ask Serena for advice but knew that Violet wasn't going to wait for an answer.

'Erm, yeah, erm, OK,' said Mia. 'I guess I'll do it. But only if Billy's cool with it.'

'Billy?' barked Violet.

He took a deep breath and let out a loud sigh. 'Yeah, count me in. I guess you're right, Violet – I always have been good at lying. And now that I've started, I might as well go the whole hog.'

*

What am I getting myself into? thought Billy.

He and Mia were writhing around in designer underwear on a bed covered in pages torn out of books. As he followed Astrid's directions and pinned Mia down as if they were about to have sex, he couldn't help thinking that he was in the middle of making a huge mistake. He remembered what his parents had always taught him about lying; that once you told a lie, you had to tell another to cover it up. And then another, then another – until your whole life was built around lies.

That's what my life is now, thought Billy, *one big bunch of lies.*

'Now if you could just move into each other a touch more,' bellowed Astrid. Billy could see that Violet was whispering in her ear. 'You know, so you're a little closer together.'

'My crotch is in between her legs,' croaked Billy. 'How much closer do you want us to be?'

'I want to see it in your faces,' barked Violet, butting in. 'Billy, look like you're about to fuck the shit out of her.'

Billy tried not to flinch. However far he'd come in the world and however much he'd grown as a person, at times like this he still felt like a well-mannered Southern boy who'd been brought up to treat women with respect. And in situations like this he felt really uncomfortable.

'I'm sorry, Mia,' he whispered in her ear.

'Me too,' she gulped.

The camera snapped away and the two of them did as they were told. Billy couldn't help thinking about a famous quote he'd read once that said something like 'every time a person has their photo taken they lose a little of their soul'. He wondered if that was happening right now.

It certainly didn't look like Mia was happy. He could feel her whole body tense beneath him. 'Oh Billy,' she bleated, 'what am I going to do when Leo arrives?'

'Shit,' he said, 'I hadn't thought about that.'

'Yeah well neither had I until Violet took control of things. If I'd known the shoot was going to be so raunchy I wouldn't have invited him along.'

'Well can you put him off at all?'

'I doubt it – he's due any second. And what's he going to say when he sees us like this?'

205

'Well if it's any help I promise I'll be on my best behaviour. I know I've been down on him till now but if you're sure you can trust him then I'll make a real effort to smooth things over between us. Who knows? We might even wind up being buddies.'

Mia laughed feebly. 'Thanks, Billy. But something tells me that right now that's not going to work.'

*

'All right mate?' grinned Leo. 'I'm here to see Mia – Mia Sinclair.'

The security guard glowered at him. Leo saw he had a face like a pork pie and when he blinked, only one eye closed. 'And you are?'

'Leo Henderson. Just a friend.' Leo wasn't sure how he was supposed to introduce himself, but one thing he was sure about was that he and Mia weren't just friends. Not anymore anyway.

'OK. Wait right here.'

The security guard gave him another one-eyed blink then lifted his walkie talkie to summon a runner. Within seconds a young man with curly blond hair and a thick ginger beard came bounding down the driveway towards him.

'Leo Henderson?' he beamed. 'We've been expecting you.'

Leo was surprised to hear that he had a Scottish accent and as he escorted him through the house he explained that he'd come to LA to pursue his dream of being a TV producer. His story abruptly stopped once they came to a closed door.

'Just give us a wee minute?' smiled the runner. 'It's a closed set so I'll nip in and see if she's ready for you.'

A closed set? thought Leo. *What does that mean?* He told himself that they were probably up against it and didn't want any distractions.

He paced around the hall and hoped he'd be let in soon. He was looking forward to seeing what kit the photographer was using and how a shoot like this worked. If things carried on as they were going with Mia, he was starting to realize that he wouldn't only have to confront some harsh truths about his job, but he might even have to consider a full career change. But that prospect seemed much less daunting than it would have done at one time. For a start, he didn't get the same adrenaline rush that he used to get from nailing a tough shot. And since meeting Mia, he wasn't even sure that he craved it anymore. Maybe she'd helped him break his addiction. And maybe photo shoots like this one wouldn't be a bad option for a second career.

Before that though there were much more important things to think about. Well, one anyway – what to do about Billy Spencer. At Cooper Kelly's party Leo had managed to get through a group conversation with Billy but he knew that wasn't enough. If things were ever going to progress to the next level with him and Mia then he'd have to get on with Billy and not just put up with him. Thankfully, he was feeling much more relaxed about the situation after their last date. Whatever had gone on with Mia and Billy, after spending the night with her, Leo was convinced it was now firmly in the past. So today he'd saunter onto the set smiling and do everything he could to get on with Billy. *Who knows?* he thought. *We might even end up being mates.*

Just then the doors opened and Mia stepped out in a white dressing gown.

'Leo!' she smiled, flinging her arms around him. 'It's so good to see you.'

'You too, princess.'

She seemed a bit nervous and he noticed that she felt tense in his arms.

'Come with me,' she sing-songed. 'Let's go and hang out in my dressing room.'

She took him by the hand and led him away.

'Just a minute,' he said. 'Don't I get to see the set first?'

'Erm, we've just finished a set-up so they're de-rigging.'

'Oh OK. But I thought I might chat to the photographer . . .'

'I wouldn't bother if I were you – terrible capped teeth.'

'But I thought you said she was brilliant?'

'She is.' She burst through the door of the dressing room and threw off her robe. He saw that underneath she was wearing nothing but her underwear. 'Now shut up and kiss me.'

She lunged at him and kissed him fully on the lips. Although he was taken by surprise, Leo soon found his groove and began kissing her deeply in return. After a few minutes, he scooped her up in his arms and carried her over to a nearby sofa. He worried that his instant hard-on would look ridiculous poking through his trousers. But there was nothing he could do about it; he didn't think he'd ever met a woman who turned him on so much.

'And what have I done to deserve this?' he joked mid-kiss.

'Oh you know, just being you.'

He chuckled. 'Well if this is what happens every time you do a photo shoot, I'll have to visit you more often.'

She jumped up to straddle him. 'Oh I wish I didn't have to do the boring shoot. I just want to stay here making out with you.'

Leo struggled to readjust his trousers. 'Well, you know,' he managed between kisses, 'that's fine with me. I mean, it's *more* than fine.'

As she began to unbutton his shirt, his whole body buzzed with the same excitement he used to feel when he was on a job and melting a great shot. Except that this felt so much better. And he was already starting to think that if he had to make a straight choice between the two, there'd be no contest.

'You're very frisky today, princess,' he breathed into her ear.

She stopped kissing and rested her forehead against his. 'It's your fault, Leo. What have you done to me?'

She nibbled his cheek and he let out a little moan.

'Mmmm.'

'Ten minutes!' a Scottish voice shouted from outside in the corridor.

'Spoilsport!' Mia called back in a sulk.

'Make-up's on its way!' barked the reply, its businesslike tone at odds with the sexually charged atmosphere in the room.

Leo cleared his throat and disentangled himself.

'Come on,' he croaked, backing away reluctantly, 'I don't want to get you into trouble.'

Mia let out a little giggle and he realized that she'd spotted his hard-on straining at his trousers.

'Sorry,' he mumbled, plunging a hand into his underwear to reposition himself. 'I guess I got a bit carried away.'

'Oh don't apologize,' she grinned. 'Just save it for later.'

She moved in to give him one last kiss.

'This is like torture.' Leo struggled. 'I think you're going to have to get dressed.'

Mia made her way over to the clothes rack with a pout. Leo took in a deep breath. *Come on, mate, calm yourself down!*

She began thumbing through the options and he moved to stand next to her. For some reason, all he could see was row after row of underwear and tiny outfits that left little to the imagination. *That's funny*, he mused, *I thought this film was set during the Second World War.*

'So what exactly are you wearing on this shoot?' he asked.

She concentrated on the clothes rack and avoided his gaze. 'Erm, not much really. It's kind of a love scene.'

'What? You mean you're in character?' He looked at her uneasily. His hard-on was finally starting to fade.

'Not exactly. Oh forget about the shoot, Leo. We've still got five minutes – come here.'

Once again she launched herself at him, smothering him in passionate kisses. But this time Leo wasn't feeling it and didn't respond. He could tell that something wasn't quite right and wanted to get to the bottom of it.

'I need to change my briefs,' a male voice called out from the other side of the door. Just then, an almost naked Billy walked into the room, his back to them as he continued talking to somebody in the distance. 'These ones are really tight around the balls.'

Billy turned round just as Leo prised himself away from Mia. The two of them came face to face.

Leo took one glance at Billy in his underwear and then looked Mia up and down.

'Just a minute,' he said. 'What *exactly's* going on here?'

*

'Oh hi, Leo,' Billy managed, desperately trying to pretend that nothing was wrong. 'How's it hanging?'

'From this angle I'd say to the left,' Leo quipped, looking at Billy's tight underwear. He obviously wasn't too pleased.

Oh no, thought Billy. *How am I going to act my way out of this one?*

'Yeah, sorry,' he smiled weakly. 'They are a little tight. I think that might be the point.'

'The point of what?' Leo spluttered. 'Will somebody tell me what's going on?'

'Oh it's nothing, Leo,' Mia soothed. 'They've just decided to sex up the shoot, that's all. Apparently it'll be good for the movie.'

'Really? But I thought you were hoping this film would get you taken seriously.'

'She was,' breathed Billy. 'And so was I.'

'Well I've got news for you, mate – you're not going to be taken seriously in your underwear. Especially not in bright red undies like that.'

Billy tried laughing to break the atmosphere. 'Yeah,' he struggled. 'They are pretty awful.'

Leo looked at him stony-faced.

What a disaster, thought Billy. *And I was ready to make such an effort with him.*

'Look, let's not over-react,' begged Mia. 'Leo, just try thinking of it as another love scene. Honestly, it doesn't mean anything, I promise.'

Leo opened his mouth but was interrupted by the Scottish voice on the other side of the door.

'Mia! Billy! Make-up's here!'

'Shoot,' said Billy. 'We really need to get dressed.'

'You took the words right out of my mouth,' huffed Leo.

'Just a second!' called Mia. 'We're not quite ready!'

'OK, we'll be back in five minutes.'

Mia moved in to touch Leo's arm but he pulled away.

Something about the look on his face at that moment told Billy that he might have been too hard on him – maybe he wasn't just a heartless pap looking to make a quick buck but he really cared about Mia and was struggling with his feelings. And even though Billy found himself on the receiving end of Leo's jealousy, in a funny way it only made him understand Leo better. And just for a second he could imagine himself one day growing to like him.

'Look,' Mia said, desperately trying to calm Leo down, 'maybe inviting you here was a bad idea. I can see now that it was pretty insensitive of me. Maybe we should just call it a day and meet up tomorrow.'

'Are you joking?' he sniffed. 'Why would I want to go home now? The fun's only just beginning.'

As Billy watched him turn and stomp out of the room, he knew that fun was the last thing they were in for.

*

Leo took his place in the crowd of hangers-on, all standing around waiting for Mia and Billy to arrive on set. He had no idea what was really going on between them but however he looked at it, it didn't add up. He understood that posing for photos half-naked would be great promotion for the film but if they weren't in character, wasn't the implication that they were together in real life? And if they were together, where did that leave him? He liked to think he knew a lot about how things worked in the movie business but he had an eerie feeling of unease about this. In fact, he felt sick with dread.

Mia and Billy stepped onto the set in bathrobes and when they took them off he saw that they were wearing flesh-coloured underwear. His heart sank. He watched open-mouthed as a team of stylists appeared and began sticking pages from books onto their underwear so it looked like they were naked underneath. He felt utterly shattered. Just this morning he'd been thinking that meeting Mia was the best thing that had ever happened to him. Now he didn't know what to think.

He wove his way through the crowd to take his place at the back, where Mia and Billy couldn't see him. He watched as the photographer directed them onto a Chesterfield chaise longue and they began striking various suggestive poses as she merrily snapped away. Even though he knew they were both actors, it didn't seem to him that they were faking an attraction to each other. He'd spent enough time around actors to know that the chemistry between these two was real – acutely real. And with each click of the camera, he felt like a bit of him was dying inside.

He turned away and at the back of the room caught sight

of a laptop lying open on a table. Displayed on the screen were the sexy shots they must have taken that morning. As he looked through them he felt like he'd been winded and struggled to catch his breath. He knew that he and Mia had only spent one night together but already he couldn't bear to even think of her being touched by another man. Having to confront the evidence glaring out at him in full colour was more than he could take. He felt vulnerable, desperate and utterly heartbroken.

He knew that he should just turn around and go home but for some reason he couldn't tear himself away. All he could think about was what a fool he'd made of himself. He'd gone and fallen for someone who was just having a bit of fun and playing with him, an actress who obviously hadn't felt what he'd felt but had faked her way through their entire sham of a relationship. Maybe Ronnie had been right when he'd said that girls like Mia didn't go for guys like him. The evidence was staring him in the face – girls like Mia went for guys like Billy Spencer.

From where he was standing he could hear a waspish woman barking orders at the photographer. He resumed his position at the back of the crowd and peered over to see Mia sitting on top of Billy with her arms wrapped around him. He thought that he was going to throw up.

'OK, we're done with that set-up,' boomed the woman, who he now saw looked just like Cruella de Vil. 'You two lovebirds go off and take five. I'm sure you can think of plenty of ways to amuse yourselves.'

As he listened to her dirty cackle echo around the room, Leo could feel the anger rising up within him. So he *was* being taken for a ride. Mia and Billy *were* seeing each other and everyone else clearly knew all about it. He'd been so stupid. Why hadn't he seen what was happening earlier? They were probably in the dressing room right now having a good old laugh at his expense.

Well he wasn't going to stand for it. Mia might be a star but that didn't entitle her to toy with his feelings like this and go out of her way to wilfully hurt and humiliate him. The more he thought about it, the more angry he became. But strangely, his anger did nothing to smother his more tender feelings for Mia. He still wanted her to run over and tell him that the whole thing was some kind of mix-up and it was him she wanted to be with, not Billy. But that obviously wasn't going to happen. And the only thing worse than imagining Mia and Billy laughing at him in the dressing room was the thought that right now they might even be getting it on.

Something inside him snapped and he knew he had to act. He stormed out of the library and down the corridor towards the dressing room.

Without stopping to think he strode right up to the door and threw it open.

*

'Leo!' squealed Mia, standing there topless. 'I thought you'd left.'

'I know,' he snarled, 'I can see that.'

She quickly grabbed a towel and tied it around herself.

'Yeah that's it,' he seethed, 'cover yourself up for me but not for Billy boy here.'

Billy was also naked and struggling to protect his modesty

with his hands. Mia threw him another towel. The three of them stood still for a moment's excruciating silence.

'Well come on then,' growled Leo at the pair of them. 'Somebody owes me an explanation.'

Billy looked at the floor and scuffed his feet awkwardly.

Mia threw her hands up in the air. She hadn't wanted this to happen and it all felt so unfair. She was frustrated and angry and all her emotions came tumbling out at once. 'Look, I already told you, Leo – we're just filming a love scene, that's all. This is acting, this is what we do.'

'Well I don't believe you. What was all that talk about you two being lovebirds? Everyone in there was acting as if you're a couple. I mean, am I being totally stupid here?'

'No, you're not being stupid,' said Billy. 'And I'm not surprised you're so pissed about it. I think it's about time we told you the truth.'

'Too right it is,' Leo spluttered. 'So come on – let's have it.'

'Leo,' Mia breathed. 'What you're witnessing today is the start of what's known in Hollywood as a show-mance. Apparently they go on all the time.'

'Yeah, yeah, I know what a show-mance is: when people *pretend* to be going out with each other.'

'Well this town's practically built on them.'

Mia realized that she was starting to sound like Violet and stopped before she went any further. She looked at Leo and felt truly awful – guilty for putting him through all this upset but terrified too that just when she'd found the happiness she'd always wanted, it looked like she was in serious danger of losing it.

'Listen, I'm really sorry you've been dragged into all this,' ventured Billy, 'but if it's any consolation, we're not particularly happy about it either.'

'Hmpf! From what I saw in there you looked perfectly happy to me, mate. Romance or show-mance, you couldn't take your hands off her!'

Billy didn't know what to say and shuffled on the spot sheepishly.

'Leo, that's not fair,' piped Mia. She wished that she could just tell Leo that Billy was gay – it would solve all their problems. But it wasn't her secret to tell and she knew that Billy would be mortified if she let it out.

'And anyway,' Leo recovered, 'if you don't like it, why are you doing it?'

'Oh don't you know anything about this industry?' Mia almost snapped. 'We don't have any choice about these things. We have to act all the time. We're never allowed to switch off. It's a way of life – whether we like it or not.'

'Oh so you're acting now then, are you? Prancing around the dressing room with good old Billy boy, both of you stark bollock naked.' He made a point of looking around him. 'I can't see any cameras in here, Mia.'

'Leo, it's not what you think. Honestly it isn't.'

'"It's not what you think"? Did you really just say that? We're not in one of your films now, Mia.'

She winced at the sting of injustice. She didn't think she could handle such animosity from a man she was starting to care about so much. In desperation, she was on the verge of blurting out Billy's secret when she pulled back; she couldn't get herself out of a mess by causing a whole new one for Billy. She opened her mouth feebly. 'But Leo—'

'And what about the other night at your place?' he thundered. 'Were you acting then too?'

'No. How can you say that?'

'Because I've just walked in on you naked with another man, that's how! What kind of fool do you take me for, Mia?'

'I don't take you for a fool, Leo. I really, really like you. And I don't want to lose you.'

'Well I really like you too, Mia. Or at least I thought I did – until I walked in on this little love-in. And now I've no idea what I feel. I just keep thinking about the other night and how wonderful it was. And today in your dressing room too. But you just told me yourself – you act all the time. I'm only sorry I fell for it.'

'But I wasn't acting with you, Leo! I promise I wasn't!'

'All right then, prove it. Prove to me that we're special, Mia. Prove to me that you've not been acting with me in the same way that you're acting with Billy.'

A tense silence descended on the room. She looked at Billy but he was gazing at the floor again. She knew that, even though it was unfair on Billy, she couldn't keep his secret any longer. She took a deep breath.

'Leo . . . Billy's gay. How's that for proof?'

*

Billy couldn't believe what Mia had just done.

He wondered for a second if he'd actually misheard her. But the bewildered look on Leo's face told him he hadn't.

'Oh come off it,' Leo scoffed. 'As if I'm going to fall for that one.'

'Well it doesn't matter whether you believe it or not,' Mia said. 'It's true.'

'But . . .'

'But what, Leo? He doesn't seem gay? Is that what you were going to say?'

'No . . . It's just that . . . I had no idea . . .'

'Most people don't,' Billy managed, stepping in. 'But it's true Leo – I am gay.'

As he heard himself say the words Billy felt his bones go soft with fear. He couldn't quite get his head around what had just happened. Mia had only gone and revealed his biggest secret – and to a paparazzo!

'Billy, I'm really sorry,' she rasped, 'I know I shouldn't have done that.'

He shook his head as if trying to snap himself out of a daze.

'No, *I'm* sorry,' butted in Leo. 'I had no idea. My God, I'm such a dick. Now I feel *really* stupid.'

The three of them sank into silence. Billy watched the dust particles circulate in the air between them. He felt like he was plunging through the air in a broken elevator.

'It's, erm, it's – it's OK,' he mumbled.

'No, it's not OK, Billy,' Leo went on. 'I was out of order. And Mia, I owe you an apology too. Something like this just never occurred to me. And I'm sorry I didn't trust you.'

'Oh forget about it, Leo. It's not as if I trusted you till you'd proved yourself. And anyway, I'm more worried about Billy right now.'

Billy stood there shaking his head. He didn't know how to begin explaining to them how miserable living with such a huge secret made him. Or how each time somebody else found out, it only increased his anxiety that the whole world would soon discover his secret and then he'd be rejected by everyone – just like he was rejected by his parents.

You're disgusting, Billy!

You're no son of ours!

No human being should have to hear words like that from the mouths of their own parents. And Billy knew that he wasn't strong enough to risk hearing them again.

'Billy,' Mia breathed, 'Leo won't say a thing. Will you, Leo?'

'No, I swear I won't.'

'Look, I don't want to discuss this right now,' Billy managed to stammer. 'All I will say is I'm not ashamed of who I am. I just don't want it to compromise my career, that's all. And no offence or anything but I don't have to explain myself to anybody.'

Leo pursed his lips. 'OK, mate, I promise it won't be mentioned again.'

Mia held out her arms and gave him a huge hug.

'Everything will be OK,' she cooed. 'You'll see – everything will be OK.'

But as Billy held onto her tightly he wasn't so sure. And now that he and Mia had agreed to this show-mance, the stakes were suddenly higher. He had a sudden image of himself suffocating under a heavy pile of lies, pressing down on him and burying him alive.

He had a bad feeling about this. A seriously bad feeling.

10

'Now are you sure you want to do this?' asked the doctor. 'You know it's only been two months since your last session – and we usually recommend waiting three or four.'

Violet Vaughn iced him with a glare.

'Well you obviously didn't put enough in last time,' she spat. 'Look at this!'

She arched an eyebrow to show just a tiny bit of movement.

'It's horrendous,' she brayed. 'I need you to get rid of it – and fast.'

The doctor gave her a frown but shrugged in resignation. He handed her a form, which she signed without even reading. All she needed to see was the one magic word: Botox.

The doctor moved over to his work table and snapped on a pair of plastic gloves. As he began filling his syringes Violet reclined on the bed next to him. She'd been here countless times before and knew exactly how it worked.

'Now close your eyes and squeeze them tight,' said the doctor.

Violet did as she was told – although her face barely moved.

'Can you manage a little more?'

She squeezed a bit harder until she felt a tiny flicker of movement.

'That's it. Now relax.'

In went the needle, just above her left cheekbone next to her eye.

The sharp pain always surprised her but it was a good pain – the kind of pain that made her feel happier after a week of being horrified at the sight of her own face. Straight away she could feel the anxiety beginning to fade.

'Aaaaaah.'

The truth was that Violet Vaughn couldn't tolerate any kind of physical imperfection. It reminded her of her teenage years – and that was a period of her life that she didn't want to revisit.

Brought up in Portland, Oregon, she'd been a quiet, mousy girl who'd hit puberty and been dealt a lousy hand – a flat chest, terrible acne and an enormous hooked nose. On top of it all her eyesight was so bad that she'd had to wear thick glasses just to see where she was going. It wasn't the kind of look that made her feel good about herself – or endeared her to her peers. The popular girls in school had called her Vile Violet and made her life hell with their relentless sniggering and sneering. Well they weren't sneering now.

'And close your other eye for me,' breathed the doctor. 'Squeeze it as tight as you can. That's it. And relax.'

She tried not to wince as the needle pierced her skin and she felt the liquid seeping in. As the Botox entered her body she could feel the tension gradually trickling away. Her teenage years in Portland seemed like a lifetime ago.

After leaving high school Violet had found a job in a company that manufactured sockets and switches as the personal assistant to a fat, sweaty executive with a ruddy complexion and sagging flaps of flesh under his eyes that looked like ball bags. She'd put up with him groping her and had even given him the odd blow-job under his desk in return for financial bonuses. She wasn't particularly proud of it but she didn't see why she shouldn't – nobody else wanted to go near her, never mind enter into any kind of sexual relations. And she was desperate to save up enough money to escape the misery of her life in Oregon and reinvent herself in sunny California.

Once she could afford it she'd jumped on a plane to LA and checked straight into a clinic to have her boobs done, her nose fixed and her acne scars lasered away. She'd ditched her glasses for contact lenses and the transformation was complete. She felt like a new woman and managed to muster up enough confidence to launch herself into the film business, soon landing herself a job as a junior publicist working in a large firm. And as far as she was concerned, that's when her life truly began.

The doctor moved onto her forehead. Violet knew from experience that this area hurt even more than around the eyes; there was less flesh and the needle felt as if it were going straight into the bone.

'Oooh,' she found herself whimpering.

'Is everything all right?' The doctor stepped back.

'Yes, fine,' she barked. 'You just carry on, don't mind me.'

As she watched him pumping poison into her forehead she realized he was actually quite attractive. He had dark, greying hair with five o'clock shadow and muscular, hairy forearms. He'd been doing her Botox for years now but for some reason she hadn't really noticed what he looked like before. Not that it mattered as she was sure he wouldn't look at *her* in that way – before or after Botox. In fact, she was convinced she was so unattractive she wouldn't be able to incite interest from a rabid dog if she got down on all fours. And it was so long since she'd had sex she'd need three days' notice and a blow-torch to get herself ready for any action. And anyway, she was past all that now. *It would only get in the way*, she told herself. Though of what she wasn't sure.

Apart from the odd one-night stand, usually when she was on international publicity tours with foreigners she knew she wouldn't see again, Violet hadn't had sex for longer than she could remember. And it had been much longer than that since she'd fallen in love. Although that she could still remember – vividly.

She'd only been working in LA for a few months when she'd been assigned the publicity of legendary actor and sex symbol Cooper Kelly. The second she'd met him she'd fallen instantly, hopelessly in love. She'd had to stop herself from gasping out loud; it was as if she could actually feel Cupid's arrow piercing her heart. She'd only been twenty and Cooper was thirty years older than her. But she'd been overwhelmed by the intensity of her emotions and they'd soon begun a passionate, steamy affair, having endless sex in every corner of his palatial home. For the first time in her life she'd felt special and alive as a sexual, desirable woman. Of course, she knew that Cooper was a major star who could have any woman he wanted. But she'd dared to believe that she just might be good enough for him – and as he was in between wives had even dreamed that he might one day marry her. Oh it all felt so pathetic and stupid now.

The truth was that Cooper had toyed with her for months without making the slightest commitment. Then, on his fiftieth birthday, she'd bribed his staff and sneaked into his home to surprise him with some diamond studded cufflinks which had cost her half a year's salary – and some racy black lingerie that she knew would drive him wild. Only she'd walked into the bedroom to find he was already being driven wild by a top-heavy blonde in blood-red stilettos. When he saw Violet he froze and started to mouth his apologies but she stormed out and rushed down to the garden, where she sat on a bench for half an hour trying to compose herself as she looked out at the moonlit ocean. She felt worse than she could ever have imagined, like a spider was crawling over her soul.

Eventually she'd pulled herself together and had gone upstairs to face Cooper and try to talk things through. Maybe this was just a one-off and the skanky blonde had thrown herself at him; she knew the way things worked in Hollywood. Maybe if she forgave him the two of them could work things out and still make a go of it. But she'd gone back up to the room and been stunned to find that Cooper was still banging the blonde, his tight ass bobbing up and down in time with her over-the-top squeals of ecstasy. Violet was struck dumb and had slipped away quietly, feeling desolate, desperate and hating herself for not being worthy of his love.

She felt a stab of sadness as she thought back to that time now. Cooper Kelly had treated her like a nobody, as if she didn't matter at all. She'd tried so hard to escape her teenage self but he'd made her feel like she was right back where she'd started, being brutally savaged by the girls in high school. As she'd burst out of his home, her face streaming with tears, she'd vowed that no man would ever make her feel like that again. And thirty years later, they still hadn't.

'Now raise your eyebrows for me,' said the doctor. 'As high as you can.'

Violet held her breath as he injected her above the eyelids – her least favourite spot and the one she knew always caused the most pain. Today was no exception. But as her whole body tensed and the needle sunk in, she found herself weirdly enjoying it. Sure, it was painful but it made her feel like she was winning.

And right now Violet *was* winning. Her PR business was booming and she was having to take on new staff to cope with the extra workload. Of all her projects, she was particularly enjoying witnessing the blossoming show-mance between Mia Sinclair and Billy Spencer. One week in and it had already generated far more coverage than she'd dared to hope for. The whole world wanted to know about Hollywood's latest love story – and the producers of *War of Words* were thrilled with the increased interest in the film. The previous day Violet had held the movie's first press junket and had been overwhelmed by the number of journalists fighting to ask Mia and Billy about their relationship. Of course she'd always known that the show-mance had been a great idea; she didn't understand why Mia and Billy had ever resisted it. Well that would teach them to doubt her. She hated it when people doubted her.

Violet Vaughn always knew what she was doing. She was one of the most important and influential women in Hollywood. And she wanted everyone to know it – especially those girls she'd left behind in Portland. *Vile Violet? They don't know the half of it* . . .

'There we go,' said the doctor, stepping back to admire his work. 'All done.'

Violet sat up and went to look at her face in the mirror. There were little prick marks all over her forehead and around her eyes and the beginnings of some light bruising on her left cheekbone. But it was nothing she couldn't cover with a little make-up.

As she gazed at her reflection she couldn't help smiling. Of course, she knew the Botox would take around ten days to come into full effect. But she felt better already.

*

It was 10 a.m. and Hector had only just slunk into the office to start work – nearly an hour late.

He'd slipped in through the back door and thankfully hadn't been spotted, except by Ramona, who he knew would always cover for him. As soon as he'd made it safely to his desk he'd poured himself a strong coffee, whacked Enrique Iglesias's *Greatest Hits* on the sound system and started working his way through Mia's mail. There was the usual pile of fan letters and he responded to the majority of them like a machine, slipping autographed photos into the fans' self-addressed envelopes and tossing them into the tray for outgoing mail. That was just about all he could cope with right now.

Because right now Hector was chronically hungover. However much water he drank, he still had a pounding headache, as if his brain was rattling around in a jar. However many times he brushed his teeth or gargled with mouthwash, his tongue still tasted like the filth-ridden contents of Bogie and

Bacall's litter tray. And worst of all, however hard he tried, he couldn't get rid of his bad case of beer fear – what Holly Golightly in *Breakfast at Tiffany's* calls 'the mean reds'– that horrible, jumpy anxiety that made him stop halfway through everything he was doing and left him incapable of concentrating on anything at all. Hector *hated* being hungover.

And it wasn't even as if he'd had a particularly good night. He'd been out with a couple of friends at the launch party of a new gay club called The Cock Pit. It was an amazing club with stunning ocean views, built around a huge under-lit swimming pool that had been the setting for the night's entertainment: a tightly choreographed display of transvestite synchronized swimming. The problem was that his two friends had picked up men and disappeared really quickly and he'd been left all on his own. And everyone he'd met had spectacularly failed to live up to his romantic ideal. He'd recoiled as he'd been chatted up by a lank-haired saxophonist from New Orleans with no sense of personal space and shocking garlic breath. He'd flinched as he'd been accosted by a skinny set designer with some sort of ginger Afro, who claimed to have been struck by lightning and somehow managed to have a serious case of what Hector had always thought to be the exclusively female condition of camel toe. And at the end of the night he'd mumbled excuses when a customs officer who claimed to be a cousin of Shereen Spicer had invited him back to his place for a binge on all the drugs he'd confiscated from passengers at the airport. Eventually, feeling drunk and desolate, he'd ended up going home with a Colombian gardener whose front teeth were missing and who looked so rough that Hector had deftly hidden his wallet under the mattress while he'd been undressing. As he thought back to the experience now he felt thoroughly ashamed of himself. Why did he always end up with such unsuitable men? After working his way through so many of them he sometimes felt like his heart wasn't so much broken as utterly shot through. Oh why couldn't he find his prince?

As if to rub his nose in it, lucky Mia seemed to have *two* princes in her life right now. As well as dating Leo, she'd recently started stepping out with Billy Spencer too. Hector could hardly believe it; she'd been loveless most of the time he'd worked for her and now suddenly she had a gorgeous man on each arm. Hector had spent much of the past week organizing her dates with one or other of them. She and Billy had presented an award at an indie film event and gone out for dinner at a busy restaurant where celebrities always went when they wanted to show off their latest beau to the ever-present paparazzi. At the same time, Hector had arranged secret dinners for her and Leo and had even booked out an entire cinema one night so that they could go to the movies together unnoticed. He wasn't sure what had got into her and didn't want her to get hurt but as far as he could tell, she genuinely seemed to love spending time with both men.

And who could blame her for wanting to date two men when they were both so insanely attractive? Leo was sexy and manly but so comfortable in his masculinity that he didn't mind expressing his affection for Hector; he always kissed him hello and ruffled his hair fondly, something that made Hector shiver with glee. Billy on the other hand was cute and boyish but with muscular arms that strained at his T-shirt sleeves and a body that Hector knew from the movies was like that of a

Greek god. Unfortunately, he was much more guarded and less forthcoming than Leo and only ever greeted Hector with a firm, businesslike handshake. He was uneasy around him in the way that some closeted gay men were, except that he didn't remotely set off Hector's gaydar – and there could be no question about his sexuality now that he was dating Mia. And the two of them weren't shy about ramming their happiness down his throat, always laughing and joking together like a pair of teenage sweethearts.

All things considered, if given the choice himself, Hector thought he'd probably opt for a night of passion with Billy rather than Leo. Not that it mattered, seeing as both of them were straight. *Lucky Mia.*

As he tossed the last of her fanmail into the out tray, Hector turned his attention to the day's packages: box after box of free clothes, shoes and accessories, sent from the world's leading fashion houses in Mia's exact sizes, just in case she ever fancied wearing any of it when she stepped out in public. At times like this he thought it a shame that he didn't work for a male star – one of the biggest perks of a Hollywood PA's job was to keep the boss's unwanted freebies. Although he had to admit that he loved hearing the squeals of delight from his mother and sisters when they called him on the phone to say that they'd received one of his regular packages back home in Miami.

As he unwrapped an elegant black dress from Dolce & Gabbana, Hector wondered whether Mia would wear it out on a date with Leo or Billy. Actually, it would most likely be with Billy as she only ever appeared to go out in public with him. Just then he realized how odd the whole set-up was. Leo was a paparazzo, so he obviously knew about Mia's very public dates with Billy. And Hector himself had arranged for Leo to go to Cooper Kelly's party, which Mia had attended with Billy, and for him to visit Mia on the set of her photo shoot with Billy. So the two men obviously knew each other. And after two years of working for her, Hector really didn't think that Mia was the type to lie to men or mess them around. But there was something funny going on and he was intrigued to find out exactly what it was.

Come to think of it, Mia always made sure that Hector wasn't in the house when she got home from a date so he had no idea which, if either, of the men ever stayed the night. And whenever he asked how her dates had gone she'd fob him off and change the subject. Reflecting on it now, he realized that she'd been much more secretive with him lately than she'd ever been in the past. The more he thought about it, the more it dawned on him that Mia's double dating wasn't quite as simple as he'd first thought. And one thing was for sure – there was no chance that Mia herself would tell him what was going on.

No, Hector was going to do some digging and get to the bottom of it himself.

*

Mia tore down the Pacific Coast Highway, or the PCH as locals called it, on the back of Leo's motorbike. The wind swept over her face and she breathed in deep, hungry gulps of sea air mixed with the smell of Leo's leathers and his own manly scent. She'd never thought that riding on the back of a man's motorbike could be such a sexually arousing experience. But pressing her body up against his and wrapping her arms around him for survival, there was no denying it now.

Leo turned off the highway at Fairytale Cove, a quiet spot he knew which he told her was one of LA's best-kept secrets. She didn't like to tell him that she'd been here a few years ago to shoot a love scene for a chick flick she'd been making. She managed to cast those memories out of her mind as she took Leo's hand and they walked along the beach, stopping occasionally to kiss, cuddle and paddle in the surf. The sheer release of surrendering to what she now knew was love felt like some kind of drug rushing through her whole body.

Walking next to Leo, Mia realized just how much taller, stronger and more confident she felt now than she ever had before. Above all, she felt so much more *herself* when she was with him and she wondered whether this was why people talked about finding their other half in life, someone who completed them. She couldn't help thinking how ironic it was that whenever she was with Leo she had to wear a disguise to fool the paparazzi, hiding behind dark glasses and a wig she'd worn in one of her film roles – as if she was pretending to be someone else on the outside just so that she could be herself on the inside.

And yeah, she still felt guilty about revealing Billy's secret to Leo but when she was with Leo she tried her best not to think about that either. Thankfully, he hadn't mentioned it since the day of the photo shoot and neither had Billy for that matter. On her very different and very public dates with Billy, the two of them had managed to have great fun, although deep down she knew they were both putting on a brave face and that neither of them wanted to go through with the show-mance. The very thought of it made her feel anxious but she told herself she wasn't going to let it spoil her date with Leo. She took hold of his hand and gave it a little squeeze. It was funny but whenever she was with Leo, all her worries disappeared – she felt safe and secure, as if nothing could touch her. And she couldn't remember feeling like that since she was a little girl. Just then she felt her love for him grow in a sudden surge.

As the sunshine began to fade, Leo drove them up into the Hills and took Mia to another quiet spot where they could watch the sunset together. As they looked out over the vast panorama, she noticed that the sky over LA had that beautiful pink tinge it always had in the evening. Somebody had once told her it was caused by all the smog and pollution in the city. She wondered how something so dirty could create such a beautiful image. She turned to Leo and snuggled into his arms.

She was so happy right now – happier than she ever remembered being. How could anything possibly go wrong?

*

'You do realize this is all going to go horribly wrong?'

Serena stood looking at Mia with her hands on her hips. That afternoon they'd had a massage and they were now in Mia's lounge getting ready to go through a pile of scripts. Serena had just been told about the show-mance and couldn't believe what she'd heard.

'You know, all I do is go away for ten days and I come home to find out you and Billy have been fucked up the ass by the Wicked Witch of West Hollywood. Man, the whole thing's crazy. Why didn't you call me before you agreed to go through with it?'

'Serena, you were in Sierra Leone. I didn't want to disturb you.'

'But I was hardly on vacation – I was working!' Serena had been visiting the set of a film starring another of her clients, Denver Jones, an African-American stand-up comedian turned movie star who'd recently seen his popularity plummet within the black community for marrying a very white, very blonde model. Subsequently, he was trying to reconnect with his core audience by playing a freedom fighter in a gritty drama about the recent civil war in Sierra Leone. The problem was that when he'd arrived on location, he hadn't been at all happy about the lack of luxury and had soon started making demands that couldn't be met by the producers. Serena had flown out there on a desperate mission to stop a new war breaking out and after ten days had just about managed to avert catastrophe. 'You know,' she sighed, sitting down next to Mia. 'I'm not saying I didn't have my hands full but I was on email or my cell out there. And I would have happily taken time out to talk you out of this dumb-ass idea.'

'But is it such a dumb-ass idea? According to Violet this kind of thing goes on all the time.' Serena could tell this wasn't the first time Mia had said this line and, more to the point, that she didn't really believe it.

'Well that's bullshit – believe me. This kind of thing *used to* go on all the time. But I know for sure that it doesn't any-more – not in a world crawling with paparazzi who can upload photos onto the internet in seconds, before you even know they've been taken. Not in a world where every regular Tom,

Dick and Harry has a camera on their cell phone and spends all their time on Twitter talking about the celebs they've spotted. I mean, what if you're caught out with Leo when you're supposed to be seeing Billy? It's way too dangerous, sister. It just won't fly.'

Mia put her finger to her lips and shot Serena a look of concern. 'Sssh! Not so loud! Bob's in the kitchen and he might hear you. He doesn't know anything about Leo.'

'But I thought you said he didn't speak English?'

'He didn't. But now that he's dating Ramona he's learning. Sweet, isn't it?'

Serena cocked her head and managed to make out a few lines of heavily accented, disjointed English coming from the kitchen.

'You very beautiful.'

'I – you – so happy.'

She couldn't stop herself letting out a little chuckle. 'Well, what do you know? There must be something in the air. Which reminds me, what does Leo think about this show-mance?'

'Oh he doesn't like it, I guess. But I'm trying not to bring it up with him to be honest. I just don't want to spoil things.'

'So it's all going well between you two?'

'Incredibly well.' She lowered her voice even further. 'Serena, I think I'm in love with him. In fact, I know I'm in love with him.'

'Well that's fantastic news. Have you told him this?'

'Not yet. We kind of had an argument when he found out about the show-mance so I don't want to rock the boat for a while. I'm just enjoying spending time with him and trying not to over-complicate things.'

'Well that's great, sister, but I hope this whole show-mance doesn't mess things up for you. Are you totally sure it's not too late to back out of it?'

'Hmm, I'm afraid so. We've done the photo shoot together now and talked about being a couple at the junket. And we've already been papped on a few dates this week so we're kind of up and running. If we duck out now then the whole thing could totally backfire.'

'You're telling me. Are you sure you don't want me to get involved? You know, Violet might scare most people in this town but she doesn't scare me. Maybe I could have a talk to her – get her to do some damage limitation with the press and call the whole thing off.' Serena thought back to the time that she and Violet had last talked, when they'd had a massive bust-up backstage at the Golden Globes after Violet had insisted that another of their shared clients, Annabel Anders, a Broadway musical star with a famously large bust, wore a cleavage-revealing dress that had been carefully tampered with to pop open at the very moment she stepped onto the red carpet. From Violet's point of view, it had been a masterstroke – the pictures were a sensation and appeared on the front page of every newspaper around the world. But from Serena's point of view it had been a disaster – she'd been trying hard to land Annabel the lead role in a heavyweight drama about domestic violence and knew that Violet's carefully planned accident had completely ruined her chances. She hadn't been afraid to vent her frustration and the ensuing catfight had caused almost as much of a stir backstage as the wardrobe malfunction had out front.

'No, honestly,' Mia protested. 'It'll be OK. She's asked me

and Billy to go to a meeting in her office later this week. And if you don't mind, it's probably better if we go on our own.'

Serena wondered if Mia was also thinking about what had happened at the Golden Globes. It had been the one occasion when she'd lost her cool in public and she'd vowed never to do it again. Her behaviour had been nothing short of unprofessional and had left her undermined in the face of the dilemma she was facing now.

'OK,' she shrugged. 'If you insist. But if there's any trouble, you let me loose on her.'

'OK, I will. I promise.'

'That's my girl. Now let's take a look at these scripts.'

As she opened the first and began reading, Serena found it difficult to concentrate. She couldn't help worrying about this upcoming meeting with Violet, who was obviously planning a new twist in the tale and wanted to get Mia and Billy on board. However she looked at it, it was all very fishy.

And Serena didn't trust Violet. She didn't trust her one bit.

*

It was 7 a.m. and Billy was thumping his way up a sandy track, snaking a trail through Runyon Canyon. He had a rucksack filled with heavy weights on his back and dark shades covered most of his face. Not that it bothered him if he was spotted or papped while he was out training; Violet seemed to think that it was actually good for his image and made him seem more 'real'. He couldn't help smiling at the irony.

Last night Billy had gone out with Mia to a charity event to raise money for the victims of an earthquake in a poor country he was sure that none of the guests had heard of until natural disaster had made it fashionable. He and Mia had made sure they arrived and left together and had posed for countless photographs during the course of the evening.

'Give her a kiss!' one of the event photographers had shouted when they were standing arm in arm on the red carpet.

Billy had made a big show of scooping Mia up in his arms, twirling her around and planting a great big kiss on her mouth.

That's for you, Violet, he'd thought.

Both the photographers and the crowds behind the crash barriers had hollered their approval. Billy couldn't remember a time when applause and adulation had actually made him feel *bad*.

As he thudded his way up towards the summit of the canyon he reflected on how much he hated his show-mance with Mia. And so far they'd only been on three dates. But it all felt so wrong already and he still had a really bad feeling about how it would play out eventually. The trouble was, after the big showdown with Leo at the photo shoot, he didn't want to say anything to Mia as he didn't want to rake things up again. He'd felt bad that his problems were interfering with her relationship and he didn't want to spoil things for her, especially as she seemed so happy now. So he kept quiet, put on a front and made sure the two of them had fun on their dates, nuzzling into her romantically whenever a pap appeared but whispering daft jokes in her ear to try and make her laugh. And maybe he was being over-sensitive about the whole thing anyway. Maybe pretending to date your best girlfriend wasn't such a big deal after all. It wasn't as if anybody had smelled a rat yet, or even showed any signs of doing so in the future. *If we can just get through the next few months . . .*

As he thought ahead to the future his mind turned to the script he'd been sent for his next film project. He'd been asked to play a womanizer suspected of serial murder in *Kissed by a Devil*, a sexually explicit thriller which his agent thought would be the perfect vehicle to dirty up his clean-cut image. The trouble was that under the current circumstances he felt uneasy about accepting it. He'd never been offered this kind of role before and couldn't help wondering if he was only being offered it now because he'd sexed up his image by faking an affair with Mia. In which case he was worried about sinking further and further into a putrid bog of lies and deceit.

He reached the top of the canyon and looked out over the city. He'd heard that panoramic views like this were supposed to make your own problems seem small and insignificant. Standing there on his own, looking out over the grid of streets disappearing into the heat haze, he realized that this particular view was having exactly the opposite effect on him.

Once again in his mind he saw himself being buried alive under all the lies he'd told and was continuing to tell. And he was suddenly gripped by a crippling fear of everything going horribly wrong, leaving his career in ruins and himself rejected and even more lonely than he was already. He didn't know what Violet wanted to talk about at this next meeting but he wasn't looking forward to it.

*

'So let me get this straight,' Ronnie said. 'Mia's with you but she's *pretending* to be with Billy?'

Leo tucked into his full English breakfast. 'Yeah, that's pretty much it. Mmm, I love black pudding.'

'We call it blood sausage here, Limey. But just rewind a second. Did you just say your girlfriend's pretending to date someone else and you're OK with that?'

'Well I'm not exactly thrilled about it but what can I do? It's her job basically – she has to promote the film.'

Ronnie made a whistling sound and shook his head.

It was Sunday morning and the two of them were sitting at a dishcloth-damp table having breakfast in Leo's favourite British café The Tea Zone. It was run by a cheery cockney called George, a fat bald man with white, pasty dinner-lady arms, which Leo always thought had the texture of uncooked pastry. This was Leo's favourite place for comfort food – although he'd thrown himself into every aspect of the LA experience, when he wanted cheering up there was nothing like a full English. And today Ronnie had joined him.

The truth was that Leo had been avoiding Ronnie all week. The Shooting Stars agency had been tipping them both off about Mia and Billy's dates and Leo couldn't face answering Ronnie's inevitable questions so had pretended to be ill in bed with a bad case of the flu. But now it was time to man up and face the music. And just as he'd predicted, the questions were coming thick and fast.

'And what about Billy Spencer?' Ronnie spluttered through a mouthful of food. 'Is it his job to make out with your girl? I bet he's loving every minute of it.'

'Oh I wouldn't worry about Billy. He's a really nice bloke.'

'Yeah, that's what everyone says but it's no reason to let him make you look like a total dipshit.'

At the next table two loud-mouthed, overly made-up bottle blondes from Liverpool were flicking through a stack of papers and magazines. One of them held up a front-page photograph of Mia and Billy holding hands over a dinner table.

'Phwoar!' she giggled. 'That Billy Spencer's well fit!'

'I know,' cooed her friend. 'Mia Sinclair's a jammy cow!'

Leo pretended not to notice them but it was really difficult not to react. All week he'd hated this – having to listen to everyone talking about his girlfriend being in love with another man while his existence was covered up like some guilty secret. Now he was starting to get an inkling of how a gay man like Billy must feel, having to hide away in the closet just for being himself. And it wasn't nice at all. But after blowing his top at the photo shoot the other week, making a fool out of himself and in the process putting Billy in a difficult position, Leo really didn't feel that he had the right to complain about anything.

'Billy isn't making a dipshit out of me, Ronnie. Honestly, he's not like that. And I promise you there's nothing going on with him and Mia.'

'OK, buddy, whatever you say.' Ronnie lifted a fork piled high with more food than Leo ever thought could fit into a human mouth and somehow managed to manoeuvre it all in. 'So in that case,' he went on once he'd swallowed, 'does that mean I can go out and pap them now? Because I've stayed away from them all week but pretty soon Chip and Biff are going to start asking questions. I mean, I'm guessing if it's a set-up like you say then Mia won't mind. And Rosie's giving me a real hard time about making some decent dough. If we're ever going to have a baby then I need to earn every cent I can.'

Leo did his best to give him a cheery smile. 'Yep, be my

guest,' he managed. 'Somebody's got to take the photos so it might as well be you.' He couldn't help wondering how he'd ended up in this position. Just a few months ago he'd never have imagined he'd be advising his best mate to photograph his film-star girlfriend while she was out on a date with another man. The whole thing felt completely unreal.

'And when are *you* coming back to work, bud?' Ronnie asked. 'I'm assuming this whole flu thing was bullshit.'

'Oh I'll be back in business tomorrow.'

Ronnie nodded his approval. 'And what do you reckon to this Hunter Kelly job? It could even be one for the top ten . . .'

They'd each received a message yesterday explaining that make-up artist turned celebrity girlfriend Dominique was setting up a honey trap for her man, Cooper Kelly's son Hunter. She was earning a hefty fee for taking reformed drug addict Hunter to an exclusive nightclub where she'd arranged for a stash of cocaine to be left in a VIP room, which would conveniently be accessible to a few carefully selected paparazzi. It was potentially a big story, as Hunter was telling anyone who'd listen how he'd finally beaten his addictions, and was later that same week due to start work on his big comeback film. If he gave in to temptation and was caught snorting coke now, it'd be quite a fall from grace.

From the look on his face, Ronnie was obviously keen to accept the job. 'Come on, man . . . ker-ching, ker-ching?'

Leo laughed. 'You know what, mate, I'm not sure I'm up for it. I'm not really sure I approve to be honest.'

Ronnie mimed disbelief. 'What? What are you talking about?'

'Just, you know, it seems a bit harsh on Hunter. What if

he *has* kicked the drugs and she's going to tempt him back and mess it all up for him?'

'Yeah but if we thought like that we'd never take a single picture. And anyway, whatever happened to our code of shooting first and thinking later?'

Leo pushed his plate of food away and stroked his chin. 'Look, no offence, mate, but I'm just not sure I'm cut out for this anymore. Maybe my papping days are over.'

'What are you talking about? You're the best pap in town – you always have been.'

'Thanks, partner. But maybe it just doesn't fire me up like it used to. You know, I was thinking the other day about becoming a sports photographer.'

'A *sports* photographer?' Now it was Ronnie's turn to push away his plate. 'Dude, are you *sure* you're not sick?'

'Perfectly sure. It's just that things are going really well with Mia at the moment. And if they carry on the way they're going, then sooner or later I'll have to think about changing my career. I've thought about it and realized I'm not cut out to be a fashion or features photographer so I just thought maybe I'd give sports photography a go. At least it might give me the buzz I used to get from papping a tough target.'

'Yeah but giving it all up already? Isn't that a little drastic?'

'Maybe. But this whole thing is pretty drastic. I think I'm in love with her, Ronnie. Well, I know I'm in love with her.'

Ronnie's expression changed, acknowledging the significance of Leo's statement. 'And have you told her that?'

'No, but I'm going to – very soon.'

*

'Oh it's so adorable to see two young people so obviously *in love*!'

Violet greeted Mia and Billy somewhat theatrically at the entrance to her office block. There were air kisses all round before she swept them into the building and past a throng of receptionists, assistants, interns and general lackeys, all of whom looked terrified at the sight of her.

'Come through and tell me *all* about it!' she trilled at the top of her voice.

Mia and Billy shuffled after her sheepishly, listening to the sound of her dagger heels on the marble floor. Both of them did their best to flash warm smiles at her clearly long-suffering team.

Once they were in her office Violet slammed the door behind them.

'Now then . . . who'd like a drink?'

'Just, just a water please,' croaked Billy.

'Yeah, me too,' bleated Mia. 'Please.'

As if by magic an assistant who looked like he hadn't slept for a month appeared with two glasses of water. As he set one down in front of Mia, she could see that his hands were shaking.

'That'll be all,' barked Violet. 'Now shut the door and make sure you switch off my phones. I do *not* want to be disturbed.'

The assistant nodded and scuttled away. As he closed the door Mia, Billy and Violet were left in silence.

'Now then,' Violet began, 'I've asked you here to talk about our little show-mance.'

'Mmm-hmm,' managed Billy. 'What about it?'

'Well, there's no easy way to say this but it's not really working for me at the moment.'

'What?' mouthed Mia. 'I thought the press were loving it.'

'They are – for now. But that's only the start. And I think it's about time we upped the ante.'

'But we don't want to overdo it,' struggled Billy. 'Wouldn't that be asking for trouble?'

'Listen Billy,' Violet steamed, 'if there's one thing I know about, it's publicity. And unless we start cranking things up soon, the press are going to lose interest. Fact.'

'OK,' ventured Mia. 'And what exactly do you have in mind?'

'Well, as I'm sure you both know, there's just one week left till our premiere . . .'

Mia didn't need reminding – in preparation for the big night she was already back on her extreme diet and working out daily with Cole. This time she was hating it more than ever and just that morning she'd made a decision: this was the very last time she was going to have it worked into her contract that she had to be a size zero for filming and the premiere. Lately she'd started learning about moderation, about relaxing and enjoying life, about not being a robot. It had all come as something of a revelation and it was all down to Leo.

'So I think it's about time we finished up the foreplay,' Violet went on, 'and started to work things up to a nicely timed climax.'

Mia gulped.

'We need another date – nothing fancy, just a little dinner, somewhere nice and public where everyone will see you, Billy, get a little carried away and work Mia up into a sexual frenzy.'

Billy wiped his brow and nodded.

'And then after dinner we need to make sure that you go

back to spend the night at Mia's place. I'll arrange a driver – someone who'll blab to the press about the two of you getting down and dirty in the back of his car. And then it's all perfectly simple. You make out at Mia's bedroom window and then, Billy, you take your shirt off and close the curtains. You got that?'

Billy tried to stop his eyes from boggling.

Violet glowered at him. 'The next morning you open the curtains bare-ass naked with your back to the window so as not to show them too much. And Mia, you look on adoringly with your best FFF.'

'FFF? What's an FFF?'

'A freshly fucked face. You know, when you've just been fucked mercilessly and have that wonderful post-sex glow.'

Mia blushed. She couldn't help thinking about Leo; she felt exposed, as if the whole conversation was indecent.

'Oh come on, Mia,' Violet snapped. 'You're a very talented actress – I'm sure it's in your repertoire.'

Now Mia was blushing even more. She reached for her water and took a big swig.

'And if you want to finish things up by kissing each other goodbye on the doorstep then that's fine by me,' Violet went on. 'Just as long as you leave the press in no doubt as to what you got up to when those curtains were closed. And that's it. Done and done.'

Mia wondered what Leo would think about Violet's latest plan. He still hadn't mentioned the show-mance since their bust-up at the photo shoot and he'd had plenty of opportunity. Maybe he'd got used to the idea and was fine with it now. Come to think of it, Billy still hadn't mentioned it either. She'd assumed he'd been putting on a brave face like her but maybe he'd got used to it too. The problem with Billy was that he spent so much of his time being bouncy and upbeat that it was difficult to tell if deep down he was unhappy. Sure, he looked a little uncomfortable right now but that was nothing unusual; everyone looked like that around Violet. Maybe she'd been misreading the situation all along and Billy was perfectly happy with the show-mance. Maybe it was only her who was reluctant to take it further.

Violet looked at them for a reaction but none was forthcoming.

'What's the problem?' she snarled. 'This is nothing new – just the natural progression of what we're doing anyway.'

'Yeah but it seems a little more sinister for some reason,' Mia managed.

Violet scoffed. 'Tsk! You're not telling me you expect the press to fall for a few cosy dinners and public appearances? That isn't going to work, Mia – I don't know if you've ever met a pap but they're not stupid. We need to put on much more of a show if they're really going to buy it. For them to see through our little charade now would be a total disaster – for all of us.'

Billy put his hands together and clenched them tightly.

Violet turned her back on them and strode over to look out of the window. 'And, you know, need I mention the Box Office . . . ?'

Mia pursed her lips while she thought it over.

'I'm sure both of you know just how important this film could be for your careers . . .'

She knew already that when Violet was like this there was no point arguing.

'You're on the home strait – just one little push and it'll all be over . . .'

Maybe she was right, anyway. Maybe they *were* too far down the line to back out now.

'All right, let's do it,' Mia said.

Billy nodded in silence.

'Good!' crowed Violet, turning around to face them. 'Now I don't know about you two, but I'm ready to shoot my load.'

11

Mia was back in Sky High reclining on a heavily cushioned sofa and listening to the venue's familiar Brazilian music. The last time she'd been here, sitting at exactly the same table, she'd been on a date with Dan Morrison the carpenter. This time, just a few months later, she was on a date with Billy.

'What about those two there?' Billy gestured towards a couple of Arab men wearing what looked like gingham dish towels on their heads. 'They've got to be fakes, surely.'

'Nah, it's way too obvious,' she frowned. 'Check out that Latin-looking guy with the stick-on moustache – now he's a major phoney.'

They looked over and sized him up.

Apparently Violet had booked a table for a couple of paps under her name and they'd be following the action on hidden cameras. She'd thought that this time it'd be better for it to look like Mia and Billy had been caught off guard in a private restaurant rather than papped flaunting themselves somewhere public like The Ivy. Which had left them guessing which of their fellow diners were the under-cover paps.

'Excuse me,' interrupted a nicotine-blonde waitress. 'Are you ready to order?' Mia recognized her as the same woman with the face like a King Charles Spaniel who'd served her when she'd come here with Dan.

'Erm, yeah,' said Billy. 'Sorry, erm, I'll just have the grilled chicken salad please. No dressing.'

'And I'll have the steamed fish with vegetables please,' said Mia.

The waitress gave them a big smile. 'Coming right up.'

'She must think we're such dorks,' Mia joked once she'd gone. 'That's got to be the most boring order she's taken in years.'

'Don't I know it.' Billy sighed. 'What I'd give for a big juicy steak right now.'

'Oooh,' Mia moaned. 'Or a fat greasy cheeseburger. Smothered in mayonnaise.'

'With chunky fries on the side . . .'

Their laughter trailed off.

'Do you ever ask yourself if it's all worth it?' Mia breathed into the silence. 'I mean, seriously?' She'd been asking herself this a lot lately, and not just about her diet. The trappings of her movie-star lifestyle had started to feel more like a burden than they ever had before, and her commitment to things like wearing full make-up every time she left the house was beginning to wane. 'You know, I'm not complaining or anything,' she went on. 'The perks of working in the movies are totally amazing. But some of the sacrifices we have to make can be pretty shitty too. Do you know what I mean?

'Sure I do, sugar,' Billy nodded pensively. 'I know just what you mean. But there's no way out yet – we've got to see through this show-mance and I've just signed a contract for my next picture.'

'*Kissed by a Devil*?'

'That's the one.'

'Congratulations.'

'Thanks. I'm not sure it's anything to celebrate though. You know, I used to feel relieved every time I signed a contract. I used to think that I'd got away with it for one more movie, like I was safe for another year or so. I don't know why but now I just feel more and more trapped.'

Mia sipped on her rather bitter pomegranate juice. 'I know, Billy. And it's much harder for you than it is for me but having to cover up how I feel about Leo has made me think about a whole bunch of stuff. And lying sucks.'

'It does, sugar. It sure does. But we're stuck with it a while longer so you're going to have to not let it get to you.'

Mia shrugged half-heartedly.

'You know,' he went on, 'when it gets me down, I try to think of it not so much as lying but more like spinning a fairy-tale.'

'So it's not so much dishonesty as fantasy?'

'You got it.'

'Well when you put it like that it doesn't sound half as bad.' She held up her glass for a toast. 'Come on then, let's celebrate your new job.'

Billy brought his glass forward to meet hers.

'To fairytales.'

'To fairytales!'

Despite her beaming smile, Mia still wasn't sure why they were celebrating.

*

Leo took a swig of his beer and put it down on the bar.

He and Ronnie were in Dirty Dick's unwinding after a hard day's work. They'd spent a total of seven hours trailing Destiny Diament, who they'd been told would be buying a pregnancy test from a quiet branch of Duane Reade in Burbank. Unfortunately her publicist hadn't specified a time and they'd had to follow her all over the city, shopping, having her nails done, eating lunch and then going for colonic irrigation before she'd finally given them what they were waiting for. It had been a long, soul-destroying day and now that it was over Leo was spent.

But he also knew that Mia was out with Billy tonight and he wanted to take his mind off their date. Obviously he wasn't jealous of Billy anymore, but he felt so in love with Mia that he wanted to shout about it to the whole world. Hiding it was becoming more and more difficult, especially when he had to put up with people thinking Mia was in love with someone else. He took another swig of his beer.

Just then his phone bleeped at exactly the same time as Ronnie's. They both picked them up to read identical text messages: 'Billy Spencer banging Mia Sinclair tonight. Sky High now, her place later. Nail them.'

So much for taking his mind off it.

Leo picked up his beer and downed it in one. 'Excuse me?' he called to the bartender. 'Can I get another beer?'

Ronnie looked at him nervously. 'Yeah, me too,' he yelled. 'Coming right up.'

The two of them sat in silence as the bartender plonked down two pints of real ale in front of them.

Ronnie began tapping his phone against his arm.

'Man, this whole show-mance thing sucks. Are you sure you're OK with it?'

Leo buried his head in his hands. 'Of course I'm not OK with it – it's totally destroying me. But I've got to live with it. I told you, Ronnie, I'm in love with her.'

'Then the whole thing's crazy. How can you stand by and let another dude sleep with her?'

'It's not as simple as that, Ronnie. And I don't really have much choice.'

'You could front up to Billy. Tell him to back off.'

'No, mate, Billy's not the problem – honestly.'

'Well it sounds like he's the problem to me. Taking your girl out for dinner a few times, that's one thing. But having sex with her is something else.'

'They won't be having sex, mate. Not really.'

'And how can you be sure about that? How do you know they're not spinning you a line?'

'Oh I'm sure. Dead sure.'

'Well I think you're kidding yourself, bud.'

'Ronnie, Billy's not the problem. Trust me.'

'I do trust you. But it sounds like *you're* trusting a total douche-bag.'

'Mate, Billy's not a douche-bag.' He lowered his voice and looked around to check that the bartender was out of earshot. 'Billy's gay.'

Ronnie looked at him open-mouthed.

As soon as he'd said it, Leo knew he'd made a mistake.

*

Mia puckered up as Billy moved in to kiss her.

'Sorry,' he whispered. 'Do I taste of chicken?'

'Don't make me laugh,' she joked. 'You're supposed to work me into a frenzy, remember?'

'OK,' he smirked. 'How's this?' He began kissing her open-mouthed and she responded with a squeal of delight.

'Was that too much?' she asked.

'No, sugar, it was just fine.'

'Well I hope those paps are taking their pictures. Can you see them anywhere?'

'Shut up and close your eyes. You're supposed to be enjoying this.'

She closed her eyes and tried to lose herself for a moment. She told herself that she was acting but all she could think about was the last time she'd kissed Leo.

'Excuse me,' interrupted the waitress, 'but would you guys like the check?'

'Oh yeah, sorry,' Billy stuttered, pretending to tear himself away. 'I guess I'm getting a little over-excited.'

The waitress looked down with a shy smile.

'Me too,' said Mia, straightening her hair. 'I think we'd better go home.'

'Yeah,' Billy smirked. 'Before things get too X-rated.'

*

'Well what do you know?' Ronnie whistled. 'Billy Spencer's gay.'

'Sshhh!' hissed Leo. 'Keep your voice down.'

Ronnie couldn't believe what he'd just heard. He'd never have guessed in a million years. 'But he doesn't come across as gay,' he went on as quietly as he could. 'He's just like a regular dude.'

'And when was the last time you saw a gay bloke, Ronnie? They're not all like Liberace.'

'But what about that film where he was dating four chicks at the same time?'

'*Four Play*?'

'That's it. Rosie made me sit through that romantic crap. But I totally bought him as a straight guy.'

'That's why it's called acting, Ronnie. You might as well say an actor can never play a dad unless he's got kids – or a murderer unless he's killed someone.'

Ronnie raised his eyebrows and nodded. 'Well I can't wait to tell Rosie. Billy Spencer gay. That'll put an end to her little crush.'

'No, Ronnie, you can't tell anyone. Not even Rosie.'

'Are you serious?'

'Deadly serious. This is a really big deal. And if it gets out then Mia will dump me faster than I can say . . .'

'Liberace?'

'Yeah.'

Just then their phones buzzed and they read another text alert letting them know that Mia and Billy were paying their check.

'Go on, mate,' said Leo. 'You'd better get a move on.'

'So you don't mind if I go?'

'Nah. As long your pictures are good. And you make my girl look beautiful.'

'Gee, thanks bud – I appreciate it. I really need the dough since that Hunter Kelly job fell through.' Earlier that week,

Ronnie had turned up at the nightclub designated by Dominique, only to find her sitting in the back of a police car in handcuffs. Apparently Hunter had suspected that she was up to something so had hired a private investigator to follow her every move. The PI had busted Dominique's honey trap right there and then and handed her over to the LAPD, who'd arrested her not only for possession of cocaine but for a string of charges relating to incitement and fraud.

'You know what,' mused Leo, 'I'm kind of pleased Dominique got rumbled in the end. It's kind of like in the fairytales your Mum used to read to you when you were a kid – you know, when the baddies always get their comeuppance.'

'Yeah but this ain't no fairytale, Leo. This is the real world. And I'm seriously broke right now. Also, I haven't told you this yet but Rosie's finally pregnant.'

'Mate, that's amazing!' Leo stood up to give Ronnie a big hug.

'Thanks, bud. We weren't going to tell people yet as we only found out a few weeks ago and we still haven't had the scan. But seeing as this is the night for revealing secrets . . .'

Leo grinned. 'Yeah but that's absolutely brilliant news. You'll make a terrific dad, mate.'

'Thanks but, you know, the first thing I've got to do is earn some dough. And fast.' He took out his wallet to pay for his drinks.

'Leave it, Ronnie. This one's on me, honestly.'

'Cheers, Leo. You're a buddy.'

Leo leaned forward to give him another hug.

'Now you go get 'em, partner.'

*

At her home in Bel Air, Violet was curled up on a black leather sofa reading the latest Jackie Collins. She couldn't get enough of her favourite author – and one of the reasons she was such a fan was that Jackie didn't get caught up in soppy sentimentality. No, Jackie Collins was a tough broad who knew the way the real world worked. Just like Violet Vaughn.

She put the book down and wondered how Mia and Billy were getting on with their own little work of fiction. She looked at her watch and realized that by now they should be in the car on their way back to Mia's. She hoped they were putting on a convincing enough performance for the driver. He was a failed TV presenter-turned-crystal-meth-addict on whose desperation for money Violet had relied several times in the past. If Mia and Billy could convince him they were consumed by lust for each other, it would definitely end up in the papers.

And right now that's exactly where Violet needed it to end up. This morning she'd read a blog post in which a self-appointed Hollywood commentator had questioned just how serious Mia and Billy were about each other. Sure, it was only a blog, but she couldn't risk anyone smelling a rat now or her whole master plan might misfire. And then people might start questioning her position as one of the most powerful women in Hollywood – which was the *last* thing she wanted.

She felt a pang of loneliness and decided to mix herself a vodka and tonic. She went over to her private bar, filled a tall glass with ice and poured in the spirit. *Halfway up the glass? Three quarters?* The loneliness hit her with another sharp stab and she carried on tipping in vodka. *Oh well, it's mostly ice*

257

anyway. She filled the glass almost to the top and splashed in some tonic. There wasn't much point adding lime seeing as she was drinking alone.

Oh I hate that word – 'alone'.

Of course, she'd never admit that she was lonely to anyone else but she couldn't hide it from herself. She knocked back a huge swig and then topped up the glass with more vodka.

Violet settled back onto the sofa and checked her emails on her phone. She hadn't received any updates about tonight from the pap she'd planted in the restaurant – some straw-haired German guy who always smelt of unwashed dick. She knew she could rely on him but was starting to question whether she could rely on Mia and Billy. The other day Mia's blabbermouth assistant had mentioned something about her having a boyfriend and Violet had wondered whether this was why Mia had been so reticent about the show-mance in the first place.

Well, Mia's love-life isn't my *problem*, she thought. And she could hardly be expected to feel sorry for her just because she'd found herself a nice man. She tried not to feel jealous and downed almost half her glass of vodka.

In Violet's experience women like Mia had it easy. She'd be willing to bet that Mia hadn't had to work half as hard as she had to get where she was today. No, everyone loved Mia and she was so beautiful people fell over themselves to do any-thing she wanted. Violet certainly didn't buy all that crap about the tough childhood with a single mother in Cleveland. *Tough? She doesn't know the meaning of the word . . .*

Violet could just imagine Mia at high school, the kind of girl all the boys wanted to go out with. The kind of girl who called her Vile Violet and made her life hell. She picked up her glass and drained it of vodka.

Well she wasn't going to let any of that get to her tonight. Right now, she couldn't care less about Mia Sinclair. All she cared about was that she was doing as she was told. And to hell with her boyfriend.

She opened up her Jackie and plunged back in.

*

Billy leaned into Mia and ran his hand along her side.

'Are the paps following us?' she whispered in his ear.

He looked over her shoulder and through the back window of the limo, which wasn't blacked out so that the paps could see in. 'Yeah, stop panicking,' he said.

'I'm not panicking – I just don't want to go to all this trouble if no one's going to pap us.'

He moved back to mime a look of outrage. 'Well I'm sorry to put you to so much trouble, Mia. And anyway, this is harder for me than it is for you.'

'Oh stop being so sensitive – you know what I mean. Now come on, aren't you supposed to be ravaging me?'

Billy moved back in and kissed her passionately. The experience wasn't unpleasant but it did nothing for him sexually. He'd heard fellow actors talk about how they struggled to stop themselves becoming too aroused when they were filming sex scenes. Obviously this wasn't something that had ever troubled him and it wasn't bothering him now – not remotely.

Through the window several cameras flashed at him and he felt almost blinded by one particular explosion. He closed his eyes and thought about Ryan Reynolds.

'I hope you're not thinking about Ryan Reynolds,' Mia whispered mischievously.

Her comment threw him off course. 'Erm, yeah, I was actually.'

'Oh Billy! Can't I be Justin Timberlake? Or at least Jake Gyllenhaal?'

'Sssh,' he hissed, motioning to the driver. 'He might be able to hear us.'

They both looked and saw that the driver, although a few yards away and separated by a glass partition, was keeping a close eye on them through his mirror.

'Well get on with it then,' Mia piped. 'Come on, I want to see an Oscar-worthy performance.'

Billy tutted loudly. With no director to guide him, he was finding this harder than he'd expected. He slipped his hand up Mia's inner thigh and began stroking it gently.

'God I'm totally starving,' she sighed. 'What I'd give for a blueberry muffin.'

'Mia! How am I supposed to concentrate when you're coming out with things like that?'

'Well it's true. That lousy meal didn't even touch the sides.'

Now he was starting to feel seriously flustered. If this was ever going to work then he was going to have to turn up the heat – and soon. He slipped his hand up Mia's back and began fumbling with her bra-strap. Again the flashbulbs exploded.

'Oh baby,' he ventured in a deep, manly voice, 'let me see those beautiful titties.'

'Billy!' she shrieked. 'What do you think I am? Some kind of slut?'

He threw his hands up in the air. This was impossible.

Just then the driver twisted his neck and opened the window between them. 'Everything OK back there?' he asked.

'Fine!' they both shrieked.

'My friend here's just getting a little carried away,' Mia croaked. 'But don't you worry, I've got him well and truly under control.'

'Well you'll be home real soon,' the driver promised, 'and then you can get as carried away as you like.'

Billy felt a wave of relief. He couldn't wait for this journey to be over.

*

For once, Ronnie arrived at Mia's house earlier than the rest of the paparazzi. He calculated that he didn't have much time to wait so quickly began setting up his camera.

He looked around for a good vantage point onto the action and remembered Leo's favourite hiding place in a tree overlooking the garden. When they'd first discovered it they'd both tried climbing it but while Leo had effortlessly scampered up and onto a branch overhanging Mia's driveway, Ronnie had only got a few feet up the tree before he tumbled to the ground, twisting his ankle in the process and ending up in the Emergency Room.

This time failure was not an option. This time Ronnie was going to scale the tree and nail the most amazing shot of the night. For too long now his career had been a joke to everyone who knew him. He was well aware of the fact that the other paps scoffed at him and said he was only in the game because he worked in partnership with Leo. Well he wasn't going to stand for it anymore. Now that he was about to become a dad, it was time to get serious. And tonight he was going to earn some serious money – whatever it took.

*

Mia and Billy's car swung into her driveway, leaving a crowd of paparazzi roaring their disapproval on the other side of the gates.

'Come back, Mia!'

'Don't go, Mia!'

'Let's have a picture, Mia!'

As the car came to a halt, she checked her make-up in a compact and re-applied her lipstick.

'Thanks very much,' she said to the driver.

'My pleasure ma'am,' he winked. 'You guys have a good night.'

'Oh we will,' grinned Billy. 'We sure will.'

As Mia stepped out of the car she could hear the familiar sound of cameras snapping all around her. And her driveway looked almost floodlit with the effect of the numerous flash-bulbs exploding simultaneously.

'Give her a kiss, Billy!'

'Go on, Billy!'

'Just a little one, Billy!'

Mia had no idea where the paps were hiding; they were probably shooting from over the walls or through gaps in the bushes. She only hoped at least one of them had a clear view of her bedroom window.

She took hold of Billy's hand and led him through the porch. Just as they were about to go inside she leaned over and gave him another kiss. *If we're doing this then we might as well do it properly*, she thought.

She opened the door, shuffled Billy in and then shut the door behind them.

'Thank God that's over with,' she moaned, slumping back to lean against the door.

'Thanks a lot!' joked Billy. 'And anyway, it isn't over yet.'

'Yeah but at least we can relax now it's just the two of us. That driver was watching us so closely I was convinced we were going to get busted.'

'Yeah, well there's no chance of that now. Shall we have a little drink? An interval after Act One?'

'No, let's go upstairs and get straight on to Act Two. Then we can close the curtains and really relax.'

'Come on then,' he said, holding out his hand. 'Let's give those boys their happy ending.'

*

Hiding in a cupboard under the stairs, Hector couldn't believe what he was hearing.

So Mia and Billy *weren't* seeing each other after all. The whole thing was a sham, probably to hype up the new film.

Well he'd been right to suspect that something was going on. And he'd been right to start digging for clues. He'd even been right to sneak into the house tonight, even though he'd felt at the time like he was crossing a line.

The whole thing was like the plot line from a romantic comedy and part of him was intoxicated and wanted to know what would happen next. But even though he was bristling with excitement at the idea of being in on such a big secret, he couldn't help feeling disappointed that he hadn't been let in on it in the first place. He knew that he was employed as Mia's assistant but he'd thought that they were friends too. *Hmpf!* he thought. *How wrong I was.*

Mia obviously just saw him as a hired help, a Cuban gofer who was good enough to pick up her dry cleaning but not to share her intimate secrets. And to think that he'd been convinced he was special, that he was living the Hollywood lifestyle with genuine movie stars as close personal friends. He realized now that all along he'd been kidding himself. He wasn't special at all; he was just the second-rate son of Cuban immigrants and that's what he'd always be. No wonder nobody loved him.

No, I am special, he told himself defiantly. *And if Mia won't let me in on her secrets, then I'll just have to find them out for myself.*

Filled with a new determination and self-belief, he opened the cupboard door and crept out.

*

High up in the tree, Ronnie felt battered and bruised from a rather ungraceful climb. But it didn't matter; he peered through the heavy foliage and realized he had an excellent view of Mia's bedroom. It was amazing what the extra incentive of impending parenthood could make him do. *Hmm*, he thought, *maybe I'm not so hopeless after all.*

He pointed his lens at the bedroom window at the very second the two of them appeared, fully clothed but acting as if they were in the deepest throes of passion. They kissed ardently and Mia began ripping off Billy's shirt. Knowing what he knew now, Ronnie could see right through their act. He was even sure he spotted them giggling to each other at one point. But what did he care? He told himself that looking at a set of stills in a newspaper or magazine, no reader would be able to spot them as fakes. No, there was no question – the pictures were pure dynamite. And he was the only pap who was nailing them.

As Billy turned towards him to close the curtains, Ronnie knew that the show was over. But it didn't matter; he told himself that in the last ten minutes he'd probably earned himself more money than he had all year. And into the bargain he'd have made Rosie proud of him for once.

Ker-ching! Ker-ching!

*

'If we've just had sex,' smiled Billy, stretching out on Mia's huge bed, 'isn't this when I'm supposed to roll over and fart?'

Mia elbowed him in the ribs. 'I wouldn't recommend it, otherwise you'll find yourself on the floor.'

She picked up a pillow and threatened to throw it at him.

'So what *do* we do now?' he asked, raising his hand to protect himself. 'I'm just not sleepy yet.'

'Well, we could watch a DVD. There's a whole stack of them over there.'

Billy went over to a bedside table and began looking through a collection of classic black and white romances. '*Some Like it Hot*? *Bringing Up Baby*?' He jumped back onto the bed and handed her a copy of *Casablanca*. 'What do you reckon to this?'

Mia sat gazing at the cast photo on the cover of the DVD. She looked towards the window wistfully.

'Is something the matter?' Billy asked.

'Oh I don't know. It's nothing really.'

'No come on, what's bothering you?'

'Well it might seem a little morbid but I was just looking at this movie and thinking that everyone in it's got to be dead now. You know, so what was the point?'

'I'm not sure I understand.'

'Well it's just that, you know, we always thought this was what it was all about.' She pointed to the cover image on the DVD. 'But sometimes I wonder if we've been concentrating too much on our careers and sacrificing too much of the good stuff in life, the stuff that's really important. Because one day we'll be dead too and what will any of this matter then?' She held up the DVD and dropped it onto the bed.

'So is this what happens when you've had sex?' Billy joked. 'You start getting all philosophical?'

'Seriously, Billy. Quit horsing around for just one second and think about it. You know, when I look back at the last few years of my life, I'm not sure I was ever really happy. Not really, truly, deeply happy. And it's only recently that I've *learned* how to be happy. And now that I've experienced happiness, I don't want to go back to the way things were before.'

Billy sat in silence, thinking it over. 'So I take it you're talking about falling in love?'

'I guess I am, yeah. And love is too serious and too special and too big a part of who I am to play around with it like this. I mean, just what are we doing here, Billy? You in the closet and me pretending to be your girlfriend? It's crazy.'

'Well let's stop the show-mance – let's just call it off. We've given Violet what she wants now. Those pictures will be in all the papers soon and the premiere will be huge. We'll just have to tell her that once we've walked down that red carpet we're done. And if we're both united on this then there's nothing she can do about it.'

'If you're absolutely sure then yeah, let's do it.' She took a deep breath before she went on. 'But I also think you should come out, Billy. Or at least start working out *when* you can come out . . . Because take it from me – a life without love isn't really a life at all.'

'But there are different kinds of love, Mia. You love me, my fans love me . . . And how do I know that if I came out there wouldn't be *less* love in my life?'

'Trust me, Billy. Nothing compares to being loved for who you really are – romantically, sexually, spiritually, in every way possible. And lying about such a big part of who you are just isn't good for the soul.'

There was a long pause while Billy thought this over. 'You're right, Mia. And I guess I know most of this already. You know, there's not a day goes by when I don't wish I could be out. Believe me, there's nothing I'd like more. But how could I possibly do it after all the lies I've told? How can I expect people to love me when telling them I'm gay also means telling them I've been a fraud for the last seven years? A low-down dirty liar.'

'But if you explained *why* you lied then I'm sure people would understand.'

'Maybe. But it's way too risky. Sure, it's something I have to deal with and something I *want* to deal with too. I just can't deal with it right now, that's all. I'm too frightened, Mia.'

'Come here, Billy. I do love you, you know.'
She held out her arms and hugged him tightly.
'My big, gay Billy.'

*

Now Hector *really* couldn't believe what he was hearing.

Standing on the other side of the bedroom door, he wanted to jump up and down with excitement. This was the biggest secret in Hollywood and he was one of the few people who knew it. Maybe he *was* special after all.

So Billy Spencer's gay . . . However much Hector thought about it, he still couldn't get his head round it. It just didn't seem real.

Hector had always thought his gaydar was infallible but it had clearly made a huge mistake with Billy. He hadn't for one minute suspected that he was gay. But now that he knew, Billy's relationship with Mia made perfect sense. And so did the fact that Billy always claimed to be too busy to have a girl-friend. Not to mention his awkwardness around Hector.

No, the more Hector thought about his discovery, the more he realized how significant it was. Knowing that Billy was gay changed everything. Absolutely everything.

*

At home in Venice, Leo was lying in bed with an even-more-gassy-than-usual Watford. As he tickled his stomach, all he could think about was what Mia was doing right then.

Is she posing for pictures with Billy?
Is she stroking his chest while the paps snap away?
Are the paps standing around talking about her like a piece of

meat, joking about how much they'd *like to spend the night with her?*

As his mind swirled his heart raced faster and faster. He was so worked up he thought he was going insane. It was as if all the anger and frustration had worked its way into his bloodstream and was contaminating his entire body. And no matter how much he tried, he just couldn't shake it off.

There was no chance he'd be able to get to sleep tonight, and then tomorrow he'd have a long wait till the pictures finally made the papers. He knew that they'd be hot property and no pap or photo agency worth their salt would let them surface on the internet until they'd done lucrative deals with papers around the world first.

Oh it was all so hideous. There was a tight knot of what felt like intense physical pain twisting and twisting inside him. He was utterly broken.

Yeah, he loved Mia – he was totally head-over-heels in love with her. But if this was the reality of being in love with her, then he wasn't sure he could do it anymore.

12

Leo felt terrible. He'd hardly slept all night, tossing and turning, obsessing over Mia. When he'd finally given up on sleep and crawled out of bed, he'd had to drink so much coffee to jolt him awake that he now felt shaky with anxiety.

To try and take his mind off things he'd taken Watford to a dog groomer's in the centre of Venice called Doggy Style. He'd needed to have his coat cleaned and his claws clipped for a while now but Leo had been putting it off in order to spend more time with Mia. Now that she was spending some time with Billy, he had the perfect opportunity to get it out of the way.

All around him in the waiting room, dogs were sniffing each other up, play-fighting and seeing which of them could bark the loudest. The relentless noise was starting to give Leo a headache. To his left a randy sausage dog tried to mount an Alsatian while its uninterested owner flicked through a magazine. On the cover was yet another photo of Mia and Billy.

This was like torture. Wherever he went, Leo couldn't escape the nightmare of Mia's show-mance and whatever he did, he couldn't stop the feelings from burning away inside him. At least the photo in this magazine was a relatively harmless one taken the previous week. But he knew that very soon the pictures of last night's clinch would hit the newsstands. And then things would get a whole lot worse.

According to the romantic films Leo remembered his sisters watching while he'd been growing up, love was supposed to be a beautiful experience, not one that made him feel a whole range of painful emotions – from dread to anger, from anguish to desolation – all at an intensity he hadn't known was even possible.

Well he couldn't take it anymore. He had to go and see Mia and tell her how he was feeling. If this was the reality of being in love with her, then he *definitely* couldn't deal with it anymore.

*

Mia strolled around the house, fluffing up cushions and re-arranging flowers. Now that Billy had left she was at a loose end and, as it was a Sunday, Hector wasn't due in to work until the next day. The house felt unusually quiet and she decided to make the most of the rare moment of calm.

She picked up Bogie and Bacall and took them into the garden, where she sat on a chair in the shade. Both cats snuggled into comfortable positions on her knee and she began stroking them under their chins and behind their ears. As she listened to them purr she felt a pleasing sense of serenity. She knew that she and Billy had made the right decision in calling time on the show-mance. It felt like a huge burden had been lifted from her shoulders and she couldn't wait to tell Leo.

But first she needed to speak to Serena, to double check that she was doing the right thing and to work out a strategy for breaking the news to Violet. She picked up her phone and dialled the number.

'Hey, sister,' Serena answered. 'How did it go?'

'Oh it was all fine thanks. Everything went according to plan.'

'And do you feel OK about it?'

'Well I didn't particularly enjoy it to be honest. And neither did Billy. But we kind of got talking afterwards and decided that that's it – once we've gone to the premiere together we're through with this show-mance.'

'Really?'

'Yeah.'

'Well in that case I think you've made the right decision. Sure, it's worked and the press have gone ballistic over it. But, you know, you've done the important part now – enough already.'

Mia nodded and bit her lip. 'The only problem is, how do we tell Violet? I know I said I wanted to handle her on my own but now that this is happening I might need your help.'

'Well I'm right with you, sister.'

'Thanks, Serena. I really appreciate it.'

'The only thing is, I think it's better to wait till tomorrow morning. By then the pictures will be in all the papers. If we're lucky we might even get some first editions and internationals tonight. Which means that by the morning Violet will have had her big climax and be basking in the glory. She won't have a leg to stand on if she wants to bully you into carrying on. And if she does, she'll have me to contend with.'

'OK, well, if you're sure that's the right thing.'

'One hundred per cent sure. I'll call her people now to fix

up a meeting. And I'll get Billy and his agent there too. Safety in numbers and all that.'

'Great, thanks Serena.'

'No problem, it's my job. I'm on it already.'

With that she rang off.

Mia was overjoyed. She cradled the cats in her arms and began looking forward to a life without deceit and duplicity – a life shared with Leo, the man she loved. *And who knows?* she thought, *the next time I have a premiere, maybe I'll be able to walk down the red carpet with him.* She knew now that there was nothing she wanted more.

She put down the cats and picked up the phone. Now that she'd spoken to Serena, she could break the news to Leo.

As she dialled his number a smile spread across her face.

*

Leo pulled up outside Mia's house and buzzed the intercom. There were a few paps hanging around but no one he knew. He kept his helmet on just in case and hoped that none of them recognized his number plates or the little sticker of the British flag on the back of his bike. It was a bit sloppy but he was past caring. And anyway, he was here to tell Mia that he was sick of hiding away and couldn't hide anymore.

As he waited for an answer he saw he had one missed call on his phone – it was from Mia. *Never mind*, he thought. *Whatever she wants to say she can say to me in person.*

After a long pause, her voice sounded on the intercom. 'Hello?'

'Hi Mia, it's me.'

'Leo! Come right in!'

There was a loud buzzing sound and the gates swung open.

He rode his bike up to the porch, his heart beating so fiercely he could see it through his shirt. *Keep calm*, he told himself. *Don't get worked up and start an argument. If you stay relaxed it'll be much easier to tell her how you feel.*

When he reached the front door, Mia ushered him inside. 'Quick,' she said, 'before anyone sees you.'

'That's it,' he blurted out, 'hide me away like a dirty secret.'

'I'm sorry?'

'You know, God forbid any paps should think we're having a relationship or anything.'

Uh-oh, he thought. *Looks like I've lost my cool already.*

'Leo?' Mia frowned. 'Is something the matter?'

He took off his helmet but didn't kiss her.

'Nothing's the matter. I just think there's some stuff we need to sort out, that's all.'

'Well I'm glad you're here because there's something I want to tell you.'

He held up his hand. 'No offence, Mia, but if it's about Billy, I don't want to hear it.'

'Well it is but—'

'Seriously, Mia. Do me a favour and keep it to yourself. You've no idea how hard this whole show-mance has been for me.'

At that moment the expression on her face changed. 'For you? How hard this has been for *you*?'

'Yeah. Sitting at home knowing you're fooling around with another man, having to listen to total strangers talking about you and Billy like it's some kind of fairytale romance.'

'Oh and I suppose you think I've been enjoying the whole thing, do you?'

'Well what am I supposed to think? You agreed to the showmance. If it bothered you that much, you could have always said no.'

'But I thought I explained to you why I agreed. Violet convinced me that I had to do it to publicize the film. And anyway, me and Billy were talking last night and—'

'I told you already, Mia. I don't want to hear what you and Billy were talking about.'

She folded her arms and glared at him across the hall. 'Can I even get a word in edgeways here?'

'You know, what really gets me,' Leo steamed on, 'is how much grief you gave me about being a paparazzo in the first place. That whole sob story about how us paps make things so difficult for you because you can never switch off and be yourself. Well it wasn't the paps who dreamt up this showmance, Mia.'

'No but Violet would never have had the idea if you hadn't taken those photos of me and Billy messing about on set. So you're just as guilty as I am. If you hadn't papped me that day then we wouldn't be in this mess now.'

'But we were only shooting what was happening anyway. Documenting reality, which is what paps are supposed to do. Revealing the truth behind the gloss that you guys show us. Not playing along with stupid fake fairytales.'

'Hmpf! You think you're so superior. But you basically invented this fairytale in the first place. Those pictures were set up to give the impression that me and Billy were together and *that's* how the rumours started. That's how the whole thing built up momentum – from a lie *you* told, not me.'

Leo was seething. She was blatantly a willing participant in the show-mance and now she was trying to blame it all on him. He couldn't believe what he was hearing. And to think that he'd even considered changing careers for her. At least he'd kept that quiet and hadn't mentioned it to her – he certainly wasn't going to mention it now.

'And while we're on the subject,' she thundered on, 'I don't know why you've got it into your head that the paparazzi are some kind of crusaders for honesty. Because that's baloney. There are plenty of paps who've played along with show-mances in the past.'

'Well not this pap,' he fumed. 'This pap has integrity.'

She snorted. 'Don't make me laugh. A pap with integrity? There's no such thing, Leo, and you know it. Are you seriously telling me you've never gone along to shoot some set-up that you've known has been fake . . . ?'

She had him stumped and he didn't know how to reply. The problem was that he understood the points she was making but none of them made him feel any better. Still the jealousy, anger and humiliation raged inside him. And after everything he'd said, it was too late to back down.

'And who's acting superior now?' he rallied. 'You know, the way you celebrities talk you'd think you didn't need us paps. But we're your oxygen, Mia. Without us, how would you promote your films? Without us, how would you even exist?'

'Your arrogance is astounding, Leo. And to think I ever found you attractive.'

'Well your dishonesty astounds me, Mia. Just like every other star, you don't know when to stop acting. You don't even realize that by dreaming up this fake romance you're just as bad as all the other celebs in town. All the Destiny Diaments or Shereen Spicers or Layla Lloyds. You've made a pact with the devil, Mia. From now on you're fair game – and there's no turning back.'

As he looked at her sad little face he realized how much he was hurting her. And it only made him hurt more. He loved her so much, more than he'd ever thought it was possible to love someone. All he wanted to do was gather her up in his arms, tell her he was sorry and that he really wanted to work things out. But he had to get this all off his chest or else he knew that it would gradually destroy him from the inside.

'Look at us,' he managed, a little calmer. 'We're right back where we started. Arguing about the same old stuff – you being a star and me being a pap. I don't know, maybe this whole thing is just too big for us to fight.'

'Is that what you think, Leo? Is that what you honestly think?'

'I don't know, Mia. Maybe these issues will always be there, yeah. Maybe we were stupid to ever think we could work this out. But I just can't handle dishonesty, Mia. And I can't live a lie.'

They stood looking at each other in silence. Leo wanted to reach out and touch her but it was almost as if he'd lost all power over his own body. However hard he tried, he just couldn't bring himself to do it. Instead, he put on his helmet and reached for the door handle.

'I just need some time to think, Mia. To work out what to do for the best.'

'OK,' she managed.

He could see her bottom lip trembling and knew that she was about to cry. He couldn't bear to see her suffer. He quickly opened the door.

'I'll see you soon,' he said.

'Yeah. See you soon.'

As he plodded down the steps, from inside the house he could hear Mia crying.

*

Mia cried so much she felt physically exhausted. She couldn't remember crying so much since her mom had died. Or since her dad had left home when she was nine and she'd first had her heart broken.

As she replayed the confrontation with Leo over and over in her head, the whole thing started to feel unreal. She'd no idea how things had blown up into a full-scale argument so quickly or how the two of them had blurted out such hurtful things at each other. How had it all gone so wrong? And to think that she'd been looking forward to seeing Leo so she could tell him she was ending the show-mance.

As she gradually came round she realized she was sitting in a crumpled heap leaning against the back of the door. Slowly she picked herself up and straightened herself out. But as she stood up she was immediately hit by an overwhelming pang of hunger. There was no denying it – she was ravenous. She had to eat something and fast.

No sooner had the thought entered her head than she was being powered along to the kitchen by a force far stronger than herself. As soon as she got there the enormous fridge drew her towards it like a magnet while the adrenaline raced around her body. In just a few short minutes she'd turned into a woman possessed, possessed by a desperate need for a binge.

As she flung open the fridge door, almost breaking it off its hinges, her heart sank. She saw that it was crammed full of boring, healthy food. Everywhere she looked she saw celery, carrots, tofu and juices. *Boring, boring, boring!* She was devastated and sank to the floor in defeat.

Just then she remembered that she'd asked Hector to arrange for a huge box of Ramona's favourite chocolates to be flown over from Mexico for her birthday. There was a particular brand she was crazy about; Mia couldn't remember the name but she could remember ogling Ramona once as she'd devoured some in the kitchen and whinnied with delight. Her birthday wasn't for a week or so but Hector was so organized Mia was sure he'd have got hold of the chocolates already – and stashed them somewhere in his office.

She raced through the house, banging into furniture, knocking over a vase of flowers and almost stepping on one of the cats. She crashed into the office and yanked open Hector's top drawer with such force that she pulled it free of the desk. Aftershave, condoms, packet after packet of chewing gum – but no chocolates.

She riffled through the other drawers and tipped everything onto the floor – still nothing. She went through piles of papers on the desk, tossing documents into the air. Magazines, photos of Hector's family, some kind of inflatable rubber ball that could have been either a stress buster or a sex toy. *But where are the damn chocolates?*

Her need to eat chocolate was by now so desperate she thought she was going to explode. She wondered if it had driven her temporarily insane. She felt so wired that it wouldn't have surprised her if her hair was standing on end. Whatever was going on, if she didn't find the chocolate soon she was going to be in serious trouble.

She thrust her hands into the trash can and began rooting around for something to satisfy her craving. A discarded candy bar, an old boiled sweet – anything would do. But all she found were snotty tissues, used dental floss and a clump of what looked like pubic hair.

She resisted the urge to scream out loud in hopeless frustration. But out of her mouth escaped a desperate, primal growl. She could feel the tears welling up again as she dropped to the floor in the middle of a room that now looked like some kind of war zone. Her nerves were frazzled and her spirit shattered.

Just then she spotted a plastic bag hanging on the back of the door with some words written on it in Spanish. She leapt up and ripped it off the hook. Inside she found a huge box of Mexican chocolates.

Oh my God, oh my God, oh my God!

She began tearing at the cellophane but couldn't get it off. Her heart was pounding and her hands were white and shaking. Her nails slid over the wrapping but couldn't rip into it. She didn't think she could bear it much longer.

Oh my God, oh my God, oh my God!

In went a nail and off came the wrapping.

She tore off the lid and grabbed a fistful of chocolates. As she thrust them into her mouth she couldn't help groaning out loud. They tasted *amazing*.

As soon as she'd swallowed the first mouthful she thrust

in more. And then more and then more. Within minutes she was on such an intense high she couldn't think straight. *What is it that I got upset about in the first place?* She remembered her bust-up with Leo and shovelled in more chocolates.

Pretty soon she'd worked her way through half the huge box. Of course she couldn't give Ramona a half-full box of chocolates for her birthday so she decided she might as well finish them. Hector would have plenty of time to order more.

As the delicious cream-filled milk chocolate slid down her throat, she thought back to the very first time she'd had a food binge. She'd been nine years old and her dad had just left home. To try and cheer up her distraught mom, Mia had saved up her pocket money and bought her a big box of her favourite chocolates. The two of them had sat on the sofa and gorged on them together, instantly feeling better. And as they did so, Mia had felt closer to her mom than she ever had done. The experience had been so comforting that the two of them had soon begun regular binges – and Mia had struggled to break her addiction ever since.

Her soul plummeted with grief as she realized just how much she missed her mom. Her head might have been buzzing from the sugar rush but her whole body felt like a dead weight.

What would Mom think about my argument with Leo?

Would she tell me I've been stupid to fall for him?

Would she think I've let her down?

Her chin began to wobble and she crammed in more chocolates.

As she worked the gorgeous gooey mixture around her mouth, two big tears trickled down her cheeks.

Then she surprised herself with a feeling she hadn't

experienced since she was a young girl. She realized that she also missed her dad. And it hit her in the heart with a heavy thud. Her whole body began shaking with grief and the tears flowed freely.

All the feelings of sadness, anger and abandonment that had collided in her as a child came rushing back and swirled around her head. But despite the pain, she found herself wishing her Dad was with her now. Whenever she'd been upset as a child he'd caught her tears and taken them out into the garden to give to the rosebush. He always said that even when she cried she was his special girl – and that her tears would make the roses even more beautiful.

As she thought back to his words now her face twisted into a warped, melting mess. The last thing she felt was beautiful.

Her dad had broken her heart all those years ago and now Leo was breaking it all over again. And she was staggered by how much it hurt.

She reached for the last of the chocolates and thrust them into her mouth.

*

Blasting down the PCH, Leo revved up his motorbike and glanced at the speedometer. He knew that he was already way over the limit but all he wanted to do was ride faster and faster.

He was so angry about what had happened – angry at himself for hurting Mia, angry at Mia for hurting him and angry at the world for hurting them both. The injustice of it all set off a combustive reaction inside him. If they both loved each other then why did it have to be so difficult? It was just so unfair.

He twisted the handlebar and shot forward. But even through his haze of anger he could tell that however fast he went he wouldn't be able to escape his feelings. And right now he was feeling none of the joy he usually experienced when burning along on his bike. On the contrary; it was only making him more miserable.

Just then he was struck by a feeling that surprised him. For the first time since arriving in LA he felt homesick. And it was so unexpected that he didn't know how to react.

Oh what am I doing here? he thought. *Am I just kidding myself that this is where I belong? Or have I been pretending the whole time – pretending to be someone I'm not?*

He remembered that he'd accused Mia of acting all the time and wondered if he was guilty of the same thing. Had he been trying to live out his own fake fairytale by re-inventing himself here in LA? And if so, who was the real Leo Henderson?

He slowed down as he thought back to his home in sub-urban England and the family he'd left behind. All right, it might not have been the most exciting set-up in the world but they were good people and they loved him. All this time had he been trying to escape them? Had he spent the last five years riding away from who he was?

He turned off the road at the next exit and pulled over by a strip of scrubland. He felt awash with gloom. But all of a sudden he had an idea about how to lift it.

*

The doorbell rang, jolting Mia back to reality. She emerged from her daze and realized that she was lying on the office floor surrounded by debris and a huge, empty box of choco-lates. She sat up and felt like she was going to be sick.

The doorbell rang again and she remembered that Cole was coming round for her final workout before the premiere the next day. *Shit, shit, shit!* This was the last thing she needed. And it was the last thing she wanted after everything Leo had said to her about sacrificing too much for her career.

She stood up and pulled the office door closed guiltily. She couldn't possibly let Cole witness the undignified aftermath of her frenzied meltdown. She buzzed him through the gates and quickly checked herself in the mirror. She looked terrible. She wiped a smear of chocolate from her chin and did her best to brighten her eyes.

'Hey, girlfriend!'

Cole was wearing pink spangly hot pants and skipped into the house with a huge grin. It was obvious that he was in exactly the opposite mood to Mia. She felt her stomach lurch but did her best to fake a smile and kissed him on both cheeks.

'Are you OK, Mia?' he asked. 'You don't look too good.'

'Oh no, I'm fine,' she struggled, failing to look him in the eye. 'It's just been one of those days, you know.'

As he led her through to the garden he began squeaking away excitedly about his hot new boyfriend. He explained that he'd now been dating someone for a month but last night they'd told each other they were in love and finally ready to go public. Cole's new man was outrageous comedian turned actor Scott Lamont, who Mia had last seen at Cooper Kelly's birthday party. She remembered Billy saying something about Scott being snide and sniffy around him, probably because he suspected he was gay. But the way Cole was talking about him now, he didn't sound remotely snide or sniffy; he sounded like the perfect man and Cole's absolute soulmate. Just as Leo had seemed to her. She felt overwhelmed by a surge of melancholy.

'Honestly, girlfriend,' he gushed, 'I think he's The One. I've never felt like this about anyone before. But when you know – *you just know.*'

'That's so brilliant, Cole,' Mia managed.

'Isn't it? And isn't it fabulous that me and you have got ourselves hot new men at the same time?'

She looked at him, puzzled. How could he know about Leo?

'You know,' he bounced on, 'you've got Billy and I've got Scott.' He flung his arms around her and gave her a hug. 'Oh I'm so happy, Mia – for both of us!'

Mia smiled thinly. Her stomach gurgled and she hoped he hadn't heard it. At some point she knew she was going to throw up.

'Are you sure you're OK, Mia?'

'Yeah,' she croaked. 'I guess I'm just a bit nervous about the premiere tomorrow.'

As soon as she'd said it Cole began bouncing on the spot. 'Well it's a good job I'm here then, isn't it?'

Again she smiled feebly.

'Come on, girlfriend – let's kick some ass!'

He bounded over to the sound system and put on a Lady Gaga dance remix at full blast.

Mia felt her stomach spasm and knew she couldn't put it off any longer.

'I'm sorry Cole, I—'

She ran to the bathroom and flung the door closed behind her.

Without a moment to lose she heaved the contents of her stomach into the toilet. She'd forgotten how much it hurt to vomit and was taken aback by the physical pain. It wasn't helped by the emotional turmoil raging inside her. She felt utterly wretched.

She heaved and heaved and wondered how on earth she'd ended up here, crouched over a toilet bowl hurling up the contents of a mammoth chocolate binge while Lady Gaga played at full volume outside. None of it seemed real; it was as if it wasn't happening to her. Except it was.

Oh how did everything go so wrong?

As she thought back once again to her bust-up with Leo, she couldn't help feeling angry and frustrated. The more she thought about it, the more she realized that both of them wanted the same thing: to go public with their relationship and openly celebrate the way they felt about each other. But for some reason all their feelings had come out wrong. And now she felt stunned by what had happened. Had she just gone and lost Leo?

Was this it? Had she just been dumped?

*

'On my head, son!'

Standing on the sidelines Leo couldn't help smiling. He was at a sports field watching the British Bulldogs in training.

'Pass it here, mate!'

'Good ball!'

The Bulldogs were an amateur soccer team made up of expats who played in the Santa Monica Sunday League. They weren't the most athletic group of men Leo had ever seen but they were all getting stuck in – and obviously really enjoying themselves.

'What a beauty!' boomed one as he scored a goal.

'Get in!' cheered his team-mates.

So much of what Leo was witnessing reminded him of home. The sound of the ball hitting the players' shoes, the occasional whistle of the referee, and the Digestive biscuits and Walkers cheese and onion crisps that were laid out on a table ready for half-time. Admittedly, the team were playing on Astroturf rather than grass so weren't wearing football boots but trainers, or sneakers as Americans call them. And, of course, rather than the dull grey skies Leo remembered from his childhood in Watford, the pitch here in LA was illuminated by the glow of yet another sun-drenched day. But none of this mattered to Leo – it was the perfect cure for his homesickness.

One of the players passed a ball to his team-mate, who then left hooked it into the net.

'*Goal!*'

Leo grinned as his mind jumped back to his childhood. On the pitch he saw himself playing while his dad stood loyally on the sidelines cheering him on. Every Sunday his dad had taken him to football – as well as training sessions after school during the week. It must have been a real bind for him but he never grumbled and always beamed with pride whenever Leo scored a goal. Leo had loved making his dad happy. He felt a stray rumble of homesickness.

'All right, kid? How do?'

He was interrupted by the Yorkshire twang of a middle-aged man who introduced himself as Tomo, the team manager.

He looked uncannily like Rod Hull and had hair like the wire wool Leo's mum used to clean pans with. He stepped forward to shake Leo's hand.

'Fancy a kick-about?'

Leo frowned. 'Erm, I'm not sure really, I just thought I'd come and have a look to be honest.'

'Well you're very welcome. We could always do with more lads in the squad.'

'Oh thanks but I think I'll just watch for a bit if that's OK. It's been one of those days.'

Tomo nodded with a smile. 'All right, kid. Well, you know where we are if you change your mind.'

'Cheers, mate. Thanks.'

As he trotted off, Leo wondered why he was so reluctant to join in. He'd come ready for action, dressed in shorts and T-shirt – a Watford FC strip his dad had sent him for one of his birthdays but which he'd tossed into a bottom drawer and almost forgotten about. When he was little the two of them had watched their local team play every weekend; father and son wrapped up in scarves and hats in their team colours, cheering and chanting from the stands and sneaking in a cheeky pie at half-time. Leo had loved it. So why had he been running away from it ever since?

OK, so life in the English suburbs wasn't as exciting as the glamour of Hollywood. But however he felt about it, it would always be part of him. Right now, he felt guilty for having put so much distance between his present and his past – his new life in LA and his old life in England. And if he had spent the last five years riding away from Watford then he wasn't sure why.

He'd always told himself that his parents' lives were too gentle for him, that settling down in the suburbs would be uninspiring and mediocre and that he was looking for more excitement and intensity in his life. But now that he thought about it, he wasn't sure whether he'd done the right thing after all. With Mia he thought he'd found everything he'd been looking for. And he'd never felt such intense, overwhelming happiness. But now he was questioning whether he'd imagined himself to be so happy – and whether the two of them had been acting their way through just another fairytale in a city that was built on imitation and pretence.

He began stretching his legs and warming up his calf muscles.

Life in Watford might not be too exciting, he thought, *but at least it's real.*

He clapped his hands and jogged onto the pitch.

*

It was late at night and Serena was exhausted. That afternoon she'd endured another long dutiful lunch with Mitchell's hyper-intellectual parents, which had left her feeling typically out of her depth and down on herself. She'd then spent most of the evening on the phone to a distraught Mia, consoling her about her showdown with Leo and trying to make her feel less bad about bingeing her way through it. If only that were all she had to worry about . . .

Right now, Serena was about to add to Mia's problems with some far worse news. And the news was so bad that she couldn't break it to her over the phone. Despite the fact that it was so late, Serena was in her car on her way to see Mia in person.

She'd texted her to say that she was coming over so that when she arrived Mia was waiting and buzzed her straight in.

Serena hated to be the bearer of bad news and as she walked up the steps to her front porch she felt sick to the stomach.

In her hand she carried a stack of papers from the US and around the world.

In her heart she carried the full weight of the news she was about to break.

Mia smiled nervously as she answered the door. 'Hi, Serena.'

She looked horrendous.

'Hey, sister.'

Serena kissed her on both cheeks.

Mia let out a long sigh.. 'So come on, what is it?'

'Look, I'm not going to bullshit you. It's bad – real bad.'

Serena walked straight through to the lounge and Mia scuttled after her. Onto the coffee table she dropped the huge pile of papers.

Shouting out at the two friends was a cacophony of headlines, photos and stories, none of which came as much of a surprise. One headline labelled Mia the First Lady of Lust. Another paper had exclusive shots of her date with Billy taken inside the restaurant from just a few short feet away. And another still told the story of the driver who'd taken them home, who'd predictably revealed that the two of them had got so carried away in the back of his limo that they couldn't keep their hands to themselves.

'What's the problem?' Mia asked. 'Wasn't this all part of the plan?'

'Yes,' nodded Serena, 'but take a look at this one.'

As she pushed forward one last paper, Mia let out a gasp.

'BILLY SPENCER GAY,' it read in thick bold capitals. 'ROMANCE WITH MIA SINCLAIR A LIE.'

Serena watched as Mia's face dropped.

13

'Are you happy now, Violet?' Serena spat.

'No but I bet *you* are,' Violet snarled back. 'Any chance to get one over on me!'

This was all Mia needed: Serena and Violet tearing strips off each other. She was still struggling to get used to the fact that in the last twenty-four hours she might have lost the man she loved as well as finding herself in serious danger of losing her career and one of her closest friends. She hadn't slept a wink and couldn't imagine how it was possible to feel any worse.

'Look, can we all just try and calm down a little?' she chided.

'I'm perfectly calm,' shrieked Serena. 'It's that witch over there who needs to take a chill pill.'

'Huh!' fumed Violet. 'I wouldn't *need* to take a chill pill if you got your fat ass out of my office.'

Mia and Billy looked at each other and rolled their eyes.

That's at least something, she thought. *Billy doesn't seem to want to disown me.* She smiled at him and remembered that today's meeting in Violet's office had actually been arranged so that she and Billy could break the news that they were ending their show-mance straight after the premiere. Now somebody else had got in there and done it first. And they hadn't stopped at that.

'I think some of us are getting distracted here,' came a voice from the other side of the room. It was Billy's agent, James Sowerby. Mia and Billy called him James Sourpuss as he was constantly miserable and never smiled, always insisting on looking on the downside of everything. For once he had good reason to be pessimistic. He held up the newspaper with the explosive article. 'What I want to know is, who's behind this? Who's the "anonymous source"?'

Mia ran her hands through her hair. All she could think was that it must be Leo. What else was she supposed to think? He'd stormed out on her after giving her a lecture about honesty and hadn't been in touch since. It had to be him. And the more she thought about it, the more she felt sick from the betrayal. She just didn't understand how he could have done that to her.

She took a deep breath and waited until she had everyone's attention.

'I think I know who the source is,' she announced. 'And his name's Leo Henderson.'

*

Across town in Venice, Leo strolled the length of the canal as Watford padded along beside him.

He'd got out of bed late after another sleepless night, scrunching up his duvet with his fists as he struggled to process his feelings about Mia. Playing football might have taken his mind off things for a while but alone under the duvet he'd felt defeated by a sense of utter desolation. How was it possible to love someone so much but at the same time find the reality of a relationship with them so frustrating?

He couldn't face buying the morning papers as he already knew what the top story would be. And reading about Mia and Billy's supposed night of lust was the last thing he wanted right now. No, he'd try to avoid seeing the papers at all costs.

He turned off the canal and headed towards the sea front.

*

Billy sat in silence listening to Mia. He'd been awake all night and was now so exhausted he felt weirdly detached from what was going on, as if it was all happening to someone else. He tried to concentrate on what Mia was saying.

'It's all my fault and I'm really sorry,' she explained. 'I can see now that I was stupid and should have seen it coming. But if it's any consolation I don't think I've ever felt as terrible as I do right now. All I can say is I fell in love – and I guess I started thinking with my heart and not my head.'

'So let me get this straight,' James Sourpuss cut in. 'You told a paparazzo that Billy's gay and didn't expect him to blab?'

'Don't blame Mia,' piped Billy. 'It's as much my fault as it is hers. I met Leo and I might have been suspicious of him at first but I kind of grew to like him. So if he is some kind of conman then he conned me too.'

'How can you be so calm?' James spluttered at his client. 'Don't you understand what this means? You stand to lose *everything*, Billy. And if Mia had been more discreet you wouldn't be in this mess.'

'Excuse me,' thundered Serena, 'but Mia's in this mess too.

What do you think her fans are going to think now she's been branded a liar? It's not just Billy's career that's in trouble.'

Violet clapped her hands and stood up behind her desk.

'Time out everybody! Time out!'

She began pacing the room as she wrung her hands. 'It's way too early to start speculating on whose career may or may not be over. And our first duty is to a certain movie that has its premiere tonight.'

A hush descended on the room as everyone turned to listen.

'Now the producers have been on the phone all morning,' she went on, 'and they're understandably anxious that all this extra publicity won't cause their movie to tank. So what I suggest is that we get through today, save the movie and then start addressing the more long-term problems.'

Although he was starting to resent Violet more than ever, Billy had to admit that her approach did sound sensible. He might have spent all night gripped by a sickening terror of losing everything he'd worked for in life but right now the thing that frightened him most was that night's premiere – having to face the media and having to face the fans.

'You never know,' Violet crowed, 'things might not be as bad as you guys seem to think.'

'Man, how can you say that?' muttered Serena under her breath. 'Thanks to you things couldn't be much worse.'

Violet scowled at her and turned up her nose. 'Here's the plan,' she carried on. 'Just before the film's shown we have a live interview on the red carpet for *The Preston and Kerry Show*. Unusual, I know, but there was so much interest in you two being a real-life couple that the networks were lining up to nail your first TV interview.'

Billy couldn't resist smirking. 'Looks like they'll be getting more than they bargained for now.'

'Exactly,' Violet went on, 'which is why everyone will be watching. So if we can get it right then we can use the TV show to our advantage. And kick-start your rehabilitation.'

There was a long pause while everyone thought over Violet's proposal.

'I'll go along with whatever,' Mia mumbled. 'I can hardly complain after messing everything up with Leo.'

'I'm in too,' said Billy. 'The way things stand at the moment I've got nothing to lose.'

Serena didn't look convinced. 'But why should we go along with your plan, Violet? The last one backfired spectacularly.'

'That's just it,' grinned Violet. 'It hasn't backfired yet – the game still isn't over. And there might still be time to turn this shit into gold.'

*

Leo strode down Ocean Front Walk, breathing in deep gulps of fresh sea air.

All around him he spotted several of his favourite characters: the Texan tarot-reader with the badly dyed hair, the big-eared contortionist in his usual leopard-print thong, and the stoned tramp begging for money for yet more weed. Leo couldn't help smiling. However terrible he was feeling, life obviously went on. Maybe things weren't as bad as he'd been thinking after all.

He was just about to turn round and go home when a voice called at him from down the street. 'Hey, Limey,' it yelled. 'Have you seen today's papers?'

It was the tattooed bull dyke who worked in the news-agents.

'Nah, I'm trying to have a day off,' he smiled weakly. 'I'm a bit sick of celebs right now.'

'But seriously,' she gushed. 'You've got to see this.'

She strode over to him and slapped a paper into his hands.

'Billy Spencer's only gay! I mean, can you believe it?'

Leo tried to open his mouth but nothing came out.

Things were far worse than he'd been thinking.

*

At his home high in the Hollywood Hills, Billy was taking his third shower of the day. He had just an hour before a squadron of stylists was due to arrive to start getting him ready for the big premiere. He stood under the main showerhead and let a deluge of water fall onto him.

He couldn't believe that today was actually happening. It was all quite eerily unreal. For years now he'd wondered how he'd feel if he were suddenly outed. Well now he knew.

And the answer was that he felt exposed and vulnerable. He felt sick and shaken. And he felt so anxious that he could almost hear the anxiety ringing in his ears – even with the jets of water gushing around him. He'd already given himself a shot of Vitamin B12, something he hated doing as he was squeamish about needles. But his doctor recommended it for fatigue or nervous exhaustion and most other stars he knew did it. Unfortunately though, on this occasion it hadn't made any difference and he still felt just as terrible. He looked at his hands and saw that they were shaking.

Weirdly though he was surprised to discover that he also

felt a sense of relief. Although he'd dreaded this day for so long, he also understood on some level that it had had to happen at some point. And now that it finally had, the anticipation at least had disappeared. He couldn't help wondering if, once things had settled down, that anticipation might turn out to be worse than the reality. There was a chink of hope and he did his best to hold onto it.

But first he had to get through tonight. And that wasn't going to be easy. In fact, whichever way he looked at it, it was going to be the most important night of his life.

He reached for the shower and turned it off.

*

Leo was sitting on a bench next to the beach, staring at the article in front of him. There were several pictures of Mia and Billy, some of them taken in the restaurant and a few from outside the house but most of them were taken in front of her bedroom window. All the time he'd been stressing out about how he'd feel when he saw the pictures. But now that he was looking at them it was the story that made the most impact.

'BILLY SPENCER GAY,' read the headline. 'ROMANCE WITH MIA SINCLAIR A LIE.'

At that moment his feelings of anger and frustration vanished. Everything felt insignificant compared to the consequences of the article in front of him. He bitterly regretted everything he'd said to Mia at her house yesterday and was utterly floored by the realization of just how much he loved her. Nothing else mattered. Nothing. And he could only imagine what she was going through right now.

He picked up his phone and dialled her number.

As the phone rang, it occurred to him that after everything he'd said to her yesterday, she might well think *he* was the anonymous source quoted in the article.

She couldn't, could she . . . ?

He felt his mouth go dry as he replayed in his head some of his big pronouncements about honesty and integrity. And as he listened to the phone ring the goose bumps raced up his arm.

There was no answer.

He tried again but still she didn't pick up.

In desperation he turned back to the paper. Whoever had taken the pictures at the bedroom window, he had to admit that they were good, clear images. *Wait a minute . . .*

He examined the angle from which they'd been taken and realized they'd been shot from his secret tree. There was only one other person who knew about that tree. And that person was Ronnie.

Ronnie also knew that the romance was fake – and that Billy was gay. *But surely he wouldn't have . . . ?*

He stood up and gave a tug on Watford's lead.

'Come on, mate,' he said. 'It's time to stop moping. It's time for some action.'

*

Mia watched the clear liquid run down the tube and into her arm.

She tried to zone out of what she was doing and pretend that it wasn't happening. She looked up at the tiled white ceiling, found a sprinkler valve and stared at it until everything else went out of focus.

She hadn't eaten since she'd thrown up yesterday after-noon. She'd read once that it took fatty food only three hours to convert itself into flab on the body and, convinced she could feel her post-binge stomach straining at her jeans, she'd decided to starve herself. She'd just about made it through this morning's meeting but as everyone was leaving she'd stumbled in the foyer and nearly fainted. Serena had already gone so Violet had stepped in and offered to help. And, as usual, Violet had known just what to do.

Of course with her face all over the front page of the papers, Mia was being pursued by more paps than ever before and Violet's building was practically under siege. To get past them all she'd had to lie under a blanket that smelled of wet dog on the back seat of the janitor's battered old truck. It was all so undignified and made her feel utterly ashamed of herself – and ashamed of how she'd managed to blow up in the air everything she'd worked so hard for.

Now she found herself lying in a clinic wired up to an intra-venous drip. Even though she didn't want to, she couldn't help looking again at the plastic tube going into her arm. She stared at the liquid trickle into her body and felt like an absolute wreck.

At least the drip would sort her out physically. It was a well-kept secret but many Hollywood stars spent time on what was known as the 'drip diet', starving themselves for days then popping into a clinic to be topped up with essential nutrients. It was way too extreme for Mia; she'd tried it once but it had made her miserable and left her on the brink of depression. But today she hadn't seen any choice. She'd overeaten and then overcompensated. She'd been too exhausted to schedule a last-minute workout, her hunger pushing her to the edge of delirium. And Violet had stressed that she needed to look her very best on the red carpet so couldn't risk eating anything and ending up bloated. Not when everyone would be waiting to judge her. In the end, Mia had felt too weak to argue.

Just then the phone rang. She picked it up and saw that it was Leo trying again. *Hmmm*, she thought, *he probably feels sorry for what he's done and wants to apologize*. Well she didn't want to speak to him. She hit the Reject button and saw from the screen that she'd now rejected twenty-three of his calls. She tossed the phone onto the seat next to her.

Why should she speak to him when he'd betrayed and hurt her so badly? For the first time in her adult life she'd opened herself up to a man and he'd only gone and confirmed her worst fears, letting her down and abandoning her just like her father had done all those years ago. Now look at the state she was in – wired up to a drip just to get enough energy to make it through the day. And the drip might be sorting her out physically but she knew that it would take a lot more to sort her out emotionally.

She looked at her watch. Rosie was due at her house in an hour to do her hair and make-up in preparation for the premiere.

She suddenly realized that she might be able to avoid Leo but she was about to spend the afternoon with his best friend's wife. Rosie would obviously be fighting his corner; Mia knew how close Leo and Ronnie were. Booking Rosie had seemed like a good idea at the time; she'd thought it would be a great way for them to spend some decent girl time together. But now she wondered what she'd let herself in for.

She called for the nurse. And as she did so she made herself a promise. She was never – ever – coming back to this clinic again.

*

Ronnie lifted Rosie's heavy make-up bag into the car and then kissed her goodbye.

As she started the engine he moved over to the porch and lit what he'd promised her would be his last ever cigarette. She'd warned him that he had to quit before the baby arrived and he'd decided he might as well bite the bullet and do it now. And besides, he was still revelling in the success of his bumper pay check so reckoned it would be easier to do it now while he was enjoying a rare lucky streak. Especially as fate was bound to turn against him again soon. It always did.

As Rosie's car disappeared down the street he spotted a motorbike racing towards him. The bike skidded to a stop in front of the house and he saw that it was Leo.

'Mate, we need to talk,' Leo said, practically flinging his bike onto the road.

Ronnie took one last drag and stubbed out his cigarette. 'Sure, buddy. What about?'

Leo took the paper out of his pocket and held it up. 'This. Have you seen it?'

'Sure I have. Do you like the pictures? Turned out awesome in the end, didn't they?'

'Never mind the pictures, Ronnie, what about the article?'

'Yeah. I can't imagine Billy's very happy this morning.'

'No. And neither's Mia. She won't even speak to me now. I reckon that's it – I think I've been dumped.'

'Dumped? But why?'

'Work it out, mate. She thinks I sold the story.'

'But you didn't, did you?'

'No. Because you did.'

Ronnie staggered back on the spot. '*I* did? But Leo—'

'But nothing. How could you, Ronnie?'

'But Leo, I didn't. Why would I do that?'

'You tell me, mate? For the money?'

Ronnie stared at him in disbelief. Just when it looked like he was turning his life around, his best friend goes and turns against him. Well he hadn't thought his fate would change quite so quickly. He was so shocked that he didn't know what to say to defend himself.

'Don't you think it's too much of a coincidence?' Leo steamed on. 'You know, I only just told you about Billy being gay and then the story appears so soon afterwards, right next to your pictures? What am I supposed to think, Ronnie?'

Every word of Leo's stung and Ronnie was finding it tough to take the blows. He hadn't for one minute expected this and he was completely taken aback by how much it hurt.

'Wait a second,' he managed. 'I'm sure you're real upset by what's happened but you're way out of line to come over here and start taking it out on me.'

'Oh yeah? Well you should have thought about that before you went blabbing to the press!'

His words brought Ronnie's heart to a canter. 'Listen Leo,' he growled, 'I've already told you I didn't sell the story! And quite frankly I can't believe you'd think I'd do something as shitty as that. I thought we were buddies – best buddies!'

'Yeah, well so did I – until you went and messed it all up

by flogging this story! I don't know, maybe having a baby on the way's changed you, Ronnie. Maybe it's made you start panicking about money.'

By now Ronnie was so angry he could feel the thick vein throbbing on his forehead. 'Yeah, well maybe having a movie-star girlfriend's changed you, Leo! My old buddy would never dump all this bullshit on me. And I haven't done anything wrong so I won't sit here and take it!'

There was a long pause. Ronnie could hear Leo's heavy breathing; he'd obviously worked himself up into a total state over this. He spotted his packet of cigarettes on the side and had to stop himself from taking one. 'Answer me one thing then,' Leo went on, 'if it wasn't you – who was it?'

Ronnie lifted his arms in the air and let them fall by his sides. He gave up – he had no idea. He slumped into a chair, speechless.

Leo moved back to his bike and picked it up. 'Listen, I've got to go. I've got to try and get hold of Mia while there's still time to convince her it wasn't me.'

Ronnie hung his head in defeat.

'OK, well, good luck.'

As he listened to Leo speed away he felt utterly defeated. He lifted his head and reached for a cigarette. He'd have to give up some other time.

*

Rosie stood waiting on Mia's doorstep biting her nails. She'd just had to fight her way through a battalion of paparazzi, all of them chomping at the bit for an exclusive shot of the next development in the big story. Right now there were two helicopters circling overhead and she could feel countless lenses trained on her in case Mia answered the door. She felt like she was being hunted and it really wasn't pleasant.

Even without the paparazzi, Rosie was more nervous about seeing Mia than she'd been the last time they'd met. When she'd first been asked to do her hair and make-up for the premiere she'd been ecstatic and had spent the entire week practising new looks on clients in the salon. But now, following this morning's newspaper revelations, her excitement had turned to dread.

Ronnie had already told her that the romance with Billy was a fake – he'd had to as she'd seen the photos in the press and knew that Mia was dating Leo, not Billy. But the first she'd known about Billy being gay had been when she'd read about it in the papers that morning. She had to admit to being more than a little disappointed. But more than anything else she'd felt concerned for Mia and Billy. She didn't have to be an expert on the movie industry to know that the revelations were potentially catastrophic for both of their careers. And if she were in any doubt, the presence of so many paparazzi outside Mia's gates reminded her just how big a story this was.

As she waited for the door to be answered, her mind raced with worries.

Will Mia know that Ronnie took those photos?

Will she regret the whole thing now that the story's out?

Will she even want to see me if her entire world's collapsing?

She decided that the only option was to try and avoid the subject altogether, to wait for Mia to bring it up herself if she wanted to. And if she did ask about Ronnie, then Rosie would plead ignorance and say that she didn't know whether he'd taken the photos or not. There was nothing else for it. For once, she'd have to keep her big mouth shut.

The door was eventually opened by an ashen-faced Latino who introduced himself as Hector, Mia's personal assistant. He looked like a different person to the camp, bubbly young man Rosie had imagined when she'd spoken to him on the phone. It had obviously been a long morning for everyone.

Hector led her through the house, an experience which in itself would ordinarily have had her spellbound. But today the atmosphere in the place was heavy, as if someone had just died. Rosie hardly noticed the domed skylight, the grand staircase or the huge walk-in closet. In fact, she was in such a daze that at one point she almost tripped over a cat. Just as her nerves were reaching fever pitch, she was led through to the salon, where a grim-faced Mia sat waiting.

The second she clapped eyes on her, she forgot all about her plan to keep her mouth shut and everything she hadn't wanted to say came bursting out. 'Oh Mia, I'm so sorry Ronnie took those pictures. We honestly had no idea this would happen. And I've been so nervous about seeing you again – I thought you might hate me now the whole thing's gone so horribly wrong.'

A smile shimmered across Mia's face and she stood up to hug her.

'I've been nervous about seeing you too, Rosie. We're going to have to stop meeting like this. But it's OK, honestly. You really shouldn't worry about the photos. I kind of expected Ronnie to be involved.'

'Well he only took the bedroom photos – he wasn't following you around all night or anything.'

Mia puckered her brow. 'In that case I've got to hand it to him – he's a very talented photographer.'

'Thanks.' Rosie felt a rare moment of pride in her husband. 'I'm glad you think so.'

'Well the truth is that we set the whole thing up so I can hardly complain about the pictures. What bothers me about it all is who sold the story. And there's no easy way to say this but I'm convinced it was Leo.'

Mia told Rosie about their big argument and Leo's parting shot about not being able to live a lie. It could hardly be a coincidence that just a few hours later that same lie was exploded in the press.

Rosie sat down and gave a loud sigh. 'I understand what you're saying,' she breathed, 'but Leo just wouldn't do that. Sure, he told Ronnie how much he was hating the fake romance. It was killing him to see the whole world talking about you being in love with someone else. But that was only because he loves you so much. And that same love would have stopped him from doing anything that would hurt you like this.'

Mia looked at herself in the mirror and fell silent.

So Leo loves me . . . He really loves me!

Even though she'd spent the last twenty-four hours hating him, she was surprised at how good it felt to hear Rosie say the words.

'Well he's never told *me* he loves me,' she said eventually. 'What are men like?' Rosie scoffed. 'They'll tell their buddies but not their girl. Ronnie only told me he loved me on our wedding night. And that was when he was shit-faced.'

The two of them laughed.

Just then Rosie's phone rang from inside her bag but she ignored it. Now really wasn't the time.

'Well if the boys can have their secrets,' Mia went on, 'then so can us girls. I'm in love with Leo, Rosie. Totally, utterly, completely in love. But he's really hurt me – whether or not he sold the story.'

'Well if it helps, I can promise you that he didn't.'

Mia nodded as she took it all in.

'But if it wasn't Leo then who was it?'

*

Next door to the salon, Hector was in the office trying to work. He was finding it hard to concentrate as he could hear Mia and Rosie's chatter coming down the hall. And no amount of Ricky or Enrique could drown out one terrible idea going round and round his head: was it possible that today's disaster was all his fault?

Last night he'd been on a date with an anonymous guy he'd met on the phone app Grindr who went under the pseudonym *lookingforlove69*. When Hector had arrived at their chosen venue, a gay bar called The Pacific Rim, to his immense surprise his date had turned out to be the comedian turned actor Scott Lamont. Better still, Scott had turned up with a bouquet of flowers and went on to be one of the sweetest men Hector had ever met. In fact, by the end of their second drink he'd been convinced that he was experiencing love at first sight and had ended up telling Scott his whole life story, complete with his most intimate secrets. By the time he was onto his fifth, he'd revealed some intimate secrets of Mia's and one in particular – that her romance with Billy was fake and that Billy was actually gay. Hector hadn't meant to cause trouble but he was still feeling hurt that Mia hadn't shared the secret with him. And besides, Scott had been so keen and attentive that Hector had wanted to impress him. He'd just got a little carried away in the process.

He'd got even more carried away when Scott had driven him home in his flashy convertible sports car. In fact, he'd got so carried away that he'd invited him in and ended up having sex with him on the kitchen table. Which is when everything had taken a turn for the worse. As soon as the sex was over, Scott had confessed that he had a boyfriend, some guy who was a personal trainer. Apparently he was totally in love with him and was only looking for some fun on the side. Hector had been devastated. And as the devastation had sunk in and the hangover taken hold, he'd been gripped by the fear that Scott would go and reveal the truth about Mia and Billy to the press. Just hours later, the story had been unleashed. Surely that couldn't be a coincidence?

Right now he sat listening to Mia and Rosie talking it over next door, plagued by the worry that it was he who was to blame for everything. And from what Mia was saying to Rosie, she'd been convinced that it was Leo who'd sold the story and had therefore been refusing to speak to him. Hector realized now why Mia had banned all her staff from talking to him or answering his calls all day. It was all such a mess. What if Mia had finally found love but now he'd gone and ruined it? Oh what had he done?

He felt truly terrible. If he were to blame, how could he possibly tell Mia? He'd almost certainly be fired for a start. But if he didn't tell her and it meant the end of her relationship with Leo then how could he ever live with himself?

*

Leo stood on Venice Beach looking out at the ocean, his camera dangling from his arm. He was feeling increasingly desperate.

He wanted to speak to Mia so badly that he'd tried calling everyone – Serena, Hector and even Rosie. But no one would answer.

He thought back once again to what he'd said to Mia during their argument yesterday. He realized now how wrong he'd been. He might have said that he couldn't go on living a lie but what he'd come to realize was that he couldn't live without Mia, whatever sacrifices he had to make.

He was filled with a burning compulsion to tell her how he felt – how he really felt about her. There was nothing else for it; if she wouldn't answer his calls then he'd just have to find her in person. And he'd stop at nothing to speak to her.

He took out the keys to his bike but before setting off there was one last thing he had to do.

He drew back his arm and threw his camera out into the ocean.

He watched it sinking under the waves before turning to walk away.

14

When Leo arrived outside Mia's house, even he was surprised by what he saw. The paparazzi were everywhere; hanging onto the gates, sitting on the wall, standing up ladders and gripping onto trees. Needless to say, his secret tree had been discovered – he counted three or four paps dangling from his usual perch. At the side of the road was a flotilla of vehicles ready to give chase and a handful of helicopters hovered overhead. It was madness.

One of the paps recognized him and called his name. She was a fellow Brit from Manchester who'd earned the nickname Bruiser because of her tenacity when in pursuit of a picture.

'All right Leo,' she boomed. 'Great story, isn't it?'

He smiled and gave a shrug.

'You know, I was just saying to the boys, I haven't seen anything like this since the days of Princess Diana.'

Leo raised his eyebrows in response.

'Where've you been anyway?' she asked. 'We haven't seen you and Ronnie all day.'

'Oh I think Ronnie's taking a day off,' Leo managed. 'He did well last night so I'm covering things today.'

'And where's your camera?'

Leo was stumped for a second. 'Oh it's erm, it's in the bike.'

'Well you'd better get it out quickly,' she grinned. 'It looks like it's going to kick off any minute.'

There was a flurry of excitement as someone came out of the house on the other side of the gates. From the almost deafening sound of so many cameras snapping, Leo could only imagine that it must be Mia. While everyone's attention was diverted, he slipped away and took his place on his bike at the side of the road. He might have thrown away his camera but there was no way that he was ever giving up his bike. And right now it looked like he'd need it.

*

Mia walked down her front steps in a loose pastel pink gown with floral details along the bust and matching kitten heels. Serena had warned her not to dress up too much as it was important today for her to look warm and approachable rather than the distant, untouchable movie star she usually played on the red carpet. It was a look she felt much more comfortable with anyway so she hadn't complained. Although comfortable was the last thing she was feeling today.

As she stepped into the back of her limo, she noticed a marked change in the paparazzi's attitude towards her. Sure, their cameras were snapping away as usual and everyone was calling her name. But there was a much more aggressive tone to their voices and she wondered whether Leo had been right when he'd said that by inviting them into her life she'd made a pact with the devil – and from now on there'd be no turning back. As the door clicked shut she felt an enormous relief.

In the shelter of the limo she took a deep breath and prepared herself for the task ahead. Tonight would be the biggest night of her life. And she was facing it alone.

She remembered what she'd always said about why she wanted a boyfriend, about being sick of going through life as a lone ranger and wanting someone who'd always be on her side. Well with Leo she'd got much more than she wanted – much more than she'd even known she'd been looking for. But right now she'd gone back to being a lone ranger. And she felt crushingly alone.

The car pulled out of the gates and she watched as the paps jumped down from the walls, trees and ladders and scrambled to their cars and bikes, ready to give chase. At the front of the pack there was one motorbike that caught her eye. Winking at her from the back was a little sticker of the British flag.

*

Leo darted after the limo with a head start on everyone else in pursuit. It wouldn't take them long to catch up but he knew from experience that he could outride any pap. And today he had an added incentive; if his plan failed then he'd lose forever the woman he loved.

He drew up alongside the limo and tried looking through the windows for Mia. But they were blacked out and he couldn't see anything. He knew she was in there. He only hoped that she was watching him.

In the distance he could see a fleet of cars and bikes racing to catch them up. He had no time to lose.

He unzipped his jacket and pulled out a big card, onto

which he'd written, 'It wasn't me.' He angled it towards the window and held it there for long enough for Mia to read. If she did, he knew that she'd understand.

He then pulled out a second card bearing the word, 'Honestly'. He hoped to God that she was looking.

As the pursuing paps reached the tip of the limo he revealed his third and final card. It said simply, 'I love you.'

He held it in the air for what seemed like forever. With all his heart he hoped that she was reading. But the limo glided on. And every second that passed felt like agony.

Just as the paps surrounded the limo, Leo spotted an indicator light flashing. And in the midst of the chaos, as if it were the most natural thing in the world, the limo pulled over.

The back door opened.

*

Mia moved along the seat to make room for Leo. He stepped in and flashed her his lop-sided grin.

'Hello princess,' he said. 'You look beautiful.'

All around him, paps were poking their way into the limo, holding out their cameras and flashing indiscriminately in case they got a half-decent shot of this latest twist in a story that had them all pumped up. Mia was past caring.

'You'd better get in,' she said to Leo, 'and shut the door.'

The door snapped shut and he sat next to her. Through the windows she could hear the confused chatter of the paparazzi. Inside the limo there was a tense silence. Mia could feel her heart begin to flutter but she told herself she had to focus on the job ahead; after everything that had happened, she couldn't be late for the premiere.

'OK,' she called to the driver. 'You can carry on now.'

As he pulled forward, Mia and Leo sat looking at each other. She could almost feel the nervous energy bouncing between them. *He loves me*, she thought. *He really does love me.*

'Did you mean what you said?' she asked eventually. 'On the card just then?'

'Yeah, I promise, Mia – it wasn't me who sold the story.'

He'd misunderstood her question but she wasn't able to stop him.

'I've no idea who it was,' he rattled on. 'Honestly, it's been driving me mad. I even accused Ronnie earlier. And now I owe him a huge apology. I reckon I owe you one too.'

'Oh yeah, and what's that for?'

'For everything I said to you yesterday.'

She looked down at her purse.

'I was wrong, Mia,' he went on, 'and from now on I don't care what I have to do but I can't live without you.'

Just tell me you love me, she thought. *Please tell me you love me.* She was too nervous to say the words out loud.

'Well I came out with some pretty horrible things as well,' she said instead, 'so I'm sorry too. But you really hurt me, Leo. And I just need a little time to think.'

He nodded sombrely.

'Look, today's insane,' she went on. 'How about I get this premiere out of the way and then we see how we feel? How we both feel. When we're not being distracted by this crazy circus.' She gestured out of the window at the paps surrounding them on all sides.

'OK,' Leo nodded. 'I can wait, Mia. I can wait as long as it takes.'

As he flashed her another wonky grin, she knew that he wouldn't have to wait very long. He wouldn't have to wait very long at all.

*

At the bottom of the red carpet, Billy was sitting waiting in the back of his limo. He'd only been there for a couple of minutes but it had felt like an eternity. He was biting at the skin around his nails so fiercely that he actually drew blood and he told himself he needed to stop. He stretched out his hands on his knees but could see that they were still shaking.

Mia's limo pulled up at the back of his and he knew that it was time to get out. His heart was thumping so fast that he felt dizzy and he was so gripped by panic that he felt frozen rigid, stuck to his seat. But he had to go through with this – there was no backing out now. He reached for the handle and opened the door.

As he and Mia stepped out onto the red carpet just a few yards apart, they were met by a pair of burly security guards. But nothing could protect them from the loud chorus of boos from the waiting fans. And there were thousands of them. It looked like all of Billy's worst fears were coming true.

'Liars!' somebody shouted from behind the crash barriers.

Another threw an egg, which narrowly missed Billy and hit the back of his limo.

He felt more alone and exposed than he ever had in his life. And it was truly terrifying.

He stumbled towards Mia and took hold of her hand. He gave it a little squeeze and the two of them shot each other tense, steely smiles.

This was going to be horrendous.

He only hoped he could bear it.

*

Man, this looks awful.

In Mia's office, Hector was sitting at his desk watching live TV coverage of the premiere. And things didn't look good. He'd never seen so many fans outside a cinema and all of them seemed to be jeering and hissing. He felt sick with guilt. Poor Mia. And poor Billy.

All morning he'd been trying to reach Scott Lamont to find out if it was in fact him who'd sold the story. It was the only way to put his mind at rest. But he'd dialled the number Scott had given him and been met by a tinny voice telling him the number he'd dialled wasn't recognized; Scott had obviously given him a decoy. He'd tried messaging him on Grindr but still there was no reply. All of which convinced Hector he must be guilty. Which meant, by extension, that the blame traced right back to him.

He turned back to the TV screen and watched as Mia and Billy walked down the red carpet and past the waiting photographers and TV crews to a deafening roar of disapproval. How could people be so cruel? And how could Mia and Billy subject themselves to this? Even as the thought entered his head he knew the answer. They *had* to put themselves through this – if they didn't they stood to lose too much.

Just then his phone gave a little ping and he looked to find a message flashing up on the screen. It was from *looking-forlove69*.

He was in such a panic to read it that he almost hit Delete.

As it opened up in front of him he stared at it so closely that the letters seemed to bounce out from the screen. He blinked repeatedly as he tried to focus and stop the words swirling around in front of him.

'Hey, Hector,' he finally read. 'No, I didn't sell the story. I wouldn't do that to Billy. I don't like him, but he doesn't deserve any of this. I hope you're good. No hard feelings. Scott.'

Hector was so relieved he thought he'd faint. He held onto the desk to pull himself up and went over to the water cooler to pour himself a drink. He didn't think he'd ever been so relieved in all his life.

As he sipped his water he looked back at the TV screen. He watched in horror as the fans began to chant an endless chorus of, 'Liars! Liars!' Mia and Billy looked terrified.

His guilt may have been lifted but none of this changed anything for them. And they still had to face the big TV interview. If they got it right they might just be able to start winning people round. But if they got it wrong their careers would be over.

*

Mia and Billy stood facing Violet, flanked by their agents Serena and James. Mia couldn't help feeling like a soldier being drilled before going into battle.

'OK,' Violet began, 'so just to confirm – we're ditching the line-up and we're not posing for pictures. Which just leaves the big interview with Preston and Kerry.'

Mia tried to gulp but her Adam's apple stuck in her throat.

'Now remember what I said this morning,' she went on.

'We're thinking a whole lot of repentance – just apologize and say you're sorry for leading everyone on.'

'That won't be difficult,' Mia muttered, 'I *am* sorry. I genuinely regret the whole thing.'

'Yeah, well don't hold back and make sure you turn on the tears. Come to think of it, a full breakdown would really knock it out of the park.'

'Wait a second,' Serena burst in. 'After all the trouble you've caused with your lying and faking, shouldn't you stand back now and let these guys be themselves? Don't you think they should just tell the truth out there?'

'Well the way I feel right now,' Billy bleated, 'a full breakdown wouldn't be too far from the truth.'

'Good.' Violet nodded. 'Good.'

'I'm sorry,' Mia interrupted. 'Did you just say "good"?'

'My apologies,' Violet breezed. 'An unfortunate choice of words.'

Mia could contain herself no longer. The way Violet was talking was insulting to both of them – and especially to Billy. 'This isn't a game, Violet,' she erupted. 'We're not play-acting here. This is our lives we're talking about. And me and Billy are really suffering because of this.'

'Oh stop over-reacting,' Violet barked. 'Everything's going according to plan. If you'd relaxed and trusted me from the start then neither of you would be suffering at all.'

Mia froze – suddenly it all made sense. 'Hold on a second. Did you *plan* this whole thing? Was it *you* who leaked the story?'

Violet threw her arms up in the air as if the answer were obvious. 'Of course it was me! What took you so long to work it out? There's not a story in Hollywood I *don't* control, Mia. Surely you know that by now?'

All four of them were dumbstruck and looked at each other in disbelief. In the background they could still hear the fans' angry chants. 'Liars! Liars!'

'But Violet,' Mia stammered, 'do you have any idea what you've put us through?'

She tossed her hair dismissively. 'And it will all be worth it in the end. All you have to do is follow my instructions and go up there and nail the TV show.' She gestured to the fans around her. 'You can win these guys round, you'll see. And then the whole world will be talking about you – and the film.'

'But you outed me, Violet,' Billy said, grim-faced. 'Don't you understand what that means?'

'Of course I understand, Billy. But I also understand Hollywood better than you. And right now I think it's ready for this.' She gestured to the fans around her. 'Have you heard what these guys are saying? They might be calling you a liar but not a single one of them is calling you a fag.'

Mia was just about to protest that coming out of the closet should have been Billy's decision when a runner appeared to say the cameras were ready for them. Mia and Billy took hold of each other's hands and gave them another squeeze.

'OK, guys, good luck,' Violet said, 'and remember, think of the Box Office!'

Mia was outraged and she could see that Billy was too. How could Violet be so cold about the whole thing? How could she have done this to them?

As they walked towards the set Mia felt consumed by anger. But she could still think clearly enough to realize that there was one important thing she had to do before starting the interview. She called over Serena to put her plan into action.

*

Serena gave Mia a wink and stood to one side as she and Billy climbed up the steps and onto the set. It was a huge covered set, an almost exact replica of the show's studio version, complete with its own lighting rig and raked audience seating. The hosts Preston and Kerry, a middle-aged couple with identical Botoxed foreheads and collagen-filled pouts, were sitting on a bright orange sofa that matched their fake tans. They were chatting nervously and waiting for the two seats opposite to be filled. As Serena looked at the empty seats her heart began thumping at the thought of what lay ahead.

She spotted the production team huddled around a cluster of monitors and made her way over to join them. She watched as Mia and Billy were briefed by a floor manager and within seconds a production assistant began counting down their entrance.

'Ten, nine, eight . . .'

As the numbers went lower and lower, Serena's heart rate soared higher and higher.

'Seven, six, five . . .'

Come on guys, she thought, tensing every muscle in her body, *you can do this* . . .

'Four, three, two . . .'

And then the wait was over.

'One.'

This was it.

The show's theme music came to an end as the floor

manager directed the audience to break into applause. Unfortunately, most of them ignored him and continued booing.

Uh-oh, thought Serena. *This isn't a good start.*

As Mia and Billy took their seats to a chorus of even louder boos, she could tell from the looks on their faces that they were nothing short of petrified.

Preston and Kerry warmed things up with a harmless preamble, explaining where they were broadcasting from and why. And then they introduced Mia and Billy to rumbles of disapproval from the audience.

'Liars!' somebody shouted again, loudly enough for everyone to hear.

On set the hosts pretended not to notice. Though the guests weren't able to hide their recognition.

'So,' Preston carried on regardless, 'let's start by saying that we've seen the movie and it's absolutely incredible – by far the best picture either of you has ever made.'

'Thanks,' they mumbled sheepishly.

'But let's cut straight to the chase,' Kerry continued. 'Everybody's been talking about the drama *off* camera . . .'

Mia and Billy nodded guiltily.

'So we'd like to hear your side of the story. How do you feel about it all now?'

'Liars!' came another voice from the audience.

During what felt like an interminable pause, Serena watched the monitors as several cameras zoomed in for close-ups. As she looked at Mia on screen she was sure she could spot her Adam's apple lodging in her throat.

Mia gave a little cough before she finally began to speak. 'Well, first of all,' she ventured, 'Billy and I would like to apologize for lying to everyone and for misleading the public and our fans.'

Billy nodded in agreement. 'There's no excuse,' he said, 'and we fully accept the blame.'

'But we'd like to explain why we got into this mess in the first place,' Mia went on, 'and then if the public will let us, we can promise to be honest with them from now on.'

Although she was saying all the right things, Serena still felt decidedly on edge. She could sense the hostility continuing to emanate from the audience.

'As a little girl back home in Cleveland,' Mia explained, 'I used to dream of growing up to be a movie star. I'd look up to the actresses in my favourite movies as if they were goddesses and I wanted them to be perfect and not to make mistakes like normal people. I used to think fantasy was more important than reality. But now I've realized I was wrong.'

Serena spotted a few members of the audience nodding thoughtfully.

'I've come to the same conclusion,' offered Billy. 'Like Mia, I'd spent years thinking that what people wanted from me was a good show, to live up to their expectations. When I was eighteen I was honest and truthful about myself but I was rejected by my parents, the people I loved the most. And I guess that ever since then I've been worried that if I was honest with anyone else I'd be rejected all over again.'

Kerry nodded at him pensively.

'But I've realized now that lying isn't the answer,' he went on, 'because once you start lying you just can't stop. And that's how I wound up in a fake relationship with Mia and let everyone down so badly.'

'So what exactly happened between you two?' asked Preston. 'Who came up with the idea of staging a show-mance?'

'Our publicist Violet Vaughn,' Mia answered. 'She bullied us into agreeing to the whole thing while at the same time planning to tell the press that it was fake and out Billy in the process.'

There were gasps of amazement from the audience.

That's my girl, thought Serena. Standing next to Violet she could sense the tension start to rise. It looked as if she was visibly giving off steam.

'This sounds like quite a story,' interjected Kerry. 'I think you need to rewind a little and start at the beginning.'

Serena watched as Mia took a deep breath and launched into the performance of her life. Only this time she was playing herself.

*

How dare they denounce me live on television?

Violet was furious. Millions of people would be watching this show – and that was before it hit YouTube. She couldn't think of anything more humiliating.

And this was supposed to be her moment of glory. Her plan had worked brilliantly, as she'd always known it would. But she'd also known that if she'd told people about it before-hand then they wouldn't have had the balls to see it through. As usual she'd been right – and as usual everyone else had let their judgment be clouded by sentimentality. Well that wasn't her fault. And it was crushingly unfair for her to be publicly branded as some kind of hate figure.

Not that everyone didn't hate her anyway. The truth was that everyone always had. And however hard she tried, she always ended up back in this same position. Maybe it was what she deserved. She felt just as wretched as she had when she'd caught Cooper Kelly cheating on her – only this time the whole world could see the spider crawling over her soul.

She wouldn't care but all she'd been trying to do was excel at her job. And in the process prove to everyone that she was one of the most powerful women in Hollywood. Well it didn't look like anyone would be thinking that now.

She winced as she thought of everyone watching the show back home in Portland. All having a good old laugh at Vile Violet.

*

So it was Violet who leaked the story . . .

Standing on his tiptoes and peering over the audience from the back row, Leo reached for his phone and began texting Ronnie.

'Looks like I owe you an apology,' he tapped. 'Am so sorry, mate. Fancy the Dodgers game this weekend? My treat?'

He knew that it would take more than a Dodgers' game to make things up between them. But he really wanted to repair their friendship and was desperate to make a start as soon as possible. He thought back to everything he'd said on Ronnie's porch and felt thoroughly ashamed of himself. He'd flown off the handle and made a hurtful accusation that he knew now was totally out of order. He'd been so blinded by his feelings for Mia and his terror of losing her that he wondered whether he'd even been going through some kind of temporary madness. But however he looked at it, there was no excuse.

He only hoped that Ronnie could forgive him.

*

Lounging on the sofa with Rosie, Ronnie could feel his phone vibrate in his jeans' pocket. He wriggled around to fish it out while Rosie's eyes remained glued to the TV screen.

'That publicist sounds like a total bitch,' she breathed. 'How could she do that to them?'

Without answering, Ronnie opened up a text message from Leo and read it. He immediately felt his mood begin to lift. All afternoon he'd felt terrible about what Leo had said to him. But Leo was apologizing and wanted to make amends. Maybe now the two of them could start working things out and one day they'd be just as close as ever.

'Don't worry, bud,' he texted back. 'Love can do funny things to a guy. See you at Dodger Stadium. Your partner, Ronnie.'

As he hit Send he patted Rosie's stomach and gave her a kiss.

*

Billy listened to Mia come to the end of her story and swallowed nervously. He sensed that the audience was gradually softening but he still had to broach the subject of his sexuality. And he had no idea how they'd react to that.

'So, Billy,' Preston said, turning to face him, 'obviously the biggest revelation to come out of this whole episode is that you're gay.'

Billy cleared his throat and nodded uncertainly. 'Mmm-hmm.'

'When did you first decide to cover that up from the public?'

He swallowed croakily and then began. 'When I first came to Hollywood. I signed with my agent and was told that if I didn't pretend to be straight then I didn't stand a chance of making it in movies.'

Again there were gasps from the audience.

'Oh it wasn't my agent's fault,' Billy went on. 'He had a point – there weren't any openly gay actors working in movies. So I didn't feel like I had a choice. But I did feel really uncomfortable about lying and ever since then I've hated every lie I've told. But I was scared and frightened and, like I said earlier, I thought that if I did come out then I'd have wound up being rejected all over again.'

He noticed that the rumblings of disapproval from the audience had completely died down. Because of the bright lights he could only make out the first few rows but the people he could see looked gripped and had moved forward to the edges of their seats.

'And now that you *are* out,' Kerry probed, 'how are you hoping the public will react?'

He sighed and looked down humbly. 'Well I'm hoping that they'll accept me for who I am. And show the world that they're more tolerant and open-minded than the people running the movie industry like to think.'

He looked up and out at the audience to address them directly.

'Because I *am* gay. And despite everything, believe it or not,

I'm proud to be gay. But that doesn't change what happens when I make a movie – when I'm pretending to be someone else. And I'm hoping to prove to you guys that a gay actor *can* play straight roles. That is, if you'll accept my apology and give me a shot.'

There was a murmur of applause from the back row of the audience. Gradually it began spreading, growing louder and louder until it rose to a roar as everyone got up to their feet. Preston and Kerry motioned Billy to stand and as he did so the applause swelled even more.

Billy couldn't believe this was actually happening – after all the anxiety, fear and worry he'd been through. But now here he was, telling the world that he was gay and being accepted for it. For the first time in his life he was being applauded for who he really was, not an elaborate lie he'd erected to hide his true self. And after years of chasing affirmation, he finally understood how it felt to be genuinely loved.

He could see Mia trying to smile at him but struggling to hold back tears of pride. He could feel himself welling up but his tears were kept in check by a rush of sheer joy. Without doubt this was the happiest moment in his life. And he couldn't help wondering if back home in Mississippi his parents were watching.

'So one more question,' Kerry began shouting over the applause.

Billy slowly sat down again, still beaming with joy. 'Yeah?'

'Now that you have come out as being gay, lots of your fans are going to want to know if there's anyone special in your life . . .'

He tried to look serious but couldn't wipe the smile off

his face. 'There isn't anyone, no,' he managed. 'But for the first time in my life I guess I'm now free to fall in love. And I can't wait.'

*

Sitting watching TV in Mia's office, Hector wiped the tears from his eyes.

For an incurable romantic, the scene playing itself out on screen was much more moving than any movie. Billy was standing up and telling the world that he was ready for love. And it was a wonderful, special moment.

As a gay man Hector could also appreciate that he was witnessing a key moment in history. Gay people he knew in Hollywood had wanted this to happen for so long and understood that nothing would change until it did. Someone needed to be brave enough to stand up and be counted, to challenge those who forced gay actors back into the closet. And now, unbelievably, Billy Spencer was doing just that. Sure, he'd had to be dragged out of the closet by Violet Vaughn, who Hector had always thought was a nasty piece of work. But now that he was out, he was handling it all brilliantly. And he was even getting a standing ovation!

Hector looked at the screen and blinked to check that it was all definitely happening. But there was no doubt; right now, before his very eyes, Billy Spencer was in the process of changing the world.

*

'And how about you, Mia?' Preston asked, turning to face her. 'Is there anyone special in your life at the moment?'

Mia froze in her seat. She hadn't expected this to happen and wasn't at all prepared. But as she looked round at everyone's smiling faces she realized that if Billy was being honest with the world then she could hardly hold back from doing the same.

'Erm yeah, there is someone, yeah,' she stammered. As soon as she said the words she began growing in confidence. 'He's British, he's a photographer and his name's Leo Henderson.'

Kerry didn't bother to conceal her delight and let out a little squeal. 'And dare I ask if the First Lady of Love is finally *in* love?'

Mia giggled bashfully. 'You know what, Kerry, I used to hate that nickname. I used to totally hate it. But I've started to love it now because it's true – I *am* the First Lady of Love.'

She turned to address the audience.

'And I love *you*, Leo. Did you hear that? I love you.'

'Hold on a second,' called Preston. 'Is he here right now?'

'He is, yeah – somewhere.'

'Well come on, Leo. Come out and show yourself.'

Once more the audience fell silent as everyone looked around them, craning their necks to catch the first glimpse of Mia's man.

After just a few seconds, Mia saw him stepping out of the shadows. And as he walked towards her, he looked more handsome than ever. Just then she realized that she'd never loved him more than she did at that moment. And she never wanted the moment to end.

Leo walked up onto the set and Mia rose to greet him. He

strode over to her and stopped to smile with his beautiful wonky grin.

'I love you too, princess.'

He picked her up and swept her around in his arms.

Mia was so happy she thought she would explode.

And from the sound of the applause all around her, the audience felt just the same.

*

Serena turned away from the monitor and dabbed at a tear in her eye. It was a beautiful moment which she would happily revel in forever. But there was one important thing that Mia had asked her to do. And after everything that had happened, she wasn't going to let her down.

She looked around for Violet and caught her rather desperately pleading her case to a lowly production assistant. 'Oh I know they seem angry right now,' she overheard her simpering, 'but they'll soon come round when they see I was right all along.'

'Yeah well I wouldn't count on it,' Serena interrupted. 'I wouldn't count on it at all.'

Violet looked at her and her face hardened. 'But Serena,' she hissed, 'even you have to admit that what I did was genius.'

'Genius?'

'Yes, Serena. I take it you understand that word. And understand this – thanks to me this picture is going to have one mother of an opening weekend.'

Serena laughed in disbelief. 'But Violet, this isn't just about the Box Office. Don't you see? This is about real people with real lives and real feelings.'

'Feelings?' she snorted. '*Feelings?*'

'Yes, Violet, feelings. Obviously something *you* don't understand. Which actually makes things easy for me. Because it means I don't have to feel bad when I fire your ass.'

'Excuse me?' gasped Violet. 'But do you have any idea who you're talking to?'

The entire production team tore themselves away from the monitors and gathered round to stare at the two women, who were now standing just a few feet apart.

'Sure I do, Violet. And I'm telling you that you're fired.'

Violet looked at her and turned up her nose. 'For your information, I take orders from my client and my client only – not some trashy broad from Harlem.'

'Well that's just as well. Because this trashy broad from Harlem has already spoken to your client. And if you didn't hear me the first time, here it is again. You're FIRED, Violet. And no doubt Billy will be firing your ass too.'

Just then James pushed his way through the production team and nodded determinedly. 'I think we can safely assume my client will no longer be requiring your services. Or any of my other clients for that matter.'

'Ditto!' echoed Serena.

Violet looked like she'd been punched in the face from both directions.

'Now get your bony ass out of my sight,' barked Serena.

Violet ran her fingers through her hair with a look of absolute panic. 'Well I . . . I . . .'

'You heard me!'

Violet looked around her and gave a loud huff. She opened her mouth as if to say something but then closed it. She turned on her heels and scurried off.

Hell, that felt good, thought Serena, beaming with satisfaction. *I might be a broad from Harlem but I sure took a bite out of her ass.*

*

Mia melted into Leo's arms and felt his lips move forward to meet hers. Her heart soared as she dissolved into his kiss.

'I'm so happy,' he whispered. 'Thanks for making me so happy.'

'Me too,' mouthed Mia. 'And in case you didn't hear me the first time, I love you, Leo.'

'I love you too, Mia. Forever and ever and ever.'

Mia hugged him tightly.

She felt like she was living out her very own happy ending.

Epilogue: Six months later

'And the Academy Award for Best Actor goes to . . . Billy Spencer.'

A rather emotional Billy slowly stood up and began making his way through the auditorium towards the stage. He hadn't heard so much applause since his now legendary appearance on *The Preston and Kerry Show*. And this time it was coming to him from some of the biggest players in Hollywood.

As he walked up the aisle he spotted Lucy Cantrell and Randy Foster on his left while on his right he saw Tyler Bracket and Hunter Kelly, whose recent comeback had relaunched him firmly onto the A list. As he climbed the steps onto the stage he looked out and recognized Hollywood legends like Bolt Stephens and Cooper Kelly as well as movie tough guys such as Buck Andrews and Denver Jones. And he couldn't get over the fact that they were all cheering him.

He walked over to collect his Oscar and gripped it firmly in both hands. It was an incredible moment.

'Thank you, thank you,' he began, utterly overwhelmed.

He cleared his throat before starting his speech.

'You know, when I was first dragged out of the closet, I

said that I wanted to prove that an openly gay actor could succeed in a straight role. Well I guess I just have.'

The applause that greeted this comment was so forceful that Billy actually staggered back on the spot. He recovered his composure and repositioned himself in front of the microphone.

'There are several people I'd like to thank,' he announced, 'and the first is my wonderful boyfriend Hector.'

Again there was a round of applause.

'Hector, you're a very special man. You're the most loving and giving person I've ever met and you've made me very happy.'

*

Sitting in the audience next to Billy's empty seat, Hector glowed with pride. Today was turning into the most incredible day of his life.

It had got off to a shaky start when he'd bumped into Scott Lamont on the red carpet. He hadn't seen Scott since he'd told Mia's trainer Cole that he was cheating on him and Cole had promptly dumped him. But just when Hector was about to disappear into the crowd to avoid him, Billy had sensed his discomfort. He'd given him a little kiss on the cheek and suddenly none of it mattered anymore.

Hector was so lucky to have found Billy and so utterly, completely in love with him. He might only be the son of Cuban immigrants but Billy made him feel like the most special man on the planet. They'd got together shortly after Billy had been outed, just when he'd been starting work on his new movie, *Kissed by a Devil*. The film was now finished and just that morning a critic from *Variety* who'd seen an early preview had called Billy's performance a 'tour de force'. With that and his Oscar win for *War of Words*, it looked like Billy's success was secure, at least for the near future.

Hector looked forward to being around to share it with him.

*

As she sat feeding baby Mia, Rosie's eyes were fixed on the screen.

'Well I hate to say it,' she gushed, 'but Billy Spencer is one smoking hot guy – straight or gay.'

Ronnie tried ignoring her and reached for another sweet. Since giving up cigarettes he'd developed a new addiction and it was proving almost as difficult to kick.

'Will you lay off the candy,' nagged Rosie, her tongue lodged firmly in her cheek. 'If you carry on you're going to finish up with one mother of a fat ass.'

Reluctantly Ronnie dropped the packet of sweets onto the coffee table, next to an award of his own; he'd recently been made Paparazzo of the Year for his now infamous shots of Mia and Billy pretending to make out in her bedroom window. Since then he'd been on a roll, nailing exclusive after exclusive and finally stepping out from Leo's shadow to make a name for himself as one of the most successful paps in town.

'Man, he is so hot!' Rosie continued, gazing at Billy on screen. 'I bet *he* doesn't eat candy.'

Ronnie sat back and let her comments wash over him. She might be an expert at winding him up but deep down Ronnie knew now more than ever that Rosie was his soulmate. And besides, there was no need to be jealous of Billy Spencer anymore. Not only was he gay and spoken for but he had nothing that Ronnie didn't have himself. In fact, Ronnie couldn't help thinking that he now had everything he wanted in life: a fantastic wife, a thriving career and a gorgeous baby girl. He listened to her gurgle and could feel the love welling up inside him.

As Rosie fondled the tips of his sticky-out ears, he turned to look at Billy on the TV screen. He felt genuinely ecstatic for him.

*

'I'd also like to thank the public,' Billy went on, 'for restoring my faith in human nature. You know, another thing I said when I came out was that what had kept me in the closet was fear – and more than anything else fear of rejection. But if I'd known how things would turn out, I wouldn't have hidden away for so long. Because it's only now that I've learnt an important lesson in life – that honesty is the key to happiness. And right now I'm happier than I've ever been.'

*

As she listened to his speech with a lump in her throat, Serena thought back to the stresses and tensions of the week in which Billy had come out. It had been such a turbulent time and back then she'd had no idea how well everything would work out for them all.

Sitting next to her in the auditorium, Mitchell threaded his arm through hers. She knew that the Oscars was his least favourite night of the whole year and once again she was grateful to him for making the effort and coming along to support her. Recent events had made her appreciate him more and more and right now she felt closer to him than ever. They were even talking about trying for a baby and tonight had agreed to miss out on the parties and go home straight after the show to give it their first shot. If they didn't make use of the next few days, they'd have to wait a whole month as very soon Serena was due to fly over to New York. She'd agreed to give a talk to the girls at her old high school about making it in the movie business, and while she was there was also setting up a new initiative to inspire African Americans from underprivileged backgrounds.

She snuggled into Mitchell's arm and gave him a smile. She was looking forward to going home.

*

Far away in India, Violet wondered how the Academy Award ceremony was going and if Billy had won the Oscar for Best Actor. She had no access to TV or the internet so had no idea what was happening. The sense of impotence was infuriating.

Violet had left Hollywood shortly after the premiere of *War of Words*, when one after the other her clients had fired her. She'd flown to a Buddhist retreat not far from Varanasi in Northern India and had spent a few weeks practising yoga and meditation, eating curried tofu, and pretending to be interested when talking to dreadlocked hippies from Sweden. But the truth was that she'd never been remotely interested in the Buddhist way of life and soon had opted out of all activities, preferring instead to stay in her room, where she became consumed with plotting her Hollywood comeback. Of course, she knew that feigning remorse and reflection would be a key stage on the road to her relaunch – and nothing ticked that box quite like Buddhism. Whatever people might say about her, Violet Vaughn sure as hell knew about PR. And right now she was her own number one client.

As she looked out over the Ganges, her thoughts darted back to Hollywood and today's Academy Awards ceremony. She really hoped that Billy won his Oscar, not for his sake but for her own. An Oscar would prove to the world that her strategy had been right all along. An Oscar would expose the stupidity of everyone who'd doubted and deserted her. An Oscar would secure her comeback.

As far as Violet was concerned, you could forget Buddhism – coming back to life in Hollywood was the only reincarnation that held any interest for her.

*

Billy knew that he was approaching the most difficult part of his speech and he took a deep breath.

'You know, it's no secret that not everybody has embraced the real me as easily as the public. Unfortunately, back home in Mississippi my parents still won't accept that they have a gay son. It makes me very sad not to be able to thank them today and to share my happiness with them.

'So instead I'd like to thank my surrogate family here in LA. Friends who are always there for me and who accept me for who I am and not the person they want me to be. In particular I'd like to thank one very special couple, Mia Sinclair and Leo Henderson. It'd be fair to say that me and Leo got off on the wrong foot but I've since realized that he's a good

man – one of the very best. And Mia, you're a unique, special and talented woman who deserves the very best. So Mia
and Leo, this is for you.'

He waved his Oscar in the air one last time and the entire
audience rose to their feet.

*

Standing side by side, Mia and Leo couldn't resist cheering
Billy at the tops of their voices. As she clapped so hard her
hands began to smart, Mia could feel a camera zooming in on
her engagement ring.

Leo had proposed to her just last month, after they'd been
to the wedding of her housekeeper Ramona to her masseur
Bob. In full formal dress, he'd driven her up into the Hills on
the back of his motorbike and stopped right in front of the
Hollywood sign, where he'd got down on one knee and asked
her to marry him. Mia had been so enchanted that she'd
accepted immediately. And ever since then she'd felt like
she'd been walking on air.

She'd been on the same high when Leo had taken her back
to Watford to meet his family. Since joining the British Bulldogs
soccer team he'd been making a real effort to reconnect with
his past – and she'd really enjoyed travelling to the UK to discover where he was from and getting to know his family in
the process. She got along particularly well with his three
chick-flick-obsessed sisters and had promised to take them on
a tour of a film set and introduce them to Billy when they
came over to LA for the wedding.

She'd already started planning the big day and had even
met with the caterers to start going through possible menus.

Since being in a loving relationship, Mia was finding it much easier to resist the urge to binge-eat and hadn't had a craving for junk food for as long as she could remember. She was looking forward to enjoying the meal at her wedding without any tension or anxiety.

As she took a moment to look around the room at some of the biggest and most powerful stars in the world, she reflected on how far she'd come since her childhood in Ohio when she'd spent her whole time dreaming of moments like this. She wondered whether she'd changed since then, or whether she'd simply grown in self-acceptance, developing the courage and confidence to be herself. She continued clapping as a wave of happiness washed over her.

Another huge event to take place in her life recently had been her dad's sudden reappearance. He'd surfaced a few weeks ago to say that he was now living in San Diego and would like to meet Mia if she'd agree to see him. After much discussion she'd said yes but only if she could take Leo along with her. With the man she loved standing by her side, seeing her father again after all those years had been a far less traumatic experience than she'd imagined, especially when he'd explained that he was now happily married to the woman he'd left home for, commenting that his split with Mia's mother had been more complicated than Mia remembered or would have been able to appreciate at the time. 'I fell in love, Mia,' he explained. 'And I'm sorry but I just couldn't help myself.'

As she watched Billy being led off stage and into the press room she felt Leo's arm wrap itself around her shoulders. He too was overwhelmed with excitement about the wedding. There were days when he felt stunned by his love for Mia and, seeing as he'd already stood up in public and announced that he was in love with her, all he wanted to do now was tell the world that he was ready to spend the rest of his life with her.

Leo was also thrilled that Ronnie had agreed to be his Best Man. Repairing their friendship after his outburst about the show-mance had been much easier than he'd thought but now that he'd given up his career as a paparazzo, he was anxious for the two of them not to drift apart. Later that month he was due to start work at *The LA Times* as one of their sports photographers. And to Ronnie's delight, his first assignment was a big Dodgers game. He couldn't wait to get started.

On the same day, Mia was due to begin work on her next movie, a heavyweight political thriller in which she played a female senator captured by terrorist forces. It was a far cry from the lightweight roles that had earned her the nickname the First Lady of Love.

It looked like Mia's days as a romantic lead were over. As she sat down next to the man she loved, she knew that she wouldn't miss them. With Leo by her side, she had more than enough romance in her life.

And it was so much better than in the movies.